# VOID

*Book One of the Void Chronicles*

## TIFFANY A. JOISSIN

Stella Luna Publishing

*For Jovi*

# PART ONE
# ENDINGS

# Chapter One

The first breath that she took came on the tail end of a scream. The sound rang out loud and clear in the middle of the night.

Her first sensation was of her falling forwards, the air whistling by her ears, the turning in her stomach. Her arms stayed limp at her sides. She fell on someone; she could feel the warmth through the clothing. She gripped the clothing in her hands.

She looked up, but tears and rain blocked her vision and Sanaa curled in closer to the warmth holding her. A heat came over her, bringing warmth to her back and Sanaa snuggled deeper into it.

The warmth was trying to move, to march her forward. But her legs were so weak and so cold that all she could do was shiver in her spot.

"Come," the person said. Sanaa could not see them. The moon was obscured by heavy rain clouds and there was no light to illuminate their face. "Come," they said again and pushed at her back. Sanaa tried, taking a shuffling step forward, never once letting her feet rise from the ground.

"That's it," the voice said. And they carried on like that with Sanaa never trusting that her legs would not give out on her. She held onto the person with as much strength as she could muster in her shaking hands.

The rain pelted down with a strength that Sanaa had not felt in ages. It chilled her to the bone, but she carried on putting one foot in front of the other. She could only hope that soon they would be somewhere warm. Somewhere she could rest.

They entered through large iron doors and Sanaa was flooded with warmth and light. Here the hallways were lit with several torches hanging against the wall and the floor was smooth against Sanaa's feet.

She looked up and took in the face of the one that was guiding her. She had a strong nose and brow but had soft eyes that reminded Sanaa of Kala. They walked, or in Sanaa's case shuffled, down the hallway and into another room with a grand doorway. This door was embossed with pictures of a group of women throwing down another woman with a crown of thorns.

The two of them passed through this door and entered a grand receiving room. The floor shone and large marbled pillars held up the ceiling. Paintings of beautiful women with copper skin amongst clouds decorated the ceiling and walls.

Women with terra-cotta skin stood around a chair as a woman with deep taupe skin sat in the lone chair on the dais. Covered in shining silver armor, the women were imposing. The woman sitting on the raised dais sat with an air of importance. In one hand she held a spear and she looked down at Sanaa and her guide with a blank face.

"Commander," Sanaa's guide said and dropped to one knee. Sanaa tilted, her feet still unused to supporting her weight. The world careened before her eyes. Sanaa reached out to grip the shoulder of her guide, to have something to support her.

The commander only nodded and the woman rose, once again supporting Sanaa's weight with her arms.

"And the others?" the commander asked. Her voice cracked through the silence. The commander's voice was low and rumbling like thunder, but her face was still blank.

"No one else made it through the ritual, commander," Sanaa's guide said with a shake of her head. Sanaa's eyes flickered around the room, taking in everything around her. Where was Mother? Who was this person who called themselves the commander when that was Mother's position?

The thought of her Mother made Sanaa's teeth grind. Mother. That icy look in her eyes and the cold sinking into her veins. Sanaa shuddered at the memory. Mother must have brought her out and needed her for something. Mother needed her again. Something warm bloomed in her stomach at the thought.

She could be with her sisters again.

"It is a pity that none of the others made it, but I am glad you were spared, Ruth," the commander said with a nod. Ruth? That was a name that Mother must have come up with. It did not sound like something that she would name one of her daughters. Mother favored names that sounded like her own and tried to name her daughters accordingly. Ruth was not a name that Mother would have allowed.

Sanaa turned to look up to her guide, Ruth, and stared at her face a moment longer. No, Mother's jaw was not as powerful as this one's and the arch to her nose was more pronounced than Mother's was. Who was this person?

Sanaa's eyes darted to the dais and the waiting women on it. Who were these people? A chill like ice water slithered down Sanaa's back. What if this was a test? Mother very much liked to test her daughters and after what happened it made sense. Sanaa had been gone for so long, Mother must want to test her.

Yes, it only made sense that this was a test. A trial that she had to go through to be accepted back into the fold. She had failed the last test she was given by Mother, and look at what happened to her. She had been frozen in time, and who knows how long Mother had left her there.

Sanaa straightened her spine and looked towards the commander. She was an imposter, another hurdle that she needed to get through for Mother to see her worth again. For Mother to love her again. She hardened her heart and changed her features to be more stone-faced.

Mother had always taught them that it was best to face every moment with a face that showed that they would not yield. Sanaa looked at the commander and waited for the next words that would escape her mouth.

"Welcome, Aunt. We are so sorry that it took us such a long time to retrieve you. It was not easy undoing the magic that imprisoned you," the commander said.

Aunt? The word broke the facade that Sanaa had carefully constructed around herself. Aunt? No, none of her sisters had children, they were busy fighting against the Faeries, and making sure that their home was safe. There was no way that they could have had children.

"It was her, she was the one who let them in!" Sanaa could remember the way that Kala had barked out the words as they all stood in the training pit. The fire that had burned in Kala's eyes then as the words forced themselves past her lips, the arch to her brow. Sanaa turned her eyes to Ruth, again taking in her features.

Yes, there was something similar about Ruth's face. She had the same soft green eyes that Kala had when they were young. Sanaa whipped her head to look at the other women that surrounded the commander. She could see hints of her

4

sisters in them. One of them looked like Tori and another looked like Adeya.

The more that she stared the more that she saw her sisters in all their faces. Aunt. They had called her aunt.

"I know this must be very confusing for you, Aunt," the commander said, her voice soft. Sanaa turned her eyes to her and the commander rose from her perch on the chair. There was silence as she descended the steps. Sanaa watched with quiet, unbelieving eyes.

No, there was no way. This must be a test from Mother. Yes, it was a test from Mother. It was the only thing that made sense. Sanaa was shaking where she stood, her mind moving so quickly that her mouth could not do anything but open and close. The commander stood in front of Sanaa in a matter of moments and undid the clasp that held her helmet closed.

When the commander removed her helmet, Sanaa looked into the eyes of Kala. The soft green eyes and the soft curve to her cheeks. Sanaa stared for as long as she could before the tears blocked her vision. This was Kala's daughter. This was her niece. Sanaa shuffled forward, her heart thundering in her chest as she raised her hands to cup the commander's face.

"You... You are—" the words got caught in her throat. If this was true then that meant Mother... "You're Kala's daughter. Aren't you?"

The commander smiled down at her and Ruth came to stand beside her. "Kala was the name of our great-great-great-grandmother." The tears felt warm against Sanaa's clammy skin and the words were like a knife to the heart.

Great grandmother. This was Kala's granddaughter. Her eyes wandered back to the ladies that stood around the commander. These were all her sister's children. They had done it. Sanaa let a laugh escape her. These were her nieces.

The commander spoke again, "My name is Greta, Aunt."

Sanaa nodded and she laughed again. Kala and her other sisters had done it. They had gotten rid of Mother, they had won. Sanaa felt the weight in her chest finally unfurl. This was not a test. This was real.

"Come, let us talk somewhere more comfortable," Greta said as she placed a hand on Sanaa's back. They walked out of the receiving room and into a room that was to the side of the dais. This room was lush in its decoration with soft chairs and pillows strewn throughout the room. Sanaa was guided to one of the chairs and sat down on one of the overstuffed chairs. The other women, along with Ruth and Greta, sat down all around her.

Sanaa could not drag her eyes away from their faces, checking the curve of their chin and the subtle arch of their noses. Sanaa felt like a child staring at them trying to find something in their faces that could not be stated, only seen.

Greta was the first to speak when they were all settled. "There is much that we must tell you, aunt. There is a lot that you have missed in your time... away from us."

Sanaa snorted at her careful wording of her being petrified in stone for...

"How long?" Sanaa's voice was nothing more than a brutal croak, the cords in her throat unused to rubbing against one another to produce sound after so long. Greta nodded and straightened in her seat. With the armor, it was hard to adjust her already straight back, but she somehow managed it. Greta took in a deep breath before she turned to Sanaa and looked at her with a stone-hard look.

"You have been gone for a millennia, aunt."

The words landed with all the force of a punch. Her mind was sent whirling from the now and to the word millennia.

Millennia. Millennia. She had been gone for a thousand years. That was how long she had missed out with her sisters. Mother had cursed her for one thousand years. Her mind kept spiraling downwards and downwards about how long she was gone from her family. They had long since died but she was still here.

"But aunt," Greta leaned forward in her chair, reaching over and gripping Sanaa's clammy hands in her warm ones. "We freed you. You are no longer trapped in stone. You are free." Tears blurred Sanaa's vision again and she began to sob in earnest.

Her sisters. Her poor sisters. They had gone on to live lives that were full and happy, but she... Sanaa did not want to pity herself but the sadness crashed over her like a wave, leaving nothing behind but a hole in her chest. She sobbed because she had missed being with her sisters. She sobbed because of the loss of her mother. She sobbed because of the life that she did not get to spend in their embrace.

After a moment, Sanaa was able to calm herself. She sniffled and sighed and then looked to Greta who still held her hands. "Tell me everything that happened."

Greta squeezed her hands. "Of course, aunt. After you were petrified, the rebelling sisters fought against the traitor. The traitor had used a lot of power to petrify you and our mothers knew that it would take a moment for her to regain her power. Our mothers knew that then was the time to strike. But the traitor knew about the assault and gathered daughters loyal to her. It was a fierce battle of sisters fighting one another but our mothers managed to kill the traitor, your mother."

Mother had died. The thought seemed so foreign, but those were the words that had exited Greta's mouth. And of course, Mother would gather those sisters that were most loyal to guard her. It all sounded like something that Mother would do. And now she was gone. Mother was gone.

Mother had always been a cornerstone for Sanaa, like the sky or the earth. Mother was always there. And for the longest time, she had followed Mother with single-minded abandon. She had believed everything that Mother had said. She never had a reason to disbelieve it. But then there was Kala, her beloved older sister, who held her hands as their home, the city of Mayara, burned.

Sanaa could not smile at the new information but she could not frown. Her sisters had done their duty. They had killed Mother for her betrayal. But a small part of her, the part that was Mother's daughter, mourned the loss of her mother, the person who birthed and raised her.

"Good," Sanaa said after a moment. "Good. Justice was served, then."

"Aunt there is so much that we have to tell and show you!" Ruth burst forth with a large smile on her face. "Oh, Aunt, so many things have changed since the death of the traitor."

Greta raised a hand and that alone was enough to quiet Ruth's bright exuberance. Sanaa quietly marveled at it. So Greta was the new commander. Greta let a smile crack through her cold facade.

"It has been a long day for our aunt. Why don't you show her to her room and let her rest, Ruth? You can tell her of all our changes when she is well-rested."

Ruth nodded and rose from her chair. "Follow me, Aunt." Sanaa rose from her chair and stood on her shaky feet. As they were exiting the room, Sanaa looked back and looked into each of the faces that were in that room. They were all the great-granddaughters of her sisters. They were her family. Sanaa turned and exited.

There was nothing but silence as Sanaa was escorted to her room. Ruth would turn to look at her, almost vibrating with energy she could scarcely contain. Ruth would pause for a moment with her mouth open, poised to mention one thing or another, but then she closed it. Sanaa could not help but find the exuberance of Ruth enchanting, with her energy and the general sense of joy she gave off.

When they reached her room, it was far removed from the rest of the compound in a wing that Sanaa could not remember no matter how hard she tried. Ruth swung the door open and Sanaa's focus was brought to her arms where she could feel the hair on her arms rising.

It was with a small amount of effort that Ruth lit all the candles in the room with a flick of her wrist. At least there was one thing that had not changed.

The room had plush rugs and the bed lay bloated in the center of the room. Sanaa entered the room with no small amount of wonder. Her lodgings had never been so luxurious when Mother had served as their commander. Their rooms were sparse and held only the essentials. They were more focused on protecting their lands than making their room comfortable.

"I'll see you tomorrow, Aunt," Ruth said from the doorway. She closed the door behind her and Sanaa was alone.

Mother had been taken down. Why was that so hard to believe? Her mother, the same one who had petrified her in stone, was gone.

"You disappoint me, daughter." Those were the last words she had heard her mother say before she felt the stiffness in her muscles. The very memory made her shudder. Sanaa fiddled with her fingers and sat down on the bed and lay down. It was too easy. Mother being gone and her being free. It was too easy. But it was true. Mother was gone and she was here, amongst the daughters of her sisters.

Sanaa let out a small laugh and lay down on the bed. There would be more time to take in the world in the morning when she sat with her nieces to break their fast. With that thought serving as comfort, Sanaa fell asleep.

# Chapter Two

T he hard length of him was cocooned in her center. August could feel the warmth pooling in his belly spreading through his veins. Helia clawed at his back, her legs wrapped around his waist.

"Harder, August," Helia said between breathy moans. August pistoned his hips faster. Her fingers raked down his back and August bent his head, taking a nipple into his mouth and rolling the flesh between his teeth. Helia tightened around him. With a great shout, August stilled and he spent inside of her. Helia gave a low moan, her body spasming underneath August's body.

She quivered and fluttered around his length, letting August knew she too had reached her peak. Lightning zinged up and down August's spine and he stayed still atop of her. When the tension in his body finally fell away, August rested down in the bed beside her.

Helia sighed in the bed next to him and August let out a small laugh. It bubbled out of him and Helia panted beside him. The two of them began to giggle beside one another.

"That was good," Helia said as she slid an arm around

August. A small chuckle escaped him and he gripped her hand that was touching his chest. He pressed a kiss to her hand.

"Better than Xander?" August asked as he leaned closer to mouth at the skin of Helia's neck. The action made her giggle and lean away from him. August leaned closer, following her every movement.

Helia unfurled her wings and August watched with amazement as the woman rose above him in the bed with a quick flap. Her wings were nothing like his, mere darkened skin stretched over lithe bones. Her wings were heavy-looking things that looked like they were dripping black sludge. It was hard to believe that this woman was a part of the ever so spotless Fae.

"Beautiful," August said, as he did every time he saw her wings. And he meant every word. He sent a wink with his blind eye at her. He liked her wings because they were different, because she was different. Helia sent a smile in his direction as she pulled on her leathers and her boots. August started to dress in the same way, but he wasn't fast enough because there was a hard pounding at the door.

"I hope everything has been handled." The small voice of Luz came from behind the door. August pulled on his pants and opened the door, enjoying the small shriek that he invoked when the door opened to reveal his bare chest. Luz turned away from his chest and August strode out, pulling a tunic over his head. This hideout was smaller than their last one, with everything gathered together in a rush. Things were pushed to the side and there were bags strewn around the room. August entered the larger room of the house and saw the scout waiting for the meeting to begin.

The scout was small. The faerie wings that unfurled behind him glowed with all the light of the setting sun, signaling he was part of the Light Court. August slid closer to the scout and settled an arm over his shoulders, the tanned skin of his arm contrasting with the alabaster white of the scout's.

"So where are you from, scout?" August asked. The scout jumped at the sudden contact, his face showing that he had not heard August's approach. The very fact made a smile twitch at August's lips. He pulled the scout closer to his side.

"O-Oh... I'm from Helios," the scout said with a small tremble of his lips. August smiled wider as he took in the small form of the scout. This scout was new, someone the recruiters must have just enlisted in their ranks. Hadn't Helia told to stop sending in their new bloods? Especially the ones that wouldn't stop staring at his eye.

"What happened to the person before you?" August asked with a small tilt of his lips.

With this, his eyes grew slightly glassy and August regretted he even asked. He hated it when people cried in front of him. He never knew what to do and comforting others was not something that he was experienced in.

"They were executed on orders of Queen Loreli. They were caught sending a missive," the scout said and August let out a low whistle at the thought. The man got caught sending a message to Helia. That was happening a lot more now. So many of their scouts were getting caught and executed. But Helia never seemed worried. She never worried about anything. And if Helia wasn't worried about it then August wasn't going to worry about it either.

"Well count Sevan's stars," August said. He leaned back. Another scout dead. That meant that Sorcha was narrowing in on them and it explained why they had to move away from the Light Court with such urgency. August let out another whistle and shook his head. Everything was getting more and more complicated.

August reached up and scratched his head. He hated how everything was becoming more and more complicated. But

Helia was never concerned no matter how complicated the situation was. He wished sometimes that he could share her nonchalant attitude but sometimes August wondered if it was because she thought there was nothing to worry about or because she was so reckless.

Helia walked into the room then and settled into one of the chairs, kicking her feet up onto the table. Her clothing was loose and not even laced up, letting the tantalizing curve of her breast show from the flaps of her shirt. August's eyes were glued to the skin before he heard her speak.

"Stop playing with the scout," Helia said in that easy tone of voice she always had. She tilted her chair back until it was perched precariously on two legs. August rose to form his position and settled himself behind Helia, his arms wrapping around her shoulders and perching his chin on her head.

"You know I was only having fun. Nothing that wouldn't have been reversible," he whispered in her ear. She laughed.

"Come now...?" Helia prompted. The scout took a moment before he straightened in his seat.

"Aydin," he said with a quick duck of his head.

"Aydin," Helia continued. "Well, Aydin since you are here I assume Julius has died. That is a shame. I liked Julius."

Aydin got glassy-eyed at the thought. August could not hold in the curl to his lip as he caught the moment of weakness. They needed to stop sending over people who were fresh to the cause. They were always so weak and emotional, things August hated to deal with.

"Well get on with it. Tell us what you have to report." Helia said with a wave of her hand. The air settled between them all for a moment before Aydin took in a deep breath. He took several before the glassy look in his eyes finally disappeared and the tremor to his hands ceased. He looked up from his hands and August was surprised to see the steel in his eyes.

He thought that this boy would be nothing more than a whimpering soul, someone, that they were going to have the guide around before he inevitably killed himself or got caught. But maybe there was something more to him, something August misjudged in his initial introduction.

"Empress Sorcha has decided to tour her lands. She is going to start in the Spring Court and then move to the Summer Court and from there to the Fall Court," Aydin said. August raised a brow at this. The empress leaving the comforts of the Imperial Court. The last time she had done this was when she was first married to Emperor Chandra. This was unheard of.

August gave a small laugh and gripped the shoulders of Helia. "Did you hear that? A moving target. We can get her easier this way."

"Shhh," Helia hushed with a pat to his bulging arms. "There must be more than that. Sorcha would never make it easy for us." Helia had a large frown on her face that made August's exuberance dim. Helia knew something. She always knew something and kept it to herself. August unwrapped his arms from around her and leaned back against the wall.

"There are rumors of unrest in the Spring Court, which is why Sorcha is heading that way first," Aydin added on. "Something is going on with Husks disappearing near General Halforth's mountains. Caravans and like are disappearing from the tunnels used for trade between the Spring Court and the Feral Stars wolves. It has caused some tension between them. Rumors are going around that Sorcha is going there first to force King Gabriel to deal with the situation."

"Unrest in the Spring Court?" Helia asked with a raised brow. August thought back to everything he knew about the Spring Court but could only draw a blank.

"Why is the Spring Court so surprising?" He asked when he was tired of trying to remember what he knew.

"King Gabriel has tight control over the Spring Court. Nothing happens there without his knowledge," Aydin filled him in. Helia sniffed and then moved to one of the shelves lining the walls. She pulled out a scroll and dumped it on the table in the center of the room. Aydin and August both had to move closer to see what she was doing. There lay a map of Ettrea, from the Fantomcrest Wolves in the north to the Gor'gan demons in the south.

"What exactly is happening in the Spring Court?" Helia asked as her eyes skimmed over the map, falling on the lands of the Spring Court.

"Husks are disappearing in the mountain ranges. They say there is someone there promising their freedom so they are leaving in droves. Caravans are being assaulted before they can reach the Feral Stars wolves. It is causing a lot of problems for King Gabriel." August let out another low whistle.

The Husks were mortals, people with short lifespans that had no power of their own. They lived and died with the whims of others. They came and went like the tide, there one day and then gone the next.

Husks, mortals, the powerless among them thought they could escape into caves and be safe. The very thought was laughable. Where could they possibly be going? It was all madness. Husks trying to escape their betters made August snort a laugh. Helia shot him a look, but that only made him smile.

"So there is someone in the caves of Halforth's mountains who is disrupting trade and encouraging the mortals to abandon their betters. This is good," was all Helia said.

August furrowed his brow. "How can this help us Helia? I thought our target was the empress?"

"Sorcha will always be my main target, but I don't like things that aren't in my control. They could ruin everything that I have planned," Helia said with a curl to her lip. August nodded. He remembered the last time something went wrong with one of her plans. She raged for weeks about it. Helia's red eyes narrowed as her finger traced the mountain range between the Feral Stars and the Spring Court.

"August, I need you to go to the Spring Court and find whoever is doing this. Make them one of us," Helia said with a wicked twist to her lips. August smiled. He loved it when Helia got that look on her face. She was planning again. That scheming mind of hers was working hard to add new additions to her side of the table.

"Why would you want them to join us? Tell me and I could take over the whole thing for you. Why waste all the time and energy in getting them to join us? Why not take over their whole operation?" Helia shot him a look, one he hated. It made him feel small and unworthy of her time when he knew that was not true.

"August, maybe this has never occurred to you, but if we can get control of what goes on down there, then it would be easier than fighting people that we do not already know. We would have less competition when it comes to playing with Empress Sorcha."

August sighed through his teeth and settled himself into a chair. He didn't want to be the one that went to the Spring Court, but it seemed that there was nothing that he could do. But Helia ordered it, and her will must be followed.

Helia nodded when she saw the pout become etched into his face. She turned back to Aydin who was watching the interaction with wide eyes. When Helia turned her eyes back to him, the scout was shivering where he stood. August was happy to have the weight of her eyes off of him and on to someone else.

For a moment, August held nothing but burning hate for Helia, the way that she commanded him around and the way that he had no choice to obey. He thought back to that fateful night when she found him and he had no choice but to rely on her.

No, it was his fault he was in this position and no one else's. If there was anyone that he should be mad at it should be himself for being weak enough to need the help of someone else. He frowned deeper at the memory.

"What town is experiencing the disturbances the most?" Helia asked, looking down at the map. Aydin came close and pointed to a small town close to General Halforth's mountains: Asren. It was the largest of all the border towns.

"Asren," August said. He rolled the word on his tongue. It was easy to say and he looked at the town with no sense of excitement. Despite his mixed feelings about being sent there, he was excited to wreak havoc there like no other. A town where Husks were running away, thinking they were going to be free? That sounded chaotic, the very thought got his blood pumping.

Besides, if this King Gabriel kept everything under such tight control, then the sneaking around that he would have to do made him shiver in excitement.

Helia nodded and went back to the shelf to pull a quill and inkwell from the shelf. She pulled a roll of paper from the ground. She began writing fast.

"I have a friend in Asren. August, you will go to him and he will help you with contacting whoever is causing the mayhem there," Helia said with a flourish of her quill. She rolled the piece of paper and closed it with a stamp of her ring. "He will help you when you give him this."

She handed the letter to August who grabbed it and rose from his chair. "Consider it done," August said with the dip of his head and it was with that, that he exited the room.

# Chapter Three

"Hold still, Auntie!" Jazmine muttered. Sanaa made a show of reaching up and patting her head. Jazmine slapped her away and continued braiding. "I'm almost done, Auntie! I promise!"

Sanaa laughed as she waited for Jazmine to finish braiding her hair. When it was finally done, Sanaa jumped up from between the girl's legs and stretched, her muscles and joints snapping back into place after being still for so long. She ran her hands through her hair, now full of braids and beads. She turned to Jazmine and gave her a bright smile.

"Thank you for the new hair, Jazmine," Sanaa said with a shake of her head. The sound of the beads clacking together made Sanaa smile. She wiped her hands against her pants and laughed. "No problem, Auntie," Jazmine said.

Sanaa could not get out another word before Ruth bowled into her. Sanaa laughed as she fell to the ground, Ruth's arms wrapped around her as she squealed. Over the past few days, there were times when Sanaa wished for the silence the compound used to have, but stripped the thought as soon as it arose in her.

It was nice having people that were happy to see her again, and she was still a novelty to them. Once the newness of her return wore off, everything would relax around her. She sighed as she rose from the ground, taking Ruth with her.

"Come now, Ruth, you are a daughter of Idir, you must comport yourself with some dignity," Sanaa scolded. But Ruth was laughing in her arms, not caring what anyone thought of her nor thinking twice about what she had done. That was something Sanaa liked about Ruth.

"Yes, but I heard you are going to perform the sword dance for us tonight! I have always wanted to see a sword dance, but none of us know one. And the way that grand-mother would talk about it- you have to teach me!" Ruth said all in one breath. Sanaa laughed again because something told her Ruth would be the first to find her when she heard the news.

"Yes, fine. I will show you how to perform some of the sword dance." Sanaa grabbed Ruth's hand and they began the walk to the training pits.

Somehow while they were going to the training grounds, Sanaa had become the follower and Ruth the leader. They reached the training grounds where women were doing drills, passed many of the occupied training pits, and found an empty one.

"Here," Ruth said as she pushed her into one of the rooms. This room was nothing more than densely packed dirt and racks of weapons. Sanaa went over to the rack, found the needles she was looking for, and strapped the two holsters to her legs.

"Now the sword dance can be performed with swords, but I prefer to use these." Sanaa unsheathed the long, thick silver needles. They were as long as Sanaa's arm and heavier than one would expect. Ruth sat near the edge of the room, her eyes never leaving Sanaa.

Sanaa exhaled and closed her eyes. The magic strings hovered before her eyes and all she had to do was reach out and pull the strings. Her magic touched the metal needle. She stretched out her hands, twitching her fingers and watching the needles tremble in the air.

And then she began to dance.

The needles flashed through the air and Sanaa jumped through the fast-moving silver. She danced and leaped and bent at the waist. It was like she was brought back to when she was young and Mother was teaching her to dance.

"This is a dance, but it is also a way to attack," she could hear Mother saying. She put one foot in front of the other in the way Mother taught her. For a moment, she looked to where Ruth was and there Mother was, beautiful and resplendent, in all her finery. Sanaa stopped dancing where she stood.

Ruth jumped up to her feet, clapping. "Oh, that was amazing! You have to teach me how to do that!" Sanaa panted where she stood, staring at the spot in the doorway where she saw Mother, with her haunting, hooded eyes and the almost-smile that was always on her lips.

No, Mother was no longer with them. Mother was dead. There was nothing left of her to worry about. But Sanaa could still feel Mother as if she was standing over her shoulder. But was that Mother's breath on the back of her neck? Sanaa slapped a hand to ward away the feeling.

"That was amazing!" Ruth repeated. "Teach me!"

Sanaa felt as though there was nothing but sand in her mouth. She pushed past Ruth. No, Mother was not here. She looked around but all she could see was blue sky, and Mother as she pulled her index finger back—

"I've been looking for you."

Sanaa's eyes snapped to the left to find Greta marching towards her. Sanaa looked around and found herself sitting on one of the grassy hills in the compound. How did she get here? She had been with Ruth in the training room. She patted her thighs and the holster of needles were still at her side. The sun was sinking low on the horizon.

"Ruth said you left the training pits in a huff. She could barely get a word in," Greta said. She settled down next to Sanaa. The ground was hot underneath her. "Though if Ruth was not able to get a word in, you probably spared yourself some trouble."

That night Sanaa danced with a furiousness that made her needles shine in bright light. She danced with her eyes closed so she did not have to see the specter of Mother waiting in the wings of the room. Sanaa finished to thunderous applause, the smile on her face stretched tight. She took her seat at the elevated table that Greta and Ruth sat at.

The room was booming with sound as all the women talked and shouted and enjoyed the feast that lay before them. Sanaa's mouth watered at the heady scent of spices seasoning the warm beef and sliced ham. She sat down next to Ruth, who tossed her concerned looks she ignored.

Sanaa stacked her plate with food and began the careful process of trying to shovel food in her mouth without looking like she had never seen food before. One thing that came out of her confinement was a new appreciation for her sense of taste. She was busy scooping bit after bit into her mouth while the others spoke.

"That was a wonderful dance, Aunt Sanaa," Jocelyn, one of the daughters of Adeya, said the moment the food touched her lips. Sanaa smiled from behind the food and nodded her agreement.

"Aunt, do you think you could tell us some more about the time when you were young?" she asked. Sanaa disengaged from devouring her meal and thought for a moment. What story could she tell that she had not already told? Sanaa wracked her memory, but Jocelyn was quick to add her thoughts on what story she wanted. "How about the story of the Battle of Duse?"

Greta shot Jocelyn a piercing look, but Jocelyn was focused on Sanaa, whose eyes had brightened at the mention of that battle.

"Oh yes. I remember that battle. I was there. The Fae— those wretched elementals— were everywhere when they descended on the town of Duse. They burned that city down just like they did our ancestral city of Mayara—"

"Sanaa—" Greta started but Sanaa continued, enraptured in the story.

"Luckily a scout was able to reach us with word they had attacked, and we were armed by night. We marched and caught the Fae while they were sleeping. It was a single-sided battle from that point on."

"Sanaa, that is enough!"

Sana's teeth clicked as she shut her mouth. Greta had a frown marring her features, but Jocelyn was the target of her ireful stare. Jocelyn sat back with a smile on her face, unrepentant from whatever gaff had occurred.

Sanaa's eyes slid between the two of them, but Jocelyn only sat there, looking as if she had said nothing wrong. Jocelyn placed her silverware down and crossed her arms.

"Why should she apologize for telling the story of what we should be doing?" Jocelyn scoffed. Sanaa frowned. What were they not doing? Times were a lot more peaceful than when she and her sisters were out doing their Mother's work, but surely they still fought?

"The Fae are our allies now, there is no need to be reliving past horrors of our history."

"Allies?" Sanaa heard herself say. Her mind could not wrap

around the word. Allies... allies? The Fae and the Batsamasi were allies? The air between Greta and Jocelyn was silent and stretched. Jocelyn was armed with only a smirk and air of confidence and Greta was armed with only her loaded looks. Talk at the table was silenced; everyone could sense the challenge that lay untested in the air.

Sanaa was still reeling from the information she had been handed. Allies. The Fae and the Batsamasi as allies. The thought did not fit anywhere in her head, the words too discordant to fit. How could they be allies? After everything the Fae had done to them? She thought of her sisters, the ones she had lost to the Fae. No, there was no way.

"Our aunt was telling us how we should be treating those Fae. She was reminding us of how it should be," Jocelyn said with a flick of her hair. "She was telling us of one of the greatest achievements our mothers had. And how we should treat those that have harmed us."

"I have had enough of your talk," Greta thundered from her place at the head of the table. "Stop."

"Is that an order, commander?" Jocelyn sneered from her position. She bared her teeth, an action that had Sanaa sucking in a breath. Mother would have never allowed for such a challenge, but Greta looked at her with an even stare that had Sanaa glancing away from her. Jocelyn stared ahead.

"Yes, that is an order." With that, Greta lifted the heaviness of her stare off of Jocelyn and went back to her plate. Jocelyn rose from the table and marched off, walking out of the light and into the darkness of the hall.

The rest of the dinner was had in such tense silence that Sanaa was relieved when the dinner ended. She rushed to her room and closed the door behind her.

Mother would have never stood to have someone talk to her like that, never mind what Jocelyn said. Sanaa went over the conversation in her head. Mother would have struck the person down where they stood. But Mother was no longer the commander; Greta was.

There was a knock on her door that sounded more like a pounding to Sanaa's delicate ears. The door swung open and there Greta stood, her face the tired mask. Greta walked into the room with no sense of entitlement or anger, but as if she was downtrodden and tired from what Sanaa could not even imagine.

Though her face was young, Sanaa could see the lines of tiredness settling into Greta's face. She looked so young, but at this moment she looked as if she had aged a thousand years. Sanaa sat down on the bed and waited.

"I am sorry that you had to see that tonight," Greta sighed out. Sanaa did not say anything but only nodded her head. "I have only recently taken control of the Batsamasi and there are those that want to test me. Jocelyn and her sect being the most vocal."

"In my time, Mother would have struck her down where she stood. It would have shown challenges like that wouldn't be tolerated," Sanaa said. Greta let out a soft laugh at that, but Sanaa did not laugh along with her. It was terrifying to watch Mother destroy someone because they made the ill-fated choice to test her. It was scary, but it kept the rest of them in line.

"We are trying to move away from those violent times," Greta said with a small laugh.

"Are you truly allies with the Fae now?" The question was burning in her mouth. She had to know if what Jocelyn said was true. The same Fae that had slaughtered her sisters and burned down the city of Mayara. The image was forever burned in her mind, the city burning, Kala's hand in her own as the screams of her cousins, aunts, and sisters rose in the air. The city glowed like a beacon in the night.

Greta did not answer her and Sanaa felt as the city of

Mayara was burning again in her chest. It was hot, and if she were a dragon, smoke would escape her mouth. "How dare you! How dare you make amends with those monsters after everything that they did to us! How can you stand here when you are breaking bread with the same people who have murdered so many of my sisters, your family!"

Greta said nothing and Sanaa took the silence as a sign. She knew. She knew about what they had done to all her sisters and yet she was allied with them. Sanaa felt so hot as if her russet skin was going to melt off of her.

"They killed our mothers! Burned down our sacred city of Mayara and yet you think that they are worthy of our allyship? Do you think those monsters are worthy of anything but our blades? How dare y—"

"I am doing what is best for the Batsamasi." Greta did not raise her voice but it still cut through the air with all the intention that her words carried. "It was your mother who conspired with the Fae in the first place and made it so that the city of Mayara burned."

Sanaa's teeth clicked together harshly as she shut her mouth. It was true. Denying it would be absolving her mother of guilt. Sanaa could do nothing but stare at Greta with fire in her eyes.

What kind of commander was she, that she allied with their long time enemies and claimed it in the best interest of the Batsamasi? The Fae were murderers and butchers. They wanted nothing more than the destruction of the Batsamasi and yet, Greta wanted them as allies. Sanaa scoffed at the very thought.

"Times have changed, Aunt. Many things have changed." Greta pulled out a rolled piece of paper from under her cloak. She fingered it for a moment before she fisted it in her hand. "Many things have changed since you were last with us, Aunt, and this is just one of them."

"Things could not have changed so much that a betrayal like this would be accepted." Greta pulled away from the door and looked at Sanaa. Her eyes were half-mast, signaling how tired she was. But then she straightened her back and unfurled her hand presenting the paper.

"As commander, I present to you your new post. It is in the Fae courts, helping the Lord of the town Asren—"

"What?"

"You leave on the morrow. Maybe by staying with the Fae you can see how the world has changed." With that, Greta dropped the piece of paper on the table nearest the door and marched out of the room. Sanaa rose and went flying out the door after her. How could she send her to the Fae courts, into the home of their enemy? But when she looked out into the hall, Greta was already gone.

Sanaa let out a sound of frustration and picked up the paper. The Fae courts. She was being sent to the Fae courts to help them. The thought made her shiver in revulsion.

They had been fighting against the Fae for as long as Sanaa could remember. And now they thought they could put aside all the horror and war behind them. She still remembered the faces of all her fallen sisters, the way that they had begged for mercy only to be slaughtered by the Faeries. And now she would have to go and help them.

A part of her resented Greta and her decision to send her off to the Fae courts. She isn't stable here, Sanaa thought to herself. She could find Jocelyn and make things the way they should be. The thought grew in her mind, plans coming together, and Sanaa could almost see it enacted with Greta being left behind.

## Chapter Four

Morning came faster than ever, the weight of exhaustion heavy on Sanaa's shoulders. She had barely slept the night before, her mind churning over the thought of going to the Fae Courts when she had spent such little time with her nieces.

The sun was not too high in the sky, cresting over the eastern horizon with the sky a soft dusty pink. Sanaa was at the stables picking a horse when the crunch of hay underfoot overpowered the sound of the horse chuffing. She turned to see Jocelyn clambering over to her. She approached with a swinging gait that showed to the world that she was unrepentant in her actions. Her long locs were twisted up into a bun at the top of her head and her clothing was billowing and loose.

"I have heard the news of your deployment," was all she said in way of greeting. Sanaa was still fixing the saddle on her horse and did not dignify her with a response. Sanaa could not help but have a burning in her chest at the sight of her. It was because of her she had to leave her nieces. It was because of her she was being almost exiled to the Fae courts.

"Aunt, you must know that I am as mad about your deployment as you are. I had wanted to grow close with you, Aunt," Jocelyn leaned against the stable wall. Sanaa tightened the saddle around the horse and looked at Jocelyn.

"What do you want?" Sanaa said with a sigh as the horse was finally saddled. Her bags were strewn around on the floor waiting to be packed onto the sides of the horse, but Jocelyn acted as if she did not even notice them as she strode towards Sanaa. She stepped as if she was coming to claim the world and nothing would stop her.

Jocelyn's eyes were hard and her spine was straight as she said, "You know this is wrong. You know that we should not be allies with the Faerie Courts. Don't go, stay here with us! We can make this right. I have people here who are ready and willing to install you as Commander." It was something Sanaa had mulled over for a while as she laid in bed at night.

She knew things had changed in the thousand years that she had been gone. She knew that with the death of Mother change was inevitable. But was this a change in the right direction? Was this how the world moved forward without her?

If that was true then she had no place here. As she was now she could never make it here with the daughters of her sisters. And ruling over them? She remembered how gleefully they spoke of the defeat of Mother. No, she would not become like her mother. She did not want to become a part of the political machinations her mother was so fond of.

No. It was better she left as who she was at that moment. The lost and last daughter of Efe. She sighed and shook her head, looking into the eyes of Jocelyn. Jocelyn's eyes were burning, sparking with the hope she would take the bait and become their commander.

But Sanaa just shook her head. "I will not help you with your rebellion," Sanaa said. She sent threads of her magic to wrap around the bags on the floor, settling them on the horse's saddle. "I agree with you: we shouldn't be allies with the Fae. They are tricksters and they have killed too many of my sisters for me to ever think of being allied with them. But I cannot fight against my nieces. I cannot fight my family. I am tired of fighting."

Jocelyn lurched away as if she had struck her. Her lip curling, she gave Sanaa a once over. Sanaa wondered what Jocelyn saw. A tired woman with her bags packed. Maybe she saw someone too old to fight, but whatever she saw she did not like it.

Jocelyn turned up her nose and sniffed at Sanaa. And then she walked away. Sanaa was left only with a saddled horse and the last of the dawn light. She sighed as she took the reins of the horse and led it outside.

The sound of the horse's hooves on the ground took Sanaa back to when she was younger, when everything was simpler with her mother and her sisters beside her.

"Keep your eyes up Sanaa," her sister Kala would whisper in her ear. "Keep your eyes up and focus on the target." Sanaa nocked the arrow and waited for the string to resist her pulling back any farther.

"Okay, now release!" Sanaa let go of the string and had it snap back into place, slapping against her skin so hard she dropped the bow. "Good. Good," Kala said with a laugh. She bent over to pick up the fallen bow.

Kala looked down at Sanaa with warm eyes and put the bow back in her hands. "This time I am going to teach you how to pull the bow without hurting yourself."

Sanaa snapped out of the memory as she reached the front of the gate. From her position at the bottom of a hill, she could see the massive home the compound had become. From here it was a sprawling mansion with new additions spiraling up into the morning sky.

Ruth and Greta were waiting for her at the base of the stairs leading into the compound. The two sisters were dressed casually, with leather pants and simple blouses. They made Sanaa feel overdressed in her leather armor. She stopped in front of them. Ruth's lower lip was sticking out and her eyes were wide with tears she could barely hold in. Greta was the opposite of her sister, with a steady gaze.

"I am sorry that it has had to come to this, Aunt," Greta said with a frown on her face.

Sanaa only shook her head, a small smile on her face. "I was going to have to see the world for myself eventually. You have done nothing wrong." Sanaa then turned to the shorter of the two, cupping Ruth's plump face in her hands. "Shhh. Ruth, stop your tears."

Ruth's tears never seemed to end despite the girl wiping at her eyes. Ruth hugged Sanaa as tight as she could. Sanaa was surprised at the action, surprised the girl could be so open with her, but then sank into the hug. She would miss Ruth with her smiles and the easy way she spoke. She squeezed the girl as much as possible before she let go.

Sanaa turned and got on the horse. Once she settled on the horse it was with the slightest press from her legs that the horse started in a trot. Sanaa pressed with her legs again and the horse shot off in a full gallop. She never once looked back.

She launched through the gates of the compound and Sanaa watched the lands of the Husks pass by. She always had to stop herself from turning around and watching the compound disappear into the horizon. She straightened her back and kept on riding into the western horizon.

The last few days spent with Helia were a blur of pleasure, the two of them not being able to leave each other's arm for long. Helia's lips rarely left August's. They spend days in the hideout touching, talking, enjoying one another. From the second the scout left, Helia put her lips on him and they were nothing more than a mass of flesh and pleasure.

On the day he was supposed to leave he woke to Helia's kisses. She kissed his cheek and traveled down his neck and chest. August sighed then put a hand to her midnight locks. She giggled as she smacked kisses all over him.

Already he could feel the heat rising in him, starting with a small pool of heat in his stomach and spreading from there. Helia kissed him ungracefully with teeth and tongue and desire shown in every kiss on his body. And it was all for him.

He liked Helia because nothing drew her away from him. Not his scars nor his blindness in one eye. August sighed again and Helia quieted him with a kiss. He grabbed her, crushing her against his chest. Her laugh was a zinging hum between the both of them.

"It is time for you to go," she said when they pulled away from one another. They were both panting, kissing until they had to separate for air. She giggled as his hands swept up and down her sides. They were both gloriously naked underneath the sheets of the bed. Around the room, candles glowed with the lights of small fires. "You need to go to Asren, August."

Helia tried to pull away but he snatched her back. He did not want her heat to leave his side. She slammed into his chest again and laughed as he held her tight.

"Leave? We have done nothing but this for days and now you want me to leave?" He gripped her tighter and she squealed as the pressure on her increased. His laugh rumbled out of his chest. "Tell me not to go to Asren and I won't. I'll stay here with you."

Every word was enunciated with a kiss. A kiss to her forehead, and another to her lips and cheeks, but Helia was like iron underneath his grip. She cut her eyes to him with a sharpness he knew meant she wanted to talk business.

August let her go and she rose from the bed. She stretched and her wings fanned out behind her, surrounding her in a sort of dark halo.

"You need to head to Asren and find my associate, Vorus. He presides over the town of Asren and he will help you when it comes to making contact with who you need," she said as she pulled on her clothes.

"And if they decide they don't want to join us?" August asked, rising into a sitting position with a purse of his lips. There was always the chance there was someone who was against joining the fold. And August loved dealing with those that did.

"You know the way we handle dissent." August nodded his head. He rose from the bed and began to dress. He took a dark blue doublet and slid it on, then gathered his leather riding breeches. For once, Helia was wearing a dress, a pink thing with pearls and frills August had never seen in all the time he had spent with her.

"And where are you going as I risk my life in Asren?" August asked as he got his boots on. Helia did not respond as she floated to the other side of the room and grabbed her face between her hands.

"You must promise me you will be careful. I have heard strange things happening to people who enter those caves," Helia said. August pulled away from her then. What could she be worried about? There was nothing except maybe a couple of Husks hiding in the caves trying to escape their lives of slavery. There was no need for concern.

August sighed for a moment and then thought of the Husks. They would probably be cowering in the caves, dirty and tired. And the leader among them must have been some low down Fae trying to make his mark on the world. August chuckled at the thought.

"Nothing will happen to me," he said with a tilt of his head. Helia shook her head and pulled a leaf from one of the plants hanging over the bed. She held the leaf between her hands and a soft glow emanated from between her fingers. When she pulled away, the leaf was a stunning gold color. She passed it to August.

"Here. You know what to do with this," was all she said and August smiled as he took the leaf in his hands.

"It is always nice to have your favor," he said as he tucked the leaf into one of the pockets of his pants. Once they were both fully dressed, they exited the room and came into the cramped hallway.

This hideout was nothing more than a series of rooms haphazardly crammed together. The rooms were tiny and the lack of space was not alleviated with the way things were strewn around each room. August made his way to the exit with Helia hot on his heels.

The town they were in was a small smattering of buildings constructed like the hideout. Just simple houses of mortal Husks and poor Faeries of the Summer court. August squinted his good eye to the sky and judged the wind. If he flew he could be in the Spring Court in a couple of days.

August unfurled his wings to their full length and Helia let out a low whistle. His wings were large with bat-like dark leathery skin stretched over thin bones. He smirked as he caught Luz watching from the windows.

"Make sure you recruit the person in Asren. We don't need something like what happened in the Dark Court," Helia said. August took the first flap with his wings and the air stirred around him. He flapped harder and harder and in a matter of moments, he was off the ground and in the air.

August never once looked back and headed east.

# Chapter Five

✣❁✣

It took Sanaa three days to reach the border where the Fae forest started and where the Batsamasi lands of her home ended. Sanaa camped outside of the forest, never once daring to go inside the cushion of trees and brush.

Sanaa broke bread in front of the forest for the third time when she finally pulled out the iron stake burning in her pocket. She gripped the object in her hand, feeling the weight of it. She remembered the raids that they would go on against the Fae and their lands. How they placed iron stakes against the ground to prevent the spread of their forest, which was truly a creature itself.

Sanaa rolled the stake in her hands before she stuck it in the ground. She then pulled out the iron compass hidden in her pack. Her magic threads dangled from her fingertips and she linked the two, the power springing to life between the iron stake and the compass. Sanaa nodded.

Sucking in a deep breath, Sanaa took the reins of her horse and trodded into the forest. All the foliage leaned away from her, wary of the iron she held. The compass whirred for a moment before it settled on the distance behind her. The magic compass could now lead her out of the forest should she get lost. Sanaa sighed and began to follow the path laid before her.

She slid onto her horse and set it at a small gallop. She rolled her neck as she thought about entering the Courts of the Fae. She remembered when she was younger and training to fight against the Faeries and their machinations. She was ready to fight and thought nothing of how they entered the city when she was young. All she needed to know was that they were the ones who burned down their home and made it so they were homeless.

That was how Mother got under her skin so easily. She knew exactly what strings to pull that would make you weak and easy to manipulate. And every time she fell for it. She was always the one defending Mother and her actions to the others. Maybe that was why Sanaa was kept so close to Mother's side, why Mother had always called her the favorite out of all her daughters. The thought now disgusted her.

How could she have not seen Mother for what she was when she was so close? How could she have not seen her machinations? The thought made her skin feel tight and something roiled unpleasant and heavy in her stomach. The shame was unbearable.

The forest was falling away and Sanaa knew that she was reaching the end. She spurred her horse and broke through the last of the trees. The town that she came upon was different from any she had ever seen before. Here the houses were not an obstruction to nature but part of it. Vines were braided together to make bridges and homes were carved into the bases of large trees. The stalls here were carved into large stones that were placed around the town.

Sanaa could not help the sense of wonder that overcame her as she saw the town. The setting sun illuminated the town in a warm orange glow that made it look smaller and more quaint. Sanaa could not drag her eyes away from it all, but then she remembered her mother's words.

"Don't stare at the Fae. That is how they ensnare you in their deals." It was with a quick twist of her head she looked down at her horse and the ground.

With the sun hitting the horizon, she thought it best she settled down for the night. She thought of heading out of the town and sleeping in the forest, but then thought better of it because that would mean setting her head down in the living greenery.

Sanaa stopped in front of a large building hoping they would have some room to spare. When she walked in the first thing that she noticed was the scent. Her nose was assaulted with the heavy scents of pollen and blooming flowers in a noxious heavy odor that caused her to sneeze several times. On the other side of the room, a man sat behind a desk, and Sanaa walked towards him, covering her nose the whole while.

"Yes?" The faery man drolled not even bothering to look up. His wings caught Sanaa's attention; they were large and green like the color of leaves. "Can I help you?"

Sanaa stopped her staring. "Is there a room available?" She felt the blood rush to her head, the shame almost swallowing her whole. How could she have been caught staring? Why was she staring? She was in the territory of her enemies. She needed to be more alert, not staring at their wings no matter how beautiful they were.

The man behind the desk slid over her key. "Last door on the left."

"I also have a horse that needs attending to," Sanaa mentioned. The man simply sighed and let out a whistle. Sanaa was already making her way down to the hall to her room.

Unlocking the door, Sanaa took in the room. It was

modest in decoration and kept to the theme with the rest of the town. Everything looked as if it had sprung forth from the ground. The heavy scent of flowers hung in the room as the ceiling was sprouting lilies, but that was something that Sanaa decided that she was going to have to deal with.

Sanaa pulled down her hair, the cowry shells and beads clacking together as she placed down her bags. Her russet brown skin coming out darker in the low lighting of the room. She unwound her hair from the high ponytail she had put it in, sighing as the tension finally loosened.

Sanaa opened her bag and pulled out a weapon from within. It was a long golden needle. The gold was worn in some places, but the gold still glimmered in the dim light. She pulled a needle out from the bag and let it tremble in the air. Her fingers pulled on the string of monyelta in front of her and the needle rose in the air. She had had these needles since she decided she wanted to be a sword dancer.

This was a gift from her mother, the only gift she had ever received from her. She could still remember the day she first got it.

Sanaa leaned back then, her body aching from riding the horse all day. She fell onto the bed and closed her eyes, only needing a moment of rest.

*"Now daughters, what I am about to teach you has been passed down from our Mothers. Mother Safira is the one who gifted us with this talent. It is called threading."* The sun highlighted the brown and blonde strands in Mother's hair as she stood in the field in front of them.

*"Our magic is different from the magic of others because it comes from within us. It is in our blood."* Sanaa could feel the grass itching against her bottom, but she tried her best to stay still. Some of her other sisters were unsuccessful in this endeavor and scratched at their bottom as they waited for Mother to finish her talking.

*"You see, my precious daughters, the world is made up of tiny*

*little threads that hold something called monyelta. Everything has monyelta. You and I have monyelta. Our magic brings this out and that is how we fight." Mother lifted from her pocket a single seed. It was nothing much, but Sanaa and her sisters sat looking at their mother as if she held the world in her hands. Each of their brown eyes was caught by the actions of their mother.*

*Mother smiled there, the sun shining so bright that all Sanaa could see was the white of her teeth and nothing more. She tossed the seed into the air and for a moment Sanaa saw it, the monyelta shimmering in the air before Mother, a cascade of strings in bright vibrant color. The strings were vibrating with energy. Mother reached out and pulled a string.*

*The ground trembled slightly as the seed sprouted forth a tree that seemed to touch the sky. Sanaa and her sisters let out a scream, all of them scrambling back away from where the earth erupted. Mother let out a laugh from deep within her throat. Sanaa's jaw stayed open as the tree swayed in the wind. She walked towards it: the heavy, aged tree that her mother had conjured from nothing but a seed. She rested her hand on the tough bark, feeling the bumps and ridges.*

*This was Mother's magic. Her magic. She could do the same thing as Mother did just now if she trained hard enough. Sanaa took a moment to look at her hands. She stared at all the lines and the dough-like flesh of her small hands.*

*Sanaa raised her head and looked at Mother. She came from behind the tree and was assaulted by a gaggle of children. Each daughter was clamoring for Mother, shouting their questions. Sanaa could do something like what Mother did.*

*Sanaa opened her mouth to speak, but she was sinking, drowning in darkness. Sanaa blinked and she was in the receiving hall with her sisters again.*

*Kala was on her knees, her green eyes furious and wet. Sanaa stood above her, sword drawn and at the ready. Mother sat on her dais, high above the rest of them. All Sanaa could see was the cut of her teeth as she spoke.*

*"Kill her and end this farce!" Mother shouted down from her raised dais. Her voice was drowned out as the stomping of feet took over the stadium. Their sisters stomped their feet with wild abandon waiting for the execution to take place.*

*Sanaa turned her eyes to Kala, whose green eyes were looking up at Sanaa.*

*"It's okay," Kala said. She turned her head back to the crowd waiting for her death. Tears leaked from her eyes. "You can do it, Sanaa. Don't think about it. I forgive you already."*

*The sword in Sanaa's hands had all the weight in the world. As she raised it above her head. She brought it down and—*

Sanaa shot out of the bed, gasping for breath. Her hand gripped her chest as a tremor of pain washed through it. It felt as though her heart was being petrified all over again. Her heart was hammering in her chest and each beat made a throbbing throughout all her body. Sanaa groaned as she laid back down and waited for the worst of it to pass.

As she lay there, with the pain burning in her chest she thought of her dream. She remembered that moment with Kala. The sword, heavy in her hands. She would never forget the look in Kala's eyes, resigned yet still strong. Stronger than she had ever been before. It was like she was ready to die but somehow with her death, she was still winning over Mother.

"End this farce," is what Mother had told her to do. At that moment Mother had become someone that Sanaa hated with all her heart. She had never felt so strongly about someone in her life, but Mother always managed to invoke even the tritest feelings in her.

The thought still felt ludicrous to her even now. Mother had wanted her to kill Kala, to cut off her head, and then simply be done with it as if that was not her sister. As if the moment where Kala had held her hand and led her through their burning home was supposed to mean nothing to her.

The sharp pain that felt like it was going to render her

heart asunder finally stopped. And Sanaa could finally breathe without feeling like her heart was about to pop. Sanaa took a gasping breath and raised her hands to her face. She was surprised by the sudden wetness that assaulted her when she ran her fingers down her cheeks.

Crying? Was she crying? Why? The tears were foreign on her cheeks as if someone else had put the water on her. But now that she had started she couldn't stop. The tears kept coming and coming and Sanaa could not stop them. They overwhelmed her as she remembered what Mother had tried to get her to do.

She had almost killed her sister, she had raised a weapon to her sister Kala when she was telling the truth. Kala had only wanted to tell the truth. Sanaa could not help but wish that Kala had not been telling the truth, that Mother had not done what she did and that Mother was not the traitor that she knew her to be.

But Mother was dead and so was Kala and the matter was already settled. Sanaa felt as though the world was on top of her, resting just on her chest and making it almost impossible to breathe.

Sanaa sighed and then leaned back on the bed, wishing that the weight of it would crush her.

# Chapter Six

S anaa spent her nights in pain. Waking to the sharp
pang in her chest and then crying until her eyes could
produce no more tears. She cried about Mother and
she mourned the loss of her sisters. She had thought that her
nieces had filled that void, that they had bandaged together
what was left of her. But her sisters left a hole in her heart, a
large void that nothing could fill.

It gnawed at her, this void, biting and itching at bits of
her heart. And Sanaa worried that it would consume her, take
the last bits of her that were her and leave nothing behind. It
was the nothingness that scared Sanaa the most; the bleak
tiredness that inhabited her when she could cry no more. She
was tired and cold, the world was no longer on her shoulders.
In those moments, nothing was. Sanaa was set adrift.

Those moments scared her. The days were another matter
altogether.

Traveling through a Fae forest she expected to encounter
some form of a brigand or wayward thief. Instead, she was
met with nothing. The roads were quiet except for the
passing merchant.

Sanaa could feel an itch under her skin as she got closer and closer to the faerie town of Asren. She had never been to a Faerie town before. The thought of entering one after being at war with the faeries for so long... it made her skin itch at the very thought.

What she was doing felt like a betrayal to her fallen sisters who had died fighting the Fae. Her sisters would have done anything to get a fae city and treat it the same way the Fae had Mayara. Standing in line to enter the city of Asren she felt the itch under her skin flare up again.

Greta had said that they were leaving the rivalry and warfare between the Batsamasi and the Fae behind. But Greta had never mentioned how the Fae were taking the change. Would they welcome her with open arms? Would she struggle to get into the city? Sanaa's thoughts began to whir around in her head. How would she be able to complete her mission if she could not make her way into the city? Would she have to sleep with a weapon in case someone still held a grudge?

Her turn at the gate came and Sanaa's breathing was shallow as she stepped up to the guards at the gate. The two guards were beautiful to look at but their faces were scrawled with boredom. The guard on Sanaa's right spoke first.

"What is your business in the city of Asren?" he asked. Sanaa felt her hands shaking as she scrounged through her pack, looking for the paper. "Your business?"

Sanaa found the edict in her pack and handed it to the guard her thoughts overwhelming her. What if, what if, what if? The thoughts did nothing but agitate her more and make her heart stutter in her chest. Sanaa passed the documents to the guard who looked them over once and then waved her inside.

"If you're looking for Vorus, you will find him in the large house in the center of town," the guard said as he handed back the papers to Sanaa. She took it with numb hands as the thoughts began to quiet in her head.

Sanaa was waved through the gates and she guided her horse through the gates. The town was beautiful in a way that Mayara was not. Mayara had been beautiful clean lines, but the town of Asren was a mess. Flowers blossomed everywhere. The houses were high in the trees with trunks that were wider than her horse.

The women and men drifted above Sanaa, their wings beating lazily behind them. The stores were carved into the trunks of the trees as men and women shouted out their prices and advertised their wares. Sanaa looked around her with wide eyes.

It was so different from the clean lines and sand-colored home that she came from. Music sounded out all around her and she was surprised to find that people were dancing in the middle of the street. Music was only played during special occasions when Mother was alive. And though she and her sisters danced, it was nothing like the wild arm swinging and foot-tapping of the Fae.

*"Don't look at them. Lest they see you and capture you in their deals."* Sanaa turned her eyes away from the faeries and spurred her horse forward. The words of Mother reminded her to keep her eyes down and to not stare. The Fae would ensnare you in their deals if they saw you looking.

Sanaa could not help but chide herself. These were the Fae. The ones that burned down her first home. The ones that had killed her sisters. Sanaa spurred her horse into a trot.

"Traitor," she could hear her sisters muttering from their graves. "Things change for a moment and you let your guard down." The thought made her heart twinge but her resolve hardened at that moment.

Sanaa could not be friends with any Faerie not after everything that she had been through. She doubted that the Faeries here wanted to be friends with her too.

Though she thought this to herself, Sanaa could not stop watching the faeries that surrounded her. Her eyes were caught by the bark skin of one of them to the deer antlers that another one had sprouting out of their head. Sanaa kept having to turn her eyes away only for her traitorous eyes to catch something else and make her stare.

It was a relief when she reached Vorus' manse. It was a large tree surrounded all around by a thorn bush. Sanaa circled the immense thorn bush once, then twice. She did not know how she was going to get inside and she brushed a hand against the bush. She snatched her hand away when one of the thorns cut her finger. The blood soaked one of the thorns.

The thorn bush shuddered, the leaves and vines trembling for a moment. Then the harsh brambles pulled away from one another, revealing a path forward for Sanaa to take. Sanaa jumped off her horse and led the horse inside. She stepped cautiously on the worn path that was before her, looking around for a sign of life.

A man appeared from the large white doors of the house. He was lithe and tall, with a shock of white hair. Sanaa watched as he descended the steps of the manse and step forward towards Sanaa.

"You are Sanaa of the Batsamasi, correct?" His voice was low but held all the authority of someone who knew what they were doing. Sanaa could barely nod her head before the man took the reins of the horse from her. "They are waiting for you inside." Sanaa nodded and walked the steps from to the entrance.

When she entered the house she stepped on slick black and white tiles. The house was decorated with all-white furnishings. Sanaa sucked in a breath. She thought that the compound was luxurious, but this was the height of luxury if she had ever seen it. The chairs looked plush and fluffy and the floor reflected her face.

Sanaa walked in and looked around. There was no one. Then she heard the sound of heels hitting the ground. The clicking sound came closer and a man with shaggy brown hair entered the foyer. He stopped in the middle of the foyer and when his eyes landed on Sanaa his lips twisted up into a smile.

"Ah, Sanaa of the Batsamasi. We've been waiting for you. I'm Vorus," he said. He walked up to Sanaa and her eyes were caught again by the antlers that curled up from his head.

"Others? There are others?" Sanaa found herself asking. Vorus was quick to have her following after him. His steps were fast, his long legs propelling him forward so that Sanaa had to trot to keep pace with him.

"Oh yes, there are other people who are going to help you with getting to the root of this problem," Vorus said. They turned down winding hallways and went through several doors before Sanaa finally saw the others that he was talking about. One of them was a demon, the other was a Faerie like Vorus. The demon had long winding horns that sprouted from his head and a scar running down the left side of his face over his eye. He was lithe, his body a honed weapon from the way that he sprawled himself in the seat. The Faerie had long blonde hair that was pulled away from her face. She was more uptight than the dead, sitting ramrod straight in the chair, but teetering forward. Her waif like form bending from unseen wind.

The two of them were sitting at a table that was bending with the weight of all the food that was on it. They picked at their plates and their heads snapped up to meet Sanaa and Vorus as they walked through the door. Vorus was quick to take the seat at the head of the table.

"I knew one day that my friendship with the Batsamasi

would pay off," he said with a chuckle. His voice was a rich baritone that rumbled through the room. The sound was beautiful like he was. "Welcome Sanaa. I'm glad that you've come all this way to help."

Help. He made it sound so voluntary as though she chose to appear here and she was not cast out of the only home that she knew. Her lips turned down in a frown as she sat herself down next to the other Fae at the table.

"I am not here because I desire to be," Sanaa started but Vorus waved his hand at her words.

"Ah, who cares about the how, you're here now and that is all that matters." Vorus juggled a fruit between his hands. His smile grew bigger but Sanaa knew a baring of teeth when she saw one. Sanaa leaned back in her chair knowing that she was never going to outsmart the Fae when it came to their word games. Vorus seemed happy with her concession as the smile on his face grew wider.

"These will be the people helping you, August and Taira," he said pointing to each in turn. The demon, August, nodded his head as he took her in. His eye was cool when they alighted upon her form. Sanaa could barely suppress the shiver that ran through her as he turned the full force of that milky white eye on her. He was blind in one eye, the sight gave Sanaa pause.

She wished that he could cover it. It was disgusting to look at, but Sanaa kept the words trapped in her mouth. The Faerie, Taira, nodded her head beside Sanaa and she turned her eyes back to Vorus who was looking at them with a bright look in his eyes.

His head of shaggy brown hair shook as he looked at the people assembled around him. "Well, now that we are all here I think I can begin to tell you what you are going to help with."

Taira sighed and nodded her head. Sanaa looked closer at

her and saw the sallow look to her skin and the bags underneath her eyes. This was a woman who was tired and seemed to be on her last leg. Vorus nodded his head and Taira fiddled with her fingers on the top of the table.

"Taira here is the captain of the Asren's guard. She has been reporting to me about the issues under the mountain." Taira's face seemed to drain of all color at the mention of the mountain.

"Yes," Taira piped up from her seat. "We have been fighting with something in the caves that has the Husks here flocking to it. It sabotages any trade that we attempt to do under the mountain. So many shipments have been stopped—"

"While that is all well and good, what is this person down in the caves truly capable of? I don't care about your trade. I want to know what the person in the caves can do," August said. His voice was low and melodic, like those he was singing with every word. Sanaa looked at him and saw that he was fiddling with a strand of his long black hair. He caught her staring and sent her a wink.

Taira shot him a black look. "Well, we suspect that what is under the caves may be a siren. It can sing people into madness though the odd part is that not everyone can be affected by the singing."

"A siren with no song?" Sanaa asked with a scoff. There had never been such a thing in all the time that Sanaa had walked the earth. Sirens had always had a song. Sanaa turned her eyes to Vorus another scoff ready on her lips, but when she saw the pensive look on his face the very action died in her throat.

"Yes, we believe it to be a siren because it can invoke madness in some of the guards that we sent in looking for it. The problem is we cannot find where it is hiding all the humans it's captured." Taira said with a shake of her head.

"What has General Solara said about this?" Sanaa asked. The words escaped her before she had a second to think it over. She sighed as everyone turned to look at her with quizzical looks. "I mean General Malforh?"

Mother Darkness above, it was getting harder and harder to remember all the new people who were in charge of the places that she remembered. They had crammed so much into her in the few weeks that she had spent with her nieces. Sanaa let out a breath.

"But there is something else. Something stranger that the siren can do," Vorus piped up from his seat. He leaned back in his chair and tented his fingers. His face, which had been bright since Sanaa had been introduced to him, seemed to be shrouded in a shadow. She looked to Taira and even she seemed more somber.

"The siren can drive people to madness. And then they stay that way," Vorus said with no small amount of dread.

The words took a moment to land in her mind, but then she let out a snort. There was no way that the siren could instill an everlasting madness on anyone. It has never been done before. August let out a scoff.

"That is impossible," he said while he crossed his arms. Sanaa nodded her head. A siren without a song and now a madness that never left. It was all too much to believe at once. Sanaa shook her head.

"You want us to believe this?" Sanaa said with a shake of her head. "There is no way that any of this is possible."

Taira slammed her hand down against the table causing the candelabras to jump up with fright. Her face was stone cold and her eyes were wet with tears.

"This is not some dream that I was telling you. I am telling you this because it has happened. Because I have seen it happen." Sanaa tilted her head at that. Taira looked as tired as she stared at the two of them, August and Sanaa. And for a moment, Sanaa wanted nothing more than to shrink away from her gaze, but then Taira stopped and turned her eyes back to Vorus.

Vorus nodded his head and then rose from the chair. "Maybe you will understand what we are dealing with if you see it for yourself." Vorus turned and gestured for them to follow. Sanaa got up from her seat and followed behind Vorus and Taira.

Walking down the halls with Taira, Vorus, and August, Sanaa's eyes darted this way and that taking in her new companions. August was the one who caught her eye the most, with raven dark hair and a lone milky white eye that spoke of its blindness. She was careful with the looks that she shot his way, but he caught her eyes roving over his figure and sent a smirk her way. Sanaa was quick to turn her eyes to the two Faeries in front of them.

Taira had long blonde hair and eyes that shone with tears that she was fighting to hold back. Sanaa felt her upper lip curl at the thought. Tears were useless. Tears were for children. Tears had never done anything to help anyone and the fact that Taira was spending time wiping tears from her ruddy cheeks pulled Sanaa away from her.

There was no use in crying. And she was the captain of the town guard. She should have more dignity. With that thought, her eyes turned to Vorus. His back was straight and his shaggy brown hair swayed from side to side as he led them deeper into the manse.

He carried himself with an air of importance that made everyone want to stop and stare at him. He seemed to walk with the knowledge that every step was going to land and that his plans were unfolding before him. It was a sharp contrast between Taira and Vorus that seemed to make him shine more and Taira dull a little more in comparison.

"Here." Vorus gestured to a door and was quick to pull it

open. When the wind from inside the room hit her face, it took everything in Sanaa not to gag. The sickening sweet smell of rot hit her face. Sanaa turned her face away from the door to protect herself from the smell. August covered his nose and gagged.

Vorus and Taira only nodded their heads as their eyes connected. Sanaa covered her nose and looked down. There was nothing but a set of stairs that were swallowed by darkness.

"Fintan's stars above, what do you keep down there?" Sanaa asked from her perch a little ways away from the door. "Bodies?"

Vorus's lips twitched up into a small smile and he tilted his head this way and that. "In a way, yes." The faeries went first down the stairs. August and Sanaa watched as they were swallowed up by the darkness and shared a look.

"You first," August said with the low timbre of his voice. Sanaa sucked in a deep breath and then descended the stairs. She pressed a hand against the wall and kept her other hand curled around her mouth. The stench only got worse the farther down the stairs she went. When she reached the base of the stairs, there was scant light that she could barely make out Vorus and Taira in front of her.

A hand touching her back almost made her jump out of her skin, but August brushed his lips by her ear with a quick "found you." Sanaa pulled herself away from him. Vorus and Taira nodded to one another again and Taira touched the wall of the basement.

The ceiling shook above them, loosing rocks and dirt on them and Sanaa covered her head. More light entered the basement and when Sanaa's eyes adjusted she could see what Vorus had wanted to show them.

Faeries. Tons of faeries held underneath his manse. They were suspended in cages made from the roots of the tree that the home was made of. The prisoners whimpered and cried out but what truly caught Sanaa's eyes were the burns. On all of their bodies, some burns festered. White-yellow pus flowed from the wounds and Sanaa reeled away from the heavy scent of infection.

"How many do you have under here?" Sanaa said as she moved to take a closer look under the cages of wood.

"Right now we have thirty-three prisoners. All of them afflicted with various levels of madness," Vorus answered. He passed by her and walked under the cages looking at the people in the cages with a bale look. This was normal for him now it appeared, to have dozens of his people hidden underneath his home.

"Taira, lower Nox down," Vorus said with a flick of his fingers. Taira nodded from her position by the base of the stairs and planted her hands on the wall again. She sighed and dug her fists into the dirt wall. The roots of the tree above them shuddered and then they shifted around. A root cage dipped down and swayed landing just in front of Vorus.

"This is Nox," he said as he unlocked the cage with a green glow from his fingers. "She was one of the first people to be afflicted with the madness. She has moments, where we can talk to her but those never last long."

Sanaa stepped closer and could see a woman dirty and covered in the same burns as the rest of the faeries cowering in the corner. She was shivering, a leaf in the wind, shuddering and shaking as though set upon with a large burden.

Her chest shook with every breath that she took and Sanaa gently placed one foot closer to the cage. Nox, shook her brown hair dusty and lacking luster.

"-s. She portends the death of the queen and shall release us all from our mortal coils. Mother Darkness shall welcome us into her loving arms-"

"Nox?" Sanaa tried. The woman did nothing but kept

muttering to herself. Her fingers glided over the rags that she wore for clothing. Sanaa dared not to step a foot inside the cage despite Vorus' eyes begging for her to do so. August marched forward his feet entering the cage without pause.

"Nox!" August's voice boomed. The woman looked up at him. Her skin was a mismatch of skin and bark, a dryad. She shudder and stretched before turning her eyes back to August and his feet inside her cage.

"You're in my cage," was all she said. "Why are you in my cage?" She looked as though the thought was something horrible to behold. New people in her cage? Sanaa saw her face darken before she lunged out, iron chains held her back and she howled as they burned her.

"Get out of my cage! Get out! It isn't time yet! She isn't ready yet!" Her hands lashed out, cracked fingernails trying to claw at August, but he simply reeled back out of her reach. Nox shook as she fell back, tears streaming down her soft cheeks as blood leaked from her ears.

"I can't do this anymore. I cannot wait anymore. When is she coming to get me? I want her to come and get me already." Nox put her face in her hands and started to sob like a child. August turned and looked back to Sanaa and Vorus. Vorus only shook his head and gestured for August to get out.

Sanaa breathed out when August exited the cage. The ceiling shuddered again and Nox's cries faded away as her cage was lifted and suspended in the air again. Vorus walked closer to the both of them, his hands crossed over his chest.

"That is what we are dealing with. This is what I need handled before the Empress arrives in Asren," Vorus said. His eyes never landed on the two of them but were focused above them on the cage above. Sanaa wondered at what he thought about as he looked at the afflicted people that he was in charge of. Did he feel sad that he let them down? Upset that they were foolish enough to fall for the siren's song?

Or maybe, a small part of her said, he feels annoyed that he has to deal with them as Mother felt with you. She quieted that thought as quickly as it rose. Mother was not tired of her, but then she remembered Mother. The way that she would look when she was tired from a day of running the compound and the way her eyes would cut into her daughters when she walked into a room.

Maybe Mother was tired of her. Sanaa shook her head and walked back towards Taira who pulled her hands away from the wall. Taira's shoulders sagged as she pulled away from the wall and she sighed out a breath, rolling her shoulders as the rest of them approached.

"The bleeding ears are a sign of madness. They only ever bleed when they are hearing the siren's song. It is a sign of the madness encroaching on their minds," Vorus said. His hands were fisted as he turned back to look at all the cages. He turned back to all of them with a smile on his face. "But now you've seen them and are committed to helping, right?"

"Of course," Sanaa said with a nod of her head. August shook his head with a laugh.

"Of course. Of course, we'll help you with this," August said as he looked at the people in the cages. Vorus relaxed and clapped his hands, rubbing his palms together.

"Good! Now let you show you where you'll be staying," Vorus passed them to lead them up the stairs. Taira and August were on his heels, but Sanaa lingered a moment, taking in the cages of people and the dwindling light of the room. She wondered at them for a moment but then she turned around and went up the stairs, leaving the mad ones in the dark.

# Chapter Seven

Dinner that night was a quiet affair with Sanaa and August excusing themselves early in the night to rest for the next day. When August entered his room, he was surprised to see that the things in his room were unpacked and put away in drawers. And that all the potions and tonics that he carried around with him were set up on one of the drawers in his room. August touched the desk and the gnarled horn sitting atop it in his room.

"Well isn't he cautious," August muttered under his breath.

"Yes, I am." Vorus stood in the doorway arms crossed over his chest. August let a smile creep onto his face as he saw the man standing there. He had expected him to come to approach him, but he did not expect to be confronted so soon.

August opened his mouth to speak but Vorus only held up a hand. August closed his mouth and Vorus pushed off of the wall. He only tossed August a look over his shoulder and walked away. August had to hold in a chuckle.

"Faeries and their performances," he muttered to himself.

He followed Vorus out of the room with a smirk on his lips. Walking a little ways away from Vorus, August could not help but think they looked suspicious. Two lone men walking in the night, one following after the other, they could not have looked more like they were planning something.

Vorus had led to one of the manicured gardens that were sporting large red roses. Vorus said on the thin metal chairs that creaked under his weight. A table of twisted cold metal sat between Vorus and the empty chair across the table from him.

August settled himself in the chair. He did it with an air of caution as though the metal beneath him was about to give way. Vorus did not even give him a chance before he pulled out the piece of paper.

It was an innocent-looking thing, something that anyone would have overlooked. But the bunching of his shoulders and the tough set to his lips made it seem as although the paper had offended him in some way. August did not say anything, waiting for Vorus to start the conversation. He had something to say if all he was going to do was put a paper on the table.

"You work for Helia?" That was all that Vorus said. August did not bother to look at him or the letter and kept his eyes trained straight ahead. He looked at the flowers, the way that the bush swayed in the wind. He already knew. The seal of the letter was already broken. So why bother to ask a question that he already knew the answer to?

"You read the letter?" August asked. Vorus said nothing to that, he simply tightened his fist around the scrap of paper. August let out a small chuckle from his lips.

"I won't allow for any chaos to be brought to the town of Asren. Any other time I could ignore this and let you do as you please, but the empress is coming here. Not some lord but the Empress of the Faerie Courts is coming so I cannot let this-"

August raised his hand to stop the torrent of words that was coming out. "You and I both know that I can't leave. Helia would be furious."

"Helia would be furious but Empress Sorcha is the one that I am most worried about. If she finds out about you-"

"She won't," August said with a sharp intake of breath. "I'll finish what needs to be done for Helia and I'll even help you with the problem with the siren."

"That isn't the problem!" Vorus almost shouted. He tossed the paper into the garden and it caught on the thorn of a rose. August finally turned his eyes to Vorus and saw him where he was. His shoulders were almost bunched up to his ears with hands in tight fists that made the skin bone white. August took this all in and turned back to the rose garden. "If someone finds you out—"

"That is what you are for. You give me a legitimate purpose to be here—"

"What if—"

"Tell me Vorus. If you are so cautious then why did you choose to become a contact for Helia?"

"That has nothing to do with anything. When you first came to me saying you wanted to help me-"

"You are an agent of Helia. Remember who you swore loyalty to."

Vorus looked at August his eyes burning with hatred that August carried in his heart every day. For a moment August pitied Vorus, the stress that he was underneath must be immense, and with the Empress coming so soon. It was something that August could not understand. But as quick as his pity arose it was gone.

Vorus knew what he was doing when he first joined Helia and her crusade against the half-mad empress. He knew what he was doing and now this was no time for him to be pulling back on his promises. August rose from his chair.

"I will help you with the thing in the caves. Helia has a vested interest in what is down there."

"But what is it that she could want in the caves. The siren is something that is hard to deal with enough already and Helia wants to add it to her arsenal?"

August shook his head. "See this is why you are so stressed. You are worrying about things that are above you. What Helia wants to do is none of your concern. Worry about getting me closer to who is in charge of what is down in the caves. Once we get that under Helia's control then everything that you are worried about will end."

Vorus did not say anything and August let a smirk grace his lips. He strode over and clapped a hand on Vorus's shoulder. He gave it a good squeeze before he turned around and left the room, satisfied that Vorus was now under control. Vorus simply let out a sigh and waved his hand. "Do as you please," was all he said.

On the way back to his room, August could not help but think about what it was that Helia truly wanted out of whoever was running the operations in the cave. Whoever was down there was recruiting Husks, the mortals. Why would she show any interest in the mortals?

The Husks of this world were weak and nothing worth having any interest in. They lived and they died like foam on a tide; they were there and then they were not. It was a short and pitiful existence that they lived. Under the thumb of those that Mother Darkness deemed worthy of power and prestige. Husks were nothing more than what they were called, hollow husks that were only entertaining when something else was in control of them.

But Helia was always doing things that he was not privy to. No matter how much August worked and tried to understand the woman she was always something of a mystery to him. And when he thought he was finally cracking the code of who Helia was and what it was that she wanted in the world, he was thrown for another loop.

August frowned at the thought, he would never understand Helia for as long as he lived. What could be so interesting about what was in the caves? August rolled his shoulders and let out a yawn. Whatever was down there could wait until tomorrow.

August walked into his room and changed into his sleep clothes. With another yawn, he stretched out his body and his wings unfurled without a thought. He was quick to put them back lest they bump into something, though the room was large enough to handle his considerable wingspan.

August threw himself into the bed, resolving to go to sleep and dream something pleasant.

*The plain was filled with bodies. The cry of birds could be heard above and they dived down ready to feed on the bodies that were strewn around the field. Rolling hills that were supposed to be green were covered in the bodies of the lost and forgotten. Plumes of smoke rose from huge pyres of fire and workers tolled endlessly as they lifted bodies from the ground and tossed them on the pyre.*

*The heavy scent of smoke invaded his senses and the world tilted around him. August coughed as the smoke-choked him and he ran as far as he could away from the heavy smoke and the burning bodies. The bodies smelled of rotting fruit and charr and that was all he could smell as he climbed the heap of bodies that surrounded him.*

*He needed to get out of there away from the smoke and ash and away from the bodies and the birds that feasted on them.*

*His feet flew past as he was tugged somewhere. It felt as though something had hooked on his skin and was tugging away at him. With hands over his nose and mouth, August followed the tug. It was pulling him away from the battlefield and somewhere else. Somewhere that was not... this.*

August allowed the tug to pull him forward, the drudgery around him blurring into a saddening mass of grey. August tried to focus his sights but he couldn't the world was turning faster than his eyes could capture. Like lightning, something flashed green around him. Bright and unyielding, August had to close his eyes from the bright light.

The world shone bright and then settled down. August was out of breath, as though he had run when the world was turning around him. August sighed out a breath and when he opened his eyes he was in a tent.

The tent was not far away from the smoke and the burning bodies. He could still smell them in the air, but it was farther away in the sense that the smoke was a note in the air. August could breathe easier once again. He sucked in a breath-

"The harpies have been completely handled after today. Those old birds won't be rising anytime soon."

August turned his eyes to the back of the tent. There stood the figure of a man and a woman. The woman wore flowing red robes that shimmered in the scant light that was in the room.

The man stood before her, his clothing was not as fine and as well kept as her's was, splotches of dirt and muck were caked on the elbows and shoulders. He stood with his hat in his hands, but he was large and gangly making the simple action look awkward somehow. His head was bowed towards the woman despite him towering over her.

The woman rested on a chaise, her legs crossed and stretched out before her. August could feel that he knew this woman. He knew her somehow, but his mind was a dense fog that he could not pierce through. The fog stayed heavy in his mind, slowing his movements and making it so that everything that he did was lagging.

The woman said nothing as she took a sip from the delicate-looking wine glass. She savored the flavor on her tongue for a moment.

"The harpies are the least of my worries," was all she said. Her voice was deep and rich. It soothed something anxious inside of

*August, something that was clawing and screaming at him. "What I wanted was Prince Titus."*

*The man gripped his hat tighter. "We did everything that we could-"*

*"No, you didn't," she said with a flick of her wrist. The man did not reply to that. The woman only took another sip from her glass. "If you did everything that you could. You would have the Prince and we wouldn't be having this conversation. No, you didn't try Havard and now I have no prince to return to my father."*

*"I am sorry Lady Aranea, but my men tried everything that they could and they could not secure the Prince," the man said with a twist of his hat. "But we were able to retrieve this."*

*The man settled something on the side table next to Aranea's head. It glowed with a faint green light. It pulsed and shivered on the table and Aranea lifted it for a closer look. August leaned closer, trying to get a better look at it, but Aranea's eyes locked on his.*

*Her gaze was burning as though she could see right him for everything that he was. She smiled at him and rose from her perch.*

*"Hello brother. Are you lost?" The words snapped into place in August's mind and he knew, he remembered why the woman was so familiar to him. Aranea smiled, holding the glowing object in her hands hidden from him. She smiled and blew.*

*The air rushed past him and August was sent flying his body suddenly weightless.*

August opened his eyes with a gasp. His body tingled all over as he tried to catch his breath.

Astral projection was something that he hadn't done in a long time. It was something that he did when he wanted to see something far away, but it was taxing on his body and mind. August could already feel the pounding ache that was spreading throughout his body.

August put a hand to his chest and he could feel the pounding of his heart. It had been so long since he had seen his sister. Aranea was just as fickle as ever talking to one of her generals. But that thing in her hands, what was that? August remembered the brilliant green glow of it and the way that it shone through her fingers.

He sat up in his bed. No, there was no use in trying to uncover whatever it was that Aranea was fooling around with now. He rose from the bed, his body aching now that it had to accommodate the weight of his soul.

His steps fell heavy on the ground with loud thumps that were so different from the quiet gliding that he was used to. August stumbled towards the washroom ready to douse himself in water and try to soak away all the aches and pain.

The tub was already full of water, though it was not steaming. August stripped off his clothing and pushed himself under the water. His body relaxed and August's muscles loosened when he rose.

A knock sounded at the door.

"August, are you there?" Vorus's voice sounded out from behind the door. "August?"

"Yes I'm here," August answered, leaning back in the pool of water.

"Can we speak?" He asked. The thought of talking to Vorus so early in the morning seemed taxing to August, but Vorus was important. He was the contact that Helia spoke of so his cooperation was essential to what he was doing. August let out a sigh.

"Come in." Vorus was quick to come in and settled himself a little ways away from August. August blew bubbles underneath the water wanting Vorus to start the conversation. The two men stared at each other for a moment before Vorus tensed up from his position against the wall.

"I'll allow for you to carry out what Helia wishes," Vorus said with a shake of his shaggy head.

August smiled and leaned back in his lukewarm bath, arms stretched wide. "So you've decided to make the smart choice and not incur Helia's wrath. You know working with me is easy. I'll just go down to into the caves get whoever is causing the trouble to stop and make her join Helia's crusade."

"And my shipments? They'll go through to the wolves and keep my end of the trade agreement?" Vorus asked with a simple wringing of his hands. August rolled his eyes, Vorus was worried about the small matters but he needed his cooperation.

"I'll make sure of it," August yawned. Vorus's shoulder dropped at the reassurance. August looked the man over. His clothing was finely embroidered with blooming flowers and the crest of the town, but Vorus sagged against the wall like a struck tree.

August nodded his head, his mind already whirring with thoughts about places where he could go to find out more about the person in the caves. It would be a tough negotiation but it was worth trying.

He rose from the tub, water dripping down onto the floor. Vorus passed him a towel, August wrapped himself in it.

"Don't worry. Once I gain control of whatever is in the caves, it'll be like it was never even there."

# Chapter Eight

✦❖✦

The sword dance was something that had been passed down from generation to generation. It was a dance that the Batsamasi did to showcase their abilities and show reverence to their mothers and grandmothers and all the generations that preceded them.

Sanaa could remember the first moment that she saw the sword dance. The way that the steel whirled in the air, the way that her aunt moved through the air. It all looked so easy and graceful that Sanaa knew at that moment she wanted nothing more in the world than to be a sword dancer.

As Sanaa landed on the ball of her feet, she allowed the needles to fall away. Sword dancing was not easy and it took years of practice to do it properly. But Sanaa was an experienced sword dancer so this should be easy, graceful. She went through the motions of sword dancing again and again in the early morning light. But she was not flowing like she used to.

Sanaa gave another frustrated grunt and dropped the needles that were suspended in the air. It wasn't working. The dance was not coming to her naturally like the way that she used to. Her blades did not sing, they clanked against one another. When she rose they did not glow but trembled and shimmered in the air before her. Sanaa's lands were not her delicately landing but harsh crashes against the ground.

Sanaa sat down on the ground and brushed back her braids. It was hard trying to do the sword dance now. The fighting style was something that she had not done in a long time—she stopped her thoughts there. It was something that she had done thousands of times. She was supposed to be good at this.

She felt something in her stomach harden and rose. She would do it again and make sure that she did it right. She looked to the large needles and she saw them, the shimmering strings of monyelta that were waiting to be plucked and manipulated by her.

Her fingers danced on the shimmering lines that connected the needles to the rest of the world. She reached out and pulled on one of the strings. The needles floated in the air ready to follow her whims. The threads of monyelta wrapped around her fingers and she could feel the magic hot against her skin. Hot, but not burning her skin.

Leaping into the first movement of the sword dance, she ducked and dodge. Weaving herself through the intricate spiral of needles that she created with a flourish of her hands. She went through all four movements, feeling the stretch of her skin and the burn in her muscles as she danced.

When she finally stopped she was out of breath. How long was she dancing? Someone clapped from the doorway behind her. She turned and saw the demon, August, standing behind her. In his mouth was a piece of food that he was crunching on and his long claw-tipped hands clapped as a smile grew on his face.

"Wow, that was stunning. It slowed down a little bit in the middle there, but it was still amazing to watch," August said with a grin. Sanaa brushed her braids back from her face and looked to the sky.

Though she was in a sandy pit that Vorus called the training grounds, the ceiling was open to the sky and the elements. Sanaa saw that the sun was high in the sky and blistering, far from the few tendrils of light that she had seen when she first entered the room.

"It looks nice, but it isn't perfect," was all Sanaa could muster to say. The dance was still not perfect, not that way that she could do it before. August swallowed the last of his food and walked closer to Sanaa, his stomping feet making a plume of dirt to rise from the floor.

"Perfection is so overdone. If everything was perfect life would be boring," August said with a quirk of his lips. Sanaa turned her head to look at the needles on the ground. They were laying still, shining in the noon light, but they were taunting her.

Perfect. She needed it to be perfect.

"It needs to be perfect or else it is not worth doing." The sword dance had to be perfect. It honored their grandmothers, the sisters who created the city of Mayara. It had to be perfect for them, for those sisters who burned when the city of Mayara burned to the ground. Sanaa shook her head, her braids swinging out wildly around her.

Standing up, Sanaa's brown skin glowed in the noon light. And she turned to face August again. Her eyes looked into August's eyes. She noted the scar that ran down the side of his face and the still white coloring of one eye.

"I tried everything but it is not perfect. It is not like how it was before," Sanaa muttered under her breath. August caught on to that and slid closer to Sanaa.

"What do you call what you were just doing?" August asked.

"It's called the sword dance," Sanaa said as she gathered

the long needles that were on the floor. She bent over to pick them up and August whistled low.

"See that's why you're having problems with the thing. It's a dance. It's supposed to have two partners." August walked over to a rack against the wall. Spears of every length lay on that rack and August did not pause in his movements and grabbed one before turning back to face Sanaa. Her eyes were caught by the thin line of scar that ran down his face, to the milky white eye.

Sanaa could not tear her eyes away from it. What had he done to earn such a scar? What battles had he survived and where had he gone. Her eyes traced over the bronze skin of his arms, the muscles bunching up underneath his skin.

"You think I need a partner?"

"You called it a dance. No dance can be done without a partner." He tossed the spear from one hand to another, looking at her with large eyes. Sanaa's stomach grumbled at her, reminding her that she had been here since the wee hours of the morning. But her muscles were tensing already. A sword dance with a partner. Maybe that was what she was missing.

"Demons are beings of chaos. Inviting one into your life will bring nothing but the god Magni's judgment." It was as though she was back sitting on her mother's lap. She could feel it, Mother's hand gripped around her throat like a vice tightening around her neck.

Sanaa shook her head. "No, I don't need a partner. I don't need a partner at all." Sanaa gathered the rest of the needles and slid them into the thin boxes tied to her thighs. She moved away from August and his spear and ran down the hallway.

It was like all she could see was Mother. All she could hear was Mother's voice and everything that she had taught her. Mother...

Sanaa reached her room and closed the door behind her, sliding down the door and covering her ears.

"Do you think that you can be anything without me? You think that you can disobey me and not suffer?" Mother's voice was a roar in her ears and Sanaa's stomach tightened as she thought of those moments before Mother did the fateful action.

Everything slowed as Mother lifted her finger in the air and pulled the string of monyelta and Sanaa grabbed at her chest, her heart stuttering in its place. Sanaa gasped as her heart shrunk in her chest and she could barely breathe.

She was dying. Her vision was getting narrower and narrower and—

"Sanaa? Are you there Sanaa?"

Air flooded her lungs. Sanaa slumped forward letting the air whistle through her chest. She pressed her hands to her chest, feeling the rise and fall of it.

What was that? She was dying and then now... Sanaa patted her breast for a moment making sure that she was there. She opened her eyes and found that she was in her room. A breeze rushed through the curtains and ruffled Sanaa's braids.

A hand pounded against the door she was leaning against. Sanaa rose from the ground and wiped her face, surprised to find that there were tracks of tears on her cheeks. She wiped her eyes and cheeks and opened the door.

In front of her stood Taira, her hand poised to knock at the door again. Taira's green eyes locked on Sanaa's brown ones and the woman put her hand down. Sanaa was still panting and wanted nothing more than to be alone in her room to figure out what the hell happened to her.

"You never made it to breakfast," Taira said with a shiver of her lips. "Vorus was worried that you may have thought against helping."

"No," Sanaa said. Her voice sounded garbled when she spoke so she cleared her throat and answered again. "No, I'm still here and I am still willing to help you with your problem." Taira visibly brightened at her words and Sanaa could not help but curl her lip at the emotions that were so obviously displayed on her face.

Mother would have never stood for one of her daughters to be so easy to read. Sanaa cast the thought of Mother and what she would and wouldn't allow out as quick as it rose in her mind. Mother was gone. Mother was gone. She needed to begin to understand that.

Mother was gone and with it all the influence that she wielded. Sanaa cleared her throat again and pushed at the door a little bit.

"Is that all you needed to talk to me about?" Sanaa asked. She wanted to close the door in her face and be done with the conversation, but she was raised better than that.

Taira shifted where she stood. The faerie had something that she wanted to say, but Sanaa was losing her patience. Sanaa felt a pounding growing in-between her eyes. She wanted nothing more than to throw herself into her room and rest.

"I'm here to show you around the town so that you know exactly what you are going up against," Taira muttered so lowly that Sanaa had to strain to hear. Sanaa thought about it for a moment. It would be beneficial for her to know where they would be inevitably doing battle with the siren.

Mother's words snuck into her head. "Always know where you will fight your enemy." Sanaa shook her head, but the words stuck with her. Sanaa nodded and walked outside of her room, pulling the door shut behind her.

"Show me." Taira smiled and turned around to lead her out of the manse. When she exited outside of the manse, the scent of several flowers blooming at once overwhelmed her.

Everywhere she looked bright flowers were bloomed. Sanaa sneezed as she covered her nose.

"I never thought that there would be so many flowers here," Sanaa said. Taira let out a laugh.

"It is a specialty of the Spring Court. None of the other courts have nearly enough flowers," Taira said. The air was heavy with the musk of flowers. They walked through the town where the people did not bother to bat an eye at a Batsamasi.

Sanaa's eyes kept scanning through the crowds that they walked through looking for something amiss. But as they walked through the town there was nothing but the hustle and bustle of a town that was unbothered. It was as though the townspeople did not know what was going on in the caves.

When she turned to ask about the general peacefulness of the town and the lack of concern, Taira was several steps in front of her. Sanaa rushed forward and on her way there she saw the temple of Roux. The temple was a silent monument that was out of place in the town. Her eyes skimmed over the temple before she rushed forward and caught up with Taira.

Blonde hair whipping around her, Sanaa caught sight of a frigid look on Taira's face as she turned to look Sanaa in her eyes.

"The people do not know anything about the problems we are having in the caves. We have tried to keep it quiet. All they know is that the Husks are running away to the caves," Taira said in a grave whisper. Sanaa could scarcely hear her over the din of people, but she understood.

They were trying to keep whatever was going on in the caves a secret. It made sense, to reveal that something was inflicting madness on their people would surely cause something of a panic. But why then were Husks so quick to jump into the caves?

The farther that they walked towards the cave, the fewer people populated the area. The waves of people soon steadied into a trickle and then nothing.

"Here they are, the caves," Taira said. The cave was a yawning maw of darkness that was carved into the side of the mountain. Sanaa looked up, hoping to catch a glimpse of one of the dragons that inhabited the mountain. She could catch nothing but the sight of white, fluffy clouds.

"There is no use in trying to see the dragons," Taira piped up from behind her. "General Malforh and his retinue very rarely leave the confines of their dens."

Sanaa turned her eyes back to the cave. The wind whistled through it causing the cave to let out a loud yawn. The sound ruffled the grass and whistled through the trees. Sanaa took a step back.

This was it. This was the place she needed to be and then she could go home. She would not have to linger any longer than she needed to and she could go back to her nieces and say that she did everything that she could. Sanaa turned to Taira, taking in the shorter woman.

"When is the next trade supposed to take place?" That was all that she asked. Taira said nothing at the question, likely knowing where Sanaa was going with this train of thought.

"You really should wait a moment longer that way we can all go with more information—"

"When is the next trade supposed to take place?"

Taira sighed as if she knew that Sanaa was not going to let up from that. This was all that she needed to do and then she would be able to go home and return to her nieces, to her family. The thought would not leave Sanaa. The thought of home, the comforts of the compound were too intoxicating.

"The next schedule trade is supposed to take place tonight," Taira said with a sigh. "Vorus didn't want to waste time and thought that maybe if they went during the night that the caravan would not be attacked."

Sanaa nodded her head and looked to the caves again. She would be on that caravan tonight. She would end whatever was in there. And then she would finally return home where she belonged.

## Chapter Nine

"**D**on't you have anything better to do?" Vorus asked.

August sat with his back resting on the armrest of the chaise, his long legs stretched out before him. The ball in his hands was a flash of red as it passed from one hand to the other and back again. August kept his eyes on the ball, juggling it back and forth between his fingers. Vorus sat behind a tall desk with several papers strewn around him.

August's lips twitched up into a smile. "I don't have anywhere particular where I have to be. Taira left with the little sword dancer to show her the caves and they left me with nothing to do except..."

"No, I am not going down there," Vorus said with a stiff line for lips. August shrugged and went back to tossing the ball back and forth between his hands. The sound reverberated through the small office along with the sound of Vorus turning pages of his book.

All was silent and August frowned, tossing the ball back and forth between his hands faster, causing the sound to grow steadily louder and louder—

"Roux take you to Mother Darkness herself! Why do you want to go down there so badly?" Vorus asked with a sigh. The man shoved away all his work. The antlers on his head looked to weigh heavy on him as he pinched the bridge of his nose between his fingers. The quill in his hands had snapped in half with how tight he was gripping it.

"Take me down to see one of the afflicted," August said with a bright gleam in his eyes. He rose from the chaise, invigorated by his new idea. "I need to see one of the least afflicted ones or maybe one of the Husks that you say are running away towards the caves."

"Finding one of the least afflicted victims is easier said than done. The only one that has any moments of any lucidity is Nox. And she is still too volatile for you to even consider possessing," Vorus said picking up one of the papers that had fallen. "Rethink your plan and then maybe I will consider entertaining it."

August let out a huff. "You aren't seeing this clearly. There will never be a perfect vessel for me to possess. Either way, I am going to take some damage. It better be in the use of ending this mission for Helia faster-"

"Be quiet," Vorus snapped. "These walls are thinner than the god Sevan's temper. You need to think before you talk. Especially about Helia."

August held up his hands and shrugged his shoulders. "You cannot blame me. I am rarely away from her side. This is usually dealt with by some of the newer boys."

"Then it appears you've lost her favor."

The words made August pause. Had he lost Helia's favor? Had he been relegated to do the grunt work for her. Helia was always something of a mystery to him. He could barely understand her and he was around her a lot of the time. Nothing that the woman did made any sense and he was supposed to be the one closest to her, at the moment at least.

But Helia always had her reasons for everything that she did. She did not take actions carelessly. She did everything with intention, with purpose. She would not send him far away from her side without a reason, without purpose.

No, he knew Helia and she was not one who throw him aside so easily. And though he tried to quiet the thought in his head, it rang out loud and reverberated through his skull. He was already indebted to Helia. How much longer until she tired of him warming her bed and wanted him to work off his debt?

August focused back on Vorus, who had righted the papers and books on his desk so that they looked less like a cluttered mess. August said, "Take me to go see Nox. I can get something out of her."

"Fine," Vorus said with the snap of his fingers. A maid entered the room, her head bowed and her uniform crisp. "Find Tiamon and tell him to handle all the work until I get back." He turned back to August and stalked past.

"Well, are you coming?"

August smiled and jogged slightly to catch up with him. The two stalked down the hallways, passing the bright colors of the stained glass windows. August took a moment to marvel at how shiny the black and white tile floor was and knew that the maids must have just finished scrubbing it. This time August was prepared for the stench when the door was opened.

They both descended into the darkness of the dungeon. When August stepped on that last step, he was amazed at the overwhelming darkness of the dungeon for a moment. All he could see was a blank, black void of darkness. Then the roots shifted and light began to be illuminated.

Those in the cages, shied away from the light, muttering to themselves or outright shouting at the sudden onslaught of light. Others moaned at the scant light that was entering in. Vorus stood with his hands against the wall of dirt.

"Bring down Nox," August commanded. Vorus only grunted his response and dug his fists deeper into the dirt. The roots of the tree shuddered and Nox was in sight. She was huddled into one corner of her cage muttering to herself as though she was going to answer back.

The door of the cage swung open and August was in the door in a matter of moments. Vorus was quick to hold the door to the cage as though he was unsure if whether or not he wanted to close August inside.

"It seems you caught Nox on one of her good days," Vorus said, craning his head to see inside the cage. August knelt close to Nox, an arm stretch away from touching her. August smiled a smile of compassion as he took in her tear stricken face and the way she shivering as though the room was cold.

"Don't worry, Nox," August said in a gentle voice. "I'm here to help you."

"P-please...please make it stop. I don't want—I don't want to be like this anymore," Nox chattered through her teeth.

"Shhh... Shhh... It's fine. I'm here to help you."

"No one can help me. Only s-she can fix this. Make her fix me."

"Shhh, just relax."

August relaxed, his shoulders rolling back as he felt his body starting to go limp. The process of leaving his body and going into another was like that of breaching water after holding his breath for a long time. He felt his body fall away and he was holding his breath.

August's soul swam towards the jumbled mass that was Nox's mind. When it breached the body it was like August could breathe again and he took his first breath in the body of Nox.

"Are you...in?" Vorus tried. The world tilted to one side

and his vision was dotted with black voids. August shook his —Nox's—head once, twice before his vision cleared.

"I'm here," August said. His voice was pitched higher than he was expecting and he felt the voice ring through his body and his bones. He sucked in a deep breath readying himself to dive into Nox's mind and soul. "I'm going to take a look."

Every mind was different. It was all organized differently and it was always a maze that August needed to work through. August was prepared for a jumbled mess of a mind, something to reflect the mess that she was in the real world. But when he entered her mind, there was nothing. It was a simple blank void. There was no mess of thoughts, there was simply nothing.

What is this, August thought to himself. The world was a blank and empty void with nothing to look at, nothing to unravel. How did she live like this? There was nothing there. It was a clean slate with nothing to uncover.

August turned this way and that, looking for a spare thought a memory something when the world rippled around him. The ground trembled underneath his feet and a flash of color passed on the floor quick as a shadow. August propelled himself after it without a second thought. The color paused its movement and spread. August was quick, reaching out and touching the color.

With all the strength of a surging tide, August was sucked into the memory. When August opened his eyes again he was in the middle of a battle. His hands were wrapped tight around a weapon and he was dodging and parrying blows that came from the darkness.

August dodged another blow and rolled away. His chest was constricted in the armor that he was wearing. Another blow came for him and he could not dodge this hit. The hit made the world go dark.

When he opened his eyes again he could feel the

remnants of tears on his face. He could hear the sounds of screaming and crying around him, but his vision was hazy. He could barely make out that a person was standing before him and they were in front of a table of some sort.

"You know, I barely have the hang of this power," the person said. August belatedly recognized that it was the voice of a woman, but his attention was caught with how it appeared that she was appearing and disappearing. One moment she was in front of the table the next she was leaning in front of him. August could barely keep up with the movements.

She lifted something to his lips. It was bitter and smelled like rotten fruits, but August swallowed it down. He choked on it but he got it down. The person in front of him had a glowing pink necklace. It slipped out from the heavy cloak that the person was wearing.

"I've only just found this power. Something that they said was rumored to be fake, but I found it." August watched as the woman blinked out of focus. Now she was farther away, closer to the table.

"Forgive me, but I have to try it. I'm only ever tried this on mortals," she said. The necklace glowed from where she stood. It grew in its luminance, growing brighter and brighter with every beat of his heart. Then he could hear it, the music. It was low at first like someone was pulling on the thick strings on a lyre. The music grew louder and louder with the growing brightness of the necklace.

"Quiet wayward wanderer." A voice sang out. He could hear the singer. She sang of lost family and the forgotten sons and daughters of the world. Her voice rose as she sang faster and faster, the world blurring together as the siren song rose and rose in power. The singer was screaming now and the light was too brilliant, the heat of it burning his eyes.

August let out a scream as he was thrust out of Nox's

body. His soul was quick to hop into the empty vessel that was his body. His skin felt stretched tight over his bones, and August was gasping for breath.

His ears were ringing and Nox was thrashing like a wounded animal in the cage screaming at the top of her lungs. August scrambled away from her and his limbs cutting through the air to pull himself away from the screaming woman. He fell out of the cage and the door swung close.

August was panting, his chest rising hard and falling even harder. His body was covered in sweat and he watched with wide eyes as the cage was lifted and suspended in the air once again. Nox's voice faded away and joined the din of the other prisoners, each one moaning out, crying for something.

Vorus stalked up to August and pulled him from the ground. August slumped where he stood. His bones felt weak and brittle, as though his legs were ready to snap into broken pieces under his weight. August's eyes were rolling, following the black spots that dotted his vision. Vorus growled, snapping his fingers in front of August's face.

"Well? What did you find?" Vorus asked.

The spots still danced in his vision but August attempted to focus on the wavering face of Vorus. August took in a deep breath and let it out. He repeated the action again and again until the dots dancing in front of his eyes dissipated.

"Well?" Vorus asked again. "Did you find anything?"

With his breath under control, August could finally focus on Vorus who was standing in front of him. "There is a woman. Someone who is in control over what is going on in the caves. She is the one who drove all these people to madness."

"A woman? So it is not a siren?" Vorus asked with a furrowed brow. August could only imagine what was going through his head. "Fucking Arif's fortune is what I have. Do you know who the woman is?"

August shook his head at that and Vorus cursed again under his breath. "The memory wasn't clear. Nox was barely conscious when she met the woman but she had something that drove these people mad. A necklace," August said.

"Fuck!" Vorus shouted with a strong kick to the air. August walked over closer to the exit and slumped against the wall. His ears were still ringing and his jaw ached. He rubbed at his face trying to make sense of what it was that he saw.

There was a woman and she had something, she did something that drove the rest of them mad. She had to be the one that was in control of the whole operation. August needed to get there and quickly.

"When is the next trade supposed to take place?" August asked. Vorus was busy hitting the wall with his fists. When he finished, Vorus sighed and ran a hand through his tousled hair.

"Tonight," Vorus said. August nodded his head, the plan already forming in his mind. "No. You cannot be planning to join the trade group."

His face must have been obvious if Vorus could tell that was what he was thinking. August shrugged his shoulders but then nodded his head.

"I know who is in charge down there. I just need to get her under Helia's thumb and then both of our problems are solved!" August said with grand gestures.

"You don't even know what that person wants down there! They could ask for anything to join the fold! And besides, you only know that this person has a necklace and it drives people mad," Vorus frowned. August rolled his eyes.

"You need to stop thinking about what could go wrong. I found the person that is causing trouble in your town. I get them under the control of Helia and then our problems are solved. Both of us never have to see one another ever again."

Vorus paced back and forth in front of August. August

tracked him with his eyes. He was looking only at the negatives and not the fact that this would end his mission sooner than they thought. The god Arif blessed him with some good fortune and Vorus wanted to squander it.

"Listen if you let me go or not, I am going. I am ending this tonight."

Vorus growled at him, turning to go up the stairs and out the door. August sighed and turned his eyes to the cages that lingered above him. He was not going to save them, but he would stop more from becoming like them.

# Chapter Ten

The air was so thick that night Sanaa thought that she was going to choke on it. Vorus and Taira ate their food as though it had wronged them. August was chipper the whole dinner, eating to his heart's content. Sanaa merely moved the food around on her plate.

Her mind was enraptured with thoughts of her family and how she could return to them sooner. She would be with them soon, was a mantra that she kept repeating in her head.

This would have been the fastest that she had ever finished a mission. When Mother sent them out it usually took weeks or months before they finished and were able to return to the compound. She could hear her nieces asking her how she completed her mission and what she did.

The strings of monyelta were practically singing when night fell. She readied herself in the candlelight, putting on the leather armor that she brought and strapping the two holsters for her needles at her sides. She danced around the room, going through the positions of the sword dance before coming to a standstill in the room.

From one of the drawers, she pulled out the figurine of

Fintan that she had brought with her. She placed it with care on the ledge in front of her window. Fintans horns rose high off his head and the figurine of the god shone in the moonlight.

Sanaa stood before the figure of her birth god, heart thudding in her chest as she said her prayer.

"Fintan, I know it has been a long time since we have communed together. For that I apologize," Sanaa started. But then she stopped. What could she say to her birth god that he did not already know? His stars looked down on her when she was frozen, stuck in that perpetual hell.

He knew everything that she went through and, because of Arif, knew where she was going to end up. Fintan knew everything that was. So what more could she tell him.

"I hope you may guide my hands and make sure that every strike that I make strikes true. Make it so that I can crush my enemies and go home to my family. Please. Heed my prayer."

The figure did nothing but wink in the moonlight, light bouncing off the brown colored glass. Fintan bared his ax and his bull's head bared his gnashing teeth. Sanaa did not feel the presence of Fintan with her. She did not feel that the god that she had so faithfully served was blessing her with his presence. Sanaa felt small at the thought.

She sat down on the bed and waited for Taira to fetch her to join the trade caravan. When was the last time she had waited with anticipation for the heat of battle? Her body was humming with excitement. Her fingers twitched ready to pull on the monyelta and make her needles go flying through the air.

She rubbed at her face, waiting in the dark. When was the last time that she fought? A millennia ago, but then she thought back to the early days when the Husks were busy with building the compound. The memory of the burning of Mayara was still fresh in her mind and Mother was preparing them to fight against the Fae, to kill them for what they had done.

*Sanaa's hand shot out to smash into Yeleni's face. She could feel Yeleni's nose crunching under her hand and she gasped then, thinking about the pain that she must be feeling. Yeleni stumbled back and her blood was all over her face and Sanaa's fist.*

"Don't stop!" Mother shouted out from the sidelines. "Keep going! Don't stop until your enemy is dead! They won't stop until you are."

*Yeleni and Sanaa's eyes connected and they rushed at each other. Their hands flying at each other's torso and face. Sanaa's weaved under a punch just to be dealt a terrible blow to her stomach. Yeleni's arm braced against a punch but her other side was weak to the second punch that came. The two girls hit each other again and again. Their arms became heavy, their punches weaker with every blow that they dealt. It was terrible madness and yet, they could not stop, would not stop until someone surrendered. No fight could end in a draw. Someone had to be the winner.*

*Yeleni's foot raised and Sanaa's hooked her foot around Yeleni's planted one and she went down, head smacking against the ground. She groaned her body lax. Sanaa stood above her panting each breath a begging gulpful.*

*Standing over her enemy, Sanaa did not know what to do. How did you win a fight? She had always thought it was when the other one had given up, but Yeleni lying there on the ground, prone and tired, did not seem like the loser when Mother picked her up and dragged her out of the ring. Uza came to take her place, fresh-faced and ready, hands up.*

*Sanaa weakly readied her stance and gave Uza a bloody smile. She did not last nearly as long as she did against Yeleni. A hard kick to her stomach blew the wind out of her and Sanaa lay on the ground looking up at the sky. Imami stood over her shaking her head and blew air out of her teeth.*

"Get up. If you haven't passed out then you can still fight. Get up," *she said. The chalk-white face paint cracked. Sanaa's body felt so heavy and tired, with the grains of dirt rubbed up against her back. Her eyes wanted to close, to send her off to sleep right here and now. But the shame would weigh her down, drag her farther and farther away from the table where Mother sat. Sanaa rose from her seat, her hands scraping against the ground. One knee bent. Then another and she was on her feet rising again. Her limbs felt long and heavy. Sanaa could sink into the ground, become thousands of pieces like the dirt. Then she would rest.*

*Uza did not hesitate and launched herself at Sanaa again. Three hits: one to the stomach and two to the face and Sanaa was spiraling to the ground again. Her face rubbed against million grains of sand, her hands passed over them rubbing them.*

*Were they real? All she could feel was the throbbing of her body. The way her muscles were relaxing, into the ground again. She couldn't get up. She should stay down, on the ground, where she could rest. The voices of her sisters cheering and laughing were far behind her. Sanaa's eyes were wandering shut, the lids were heading closing and closing together, close enough to kiss. She could see a sandal slam down in front of her and then, finally, thankfully, the world shuddered into blackness.*

Sanaa could remember those days with her sisters. It was something that Sanaa kept close to her heart. She remembered the fire in Mother's eyes as she pushed them through the drill and stances.

"You must always be ready for a battle my daughters," Mother would say with fire in her eyes. Her calloused hands would be in clenched fists at the words of Mother, inspired to take on all the Fae in those moments.

Sanaa clenched her gloved fists. A part of her was upset that she was even thinking of helping the Fae after everything that they had done to the Batsamasi. But Greta had said that the animosity that she was feeling was a long-dead history for the rest of them. That must mean something, that may be the Fae were not as bad as she had always thought them to be.

84

She wanted to believe that. She wanted to believe that her nieces. But the Fae were wily and trickers and they had burned down the first home that Sanaa had ever known. She needed to protect the daughters of her sisters, they needed her to guide them.

Something warm settled in her stomach and blossomed. Yes, this is why Fintan brought her back, to guide the lost daughters of her sisters. They did not know who exactly they were dealing with. But Sanaa did and she could show them exactly who they were dealing with.

Quick rapping on the door brought Sanaa out of her thoughts. She was unable to utter a word before the door swung open revealing Taira. The woman had her hair pulled back and a sword strapped to her back. Her brilliant green wing shone in the scant firelight of Sanaa's room.

"You're coming with me?" Sanaa asked. She did not think that Taira was going to go with them but then she looked her over. Taira was covered in light leather armor that was molded to her body. The armor was covered in marks that showed that it had been put to good use.

"It would not look good for the people we conscripted to lose their minds in the caves. I am also the most experienced with the siren in the caves. And it would be wrong of me to leave you unawares" Taira said with a shrug of her shoulders. "Follow me."

Sanaa and Taira went down the winding hallways that seemed to go on forever. The hallways were long snakes that they traveled through. The shadows stretched against the wall, flexing their might, only the small flame of light from the candelabra that Taira was holding warded them off.

The two marched through the foyer and to the outside of the manse where both Vorus and August were waiting for them. Sanaa raised an eyebrow.

"Are both of you coming with us also?" Sanaa asked as she

walked down the steps. Vorus pinched the bridge of his nose and August greeted her with a wide grin that bared all of his teeth.

"No. Only I shall be accompanying you." August stepped forward. Sanaa took in the shiny metal armor that he wore and the glossy spear that looked as though it was just passed over a whetstone. Sanaa shrugged her shoulders at that.

"Don't get in my way," was all that Sanaa could say to that. Vorus groaned and shifted away from August.

"I tried to stop him but he insisted," Vorus said. Taira nodded her head and gestured to Sanaa.

"She insisted on the same thing. Wants to get this done all in one night," Taira said. Sanaa frowned. She wanted to get back to her nieces, her family. She needed to get back to them so that they could see reason again so that things could back to the way that it needed to be.

"Let us go. We are wasting time here," Sanaa said. The three of them left Vorus who did not stay and watch them go but went back into his manse without a backward glance. Sanaa let Taira lead and was just a step behind her with August bringing up the rear.

When they reached the caves, people were already there. A dozen guards with their green leather armor and more than a dozen merchants. People were muttering under their breath and casting wary glances at the darkness of the caves. As Sanaa looked into the darkness of the cave, a faint, fluttering feeling entered her stomach. It made her breath quicken and shift her feet.

Whatever was down there was waiting for them. Sanaa knew this to be true. But Sanaa was not one to back down from a challenge. Whatever was down there was going to meet its end at the end of her blades and then she would go home. Thoughts of home took hold of Sanaa that she was startled when August slapped a hand onto her shoulder.

"Are you excited?" August asked. His face was stretched into a big grin, the complete opposite of Sanaa's grim face. "We are gonna face the siren and end what the Fae could not."

He said the last part of his sentence a little louder than the rest, casting his eyes to the Fae merchants and guards around him. The air bristled with the challenge, every eye turning to Sanaa and August and none of them friendly.

Sanaa stood straighter under the increased scrutiny and did not waver. August seemed to enjoy the animosity thrown their way and preened under the new attention. Sanaa slapped his hand off her shoulder.

"Stop. We are meant to be protecting these people, not threatening them," Sanaa said. August still kept the grin on his face. He rubbed his hands together and cast his eyes to the blackness of the cave in front of him.

"Does it matter? We're going to end whatever is in those caves before any of the Fae could have even dreamed of doing it. Is that not reason enough to celebrate," August said stretching his arms wide. Sanaa cut her eyes to August.

His taupe skin glowed in the torchlight. His shoulders were relaxed and his teeth bared still in that never-ending grin glistened. He looked relaxed, ready for any challenge that would come his way. Sanaa's shoulders tensed under his relaxed gaze.

"I would rather not have the Fae planning my murder. They might decide to leave your body behind for the siren to eat. I hear they especially like demons," Sanaa said with a touch of indifference in her voice. Why was this demon always speaking to her? Why was he attempting to make the whole caravan hate them?

"It is like demons to want to cause chaos," she remembered Mother saying. Was this what that was? The undeniable urge to cause chaos where ever he went? Though he was not wrong. They would accomplish something tonight that the Fae could not have done in months and maybe that was reason enough to celebrate. A smile twitched at Sanaa's lips.

"Ah! I finally got her to smile!" August crowed. He leaned closer to Sanaa, practically towering over her with his superior height.

"You may be right about doing something that the Fae could not. That fact alone does bring me some joy," Sanaa admitted. August smiled down at her.

"So then celebrate with me." August pulled out a small flask from some hidden pocket in his armor.

"I don't drink before a battle."

"Come now, a little bit can't hurt." August wagged the bottle underneath her nose. A sweet smell was coming out of the open lid and Sanaa was curious about the contents but she held steadfast.

Someone clapped their hands loudly. Sanaa turned her head to find Taira standing in front of the cave.

"As you all know there is something in the caves. So we need everyone to stay together. Sanaa, August, you will be in the front with me. Guards stick to the sides of the caravan..." Taira said. The guards tightened around the caravan. Sanaa and August walked to the front of the caravan where Taira was waiting for them.

"Hopefully this one will go smoother than the rest," Taira muttered under her breath when the two finally reached her. Sanaa turned her eyes to the black void of the cave. Hopefully, it wasn't so peaceful and Sanaa could end this sooner than they hoped.

With a signal to the caravan, the three of them stepped out of the light and into the darkness of the cave.

The air in the cave was damp and musty, Sanaa felt the moss growing in her lungs with every breath that she took in. The path they were talking was a straightforward one. There was a steep incline after they entered into the darkness and from there it was simply a matter of heading forward. Torches were lit and that allowed them to see only a few steps in front of them.

Taira led the charge, her eyes constantly scanning their surroundings trying to find the enemy that lurked in the darkness. Sanaa walked a step behind her with her hands at the ready. Sanaa's eyes skimmed over the threads of monyelta all around them, trying to parse out if there was anyone there in the cave but could find nothing.

August yawned his hands behind his head. His steps were large and full of leisure. He leaned down to whisper in Sanaa's ear, "Boring right?"

"Sometimes guarding has no excitement," Sanaa replied. She pulled on the strings of monyelta and a small breeze buffeted the two of them. Taira jumped at the sudden wind and looked around the caves, her eyes darting this way and that. August and Sanaa let out a chuckle.

"What else can you do?" August asked. Sanaa smirked and then turned back to the darkness of the cave. The light was scant, with the flickering of the torches being the only light in all the caves. Sanaa gathered the threads of the moss in the caves tangling them together and pulling on the green thread. It was faint and flickering, but slowly the moss and flowers in the room began to glow.

Sounds of shock and awe began to go up around them all as the plants began to glow with blue, green, and purple lights. Taira jumped where she was and drew her sword looking around the cave for enemies. Sanaa and August let out a hearty guffaw at her expense.

Taira flushed at their laughing, but her lips were hard set into a line on her face.

"I would expect our guests to show some seriousness when we are on a supply run," Taira said with a stiff turn of her head. Sanaa and August covered their mouths, their heads bent together as they laughed at Taira.

August chuckled, "Have you sensed anyone since we entered?" Sanaa shook her head.

"Nothing. Not even an inkling of power. It is almost maddening that nothing is happening," Sanaa said. Where was this siren that was supposed to be haunting these caves? If it did not show itself soon, Sanaa was tempted to make it reveal itself by causing a ruckus but the thought was quickly done away with. She did not know what exactly she was dealing with. It would be foolish to try and lure it out.

"I haven't sensed anything either. Nothing at all," August said with furtive looks to the walls of the caves. His face was washed with the blue-green lights of the plants and his hair looked raven black that it almost blended into the shadows of the cave. Sanaa turned her eyes away from him to hide her stare.

"It is concerning," Sanaa mumbled.

August had his mouth open about the reply to what she said, but then Taira raised a hand stopped the caravan from moving forward. Just in front of the lay a cavern with all the same glowing plants that Sanaa had brought to light. Taira looked into the cavern and seeing nothing turned to the rest of the caravan.

"I want everyone to be as silent as they can. This is where the caravan mostly gets attacked by the siren," Taira said in a hushed tone. Sanaa's hands clenched.

They moved with an air of caution. Sanaa held her breath for fear that it would be too loud. The cavern was dotted with the remnants of other caravans. Broken wheels and toppled carts were strewn around the open space.

Sanaa cringed away from the carcass of a dead horse that was swarmed with flies. Taira shuffled forward, a hand-stretched behind her cautioning the rest of the caravan.

"Wait stop," August said with a gasp. Sanaa and Taira paused, both their heads whipping around wildly looking for an enemy to fight or the siren itself. August turned also looking around like he was missing something. "You don't hear that?"

Then rising from the floor, a wall of darkness stopped their path. The horses reared back, shocked at the sudden appearance of a wall of darkness. People descended from the slopes, sliding down, with dark tattoos that looked like oil on their skin.

# Chapter Eleven

August pulled the spear off his back, his eyes scanning over their assailants. His ears were still ringing but he got into his stance ready for anything. People covered in the tattoos that swirled on their skin slid down the slopes and into battle positions.

There was a moment where none of them moved. August could swear he was not the only one who heard the ringing in his ears. And then they charged.

A burly man charged at August his hands open and swirling with the dark energy that blocked their path. It was a writhing mass of darkness rising from his fists like smoke. August ducked out of his way and was able to nick his side. Then hit him in the face with the blunt side of his spear. The man growled out and tried again.

They danced around one another, the man attempting to kill him in one blow and August only landing glancing hits on the man, dodging every menacing blow. The man was wearing ill-fitting leathers, the leather bunching at his shoulders and his waist. The tattoos were barely tattoos and more like living paint on his skin. They were matte black and livid, black snakes dancing on his skin.

August lashed out, his cutting at the meat of the man's thigh. With a roar, the man continued his onslaught pushing August back towards the caravan and almost pinning him there. August could scarcely breathe. The man was relentless his fist coming down with force.

Every punch that whizzed by his face stirred the air and each hit that landed on the cart behind him splintered the wood. August ducked down, spinning the spear above his head which caused the man to pull away. August took a moment to cut his eyes to Sanaa and Taira, but they were both engaged with similar enemies of their own.

The rest of the guards were busy also doing battle with their enemies. This was a mess. They were in here looking for a siren and instead they found bandits with shadows on their skin.

August let out a huff of breath and turned his eyes back to his enemy. The man had coalesced darkness in his hands. The man launched the shadows at him but August was faster. In a flash, August unfurled his wings and was in the air.

The ball of darkness slammed into the cart that was behind him and exploded outwards. The darkness sucking in the cart and making it explode outwards.

August's eyes widened at the sight and he turned his attention back to the man who was gathering darkness in his hands again. August gripped the spear in his hands and imagined the burning blue fires of his home.

"Ignis," August said and the tip of his spear burned red hot. Fire spiraled down the shaft but it did not burn him. No, this fire was warm and familiar. It was the flames that he was born in hellfire. The tip of his spear was covered in the hell flame and August charged.

His spear hit the ball of darkness and it scattered, slithering back up into the arms of the man. August was quick with his assault, every cut was accompanied by the never-ending burn of hellfire. The man cried out with every hit.

It was with these cuts that August saw his opening, the man stumbled back, and August chucked his spear with all the strength that he could muster. The spear found its mark. It lodged in his chest with a sickening squelch and the man was consumed by the blue flames of hellfire.

August pulled his spear out of his chest and turned back to the battlefield. The bright light from the burning man reached out to other parts of the caravan. August saw the tattoos on some of the men and women wither away at the touch of light. August's eyes widened.

"The light!" He shouted. "Their magic is gone with the light!" August made the light of the hellfire burn brighter. Their assailants shrank away from the light and August was launched into the fray once more. He threw himself into the nearest fight, Sanaa's.

He used his lit spear to chase away the dark tattoos. The two of them danced around one another, Sanaa landing hits on the small woman and August preventing her from attacking. They were in tune with one another, able to anticipate the move that the other was going to make moments before they did it.

The woman was down in moments and Sanaa and August turned looking for the next person that they needed to fight. It was then that August heard the singing.

It was faint. It could have been mistaken for someone wailing as they battled, but then it grew louder and louder. August turned this way and that looking for the singer as the song reached its crescendo.

"Do you hear that music?" August paused the thrust of his spear. The woman took advantage of his distraction and landed a strong hit to his chest.

"August!" Sanaa cried out. August was sent flying. His body slammed against the unforgiving ground and his skin stretched, chafed, and tore under the roughness of the ground. With a groan, he rose from the ground, the skin of his arm bleeding and torn. The metallic tang of blood pooled in his mouth and August spat it out.

"Invoco!" The woman shouted. The tattoos slithered off of her arms and neck. The dark snakes of power traveled off her skin and jumped into the carcass of the dead horse. The thing rose from the ground, eyes glowing a deep purple color.

The horse let out a loud neigh before it charged towards Sanaa. August let his wings lift him off the ground and rush towards Sanaa blocking the shot with a twirl of his spear. The horse reared back falling away and coming to stand next to the woman.

The woman hopped onto the rotting back of the horse and tattoos slithered back into place on her skin. The black dark as night against her porcelain skin. The singing that he heard grew louder, but he ignored it seeing the woman charge on her horse.

What were these people capable of? And where did they get this power from? Only the Dark Fae wielded the power of darkness like this. But this was different from the power of the Dark Fae. It was volatile, changing shape and function to the will of the people that wielded it. It was magic that had never been seen before and it was getting harder and harder to fight.

Sanaa had a sheen of sweat covering her brown skin. August could feel his raven hair sticking to his cheeks and forehead, but the two of them never stopped fighting. The woman on the horse never let up her attacks coming at the two of them with heavy hits and stomps from the horse.

August tried to keep the hellfire alight on his spear but it was losing strength and brightness with every moment. His ability to hold on to it was tenuous at best and he could feel the flames withering inside of him. It was only a matter of time before the flames went out.

He wanted to keep fighting but he knew that they were sorely under-prepared to deal with shadow monsters and people who could control shadows.

"Fall back!" Sanaa shouted. Her thoughts aligned perfectly with his. They could not fight them in such a crowded space and they needed more information before they could continue to fight.

One by one the others began to pull away from their fights and make their way towards the narrow passageway that they had come from. Sanaa and August stayed where they were fighting against the worst of the enemies.

The woman on the horse sang out a tone one that matched the pitch of the song that August heard ringing in his ears. What was this song? How did they know about it? Were they connected with the siren in some way?

The questions bubbled up in August's mind and he had to know. It was something that was burning him upside like the hell fire he wielded. He needed to know.

The dead horse shook from where it stood. It's purple eyes glowed and it pawed at the ground getting ready to charge again. Sanaa and August got into position, ready for anything. The horse began to charge when suddenly a wall of thick thorny vines sprouted from the ground stopping the horse and the woman riding it right where they stood.

"Let's go!" Taira said above their heads, wings beating furiously as she hovered above them. Sanaa and August both turned and began to rush back towards the way they came. Laying there with a gash on his side lay one of the enemies.

August slowed his running and turned to look at the man. He was holding his side, his breath coming out in harsh pants and his body constricted by the too-small armor that he wore.

It would be so easy to slip into his mind. The information that he could get. And the way that he could end this faster if he just found out who was in control of these people. Maybe this was the one who Helia wanted to get under her thumb. August stopped and reached out, gripping Sanaa's arm, stopping her where she stood.

"I'm not going," was all August said. Sanaa's eyes widened.

"Are you crazy? These people will kill you without thinking," Sanaa said, her eyes glancing back at the enemies behind them. August did not bother to look behind him. The wall of thorns must have been falling away and August opened his mind allowing his soul freedom.

His body slumped forward into Sanaa's arms and he directed his attentions to the man who was clutching at his wound. August was caught in the feeling of holding his breath that always caught him when his soul was without a body.

The man clutching his wound was like a beacon, the hint of light that August needed so that he could finally breathe again. It was like he was swimming through the air, pushing his soul towards the light that the man exuded. When he touched the body it was as though he broke through the surface of the water.

This man was unlike Nox, as his mind was present and aware. It could feel August's intrusion and lashed out. His mind was a tangled knot of thoughts and feelings, his thoughts fading in and out as he lost more and more blood.

The mind lashed out at August, striking his soul with static. August felt the buzzing against him and pushed the mind down. It struggled but it was weak at best. August kept pushing, shoving against the mind with everything that he had to make sure that the personhood of this person would stay quiet and not interfere with August's control over the body.

August gasped for breath in the muddier vision of this

man. He turned his eyes to the wound that peppered his side and groaned at the blood running rivulets down his side. August then whipped his head to look at Sanaa who was still holding his body and looking as though she didn't know what to do next.

"Go, Sanaa!" August said. This body's voice was higher than his own, but still held the low tone enough to be identified as a man. Sanaa whipped her head to August looking into his eyes.

"August?" She asked. But it was too late, the rest of the tattooed bandits had broken through the thorny brush and were making their way towards them. August dug around his pockets trying to find anything something and found a medallion in his pocket. Sanaa dropped his body, his fingers twitched and she made a pulling motion with her arms. A wall of flame erupted in front of them, blocking the tattooed bandits from progressing any farther again.

August rose as fast as he could, the pain lancing his side was a dull thought in the back of his head. He pressed the medallion into Sanaa's hand.

"Keep that as a memento of me. Now go!" Was all that August said. Sanaa turned her attention back to August's limp body on the ground.

Sanaa frowned and shook her head "No, I am not leaving you with them!" A woman slithered closer and brought her arm up. Her hand gathering darkness and she shot it out directly at Sanaa. The hit landed and Sanaa grunted. August looked at her , begging her to leave with his eyes. Sanaa caught his gaze and it was like something finally clicked in her head. She only nodded, shouldered August's unconscious form, and ran as fast as she could out of the cave.

August collapsed down into the sticky pool of blood and let out a heavy sigh of breath. The other bandits catapulted themselves over the wall of fire, but Sanaa had already been swallowed up by the darkness. They landed with heavy foot-falls on the ground and August let out a wheezing chuckle.

"Tobias," a shrill voice cried. A woman with black tattoos that spiraled up to her chin rushed at him. She fell to her knees when she reached him and gathered his face in her calloused hands. She leaned close, pressing her lips to August's chapped ones. August's eyes widened before he relaxed his stance.

He was supposed to be among friends. He lifted his arms and wrapped them around the woman. He kissed her hard, his mind grasping for the name of this woman and the rela-tionship between them.

August turned his attention to the tangled mass of thought and memory that this man—Tobias— was. He had no time to sort through the tangled web. He allowed Tobias a view through his own eyes, the face of the woman.

A thread of thought sparked up and August grabbed at it. August was assaulted with warm feelings and contentment that came with affection. Penelope. The name washed over him, and the words rolled on his tongue.

"Penelope," August breathed when they finally pulled apart. Penelope looked at him, eyes glassy from her tears. Her eyes scanned his form, landing on the blood pooling near his side.

She gasped and put her hands on the wound, pushing down with as much strength as she could muster. August coughed as the others gathered around him. The woman on the dead horse rode up to him, tattoos swirling furiously on her arms and legs.

August leaned back and closed his eyes.

# Chapter Twelve

H e kept his face as still as he possibly could.

"Tobias!" Penelope shouted out. There was a commotion around him as the others closed in. They were all murmuring words of concern, wanting to know if he was okay. Penelope took to weeping on top of his, slapping his face lightly.

"Tobias wake up! Wake up! Please you can't leave me!"

August heard the chuff of a horse and the sounds of it nearing closer. Someone wrapped their arms around his shoulders and he was propped up against something soft but firm.

"Everyone calm down. Tobias is seriously injured. He must have passed out because of his wounds." The sound of dirt crunching underfoot made its way to August's ears. He was lifted and put on top of something.

August could smell the sweet scent of rot and knew that they put him on the horse. The horse was jostled again as someone took the reins of the horse.

"We need to return to the hideout. Everyone fall in line," a woman's voice commanded. The was the sound of shuffling as people gathered and "fell in line" as the woman had commanded.

August dared to open his eyes the slightest. He was laying on his stomach on the back of the horse. The other bandits had lined up behind the horse with Penelope being the one nearest to him. Her face was streaked with tears. The rest were in a rough line behind her. August cut his eyes in the other direction to see the woman that Sanaa and he had fought, holding the reins of the horse.

The wound in his side was a dull throb. His side ached with the heaviness of the wound and August could feel Tobias' thoughts flickering in the back of his mind.

Release me, came the weak plea, but August ignored the voice in the back of his mind. They said that there was a hideout. August wished that he was sitting upright so that he could try to memorize the way to the hideout. But all August could see was the cave ceiling that they walked over.

The path that the woman lead them down was a winding snake, with several turns and precarious slopes. Instead of leading a way out of the caves, August was surprised to see them go deeper and deeper into the belly of the cave.

August let out a grunt as the horse clumsily made its way down the side of a sheer slope. Penelope was on him in seconds, cooing and shushing him, brushing back his hair and trying to soothe away his pain. August groaned and settled back into the rocking motions of the horse.

With a whip of her platinum blonde hair, Penelope turned her eyes to the one holding the reins of the horse. "Mary, can't you lead us through one of the smoother paths? All these bumps are hurting Tobias."

"This is the fastest way to the hideout," Mary said with a quick jut of her chin. "Tobias needs to get that tended to as fast as possible."

Penelope turned her watery gaze towards him again and

August managed a weak smile in her direction. She caressed his face again, pressing a kiss to his sweaty forehead.

August's mind wandered. Who were these people? And what did they want? Why did they attack them? Were they servants to the siren? But they lacked the distinct bleeding in their ears that signaled that the siren's song afflicted them. And the shadows tattoos. August spared a glance at Penelope and the whirling tattoos that danced across her lower chin and sunk underneath her clothes.

What were they? August in all his travels has been to even the far reaches of Ettrea. He had seen the howling packs of the Winter Wolves and the hellfire worked by demonkind and he had never seen the magic that they carried on their skin.

It was nothing like the Dark Court of faeries, who's darkness was something smokier and shrouded them like an aura. These seemed alive and they did whatever the user asked for from walls to making a dead horse walk again. It was nothing that he had ever seen before.

August was shaken from his thoughts when the horse that he was riding stopped finally. The dull ache in his side stopped with the horse's movements and August turned to see a smattering of people gathered around fires.

They were on a precipice that looked out into the darkness. Tents and other makeshift shelters were erected all around one large bonfire in the center of all the action. August watched as children ran past unmarked and some of the adult cooked spits over the fire.

They each had swirling tattoos on them from the oldest person there to the children. All of them had those oil slick tattoos that breathed on their skin. August's eyes widened and was tempted to crane his neck to see more but he remembered that he was supposed to be injured and kept his eyes on the ground.

A whole camp full of people with those living tattoos. Where did they come from? Was this a new race? The thoughts were swirling in his head and implications of them being a new race ricocheted through him.

August was lifted off the horse by many hands. He let out a groan and Penelope piped up telling everyone to be careful with him as he was carried into one of the tents. It was a hovel with only a long table. They set him down onto the table and Penelope was by his side in moments.

"Don't worry baby. Nova will be here soon and then she'll fix you okay," she said with a wobble to her lip. As the others filed out, Mary stayed behind her eyes narrowed as she took in his prone form.

"What happened back there?" she asked. Her eyes were a hard slate color that revealed nothing of what she was thinking. August scrambled to think of a response and his thoughts wandered to Tobias. He reached out but the tangled web that Tobias was, was silent, barely a hum coming from him. August cursed.

"I was injured fighting one of the guards. I barely held off against that last woman," August said. Mary's eyes never wavered from his form and he wanted to shift with how uncomfortable he was with the attention.

"Stop it! He's injured! Now is not the time for this," Penelope said from his side. August thanked Sevan above for Penelope and her mother hen attitude. She turned to Mary and jutted out her chin and squared her shoulders.

"You can talk to Tobias when he is rested and heal. Now you should go. It is going to be crowded in here once Nova comes," Penelope said. Her voice was hard, never yielding in tone or pitch. Mary rolled her eyes and turned, leaving the tent without so much as a backward glance.

With Mary gone, both August and Penelope let their shoulders slump. August leaned his head back and rest against the hardwood. He sighed out through his teeth but then winced at the pain in his side. Penelope turned back to him, her eyes taking in his form.

"Oh, Toby. You should have stayed closer to the group. You always want to go off and be the hero," Penelope said with a sigh. The words sparked something in Tobias' mind and August caught on to it and he was swept into memories.

August saw Tobias in bandages often and pushing himself when it came to using his powers. August watched as Tobias was the first to separate from the group and engage in battle with reckless abandon. The way that he threw himself into battle was like a child when they had a weapon, reckless and without thought. There was no strategy to his movements only him throwing his weight around and somehow landing hits on his enemy.

The scene changed and it was Penelope tending to his wounds her face just like it was now, with the same shy smile as though she could scarcely believe that he was still alive. Tobias' eyes traced over the soft curve to her brow that signaled that she was grateful that he was still with her. August turned his eyes towards Penelope and turned a smile towards her.

"Well you know me, I always have to be—" August paused as the last of the memories trickled into center view. Who the hell was—

"You always have to be Kid Eternity," Penelope finished for him. She let out a small giggle. Penelope got on the table to lay down beside him on his unwounded side. She snuggled close and August reached an arm around to hold her close to his side. Penelope took in a deep breath.

"One day this is going to get you killed."

"It hasn't yet."

"But it might! You need to be more careful, Toby." Penelope reached around him to wrap an arm around his waist and August let out a breath. She thought that this was Tobias, her lover, someone that she trusted. August could feel the real Tobias was in the back of his mind, screaming to be let out and not to be deceived by the imposter, but August quieted him, focusing on the thought of meeting Nova.

Who was this Nova? And what role did she hold here in the camp? August's thought lingered on the tattoos that decorated every person in the camp. Where were they getting those tattoos? Even the children had them, it was nothing like the powers bestowed when a demon makes a contract with someone else.

The flaps of the tent opened and a woman escorted by two large burly men entered the tent. The woman was a mouse, her shoulders bunched up to her ears and her eyes looking not at them but the ground. She fiddled with her fingers in a manner that August found annoying the moment that he caught sight of it.

Penelope rose from his side. "Nova, you're finally here. I need you to treat Tobias. He was injured in the latest raid."

The girl mumbled something under her breath that no one in the room could catch. Penelope leaned closer, cupping a hand to her ear to try and hear the girl better. "Huh?"

"I'm not...Nova," the girl mumbled out again. Penelope sighed and leaned back onto the balls of her feet, a sigh leaving her lips as she rubbed her forehead.

"Alicia as much as I hate to say this, you're not the one that we need. I need Nova." Penelope cast a look back at August laying on the table and then turned back to the two guards by the girl's sides. August furrowed his brow as he looked down at the woman.

Penelope sent a nod to the two guards by her side. The guards grabbed her by the shoulders and the girl chewed at her lip.

The girl struggled in their hold, twisting this way and that trying to get out of their hold.

"Wait! Please, stop! I don't want to go under again! Stop!" Tears gathered in her eyes and she struggled harder as the two men brought a vial of black sludge out of one of their pockets. "Please don't!"

One of the men held the girl's nose, forcing her mouth open. The other raised the vial of black sludge to her mouth. They forced her to swallow every drop while she struggled and screamed for help. August watched this all with a furrowed brow.

When the girl had swallowed all the sludge, they let her go and she fell to the ground, sobbing. She moaned for a moment and then her head shot up and August could see her eyes turn black, from her pupils to the white of her eyes, everything was black. She moaned and sighed, her body trembling as something overtook her.

Finally, the girl slumped to the ground. Tattoos like black oil rose on her skin. It was the swirling tattoos like the rest of the people here had. Her hair changed color darkening from the burnt brown color to match the black of the tattoos.

When the tattoos settled on her skin, the girl rose from the ground with a flick of her hair. Her eyes were no longer the chestnut brown but a daring amber color with the whites of her eyes completely black. She sighed as she settled into her skin.

"How long was I gone for?" Was all that she asked.

One of the guards at her side piped up, "Not long. Only two days."

"Two days is too long," the woman said with a cut of her eyes. She turned her eyes to Tobias and she sighed again. "Again Tobias?"

August let loose a smile. "You know me."

The girl scoffed. "Yes, I do."

"Nova can you please help him," Penelope asked. August's brow furrowed deeper. So this was Nova, she was that girl and was brought out with that black oil that her guards made her drink.

August smoothed out his brow when Nova turned her attention towards him. She looked him over before her eyes landed on the wound that was slowly oozing from his side.

"Oh, Tobias," Nova said. She pulled out a necklace from under her clothing. It was a small trinket, it was pink and in the shape of a woman. She said nothing as she walked over towards him and the trinket on her necklace began to glow. It shined with a brilliant light. Nova laid her hands on August.

August was awash with warmth. He felt as though where Nova's hands touched him was emanating with warmth. The wounds at his side stopped throbbing and it felt as though parts of him that he did not even know was aching were suddenly at rest.

August marveled at the feeling, he had never felt something like this before. He had wanted nothing more than to stay with this feeling. It would be easy to become addicted to this August thought to himself. Where his hands touched, August felt the warmth sink into him. It was a warmth that entered his bones and traveled through his blood.

In a matter of moments, August felt energy zinging up and down his spine. He tossed and turned and then rose from the table. He felt over his skin, not even a scratch lay on him. Nova pulled her hands away from his person and the light from the necklace receded.

"I'm amazed every time you do that," August said. Penelope rushed to him, wrapping her arms around his torso. She was smiling wide and showing all her teeth. "Thank you."

Nova smiled, "Don't thank me yet. You are going to have to report everything that happened in today's raid to me and explain how you got those wounds. But tonight I'm in the mood for a party." Nova turned to her guards. "Go and tell everyone we are going to have a celebration!"

The two guards bowed low and exited the tent. August smiled, he just needed to get Nova alone for a moment and tell her Helia's proposal and then this would be all over.

# Chapter Thirteen

The weight of August's body on her shoulders was nothing compared to other things that she carried while she ran. Sanaa focused on the steps that she was taking one foot in front of the other without stopping. In a matter of moments, she was in line with Taira and the guards and merchants. She cursed under her breath and resettled the weight of the body on her shoulders.

They ran through the tunnels under the caves and it seemed as though they arrived at their starting point in a matter of moments. When they broke through the mouth of the cave they all collapsed on the ground.

Sanaa let August's body slide off her shoulders as she fell onto her hands and knees, gasping for breath. She took in grateful gulps of air, her lungs and sides burning from the running. Sanaa through the curtain of her braids caught sight of Taira leaned against a tree and rose. She stalked over to Taira and yanked her away from the tree.

"What in Darkness' name was that! You never said that there were bandits!" Sanaa panted out. She gripped the arm of Taira as tight as she could and bared her teeth. "Did you think to teach us some sort of lesson by allowing us to be ambushed?"

Taira shoved Sanaa away from her and frowned at her. "Are you stupid? I was almost killed too. I have never seen anything like that in my entire life."

Sanaa shrugged off the leather armor around her torso, pulling on the strings that held it close. What the hell was that, and who were those people, and what was that power?

She thought back to the way that the woman she was fighting moved, snakelike, and ready to expect her every move. And those tattoos, the way that they moved on her skin and obeyed her every whim. It was powerful and nothing that Sanaa had ever fought against.

The mission was not over and she could not yet return to her family and help guide them. The very thought made Sanaa punch at a tree. She wanted this to be over, but there was always something in her way, always something stopping her from moving forward.

Taira came close, her hands raised in an obvious peace offering. "I have no idea who those people were. We've never even seen bandits in the caves before. We need to go back and tell Vorus about this new development."

Sanaa punched the tree again, and pain radiated from where her fist landed. When she looked at her knuckles they were split and bleeding, the blood pooling. Sanaa turned away from the wound on her hand and began the march back to Vorus's manse.

The sky was beginning to lighten with hints of dawn already arising. The town was still slumbering yet and Sanaa and the band of merchants and guards that surrounded her did nothing to disturb the sleeping town. As they neared the manse more and more of the merchants and guards fell away, heading to their own homes to rest and recover until it was only Taira and Sanaa standing in front of the doors of the manse.

They climbed the steps but neither one of them had the opportunity to open the door before it swung open. Vorus was there with heavy bags under his eyes. He was wearing his loose nightclothes and the thin linens billowed in the brief wind that the door made. His hair was a mess of dark brown curls.

"Is it over? Is the siren dead?" The words pushed out of his mouth, each word coming before the last finished. Taira made a face at Vorus and pushed him aside from the door and entered the house. Sanaa followed after her dropping August's body somewhere near the door.

"Well, is it over?" Vorus asked again in that same rushed manner. Sanaa rolled her eyes and began the tedious process of pulling the knots that held her armor together. Taira began the same process but a maid appeared to help her out of her clothing. "And what happened to August?"

"August possessed one of the bandits that attacked us," Sanaa said with a hard yank to her armor. The armor clattered down to the ground. Sanaa ran a hand through her braids, fingering some of the little beads that decorated her hair.

Vorus's face screwed up as if the very thoughts that there were bandits in the caves was impossible. "Bandits?" Was all that he could ask.

Sanaa drew her braids behind her and pulled a leather strap from her pocket and tied her hair up. "Yes, bandits. They ambushed us in the cave," Sanaa said with as much fire in her voice as she could muster. "They had some sort of power, like these living tattoos that they could manipulate to their very will." Sanaa grit her teeth just remembering the battle.

"Do you think that they were people under the control of

the siren?" Vorus began. "There have been people who have stayed in the caves to listen to the siren."

Taira piped up then, "No. This was nothing like that. These people were organized and powerful. They didn't even have a hint of the siren's madness inflicted on them."

"They were powerful. We made the best decision and left before we could have any dead," Taira said. Vorus froze then, his hackles rising.

"You just left? You did not kill them?" He spat.

Sanaa turned at this, her hackles rising at what he said. "We didn't know anything about this enemy and they ambushed us! We are lucky that we got away without any deaths on our part."

"So what? I didn't hire you to fucking run when you're faced with a tough fight—"

"We did it to save lives and to make sure—"

"The empress is coming and I can't have bandits running around disrupting trade and—"

"If you are so unsatisfied with how I do things well then maybe you should do it yourself!" Sanaa shouted. "Or will you stay here, waiting for the real warriors to come home?"

Vorus leaned back as if her words lashed out at him. But then his face became dark and foreboding like a heavy rain cloud. He puffed up his chest like some bird ready to swoop down and capture his prey. He might have been bigger than her but Sanaa never backed down from down a fight. She steeled herself and leaned her shoulder backs, jutting out her chin.

She would not be intimidated by a Faerie. She had slaughtered thousands of them when she was merely a young girl. She had fought in battle after battle and had come out alive. The only woman that could stop her was long since gone.

Vorus looked down his nose at her and it was like he gathered all his power into his lithe frame. Sanaa stared back her eyes glacial.

"I hired you to do the job and I expect you to do that job."

Sanaa merely cocked her head and looked Vorus in his eye. "Then let me do my job." With that, she turned away from him and marched away.

How dare that man think to try and intimidate her. She was doing everything that she could. Did he think that she wanted to be here at his beck and call? Waiting for the moment when it was best to strike. She could be with her family, guiding them on the right path.

"You see," Sanaa could hear mother's voice whispering in her ear. "Nothing good ever comes from dealing with the Fae." Sanaa marched to her room, slamming the door behind her. She looked at the statue of Fintan that she had in her room. She grabbed it and held it in her hands.

"What am I supposed to do now?" She said to no one. The siren was not dead and now there were tattooed bandits in the caves that she needed to fight off. Nothing made sense and nothing was as easy as it was in the beginning. Sanaa leaned back against the door and sighed.

She just wanted to be with her family. But Greta thought that she needed to go to the Faerie courts and see how different the world was. The world might have changed, power may have changed hands but nothing had changed about the people. The Faeries were still mischievous and conniving, and Sanaa hated it.

It would be right for the Faeries to send them in blind. To allow them to fight against a threat unnamed all so that they would be humbled and listen to their betters. But Taira was surprised at the arrival of the bandits and there was no way that they would risk on of their own in some backward attempt at humiliation.

Things have changed, Sanaa thought to herself. Maybe these new Faeries were more cutthroat than the ones that she had dealt with. Maybe they would do something like that.

Sanaa looked at the figurine of Fintan. She rubbed her hands over the bullhead and ran her fingers down the human body. At the temple of Fintan, they always told her disasters were something that Fintan created to test his faithful to make sure that they were always ready to do battle. Now Sanaa had weathered many battles and a small part of her was tired of doing so.

How long was she going to be fighting against the world? She was tired and all she wanted was to be with her family. Sanaa thought that she had proven herself to be battle-ready and worn.

Sanaa leaned her head against the door and felt the beginnings of burning in her eyes. No, she would not cry. Crying was for those weaker than Sanaa. She was a Batsamasi, and Batsamasi did not cry.

Sanaa put her hand into the pocket of the pants she was wearing and was almost surprised to find something in her pocket. She pulled the heavyweight out of her pocket.

It was a bronze medallion swinging on a leather strap. The medallion was the size of her palm and was embossed with the figure of a woman dancing in a waterfall. Sanaa had never seen anything like it before. She remembered the words of August as he handed it to her. *Keep that as a memento of me.* She scoffed at the thought.

The demon had no caution but he was on the inside now and could bring back useful information about who the bandits were and what was the source of the power.

Sanaa held the medallion in her hands, feeling the weight of it in her palm. Why did the man that August possessed holding this medallion? Maybe... Sanaa rose from the ground, gripping the medallion in her hands. She wanted to know where this medallion came from and what the woman on this thing meant.

She opened the door to her room and strode out. She walked the length of the hall before she encountered a maid and Sanaa asked for directions to the library. After she was told the way, Sanaa kept her eyes trained on the medallion.

The medallion held some rusted blood on the sides but other than that the medallion was well taken care of. It shone in the candlelight and the embossing was well done. Maybe it meant nothing and was an item that the man had taken off a body he had scoured but she doubted that. No, this medallion meant something.

It had to mean something. The man that August possessed held it in his pocket and it was well taken care of. No this was important. It had to mean something, because why else would it be so well taken care of.

Two grand doors stood as the entrance to the library. Sanaa pushed it open and was welcomed to the sight of books. The shelves were stacked with them, books on top of books on top of books. Where one shelf was full, books were shoved on top of the previous books. Sanaa thought nothing of the robust collection and lit a candelabra with one of the candles from outside.

Shadows loomed large in front of her, the shelves were dusty and sagged with the weight of all the books they held. Sanaa had no idea how she was going to find what she needed when the shelves were so disorganized. She brought the candelabra closer to the books, trying her best to see the titles of the books in front of her.

"Elemental Magicks...Julian Optics and Policies... How does anyone find anything in here?" She asked. The shadows in the room did not deign to answer. She reached the end of the shelves of books never discovering a book that could help her uncover the importance of the medallion.

She turned the corner and was pressed in on both sides by the oppressive nature of the shelves. She sighed. There had to be a faster way of finding the books that she needed.

A clicking of the door opening brought Sanaa out of her musings. She brought the candelabra close to her as she turned back towards the door. "Hello?" Someone called out.

Sanaa replied, "Hello?"

Someone rounded the corner and there stood a man, he was taller than Sanaa with large spectacles hanging off his nose. He was dressed in long royal blue robes and his hair was a shock of blonde. Sanaa looked him over, he could be hiding weapons in his robes, was the first thought that she had, but then she discarded it. There was no use being suspicious when this man could help her.

"Oh," the man said with a pleasing lilt to his voice. "Sorry for the mess. I rarely get guests coming this way."

"Sorry I've come so late. I just need to find a book," Sanaa said with a twist of her lips. "But I can't find anything with the way that this library is organized." She gestured with the candelabra at the precarious shelving of the books. The man let out a laugh, looking this way and that at the books.

"Yes, it could get very confusing. We ran out of shelf space a few years ago, but the books kept coming in. What exactly are you looking for?"

Sanaa pulled out the medallion. "I'm looking for something that could explain what this is."

The man looked the medallion over and raised his eyebrows. "Are you a scion of the Temple of Roux?"

"No, I was born under Fintan's stars. What does this have to do with Roux?"

"This is something that's given to those who are part of the temple of Roux," the man said. He took the medallion from her hands and looked it over again in the candlelight. "Yes, this is something that is definitely something that belongs to the temple of Roux. You can see the icon of Roux on the back here." He turned the medallion over and showed her a picture of a woman howling in the water. Sanaa nodded her head.

"Okay, so this is from the temple of Roux?"

"Certainly. Though if you are not from the temple, I have to ask how you came upon it since only someone from the temple would be able to receive something this detailed."

Sanaa snatched the medallion back. "Thank you for your help." Sanaa tossed back. She passed the man as fast as she could and ran out of the library. It would not do to alert the town that there was trouble in the caves.

Sanaa held the medallion in her hands as she walked back to her room. So this came from the temple of Roux. But what did the temple of Roux have anything to do with this? Why would the temple of Roux have anything to do with the bandits?

Sanaa pressed the medallion close to her chest. It could mean nothing. It could mean that he raided someone from the temple of Roux, but something deep within her told her that it was deeper than that. A bandit would not cherish something bronze when there were several items of gold that he could have his pick from.

So what was so important about this medallion that he held it in his pocket and kept it close at hand? Sanaa knew that there was no way that she was going to get answers for it right now. The light from the sun was just beginning to creep into the manse. On her walk back from the library Sanaa saw the manse beginning to stir, maids and servants were beginning to awaken.

It was a long night for Sanaa so when she entered her room she flopped onto the bed and decided to investigate more when she was less tired. With that, she closed her eyes, medallion in hand, and went to sleep.

# Chapter Fourteen

The beat of the drum thrummed through August son loudly that he was surprised no one found their camp yet. The men and women were dancing around one another, their hands wrapped around each other. The children giggled while they played, running this way and that.

The only light in the whole cavern was the large bonfire that stood in the center of the encampment. August hung back from the main merrymaking near the fire. His eyes took in everything, from the swirling tattoos to the easy way that the people near the fire danced. It was perplexing.

How could these people be here? What were they? And what was the power that they were wielding? Nothing made sense. August's eyes caught Penelope as she strode over to cups in her hands.

He was sitting on a plush pillow that was pillaged from one of the supply runs that they raided. Penelope sat down on the ground beside him and offered him the drink. August took it in his hands and took a sip. The taste of it coiled in the back of his throat.

He pulled away with a quick smack of his lips. "Ugh, sweet," August said.

"What's wrong? You usually like sweet things." Penelope said with a frown. August closed his mouth. He couldn't ruin the facade before he could talk to Nova.

"Nothing. I'm just not in the mood for something sweet right now," August said. He tried to give her a tired smile, but it might have come off as more of a grimace with the taste of the sweet drink still trapped in his throat.

A frown marred Penelope's face and she put down her drink. She pressed a hand against his forehead. "Are you okay? You have been... quiet ever since you came back from the raid."

August was tired, keeping up the charade was harder than he thought. He had hoped when he possessed this man that he was unattached, that he was alone in this world and that he would have fewer people to answer to. But it turned out to be the opposite and Penelope stuck to his side like a fly. She was always buzzing in his ears. He sighed out through his nose.

No, he knew the risks he was taking when he possessed the man not knowing a thing about him or the other bandits.

"When will we go back? You know, to get the other supplies?" August asked. Penelope pulled away from him then and took another sip of her drink.

"Oh, you know probably again at night when we are less likely to get caught and defend ourselves."

The words brought back images of the fight. Light. The light made the tattoos shrivel and disappear. They were like shadows, only present with indirect sunlight, running away when confronted with the actual thing. Even now when he turned to look at the tattoos they were no longer the dark pitch black that they were before. Instead, they were a pale grey on his skin, a faint memory of what they were before.

At his gaze, Penelope looked down at her tattoos and sighed. "Yeah, I always get sad to see them go too. I never thought I would enjoy having these powers, but surprisingly I do. I love having them a lot."

August cast his gaze back to Penelope. What did she mean by that? Were these powers gifted to her? Were the gods playing again, handing power to those that wanted it? It would not be the first time that something like that happened, but it was odd that they were so powerful, and yet here they were, hiding in squalor.

"I hate wasting time down here," August tried. "I wish we could just go into Asren and show them what we can do."

"You know we can't. Nova hasn't found a way to make our powers last longer."

Nova? Nova was the one that was gifting them with these abilities? But how? August thought back to when he first saw Nova, the sniveling woman that she was before her guards made her drink that vial. How could she be the one that gifted these people thing amazing power?

Then the thought occurred to him. These people were powerless before Nova. They did not have the power before she gifted them with these abilities. Were they Husks? The powerless mortals that slaved away on the surface.

Husks with power? The thought would have been enticing if August was a mortal, but there was no way. Mortals were exactly as they were called, Husks, hollowed out and empty. Almost useless until they had something to do or were controlled by someone else.

He discarded the thought as soon as it arose. No, this had to be a new race something that had never been seen before.

"You know before all of this, I thought I was going to die where I was. I thought that it was the end for me when they sent me into the Fae forest. But then Nova found me and she healed me. I'll always be grateful for that."

Penelope turned to him, landing her eyes on his own, and grabbed his hands. "One day we will take the surface and free all those other humans. We'll save them from the hell that they live in now and we'll go home."

August's mind was sent reeling from the information. They were Husks, the thought rang out throughout his head. He wanted to pull his hands away from Penelope disgusted with her weakness. But he kept them there and squeezed her hands in his.

"We'll save them all," he murmured back to her. The thought of releasing all the Husks was something that he wanted to guffaw at. They wanted to be free. And they had to have their power gifted to them by some random woman that they did not even know. They were weak; always relying on someone else to save them.

He cupped Penelope's face in his hands and brought her in for a kiss. They were weak, he could not help but think. All of them. He kept his eyes open the whole time as he watched the tattoos disappear from their skin.

When Penelope pulled away she looked down at her skin and gave a small sad laugh. "I always miss them when they leave."

August rose from the ground. "I need to talk to Nova," he said as a way to get away from Penelope. He turned his head this way and that trying to catch sight of Nova and the two guards that flanked her every step.

August turned his head this way and that and found Nova lounging among several pillows surrounded by children. August gulped down the rest of his drink, barely wincing at the sweet tang on his tongue, and walked over to Nova.

Nova's black locks were pulled back away from her face. She saw wearing loose clothes that hid her figure, though they did not hide her ample chest. Nova barely bat an eye at his arrival, speaking to the crowd of children that surrounded her.

"-And then he went to confront the giant. He only had the pebbles with him," she said. The children looked at her with rapt attention, their gazes never diverting from Nova and her story. August hung back a little bit, allowing her to finish her story with the children.

When she was done the children all rose from the ground, chattering on about the stories and some starting their reenactments of the battle that Nova described. Nova laughed and turned to him her eyes shining in the firelight.

"Yes, Tobias?"

August stepped closer, his black eyes meeting her brown ones. "May I speak to you alone?"

Nova nodded and rose from the pillows. The two of them walked over to the biggest tent out of the whole encampment. The inside was covered in lavish, plush rugs, and many pillows. In the center of the tent was a low table that was embossed with gold and shone in the lantern light that decorated the room. The lanterns were hung against the tent poles and gave a soft red light to everything in the room.

Nova and her two guards sat on one side of the table and August took the seat opposite from her. The two guards were wearing armor that was not ill-fitting like the rest of the people here wore. Nova threw herself into the pit of pillows a sigh escaping her lips as she sunk deeper among the softness.

"I suppose you're here to demand that I allow you to go to the surface again aren't you Tobias," Nova muttered from her position in the pillows. She waved a hand as though trying to swat away an annoying fly. "Well give up on that already. I need to find a way to make your powers permanent before I can send you to the surface."

"No that isn't what I wanted to talk to you about," August

said. His back was straight as he sat down. These were Husks and this woman was the one that was granting them their powers. Helia would laugh at them until she saw what they could do with that power.

Once she knew what they could do with this power then she would understand. For now, he just needed to get Nova on his side, to get her to understand the benefits of siding with him and Helia.

"I wanted to talk to you about something else. Something more important," August said.

Nova was lying on her stomach her back exposed to August and a part of him wanted to snap at her. Face him, give him her full attention is what he wanted to say, but he had to keep quiet. He could not reveal who he was to her just yet. "Oh? Did you want to give me your report about what happened today—"

"No—"

"Or did you want to talk about that thing that is inhabiting your body?"

August paused. What?

"Yes, I know that there is something other than you that is inhabiting your body. I felt it when I was healing you. Do you want to talk about that?" She turned over, exposing her stomach to him but finally looking him in the eyes. Her eyes shone with triumph, she knew that she had him.

August now had two choices in front of him and he didn't know which one to make. Nova settled her hands on her stomach and sighed.

"You know when I heal someone or when I imbibe them with the power I get to feel them. I sometimes feel thoughts and memories. Other times I feel their bodies, all their aches and pains become my own. When you heal someone like Tobias enough you get a feel for what that person should feel like, their thoughts, their emotions, their actions. And everything that you have done was good, but not Tobias."

Nova did not bother to stop her guards who rose from their position beside her and pointed their weapons at August without a second thought. August raised his hands in obvious surrender, his face calm as an untouched lake. August took in a deep breath. "You caught me," was all that he could say.

Nova let out a wide grin at his words. She looked childlike with her small frame cocooned in the pillows. Nova gave a small giggle but still did not call off her guards. "Yes, I did. Now tell me. Who are you?"

"My name is August. I am an envoy from Helia."

Nova twisted her lips at the name. "Helia?"

"You must have heard of her," August began. His hands never lowered from beside his head. "Helia the bane of Empress Sorcha's existence."

"Yes, I have heard of her. I have heard of some of the things that she has done to be a thorn in the Empress' side. Now, why would one of her people be in the body of one of mine."

"I admit that this is not the best way to introduce myself," August said with a chuckle. "But I had no idea as to how to contact you. Hell, I barely knew if there was someone in control of this whole operation." Nova tilted her head and settled deeper into her mountain of pillows. "Helia would like to propose an offer."

"Oh?"

"Yes one that would be mutually beneficial to you and her," August said. He tried lowering his hands slightly but the guards were ever vigilant and pressed their weapons closer to August's throat.

"Stand down," Nova called.

"But—" one of the guards started

"I said stand down." Nova enunciated with a hard look at each of the guards. They each pulled back with weapons with a hint of resistance, but they followed orders. August let out a large smile and leaned back into the pillows.

"Tell me about this offer," Nova said with a slight wave of her hand. The two guards settled down into the ground. August's smile could not be wider.

"It is a simple proposal. Helia would like for you to join her. She thinks that the two of you could make something beautiful together."

"Oh?" Nova said with a raised brow. August sucked in a deep breath and continued.

"Helia has heard about what you have been doing down here, stopping trade. Helia wants to join in on that. She thinks that what you are doing down here has a lot of potential and she wants to see it expand."

"Helia doesn't even know why I am doing what I am doing and she wants to be a part of it all?"

"So tell me, why are you doing all this? Making yourself a nuisance to King Gabriel and making life a living hell down here?"

Nova sighed and leaned back into the pillows. She turned her eyes away from him and looked up at the ceiling of the tent. Sitting among all those pillows made Nova look so small like a child almost.

"I want to go home. More than anything I want to go home and I want to bring the others with me."

"Well, Helia will help you get to this home that you want to get to so badly. She will help you strike down whoever is preventing you from going home. You won't just go home you'll rule there." August tried. He thought that he sounded convincing, but Nova only laughed at his words. It was a deep chuckle that unsettled the air between them.

"No. You don't understand. I just want to go home. That is all."

"The Helia will help you get there."

Nova rose from the pillows and turned her back on him. She stalked from one side to the other with a frown pressed onto her face. "Helia has a history you know. Do you remember the Brownie Brothers? They were taken under the control of Helia and they disappeared in a matter of months. There was the revolution that was brewing in the Summer Court and the moment that Helia inserted herself into the situation that is when everything went to hell for the rebels."

"All those things were due to their incompetence. Helia had nothing to do with that," August quickly added.

"Maybe. But Helia is the thing that always seems to come first before their downfall. She is always there when they fall and yet she always comes out unscathed." Nova said with a long look over her shoulder.

August frowned at that. Why was she resisting? It was a simple offer, join, or not join. Why did she have to bring up the past and things that Helia had nothing to do with?

But all those things did fall when Helia joined them, a small part of him whispered. He shut that side of him down the moment that it arose. The Brownie brothers fell because of their pride and the fact that they did not want to follow Helia's orders after joining her. And the rebellion in the Summer Court fell apart because of infighting.

"Helia knows how to play people," Nova said with a long look at him. She turned around to stare at him. "I and refuse to be played."

August sighed, his shoulders sagging as Nova settled herself among the pillows again. "So I take that you will not be joining Helia?"

"Yes that will be a no," Nova said with a smile. August tried to rise from sitting on the pillows but the guards trained their weapons on him again, making him raise his hands. "Oh, you won't be exiting that way."

"What?" August said, his eyes trained on the weapons.

"You know a little too much about how things operate here. I can't just let you walk out of here like nothing happened. It wouldn't be good if you found out way out and then told others where we were."

Nova rose from the pillows again, reaching into her shirt and bringing out the necklace that glowed with pink light. The guards rose from the ground and moved to either side of August.

"You have to understand August. I'm a leader; I have to do what is best for my people." The necklace glowed brighter and brighter, the light overtaking everything in the room. August raised his arms and turned his face, trying to turn away from the light.

It was then that August felt it, the feeling of being unmoored. Something was lifting him from this body, strengthening Tobias. The man's consciousness was lashing out battering at him with everything that he had.

August tried to hook on to the body, to anchor himself there, but the light was not just bright, it was loud. Something like a howling arose from somewhere in the light and surrounded him, making it hard to focus on being in the moment. August's soul tried to grab on to the body, but he was being dragged—pulled by the light and the sound—out of the body.

August let out a scream himself as he was cast out of the body and cast into the void. Everything was dark and silent but August held his breath. He needed to find a body, he needed a new place to hide and recover.

He sent himself flying through the air, searching for his own body. He lurked in the shadows and felt his soul become heavier and heavier with every moment that he was not in his skin. August went up traveling the length of the caves hoping that he could get out that way.

The world tilted and August was outside, looking at the sun and the sky. There was no time to bask in being outside those damp and dark caves. He needed to find a body. August traveled along the side looking for Vorus's manse.

He felt as though his soul was becoming heavier and heavier with every moment that he spent outside of his body. He pushed himself harder, rising above the trees and finding the manse in a matter of moments.

August raced into the manse, his eyes moving from one side to the other, looking for his body. He traveled into every room of the manse before he found it. The body was lying still in a room. He felt his soul weighing down towards the ground and reached out with a single hand to touch the body.

The moment that his soul touched his body, it was like rising out of water. He was sucked into the body and awareness washed over him again and he sucked in a breath for the first time since he was cast out of Tobias' body.

"August is that you?"

His vision was not fully back to him. The world moved around him and his vision went in and out and his breath stuttered in his throat. Someone grabbed him but all he could make out about them was the golden russet brown of their skin and the black of their hair. August kept trying to get air inside his lungs, sucking in gulpful after gulpful of air.

August tried to stop the world from turning this way and that and grabbed on to something. He laid down on the bed and sighed as he closed his eyes and sighed out from his nose. He stayed like that for a small moment, eyes closed, breathing in through his mouth and out through his nose. When he opened his eyes again the world had ceased its turning and his eyes could focus.

He turned to the side of his bed and saw that he was

holding a hand. His gaze traveled upwards and he saw that he was holding Sanaa's hand. She was looking at him with a look on her face that he could not decipher. He let his eyes wander and found a pile of books toppled over by her side. Sanaa opened her mouth to speak.

"You're an idiot."

# PART TWO
# THE RELEASE

# Chapter Fifteen

It took a matter of days for August to get well enough to speak and walk again. When he was better the group gathered in the dining room. There was no food decorating the table or maids and servants walking around serving. For all her time living there, Taira could not remember a time when the dining room was so still.

Vorus sat at the head of the table, his hands folded in front of him. Taira sat to his right and across from her was August. Sanaa sat beside him and the rest of the table was empty. They all sat quietly around the table.

"So what you are saying is that I have bandits in my caves?" Vorus said with an easy tone of voice. Sanaa nodded her head and August grunted his agreement. While everyone was looking at his face, Taira knew better than that. She looked at his hands. They drummed against the table in a quick staccato rhythm.

"These bandits are led by a woman named Nova," August began. "They were all originally mortal husks before she gifted them with their powers." The drumming on the table became faster and faster but Vorus's face stayed serene. Taira felt her stomach begin to tie itself in knots.

"Their power is immense. They can control shadows and bring the dead back to life to work under their will," Sanaa added. Taira thought back to the fight back in the cave. The way that they used the shadows and moved. They were getting training from a person. Someone who knew how to work with their powers. They were too good with their powers. Maybe it was a Dark Fae?

"If this gets out to the Husks there will be rebellion," Taira muttered to no one in particular. They all knew it. The Husks, mortal though they were, were several. There were hundreds of them in the town of Asren and the Spring Court alone there could have been thousands of them. Taira turned to Vorus, but his face was still the serene mask that it had been since the conversation started.

"Is there anything else that you may have discovered?" Vorus asked in a low tone. Taira felt a shiver go down her spine. It had been so long since she last heard that tone from Vorus. Taira wrung her hands under the table.

"I discovered that this medallion is from the temple of Roux. I think that they may have something to do with the bandits." Sanaa placed a medallion on the table with a heavy clink sound. Taira reached out to grab it in her hands, but Vorus was faster. Snatching the medallion, Vorus brought it close to his face.

The medallion shone in the afternoon light and Taira looked at the heavy bronze hanging from a leather strap. Vorus sighed and placed the medallion down again.

"Anything else?" He asked with a movement of his fingers. Sanaa and August looked at one another and then they both shook their heads. Vorus nodded. "Then there is nothing else to discuss." Vorus rose from his chair and Taira followed suit.

"Wait that is it?" Sanaa asked.

"Yes, that is all that I needed to know. I'll make sure to give you your next directions when I formulate a plan," Vorus said with a look over his shoulder.

August was the next to pipe up from where he was sitting. "You need time to understand what is happening? Just head down there and finish them off. Their power disappears in the day time!"

Vorus turned around to face the two of them again. "Oh? And do you know where they happen to be located in the caves?"

August looked properly mollified with his question and Vorus cast his eyes over both August and Sanaa.

"I will tell you what will be the next stage of the plan when I properly come to a conclusion. Thank you for everything that you have discovered." Vorus said. With that Vorus made a stiff turn and began to walk out of the dining room. Taira was only a step behind him.

The whole walk from the dining room into Vorus's room was silent. Taira's stomach was twisting into knots. Vorus was angry, angrier than anything that she had ever seen before. She needed to find a way to relax him to make sure that he directed his anger somewhere else.

"Vorus—" Taira began but Vorus held up a hand, never once stopping the punishing walking pace that he set.

"Not now Taira," was all that he said. Taira looked down at her hands. Her stomach was in her throat at this point. When they reached Vorus's room, he opened the door and walked in without a second thought. Taira took a moment standing in the threshold of the door but eventually put one foot in front of the other and entered the room.

Vorus stood in the center of the room, holding his hands together in front of him. The ground underneath him began to tremble, Taira could feel the tremors from where she stood. The oaken floors split open and a large thorny vine sprouted from the ground.

The vine lashed out, stripping wood from the ground and knocking things out of place. It slammed against the dresser, squashing it into splinters. Taira had to jump out of the way from one of the swipes that the vine took in her direction. Another vine sprouted from the opposite end of the room, slapping and smacking its way around.

Taira huddled against the corner out of the range of the vine. She looked to Vorus who was still standing calmly in the room as it was being destroyed by the vines that he summoned.

In a matter of moments, the whole room was destroyed, looking nothing like its former self. The bed was split in two, the dresser was crushed and the pair of chairs that sat in the room were upturned. The ground was scratched and torn up. Taira looked at Vorus, and the vine receded into the hole that it created in the floor.

"Bandits. The Empress will be here in a matter of days and I not only have a siren that no one can kill but I also have bandits that have decided to make their home in the caves."

Taira eyed the hole where the vine had sprouted out and walked out from the corner. Vorus sighed out and let himself fall forward onto the broken bed.

"Well, what do you want to do about it?" She deigned to ask.

"You know I would send you into the caves the moment that I found out the hiding place of those bandits. But I have no idea where those bandits are. And the wolves are breathing down my neck about that fucking trade agreement."

She stood in the center of the room, pondering the carnage of Vorus's temper. The curtains were torn and Taira frowned at them.

"And now we could have a Husk rebellion on our hands and the Empress will be here with King Gabriel..." Vorus trailed off.

Taira brought herself closer to Vorus. She leaned against the torn wall and looked out through the ripped curtains.

"If the other Husks find about what is going on in the caves-"

"Husks! With power! There would be mutiny in the streets. I would have hundreds of Husks fleeing from the city and into that woman—Nova's—hands. We would never be able to handle an onslaught like that."

"But what can we do? The caves are the fastest route to the wolves. Going around the mountain would take weeks."

"You don't think I know that. How can I stop the Husks from going to the caves and keep them where they are?"

The two of them were silent for a moment before Vorus huffed and rolled over onto his stomach. There had to be a way for them to control the Husks make sure that they did not flee. And they still had not even addressed the initial problem that they had: the siren.

Taira tried to juggle all the problems in her mind, but every solution that she came up with forgot to deal with one problem or the other. There was no way that they could corral all the Husks and keep the news of what was found there under wraps.

"What if we stopped allowing all them out?" Vorus asked. Taira tilted her head at that. "I'm not saying that we ban all Husks from going outside, but I'm thinking of a curfew for the Husks to prevent them from going outside from sundown to sun up."

"How would you enforce that?" Taira asked but she knew the moment that she asked. Vorus gave her a droll look and Taira sighed out. "It is going to be hard considering that most of the guard has already been afflicted with the siren song."

"Yes, but now we have a demon and a Batsamasi to help deal with the shortage," Vorus said with a wave of his hand.

Taira felt a dull thudding starting to grow in-between her eyes and rubbed the skin between her eyes. It was with a toss of her blond hair that she delivered the next words.

"Two people. For the fifteen guards that I have trapped under this house, you have given me two people. And we still have to investigate the Temple of Roux for their relationship to the bandits."

"Sanaa and August will investigate while we keep the peace and prevent any more bandits from arising," Vorus said. His voice was low and slow like the conversation was already beginning to bore him.

While having the two of them there was going to be a great help, it was still hard to maneuver around the city with such a limited amount of people. But she could tell that Vorus did not care about the shortage of people.

He wanted to have the job done and did not want to hear anything more than that. Taira felt something like fire heat her chest and her throat. She wanted to shout and lash out in the same way that Vorus did but she could never lose control the way that he so easily did.

"I'll have the edict written within the hour," Vorus said. Taira straightened her back and turned to leave the debased room. "Oh, and Taira?"

Taira turned to look back at Vorus who was laying face first in the split of the bed.

"Can you call someone to come and clean this up?"

Taira rolled her eyes at that and left the room. She did not know where her feet were taking her, but she allowed them to guide her path. She passed by the maids' quarters and was quick to tell a group of maids their new job, but from there she wandered listlessly from room to room, from hallway to hallway.

It was no surprise to her when she arrived at that door in the back of the house. Cobwebs were squatting in the corners, and dust was stuck to the windows and danced in the afternoon light, giving Taira the taste of stale air every time she breathed. The objects in this hall were worn, marred with dust and scratches, leaning on one another for support.

There was an oaken door at the end of the hallway. It was the only room in this hallway. Taira's hand hovered over the doorknob. Her fingers trembled as though she was being shocked with lightning. With a sigh, she leaned her forehead against the door.

She could not will herself to go inside. She did not have the strength. She had no right to go and see the person who was laying behind the door. Her hand rested on the knob, but her wrist was limp. The door would remain closed for now.

Taira wanted to open the door. Her heart was thudding in her chest at the thought of opening it. There were times that she dreamed about who was behind that door, but she stopped herself. She had no right to want to see her. Not while everything was going on.

Taira pulled herself away from that door and marched away from it. One day she would open that door, is what she told herself, but she knew that the day was not coming soon.

Taira returned to her rooms, sighing she sagged against the door. She pulled her blonde hair out of the tight top knot that it was in. The Empress was coming. The thought made her stomach do a flip.

The Empress was coming. And this would be her only chance to set everything right. The last chance she would have before she would be able to open that door. She needed to deal with the Empress and fast.

Taira got on the ground and pulled from underneath her bed a blue box. It was heavy but nothing that Taira could not support. She opened the box and took in the tinted blue steel of a sword.

Taira pulled the sword out of the box and held it in one hand. The sword was the standard sword, though its hilt was made of a cobalt blue material. The blade was shining and new, untouched by anything before.

She tried the weapon in the air hearing the way it sang through the air. She would be able to open the door and she would deal with the empress. It would end soon.

Taira would make sure of that.

# Chapter Sixteen

✦✦✦

"We made a pretty good team in there don't you think?"

Sanaa sighed and turned to face August. He was resting on the hind legs of his chair, his feet propped up on the table. Sanaa sneered at the casual way that August could place his feet on the table.

"I have no idea what you're talking about," Sanaa said as she rested her arms on the table. August rocked back and forth on the legs of his chair.

"Come on. You know what I'm talking about: in the cave, fighting those bandits. We fought well together," August said with a smile on his face. Sanaa rolled her eyes.

"It was in the heat of battle. I barely remember what was happening then," Sanaa said. It was true that she did not. She remembered his foolish attempt at espionage and the medallion that he pushed into her hands. She lifted it now, watching the way that the light reflected in the polished bronze.

"Well, I remember. We were good together. We worked well together."

"Is this about you being my partner again?"

August did not answer but tossed a grin in her direction. Sanaa rolled her eyes again.

"I don't need a partner. I just need to perfect the sword dance and fight better," Sanaa said with a flick of her hair. Thinking about the sword dance made her heart thud in her chest. She could not wait to be doing it again, to practice it and feel her muscles stretch as she jumped and flipped. She wanted to dance again and could feel the ache in her muscles to move again.

Sanaa rose from her chair in the dining room. She wanted to dance again, the desire filling her and coloring her every thought. She did not need August getting in the way of her practicing.

"Where are you going?" August asked with a turn of his head. Sanaa gave him a trite look over her shoulder.

"I'm going to dance," was all that she said. She turned her attention back to walking and heard the scrape of the chair against the ground and the hurried footsteps following behind her.

"Is that what you call fighting? Dancing?" August asked, coming up beside her.

"Isn't that what a battle is just a form of dance between two or more people?" Sanaa said, pushing herself to stride a little bit faster. August kept pace with her.

"I never thought of it that way, but I can see what you mean. The way that blades connect, the dodging, the hits. It is an elaborate dance if I have ever seen one," August said from beside her. "Is that what they teach you in the Batsamasi cities?"

Sanaa stopped where she was and turned to give August a sizing look. "What do you want from me?" She asked with her hands on her hips and a narrowed gaze.

August did not shrink under her gaze. Instead, he chucked

his chin higher and grinned wider. "I only ask that you dance with me once, milady."

She thought about it. Better to let him get a taste of her steel now than to deal with his nuisance for the longer time. She nodded her head then and somehow the grin on his face grew larger. Sanaa narrowed her eyes at him.

As the two of them walked to the training pit, Sanaa's body was singing with the thought of dancing once again. When they reached the training grounds Sanaa went to one side of the pit, pulling on the strings of monyelta. The needles rose and floated around her head in an array.

August still with that smile on his face, pulled a spear from one of the training racks in the room.

"You know," he started. "It seems a bit uneven for you to have a blade and for my weapon to be blunted."

Sanaa did not dignify that with a response and launched into her attack. She flipped and somersaulted over to him, bringing down her needles with all the strength that she could muster. August dodged the attacks, coming in hot with his spear. He jabbed at her sides, but Sanaa twisted away from the hits, leaning over and under them with ease.

Sanaa's muscles were screaming with joy. They were dancing again. They continued like that, each trying to hit one another, but never a hit landing. Sanaa changed the needles from an array to a melded blade and came down hard on August's spear.

He went to block it, holding his spear with both hands, but it split from the hit. It did not deter him at all, he twirled the split wood in his hands and kept on attacking. August shoved on, knocking away the blade and striking out with the other half of the spear.

Sanaa dodged the attack, separating the blade back into several needles again. She struck back. They were dancing around one another, trying to see the limits that they could take this battle to.

August was never on the defense for long, always skirting out of her reach and coming back with vengeance. Sanaa was surprised at how creative he could be with his attacks. It forced Sanaa to try somethings that Mother would have considered below her to even try.

Their two weapons crossed once again, Sanaa's needles were embedded in the wood of the spear. August and she were panting, their breathes intermingling as they took this moment to breathe. Sanaa trained her eyes on August. Brown eyes crossed amber and something like lightning sizzled down Sanaa's spine.

They broke away from one another again. Sanaa flipped away. She gathered the needles in the air in front of her and shot them off two by two at August. He parried each blow. Sanaa grabbed the last two of her needles and ran up to August.

The two blows clashed together, Sanaa's steel against August's wood, and the two were eye to eye. Sanaa twitched two of her fingers and the needles that he parried to the side rose, gathering to a point behind August.

"I win," Sanaa said. August turned to see the needle hanging in the air behind him. He let out a soft chuckle and pulled away from her. Sanaa let the needles drop.

The sun was lower in the sky when Sanaa looked up and August grabbed a towel from one of the cabinets in the training pit. He tossed one of the towels to her and Sanaa began to rub her face.

"Was it bad?" August asked after some silence.

"What?" Sanaa replied.

"The dance that we just did, was it bad?"

Sanaa looked towards the sky. The demon could fight. And the way that he moved against her was something that she had never experienced before. It was challenging. It was fun. Something that she would have been able to experience back at the compound.

Sanaa sighed and shook her head. "No."

"Good. I aim to please."

Sanaa cut her eyes to him. "I said it wasn't bad that doesn't mean that it was amazing."

"That means that there is a chance that this can happen again." He said it with the full confidence of someone who was assured of their place. Sanaa rolled her eyes.

Sanaa turned her eyes to the sky, the sun was coloring it a myriad of oranges and yellows and the sun hung low with a burnt red color. They had been fighting for so long that the sun was beginning to set. Sanaa wiped the towel across her face and sucked in a deep breath.

"The magic that we use is different from the Batsamasi that I knew growing up," August said. They were both lounging on the sandy floor of the training pit, but Sanaa nodded.

"I would expect my cousins' magic to be different from my own," she said.

"Cousin?" August asked.

"They are my cousins. They were birth by my Great Mother's sister so their magic is different from my own." Sanaa said. She thought back to the day that Mayara burned. Her heart was thudding in her throat that night when they fled the city. The orange-red of the fire and the way that the smoke overtook the sky, blotting out the stars and the moon.

Sanaa remembered holding on to Kala's hand and hoping that they were outpacing the fire. She did not even cast a thought to the cousins on the other side of the city and how they were faring.

"The magic that the Batsamasi I know uses blood magic and they are covered from head to toe in scars," August said with a twitch of his lips. "Their magic is heavier than your magic."

Sanaa let out a low chuckle, "Yes, their magic is a lot more terrifying than the magic that I wield. Their Great Mother had the power of blood magic and my Great Mother had the power of threading."

"Threading?"

Sanaa nodded her head and turned her eyes to the sky. "The world is made up of connecting threads full of monyelta, magic potential. My Great Mother had the power to see those threads and bend them to her will. Her sister had the power to manipulate the world through her blood and the two sisters set out to create a home for themselves."

"A city?"

"Of course. They built themselves a beautiful city and lived there with their daughters."

August hummed at her words and rose from the ground. "Well this has been fun, but I'm feeling peckish. Time to find something to eat." With that, he turned and left the room. Sanaa stayed in the training pit thinking to herself.

Her Great Mother was Thandi, the younger of the two sisters. She wondered what she would have thought about what was going on. The fact that Sanaa was helping the very people that burned the city that she worked so hard to build down.

Would she feel shame? Sanaa felt it bubbling in her chest when she thought about it too long. But the one who allowed the city to be burned down had long since passed. If there was one thing that Greta was trying to instill in her is that people have changed.

Sanaa sighed. It seemed that she was always stuck with the hard questions. Turning thoughts over and over in her head was exhausting. Sanaa rose then, maybe there was an easier answer. Sanaa rose from the ground tossing her towel aside.

She walked out of the room and towards the foyer of the manse. She walked straight out of the home and into the bustling heart of the town.

People bustled around her and for a moment Sanaa just enjoyed the feeling of people flowing around her. Some flitted with their wings overhead while other Fae lumbered on with their bark skin and antlers. Sanaa turned and looked around the town center.

She went to the booth of a woman and asked for directions to the closest temple of Arif. If anyone had answers to her questions it was going to be the witches that worked in Arif's temple.

Sanaa followed the directions that the woman gave her and Sanaa found herself staring at the temple of Arif. It was a shining building embossed with what could only be gold. Two sphinxes sat in front of the heavy wooden doors and stained glass windows showed the lion-headed Arif in battle with his sword.

She climbed up the steps to the temple and was about to knock on the door when it swung open. The woman who opened the door was covered in a gauzy material that was almost see-through, but she had packed it on in layers to keep her modesty.

The blue material of the clothing matched her eyes as they stared at Sanaa with a smile on her face.

"Hello, Sanaa," she said without a thought. Sanaa flinched at the use of her name and wanted to ask the woman how she knew it, but thought better of it. Arif was the god of the future. Of course, they would know her name.

"Come inside." The woman waved her hand. Sanaa entered the temple. The inside was covered in a plush rug and soft pillows to sit on. The women and men of the temple sat together, chatting lowly amongst themselves. And Sanaa felt out of place with her linen shirt and breeches.

The witch came up behind her and patted her shoulder, "Don't worry. We have everything that you need ready in the back." The witch led her through the conversing witches and wizards and into the back of the temple.

The back of the temple held the large floor to ceiling windows that depicted Arif doing many feats. Sanaa could not pin which story they were trying to tell, but she noticed that some of the other gods were in the windows. She spotted Fintan, Soliel and Iah, and even Magni.

The woman led her past the hallway of windows and into a small quiet room that held nothing else but a pit with pillows and a cauldron. Water bubbled in the cauldron and the witch came forward sitting on one of the pillows, gesturing for Sanaa to sit too.

Sanaa sat down and the woman threw in a couple of ingredients into the cauldron.

"Arif has told me that you have several questions," the witch said with a twitch of her lips.

"I want to speak with my Great Mother. I want to know if what I am doing is right." The witch hummed and pulled the spoon from the cauldron. She brought the spoon close to Sanaa's lips.

"Drink deeply," was all that the witch said. Sanaa drank. The concoction was heavy on her tongue, the liquid was thick and more like slime than water. But the taste was salty, something that she could bear. Once the witch pulled her spoon away, Sanaa felt heavy like her stomach was full.

Sanaa could barely keep her eyes open. She blinked slowly and her vision was tunneling. The witch came close to her, pushing her down onto the floor. The heavy feeling in her stomach felt warm and it spread through her veins and to her head. Sanaa felt so tired and warm.

The witch started murmuring something under her breath and Sanaa tried her best to listen to it, but her eyes were already falling close. She grew warmer and warmer with each utterance from the witch. Sanaa sighed and fell into the dark warmth that was waiting for her.

*When Sanaa opened her eyes again it was to a warm breeze. There was a wide grassland, that rippled and bent under the warm winds. Sanaa walked forward in the tall grass.*

*It was just how she remembered it from when she was a child: warm and bright, with a warm breeze and the sun shining down on her. Sanaa sighed and fell into the grass.*

*She wanted to stay in here forever. It was everything that she needed and wanted right now. She rose when she heard a giggling. Sanaa watched as young girls ran out in the grass, giggling and screaming with one another. Their long braids trailing out behind them.*

*"Beautiful isn't it," a voice said from behind her.*

*Sanaa whirled around to find herself face to face with Mother. Sanaa gasped as her eyes locked on her figure. Her fingers twitched but the magic did not respond to her.*

*"That won't work here. The witch makes sure that we cannot hurt one another here," Mother sang out with a hum. Sanaa frowned and turned away from her mother.*

*"I did not want to talk to you. I wanted to talk with my Great Mother," Sanaa said with a huff. She crossed her arms and stared out into the grassland, watching the girls play again.*

*"Our Great Mother is very hard to get a hold of. You are going to have to settle for me," Mother said. Mother sat down on the grass her legs stretched out before her. "Come sit with me."*

*"No, thank you, Mother," Sanaa grit out. Mother shrugged her shoulders and leaned back into the grass.*

*The girls began to play some sort of game in the grass, hiding in the grass and jumping out at one another.*

"You know you used to play something similar when you were young."

Sanaa cut her eyes to Mother. "Why are you here?"

Mother sighed, "I'm here because you used Arif's witch to call me here. I'm here because you want me here."

"If I wanted to be lied to I would have stayed with the Fae," Sanaa bit out. Mother gave a deep laugh at that.

"I saw from my place in the Void that you are working with the Faeries now. How is that going?"

"You do not get to ask me anything. Not after everything that you did."

Mother rolled her eyes and rose from her place on the ground. Sanaa shifted to put some distance between the two of them. Another breeze rustled past the two of them.

"Sanaa, I am already dead. I have paid for everything that I have done with my life. Your sisters made sure of that," Mother said with a toss of her hair over her shoulder. "I cannot do anything but speak to you here and now."

Sanaa stayed silent for a moment. There was a lot that she wanted to ask her mother. She wanted explanations and reasons, but she knew her mother. She knew that she was never going to get a straight answer. But there was no harm in trying.

"Why did you do it?" Sanaa asked lowly.

"What?"

"Why did you do it?" Sanaa asked again. Her foot tapped against the ground in a furious beat. Mother looked her over, once, twice, and then shrugged her shoulders.

"Because I could. I wanted something so I took it," Mother said. The answer was so simple. Because I could. She simply did it on a whim. She did it for herself.

"How could you be so selfish! We all trusted you to guide us and teach us and instead you manipulated us. Your daughters!" Sanaa shouted turning to look at her mother for the first time.

Mother looked at her, those acid green eyes seeming to glow even *in the bright light of the sun. "Who better to manipulate than those that have no choice but to love you."*

*The words pierced something in Sanaa's chest. She felt as though she had been cut deep and could not staunch the bleeding. She had loved Mother, looked up to her, aspired to be here. And then there came the revelation and then Sanaa had been turned to stone.*

*Mother looked out into the playing girls. Sanaa felt tears come down her face warm and wet. Sanaa let out a sob. They were nothing more than playing pieces to Mother. They were only pawns in her game. The thought shook her, rattled everything that she thought she knew and loved once again.*

*Sanaa turned to look at her Mother, but the woman was gone like the wind. Sanaa cried out, slamming her fists against the ground and cursing her mother the whole while.*

Sanaa woke up with a gasp. She quickly turned over and vomited up whatever it was that the witch had made her drink. Sanaa struggled to breathe spitting up bile and whatever was left of that slime.

The witch patted her back and rubbed it trying to soothe her. "Did you see who you needed to see?"

Sanaa panted, "Yes."

If they were just pawns in Mother's games then there was no need to follow her teachings anymore. Mother was dead and the rules along with her.

# Chapter Seventeen

Steam floated up from the heated water and August sank lower into the bathtub. His skin felt renewed by the water though it still felt as though his skin was stretched tight over his bones. The cost of being in another body for too long.

August lifted his hand and conjured a flame, flicking it underneath the bath and sighing as the water grew hotter. The heat of the bath soothed over his tense muscles and warmed away all his aches.

Though relaxed, August could not help but think about what Nova said. Helia could not be the reason for the downfall of so many people. It was the pride of the others she worked with that was inevitably their downfall.

Helia hated the Empress and the royals more than anything else. She had gone out of her way to mark them for death in any way that she could. Though with the Empress on the move now would be the best time to kill her.

He thought back to what Nova said in the caves. The Brownie Brothers were volatile with their tempers and their raids... They were lucky that no one got caught. For those two everything they did was a matter of pure luck and nothing else. When Helia stepped in, she tried to inject some sort of order and hierarchy, but the brothers were resistant.

It was not long before everything fell apart. The Brownie Brothers were caught and executed and Helia absorbed the remaining remnants of what was left into her organization. The brothers were never going to make it. Besides, the brothers had horrible tempers. It was a matter of time before they got caught or there was a mutiny among those that followed them.

The rebellion in the Summer Court was a separate matter altogether. August could remember the way the rebellion started with the dissatisfaction of some of the nobles in the Summer Court. Then it grew to encompass farmers and merchants too. It was a well-oiled machine by the time Helia entered.

At the time it seemed nothing was going to stop them. They were going to overthrow the King of the Summer Court and install their leader, but then there was a spy. And infighting started to take place among the leaders.

Just as quickly as the swirlings of the rebellion started it ended. The men and women who started the rebellion were gone, executed by the King of the Summer Court.

August remembered the meetings and the distrust that festered in the room like an open wound. No one could trust one another and everyone was on edge. Everyone except Helia. Helia was like she always was calm and collected, assured of herself and everything around her. Even when others accused her of working with the spy the accusations rolled off of her like water.

There was no way that Helia would have done something to ruin their chances at a successful revolution. It was too much work, it was too hard. August cast the thought aside. It was just Nova trying to justify not wanting to join with Helia. It meant nothing.

August lifted himself out of the tub. It had been a while since he contacted Helia. Going to the mirror August let a spark of hellfire burn on his finger. He touched the glass with the hellfire and watched as the glass glowed with light. It was bright enough that August cast his eyes away from it for a moment.

The glass fogged up, steam from the bath and the fire making the glass cloudy. August wiped away at the steam and saw Helia instead of his reflection. Her red eyes were trained on something in the distance. Her straight black hair ran down her back and August wanted to reach out and grab it in his hands.

"Helia," he sang out. She turned to look at him, her eyes roving over his naked body. "Do you like what you see?"

"Of course I do," Helia said with a smile on her lips. Helia leaned closer, her shirt sagging a little bit to tease the curve of her breast. August let out a low chuckle.

"Have you missed me?"

"Dearly," Helia said with a hand to her forehead. "Every day without you is like being stabbed with thousands of swords." August chuckled. The words though joking made him feel warm. He wanted nothing more than to reach out to Helia and grab her into his arms.

"I have some news for you," he said as he wiped his wet hair back from his face. "I was able to make contact with the leader of the operation over here."

"And what did they say?" Helia said, playing with the ends of her hair. Her eyes were no longer on him, but looking at some distant point. He shifted from one foot to the other.

"Their leader, Nova, declined the invitation. They say they want to work independently." Helia turned to look at him then, a frown marring her features.

"Well, that isn't what I wanted to hear," was all that she said.

"Their operation is very unorganized," August started. He attempted to placate her, soothe her over so that she did not order something rash. "And the craziest thing is their whole operation is being run by Husks."

"Husks?"

"Yes. These are Husks with power. They were gifted some sort of abilities by their leader."

"Husks? With power?" Helia repeated with more incredulity.

"Yes, I know. I was surprised when I found out also." He said with a huff. "I could hardly believe it because they were giving us such a hard time in the caves."

"August, if what you are telling me is true, then I do not want them to join us," Helia said. "I want them to disappear."

"Disappear?" he asked.

"Wipe them off the face of the planet," Helia said with a shrug of her shoulders. "I cannot abide by what they are doing down there." Her lips twisted in a grimace and she rolled her shoulders back.

"I will do just that then," August stated with a sigh. It was hard dealing with them before and now he needed to get rid of them all. "Is there any way that you can send reinforcements?"

"Reinforcements? What would you need them for?"

"They are hard to deal with and I don't know how many of them there are. I think it would be better with more people here."

"August, the Empress is expected to be in Asren in a matter of days. I cannot send you help and expect you'll get away without her noticing."

"I know that but—"

"Besides you are dealing with Husks. How hard could it be?"

He wanted to tell her of their abilities and the way that the tattoos danced on their skin. But then he thought better of it. They were simple Husks. She was right. He would need to find another way to deal with them.

August sighed. He'd have to deal with this on his own. Maybe he could convince Vorus to loan him some of his men to deal with the bandits. Yeah, that is what he would do. Silence reigned for a moment before August decided it was best to ask her about what Nova said.

"You know, Nova had a lot to say about you," he started. Helia raised an eyebrow.

"A lot of people have things to say about me."

"She mentioned the Brownie Brothers and the rebellion in the Summer Court." August felt as though there was a knot in his chest, something weighty that was on the edge of tipping over. He wanted to shove the feeling down, hide it, but the weight of it was too much, it was something that he was going to have to deal with.

"Oh? That was so long ago I barely remember it," Helia said.

"I hadn't joined you when the Brownie Brothers were taken down, but I remember the Summer Court rebellion."

"I remember you when you first joined us. You were so eager and now look at you never willing to go anywhere." August let out a chuckle at her words. But as quick as the mirth landed it was gone in a matter of moments.

"Did you ever root out the spy? Did you ever find out who was leaking the information to the king?" August asked but he already knew the answer before he asked the question.

Helia shrugged her shoulders. "We never found out who was leaking the information. But the rebellion was never going to last. It was doomed to fail when the infighting started... Why are you asking about it anyway."

August shook his head. Why was he asking about it? Nova was no one. She did not know a thing about the workings of Helia and how she ran her organization. Why was he letting her get to him like this?

"No reason," he said. "I'll speak to you when Nova has been dealt with."

"Good. I hope to hear the good news soon," Helia said with a toss of her hair. The mirror fogged up again and when August went to wipe away the steam and smoke, Helia was gone and his reflection stared back at him.

"That was stupid," he muttered to himself. What was he trying to get from Helia? An admission of guilt? Helia would have never set up the rebellion or the Brownie Brothers to fail. That was not like her.

She hated the Faerie royalty more than anything else in the world. She made it her mission to be a thorn in their side for as long as she lived. How could he doubt her? And all because of some... Husk planted the thought in his head.

But a small part of him whispered, you are under her thumb because of the deal you made. It whispered to him that he did not know Helia like he thought he did. And though he tried to shut down that part of him. It was true. He didn't know why Helia hated the Faerie royalty.

Sevan's stars above, he did not even know the reason why Helia decided to keep him around. He never even knew what she was thinking half the time. He said it himself, Helia was fickle, she was hard to understand and contain.

Talking to her about it was going to be a waste of time. It was a waste of time. August leaned into the mirror, the cool glass pressed against his warm skin.

The bath steamed behind him, but August wrapped a towel around his waist and left the bathroom. With a flick of his wrist, the darkness of his room ebbed away at the light of the candles. The room was bathed in the warm glow of the candles and August sat back as he took in everything he and Helia talked about.

He decided that it would be best to go to sleep. The light of the sun had long since faded and stars speckled the black expanse of the sky.

August laid in bed for a moment and then shifted, his hand reaching out for what was in the drawer. He stopped his hands from opening it. And they rested against the lip.

It had been a while since he used it. He didn't want to run out. August knew he could not sleep without it. He needed it. And if he wanted to take out all the Husks that were lingering in the caves he was going to need to use a lot of it.

Sighing, August pulled the drawer open. In the drawer laid the curled form of a horn. It was a dull gray in the candle-light, and August could count the rings on the horn. The horn was hard, but smooth in his hands and he grabbed the grater in the drawer with it.

He shaved off a little from the tip of the horn. The horn was brittle and the shavings fell off easily. He pressed on the side of his nose and took in a deep inhale of the shavings.

Fire lit his veins. The shavings traveled through his blood, warming him down to his toes. He leaned back and rested against the bed. His head was weightless, only being held down to his body by the string that was his neck. His body hit the bed and a tingling rose in him. A million bristles of a hairbrush pushed against his body and dragged their lightning fingers down his sides.

He could see why demons were hunted when they could make people feel like this. August sucked in a breath and closed his eyes. The tingling sensation turned into a full on burning, his blood boiling in his veins and traveling all along his arms and legs. All his problems were floating away from him.

He closed his eyes and sunk into the warmth and the tingling. This was all that he needed. Why worry about Helia and what she was doing when he could feel like this. August let out a breath that he didn't know that he was holding.

His thoughts floated away and he was wrapped up in the euphoria of his high. He forgot about Helia, his mission here, and everything going on. All he could feel was the warmth in his body and the tingling that shot up from his toes to his head. And that was all he needed.

## Chapter Eighteen

"I have issued a new edict," Vorus said over breakfast the very next day. Sanaa was lost in her thoughts, thinking about everything that she spoke about with her mother. When Vorus spoke the words did not register in her mind. It was Taira's hard nudge to her side that caught her attention.

Vorus stood at the head of the table. He was dressed in fine clothing and the smirk on his face told that he thought whatever he was going to say next was clever.

"This new edict is a curfew for the Husks. We cannot have them escaping to join those bandits," he said. "Sanaa, August, I expect the both of you to help Taira with the patrols."

Sanaa nodded her head without a thought, but then she paused. If they were stuck helping keep the Husks from escaping, then when would they confront the bandits and the siren? It appeared that August had the same thought as their eyes connected from across the table.

"While I would love to help with making sure that no one escapes to join the bandits in the middle of the night. If we are watching the Husks who then would deal with the bandits? If we leave them unattended long enough they may decide to leave the caves." August said, shoveling some food on his plate.

A frown marred Vorus's face. Sanaa nodded her head and turned her eyes towards Vorus.

"He is right. We haven't found the siren yet and these bandits cannot be left alone," she said.

"Well they gave you so much trouble last time I thought that you'd be happy with this new edict," Vorus replied with a short look to Taira. Taira said nothing as she moved the food across her plate.

Sanaa grit her teeth. "We were ambushed."

"Yes, yes, and now you can spend time looking into the medallion and what the temple of Roux has to do with any of this." Vorus waved his fork around. "I want you and August stationed close to the Temple of Roux, I want to know exactly what is going on in that temple."

August sighed, leaning back in his chair and began to play with his food. "This is a waste of time. The temple might not have anything to do with the missing Husks. Defeating the bandits and the siren is more important than trying to discover what is going on in the temple. The temples of the Twelve are known to be secretive."

"And that is why I want to know exactly what they are up to," Vorus said with a pound of his fist. "The temples of the Twelve have always promoted peace in Asren, and because of their power, I cannot go against them. But you two are not from here. You can investigate the temple of Roux better than I can."

"And if it turns out that he was just some slave who escaped the temple?" Sanaa asked.

"Then he was just some slave who escaped the temple. But we cannot know if we do not investigate what they are doing. I want to know what they are up to and I want to know sooner rather than later." Vorus said.

Sanaa sighed. What Vorus said made sense. If the temple of Roux was aiding the bandits in the caves then it was better to know now. But why would a temple help the Husks? They were nothing more than mortals. They had no power or influence on their own and most of them were enslaved, toiling away for their betters.

Sanaa thought of the Husks that built the compound where her nieces now lived. This was something that had to be contained to the Faerie courts and dealt with. The Husks would flock to the leader of the bandits if they knew that she could grant them some power.

No, this needed to end here. Sanaa nodded her head. "Fine then. We'll investigate the temple of Roux. We'll find out what is happening in there and report it back to you."

August pushed his chair back and rose, making his way to the door. "Maybe you will, but I will not. I was hired to take out a siren and that is what I will do. I want no part in your politics."

Vorus rose from his chair. "I am ordering you to stake out the temple of Roux."

"And that isn't what I was paid to do-"

"August!" Sanaa said rising from her seat. She stalked over to the demon and though he was a head taller than her, looked him right in the eye.

"I know what we were brought here to do hasn't been done, but we have a bigger issue on our hands. Think about what would happen should the rest of the Husks find out about what is going on in the caves. Think about the madness and chaos that those bandits can create should they be left alone."

August did not budge from his spot so Sanaa continued. "The Husks are many. They outmatch us five to one at least.

We need to make sure that the temple of Roux is not helping them in any way possible. Once we confirm that then we can make our way back into the caves and ruin them for all that they have done. It will take all of us."

August's shoulder sagged. "Fine. I'll help with watching the temple of Roux. And then we have to deal with these bandits as soon as possible." Sanaa let a smile stretch across her lips and they both turned back to Vorus.

"When is the first watch?" Sanaa asked. Vorus sat back down in his chair and smiled.

"Tonight. I already sent out messengers to deliver the edict to everyone in Asren. I expect that by noon everyone will have heard about the new curfew for Husks," Vorus said. Sanaa nodded her head and turned to look at August.

"Then our investigation of the temple begins tonight. We'll get it done," Sanaa said. August mumbled out his agreement but it was heard nonetheless. The two of them then turned and exited the room.

Sanaa made her way to her rooms, her fingers itching to gather the strings of monyelta in her hands again. August jogged a little bit to catch up with her, his hands resting behind his head.

"You're okay with this?" August hissed under his breath.

"Of course I am okay with this. The bandits need to be stopped and we need to know if the temple has anything to do with it," Sanaa said. August came in front of her, stopping her from continuing her march forward.

"I'm surprised that you of all people are okay with taking orders from the Fae," August said with a tilt to his chin. Sanaa crossed her arms and leaned back on the balls of her feet, her lips turning downwards. "You know considering that the Fae and the Batsamasi have been at odds for over a hundred years."

"Doing research I see?"

"More like listening and taking notes." Sanaa tried to step around him, but he moved to block her. "Why are you taking orders so well? Didn't your commander warn you against listening to the Fae?"

"No, in fact, my commander sent me here to see that the world has changed," Sanaa said. August raised an eyebrow at that, but he refused to budge from his spot. "Move out of my way."

"We are caught in a web of Faerie politics. You do them one favor and then it spirals out of control and you find yourself entrenched in their world. Trust me. I know for a fact that if we do this one thing for them. They will never let us go."

The words struck a chord in Sanaa. She remembered the moments that she spent at Mother's knee, learning about the world of Ettrea and the races that populated it. She remembered the venom that Mother would inject into her words when she spoke about the Fae.

*"The Fae deal in favors. They are tricky with their words and their actions, all to ensnare you in their deals. Never do the Fae a favor, because that is how they trap you."*

What a load of shit that had been.

"Sure. Let them get us with their deals. I for one would welcome it," Sanaa said. "It'd be the one thing that makes sense."

Sanaa stepped to the side again and this time August did not follow the movement. She walked past him, never once looking back.

When she reached her room, she collapsed onto the bed. Her fingers itched to practice her sword dancing again, but her fingers were frozen, heavy things that she could not muster the will to lift.

Mother lied to her. She lied to all of them. She had twisted her words so skillfully that they were willing to die for her and her quest to do what? Mother had no bigger goal. No higher calling or ambition. Mother just wanted her daughters under her thumb where they were easy to control.

She was no better than the Fae she claimed to hate so much.

Sanaa reached for the boxes of needles. She strapped them to her legs and then left the room. She needed to move. She needed to be physical with her body. Sanaa's feet flew to the training pits. When she reached the training pits it was without a second thought that her fingers wrapped around the strings of monyelta.

The air stirred around her as the needles rose from the boxes strapped to her thighs. The needles fanned out behind her in a perverse halo of death. She launched her first attack against a dummy back against the wall.

She had no idea what she was attacking, maybe it was Mother, maybe it was Greta. Maybe it was everyone. But Sanaa needed to attack something. Her body was screaming for it, aching for it.

When one dummy was shredded beyond recognition she moved on to the next one. She continued, cutting and dicing at the training dummies until they were nothing but shredded straw at her feet.

Sanaa wanted nothing more than to be home in her room. That place filled with the ghosts of her life before. Sanaa let out a shout as she cut off the head of one of the dummies.

Following orders. That was all that she did. Follow orders. Let other people dictate her future, her fate. When would it be her turn to make the decisions and decide things for herself?

Maybe she was happier when she was following orders. She didn't have to think too much and if anything went wrong then the blame rested solely on the shoulders of the person issuing the orders. Maybe it was better that way.

Sanaa threw out a fist, her fingers dancing on the red hot string of monyelta. The magic surged through her, scorching hot, and it came out in the needle. The needle grew red hot, glowing with heat, it cut through the last head of the training dummy. It lay on the ground sad and singed.

"I did not know that our straw had done you wrong."

Sanaa turned around. Taira stood in the archway, her blonde hair tied up in a topknot. Sanaa took a look around the room. Straw was strewn everywhere. It was on the floor and when Sanaa reached up to push her braids away from her face, there was straw in her hair. She shook her hair in an attempt to dislodge the straw.

Taira walked slowly into the room. Her head swiveled side to side like she was expecting an attack. Sanaa settled the air around her, sliding the needles back into the boxes strapped around her thighs.

"This is a lot of anger for one person," Taira said. Sanaa let out a breath that she didn't know she was holding. She shook out her hair and rocked back and forth on her heels.

"I was holding it in," Sanaa commented.

"Well with anger like that maybe we do have a chance of defeating the bandits."

The two let out a low chuckle at the joke. And then everything was silent. Sanaa had never taken a moment to size Taira. She stood with her shoulders sagging and her head bent. Her eyes though, they were bright and the skittered arounds the room, trying to take in everything around her. Her shoulders sagged when she saw no one else in the room and her head raised to look Sanaa in the eye.

"Why were you so angry?" Taira asked.

"Yeah, like I'll tell you. So then you could use it against me and ensnare me in one of your deals?" Sanaa scoffed. Taira let out a low chuckle but did not leave the room. It did not even appear that she took offense at her words.

"I'm not the type to strike deals," Taira said with a flick of her hair over her shoulder. "I've been burned one too many times."

The words made Sanaa pause. A Fae that did not make deals. The thought was astounding to Sanaa. It was like a siren with no song. She did not think that one could exist without the other, but they existed. Sanaa crossed her arms. Well if she wasn't going to be making any deals.

Sanaa paused. Should she speak? Sanaa shuffled her feet. Her Mother had always told her that Fae were the type to make deals. That was their currency, their way of life. For one not to make deals. She shot Taira a wary glance. Taira rolled her eyes and settled down on a bale of hay.

"Here," Taira offered her hand. "I'll make a deal with you. I won't tell anyone what you tell me here. And you'll tell me what has been bothering you. Deal?"

It was a simple deal and one said in the simplest terms. Taira would gain nothing but conversation and Sanaa would get the safety of knowing that Taira would not tell anyone. It was simple, safe. Mother's words still rang in her ears though. Sanaa frowned and shook her head.

"No," Sanaa said with a shake of her head. "No deals."

"Okay," Taira said pulling back her hand. Sanaa nodded her head and Taira looked up at her. "You know I won't tell anyone right? Like you can just tell me."

Something in Sanaa's chest unfurled at the honest look in Taira's eyes. She needed to tell someone; she needed to speak—

"My mother is not who I thought she was." The words poured out of Sanaa without preamble. Sanaa slapped a hand to her mouth, her eyes going wide. But Taira did not move. She simply stayed where she was and looked at Sanaa with those wide green eyes. Sanaa lowered her hand. "My mother lied to me. She manipulated me. She was telling me what I wanted to hear never once thought about what I needed to hear. She wasn't the mother that I thought I had."

Sanaa remembered the stone covering her body. The way that it wrapped around her and how her heart thudded in her chest. She remembered the cold look in her mother's eyes and she pulled on the gray string of monyelta that connected both of them. The way that Sanaa struggled to breathe as her chest turned to stone. She shuddered at the memory.

Then she thought of the mother that she saw in her vision. The mother that look tired and could only offer very little. That mother that she spoke to was the mother that she had wanted all along. A mother that wasn't going to turn her to stone.

"Aren't parents always different from what we expect?" Taira said. Sanaa sighed. As though a part of her knew that Mother was not the person that she said she was. But another part of her wanted to rebel against that thought. Mother could not have been two different people at the same time. She couldn't have been the tactical and calm person that lived in her memories and the tired-looking woman from the visions. It was not possible.

But somehow it was. Mother was different, now that she was dead. And it was something that Sanaa was going to have to learn to live with. Mother was a different person; she always had been a different person.

"I don't understand how she could be— just— she is nothing like the mother that I knew when I was a child."

Taira played with the ends of her hair. "I understand the thought of someone who you love not being who you thought you were. You feel as though the world has been taken from under you. Nothing makes sense anymore and you question everything that they must have said and shown you."

"Yes!" Sanaa jumped at the words. That was what she was

feeling. "Nothing makes sense anymore. If Mother was not who she said she was then who is she?"

"Maybe you are going to have to be okay with the thought that you will never know anyone the way that you know yourself," Taira said. Sanaa deflated at her word, her shoulders sagging.

That was not what she wanted to hear, but it was the truth. She could not know Mother and all her complexities. And the rules that mother gave her, they no longer applied to the world anymore. The world was a vastly different place than the way that mother presented it. Sanaa may have to discover it for herself.

"Thank you," Sanaa said. "I think I understand what you mean."

Taira nodded her head. "People are more complex than we think. And with that usually comes trouble." Sanaa let out a laugh.

"A lot more trouble," Sanaa agreed. She sat down in the dirt and then laid down. She looked up at the stars and wondered if Mother was looking at her from across the Void.

The world was a lot bigger and more complex than she was raised to believe. The thought scared her a little bit. She was standing on a great precipice and she was teetering on the edge. But there was a light at the end of the never-ending darkness. And she was stretching out her arms to reach it.

## Chapter Nineteen

W hen the sun began to set, the town was a flurry
of activity. Husks ran from one place to the
other, moving as fast as they could to be within
their homes by the time the sun dropped out of the sky.
August sat high in a tree sitting on one of the branches
watching as the Husks ran amongst themselves.

They scurried like ants, with no reason, no sense of direction just the feeling of urgency among them all. They dashed
from stall to stall their eyes watching the sun as it sunk lower
and lower in the sky.

This edict would do nothing more than entice the Husks
into leaving and joining the bandits. They may not know
about the bandits but the word would soon arise of the power
that could be gained if they made their way to the caves. And
then it would be a matter of time before they made their way
out of the caves and into Asren.

August doubted that this edict would solve their problems. The temple of Roux had probably nothing to do with
the bandits. But then how were the bandits so well trained?

The way that they fought and the skill that they had, there had to be someone training them.

He remembered Nova and the way that she arrived. The black sludge that the girl had to drink down and how the whites of her eyes changed. And what did she mean about going home?

Where was this home that Nova spoke of? And why was she trying so hard to go back? August knew better than to try and pry into the business of others but he was curious and everything about Nova piqued his interest.

How was it that she was gifting power to the Husks? Why was she only giving power to the Husks? He had many questions, but he was no longer in Nova's lair. Instead, he was stuck here, watching the Husks trip over themselves as they tried to haggle with the poultryman for the last piece of goat.

The sun sunk below the horizon and by that time all the Husks were gone, cooped up in their homes waiting for the sun to rise again. August launched himself out of the tree branch and into the town square.

He walked around the town, keeping his ears open to hear what the people were saying.

"This new edict is ridiculous! Are you telling me that I have to go out myself at night instead of sending my servants?" Someone piped up from one of the stalls.

August let out a low chuckle at that. It would not kill them to get off their feet. The Fae were too complacent with how everything worked. If one edict was enough to send their life out of balance then their lives were too easy.

The thought of easy living brought back thoughts of Helia. Was he like the Fae? So content with his life that the moment that when something new entered the stage that he was set adrift? No. That was impossible. Helia was too fickle for him to ever be complacent with his place in her life.

With the Husks inside their homes, there were more Fae

out as a result. And August took a moment to watch them all go about their business. He had never seen so many different types of Fae. Some had bark for the skin while others had the spotted coat of a deer complete with matching antlers.

August touched his horns, he followed the way that they curved around his head. He wondered what it would be like to have antlers. Were they heavier or lighter? The thought left him as soon as it came. Being with the Fae for so long was beginning to get to him. He was thinking that he wanted to be one of them now. The thought was laughable.

He made his way back to Vorus's manse, the Husks attendants already cooped up in the massive home. August went to his room grabbing his spear and shrugged on his armor. He wanted to rush to defeat the bandits that were hiding in the caves, to follow Helia's command. But he could not afford to bring any suspicion to himself.

He was already on thin ice with Vorus. He was not sure of the man's temperament and how committed he was to the cause. In a matter of moments, he could reveal that August was working for Helia and then he would have all of the Courts hunting for him. No, August could not have that happen.

August walked back into the foyer where Sanaa and Taira were waiting for him. Sanaa had her braids pulled back into a top knot and all the cowry shells and gold bits were taken out. Taira had her hair down in a low ponytail.

Sanaa shifted from one foot to the other as though she could not wait to get to staking out the Temple of Roux. August reclined back on to the heels of his feet when he reached both of them.

"Ready to begin Husk watching?" He asked. Sanaa rolled her eyes and Taira nodded her head and turned to look at the both of them in their eyes.

"The Temple of Roux has been dormant lately. They

haven't been strolling and they haven't been accepting any visitors, so neither one of you will be able to walk into the temple to investigate," Taira said.

"Yes, yes. We will only be able to watch the outside of the house and report any suspicious activity," August yawned. They all knew the mission and what they had to do. He wanted tonight to be over as soon as possible so that they could go back to the caves and kill those bandits already.

Sanaa shot him a burning look, but August ignored it. Taira shook her head but continued to speak.

"The witches will not expect the two of you to watch them, but make sure you don't get caught watching them. If you do that could spell trouble for both you and Vorus." Taira said. "If they catch you, Vorus cannot afford to be caught in the mess so he will leave you to work your way out of that mess."

August frowned at this. Of course, Vorus would leave them to club out of the grave. He couldn't be caught fighting with one of the Temples of the Twelve this close to the Empress' arrival. From the whispering that he had heard, the Empress was already in the Spring Court and it was only a matter of days before she made her way to the town of Asren.

But still August and Sanaa nodded their heads at Taira's words. They wouldn't get caught; the two of them were too good for that. They made their way to the town square, the lantern lights guiding their path. It was there that Taira decided they would part ways.

"Keep going south as though you are heading towards the caves. On that path you will find the Temple of Roux," Taira pointed. The path was darker than any of the others. Sanaa though walked down without any fear.

August followed after her with his head held high. The two of them walked down the path, their eyes shooting this way and that looking for anyone suspicious, but they could not find anyone on their way. It seemed that even the Faeries of southern Asren had taken to their homes.

"This is stupid," August said under his breath. "We should just gather all our power and kill those bandits." Sanaa looked over her shoulder and gave him a withering glance. But August continued. "You know I'm right, Sanaa. There is nothing to be found with the temple of Roux. If anything we may just be spying on Vorus's political rivals."

"The man that you possessed had a medallion from the temple of Roux," was all Sanaa supplied as an answer.

"He could have gotten that medallion from anywhere!" August groaned out. Sanaa turned to him and pressed a finger to her lips. August lowered his voice. "He could have gotten it from one of the carts that were trying to make it across to the wolves."

"Well where ever he got it we must investigate. We don't know about their connections to the Temple of Roux and we need to know. I know I was not the only one to notice how well trained the bandits were."

August remembered the way that they moved. The bandits knew how to support one another to bolster their strengths and cover their weaknesses. They moved like a well-trained militia and that was something that August couldn't ignore no matter how much he tried to discard the thought.

He wanted to add something else, but Sanaa had already turned her eyes back to the path in front of them. They walked a little way more before Sanaa caught sight of the temple first. It was hidden behind the shadows of two large trees.

Here the temple was shrouded in darkness. The place of worship was a large, squat building, wider than it was tall. It sat in the middle of a grove of trees.

Sanaa and August stopped where the trees were and hid among the trees. There were some lights on in the windows.

There was a stiff wind that danced by the shook the leaves in the trees but the cool air did not deter them from watching the temple.

For a long time, the two of them sat behind the trees, watching lights go on and off in the windows of the temple. August sighed and turned his eyes away from the trees.

"There is nothing here," he started. "They are just going about their nightly duties. We can't even see that from here."

Sanaa looked at him and then turned her eyes back to the temple. "You're right." Sanaa got down close to the ground and crawled closer towards the temple. August sputtered.

"S-Sanaa! Come back here!" He whispered, but she didn't look back just kept crawling towards the temple. August looked at the spot she had left behind and then sighed. He got low to the ground and began to crawl after her. The two of them reached the temple and sat down underneath one of the windows of the temple.

"Sanaa are you crazy," he whispered under his breath. "We are too close to them, now we could get caught!" Sanaa waved her hand at him like she was waving off his comments. Sanaa rose from the ground slightly to peek into one of the windows. August did not bother trying, his horns would cast a large shadow in the moonlight.

"This one is just a bedroom," Sanaa announced. She sat back down with August and she looked like she wanted to look into more of the windows, but August grabbed her hand.

He narrowed his eyes at her and jerked on her arm. He held her arm the whole way as the two of them crawled back to their hiding spots in the trees. When August turned back to look at her the woman seemed to almost be pouting. August frowned at her.

"Are you insane?" August asked.

"You were right when you said that we were too far away to hear or see anything. I thought that by getting closer—"

"You thought by sitting underneath their window that we would hear something about their relationships with the bandits?"

"—I was hoping that we would overhear something," Sanaa continued as though he never interrupted her. August sighed and ran a hand through his hair.

"You think that they'd just be discussing something so important in casual conversation? That they'd just be talking about it so clearly at night?" August said.

Sanaa stayed silent and August hoped that his words properly chastised her. He sat back down behind his tree. He leaned his head against the tough bark of the tree and sighed.

"Is that what they teach you at the compound? That you should always dive headfirst into your missions. To go on ahead without any plan?"

"Like you? You want to go headfirst into the caves without a plan at all."

"Because that is our job! We were hired to deal with a siren and make sure that trade goes about smoothly. I'm wrong for wanting to get this job over with?" August shot back at her.

Silence reigned for a few moments, the two of them shared a heated stare. Then they both started to laugh quietly. Their eyes crinkled and they held their stomachs as they let the laughs rack through them. Finally, the laughter subsided and the two of them relaxed against the trees.

"They teach us to be cautious in the compound. My mother could not have us dying in the field and humiliating her name. I was being reckless," Sanaa admitted in a small voice.

August nodded his head. "More than anything I want this to be over."

"Why do you have someone waiting for you back at home?"

Helia entered his thoughts. She would never allow him to treat her like something to own. No, Helia was the one that owned him and treated him like an object. But he wanted this mission to be over so he could go back to her. It was a strange relationship that the two of them shared. "No. I don't have anyone waiting for me back at home."

"Then there is no need to rush back. Enjoy this time away from them," Sanaa said as she stretched out her arms.

Enjoy the time away? It would be hard with Vorus looming like a specter of Helia. Now that he thought about it, Helia controlled most parts of his life. She lingered in everything that he did. Hanging over his head like a noose, tightening when she felt him about to struggle free.

For the first time in a long time, August felt something hot boil inside him as he thought about Helia. She had the power in their relationship and had him following her around like a dog.

But it was all his fault that the relationship ended up this way. It was all because of his weakness. He wished that he could have controlled the curse better.

"I wish I could enjoy my time away from them." Thoughts of Helia ached like an open wound that he wasn't ready to address. Sanaa and August stayed there hidden amongst the trees. August kept his eyes on the sky though, watching the stars slowly wink out as the sun rose higher and higher in the sky.

# Chapter Twenty

T he air was heavy the next day. The sun beat down steadily and Taira shaded her eyes as she stared out at the garden the next day. Maids and servants scurried around her as she watched over the renovations taking place in the gardens.

The groundskeeper was shouting orders left and right as they pulled weeds out by the root. Taira leaned back against the wall as more servants were sent out under the hot sun.

The Empress would be here in two days and the thought sent tingles through Taira's body. The Empress was coming. This would be the first time in almost a decade that she would have seen the Empress. Her hands went to rest on the swords that lay against her hip.

The last time that she had seen the Empress was when she was younger and much more naive than she was now. Her hair had been shorter and she thought that the world was underneath her feet. But now. She looked around the garden once again. Now, everything was so different.

Taira turned and walked into the manse. The house was no less chaotic than the gardens. People ran from one side of the room to the other, bundles in their arms and shouting over one another. Some of them zipped through the air, their wings nothing more than a swatch of color. Some maids were on their hands and knees on the ground scrubbing as though their lives depended on it.

Taira stepped past it all and walked to her room in the house. The room was cluttered with decorations and things that she had kept from her travels. Taira launched herself onto her bed and sighed when she landed.

The empress would be here in two days. Two days was all that she had to fix the problem in the caves and then she would have to settle the deal with the empress. She still remembered the words from that night and the way the golden eyes of the empress bled red as she spoke the curse.

*"From this night to every night, you will dream like the dead. Your body will slow and then you will join them."* She thought about those words every night. She dreamed about the way that the Empress looked down her nose at Taira as she spoke those words.

And then she thought about the room. The dust that was gathering in there and how desolate and alone it must be to be trapped in there. Taira could not let her rot in that room any longer. Taira needed to deal with the Empress and the curse.

Taira knew the laws and the codes of the Fae better than anyone. She knew that she could issue a challenge to the empress and that she would have no way to refuse. Taira rose from the bed.

She needed to know if this was the correct time to challenge the empress. She needed to know if her challenge would work. She turned and left the room, marching over to the Temple of Arif. She did not take in the revelry of the town. She ignored the garlands hanging from the trees and the way that the flowers seemed impossibly bright. When she reached the temple it was polished with the windows displaying Arif's achievements.

Taira knocked on the door to the temple and did not wait for someone to open the door. She walked right in. The temple was in a state of disarray just like Vorus's manse was. Witches rush from side to side, some were polishing the windows while others were polishing the oaken floor.

Everyone was in a flurry because the empress was coming it seemed.

Taira caught the eye of one of the witches and she walked over to Taira with a smile that spoke more than words. The witch dipped into a curtsy and giggled.

"And how can we help the captain of the guard today?" The witch asked. At the mention of her title, Taira straightened her back.

"I have to need to know if a venture of mine will be fraught with misfortune," Taira said. The witch just gave another beautiful smile and led her away from the pews and the stained glass windows.

In the back of the temple was where the real magic happened. The back was darker than the front of the temple, here there were small slits on the top of the ceiling that let light in. There a great fire burned and heavy smoke blotted out what little light there was.

The witch led Taira into the room and threw some herbs into the fire. The flame went from deep red to a mint green color. Taira walked closer to the fire and breathed in the smoke. The smoke smelled of moss and the forest. Taira could see the forest that surrounded the town of Asren when she closed her eyes and breathed.

*Taira opened her eyes to the town of Asren burning. The city that she protected was burning. Taira turned all around but all she could see was the flames. The sound of the crackling fire almost overpowered the screaming.*

*The treehouses that people had built for themselves had tumbled to the ground. Taira walked through the flames, watching as the flames consumed everything. She did not know where her feet were taking her, but she let her feet guide her.*

*When she got to Vorus's manse, the windows were broken and the door was left wide open, swinging on its hinges.*

*"Grahhh!" Someone shouted from inside. Taira ran towards the sound looking for someone, anyone to explain the madness that was going on around her. The house was crumbling on the inside, the ceiling was caved in and Taira had to climb over the rough rock to get to the voice.*

*"Ahhh!" The voice shouted again. Taira slid down the tower of rocks and ran as fast as she could towards the voice. She could hear the sounds of steel meeting steel over the crackling of flames.*

*The gardens. The voice was coming from the gardens. Taira ran as fast as she could towards the voice. The gardens were burning just like the rest of the city. But sitting in the garden was a sphinx with a scale in front of it. Taira ignored this sight and looked to the sky.*

*There flying amid the smoke was herself. Her hair was sagging out of the top knot that she had put it in and she was covered in shallow wounds and soot from all the flames, but she was standing her sword drawn.*

*"Do you think that you can lift the curse by killing me?"*

*Across from her, the wind blew and the smoke cleared bringing the visage of the empress into view. Her hair was still in its immaculate curls. Her golden wings spread out behind her like a halo and she smiled that horrible smile.*

*"I know I can kill you!" With a flutter of her wings, Taira shot towards the Empress. Her sword clashed with the empress's long claws. They did battle like that, Taira throwing attacks her way with her sword and the empress simply dodging or parrying the blow with her long steel-like claws.*

*Taira shouted with each hit that she was landing, growing more and more furious as she could not even land a blow against the* empress. Taira watched as her movements got sloppier and sloppier, leaving openings that the empress could exploit. Taira watched as she brought her sword over her head and brought it down with all the strength that she could muster.

The Empress caught the sword a hairbreadth away from her face. Taira tried to pull the sword from the empress's hands but she had a vice-like grip on the sword.

"I thought that you would have improved in the years since I have last seen you," the Empress said with a downward twist of her lips. She bent her wrist and the sword broke in her hands. Taira gasped and the empress was quick with her movements and shoved the tip of the sword into her chest.

Blood pooled where she was hit and Taira watched as she fell out of the sky and onto the ground. Taira screamed out as the empress landed beside her, looked over her body for a moment, and then walked away as though nothing happened.

"You lose." Taira was so caught in watching her battle the empress that she forgot about the Sphinx. It stood close to her bleeding body, the scales heavier on one side than the other. "I have watched you lose a thousand times now."

The Sphinx raised a paw and place a stone on the heavier side of the scales. Taira gasped and held her chest. She watched as her own body bled out in the dirt and the empress walked away.

"No, I can't lose. I can't." Taira said to herself. The Sphinx heard her and tilted its head.

"It has already been decided by the scales that you will lose. Empress Sorcha is much too powerful for you to handle alone," the Sphinx said. Tears gathered in her eyes, but Taira wiped them away to stare at the back of the retreating empress.

"I need to win. I need to kill her so that I can finally be free. So that she can be free," Taira said. The Sphinx nodded its head and turned back to the scales.

"A desire to win. A chance to undo what has been done," the sphinx muttered to itself. "Yes, this might do."

Taira stood there tears in her eyes and hand on her chest as the sphinx prowled around the scales leaning down to look at them, measuring the heavier side to the lighter side.

"You want to win more than anything?" The sphinx asked. Taira nodded her head and wiped more tears away from her eyes. "I can give it to you, but there will be consequences for this."

"I don't care," Taira said as she looked at her own dead body. She had to avoid that fate. She had to win against the empress more than anything. She needed to kill the empress and release her from the curse. She needed to win.

The sphinx smiled at her, the human face stretching its lips in a too-long smile as it's lion body stretched out. Taira took half a step back from the sphinx.

The wind whipped around Taira and she looked around as the setting of the gardens and the fire began to blur. Taira could hear voices in the wind muttering and laughing and jeering at one another.

"Kill Sorcha!" One voice called out.

"She killed me!" Another shouted over the din.

Taira covered her ears, yet the voices had invaded her thoughts and she could hear them even with her ears covered. They were all speaking at once, one voice began talking and then another would interrupt it, shouting about some different and completely unrelated. The voices shouted over one another, each voice trying to be heard. The din of noise caused an ache to rise in her head as she tried to sort out the voices and what they were trying to say.

The wind whipped around Taira and the voice grew louder and louder and Taira let out a scream. She tried to drown out the voices with her voice, but they screamed louder than she did.

Taira shot up from the ground with a screech. She pressed her hands to her ears and pressed as hard as she could. Something reached out and tried to touch her, but she slapped it away. The voices died down little by little; the voices withering with every moment that she pressed her ears close.

A hand ran down her back and Taira flinched away from it

at first, but it continued to rub her back. She muttered under her breath the words that she remembered the voices saying.

When the voices finally faded away, Taira lifted her head to see the face of the witch. The witch sat beside her, legs stretched out. Taira shuddered as she remembered the image of her own body bleeding out on the ground.

"Did you see who you wanted to see?" The witch asked with a smile.

Taira thought of the large sphinx that waited for her in the burning gardens. She thought about how it's wide mouth stretched the length of his face when it smiled and the whirlwind of voices that it bestowed upon her.

What had the sphinx done to her? What had those voices been? Taira's chest rose and fell, as she thought back to what she saw in the burning garden. She thought of the stained glass windows and the body sphinx body of Arif that it depicted.

Had she met a god in her visions? Did Arif reveal himself to her? The thought sounded ludicrous to her but it made so much sense. Who else would reveal himself to her while she was at the temple of Arif?

"No. I think I saw who I needed to see," Taira said.

# Chapter Twenty-One

"The Empress will be here soon enough."

August tossed a coin in the air. On one side it was the face of the empress on the other side it was the sigil of the ruling family: a sword and a quill. The coin caught the scant light of the moon as it tumbled through the air and August caught it every time.

August and Sanaa were hidden in the trees once again. They were perched on the branches of a tree looking at the temple of Roux. The lights were low in the temple and there was no movement to be found in the windows. It seemed like tonight was going to be another boring night.

"What do you mean?" Sanaa asked. She was standing on the thickest part of the branch close to the trunk. Her arms were crossed and she was leaning against the trunk of the tree. August sat lazily on a branch, legs dangling over the edge as he looked into the windows of the temple.

"You haven't heard? The Faerie empress is coming to Asren," August said with a toss of his long black locks. His hair was tied back in a low ponytail so that he could keep his eyes on the temple. "She is here to inspect everything that is going on here and to tour the Spring Court."

Sanaa shrugged her shoulders. "If she comes, she comes."

At that August raised an eyebrow. "You honestly don't care that the Empress of the Faerie Courts will be arriving here soon."

"What change will my caring bring about? She will arrive here when she arrives here. My job is to deal with the bandits in the cave and the siren. That is all." Sanaa said all this with a cool tone of voice.

August dared to look at Sanaa. Her hands were fisted at her side, but she was still leaning against the trunk of the tree. August's eyes danced across her face and found nothing but fire in her eyes.

"You do care. This is the Empress," August insisted. He watched as her hands tightened and the cold effect to her voice got even colder.

"No, I don't care." August leaned back against the tree he was on. Oh, so she was going to deny it was she? He shrugged his shoulders and decided not to pry anymore. If she wanted to tell him then she would.

All that could be heard was the wind rustling through the leaves and the groaning of wood from the temple. The trees sighed with the wind and the silence of the night was soothing to August. He was born in the night and shadows were his element. He felt at home in the dark.

"I heard that the King of demons fell," Sanaa started after a moment of quiet. August cut his eyes to her. She was still keeping her eyes on the temple, but her hands were no longer fists at her side. August took that as a good sign. "I heard that King Romulus had died and left no successor. And that all the demons are fighting to win the crown."

"Yup," August said. It had been a long time since he had thought about his homeland. He could remember the plains and the mountains, the dipping valleys that he had grown in. But as soon as those thoughts graced his mind he remembered the blood and the screaming. He remembered cowering in the corner, his face pressed into his sister's side.

"I learned that they split into three factions. The Moros, Rizzan, and Gor'gan demons," Sanaa continued. August nodded his head. "Which faction do you belong to?"

"Whoa—it's impolite to ask someone's politic affiliations," August said with a chuckle. Sanaa laughed along with him. The question was something that he never had to answer before. "It's complicated."

"I didn't know choosing a side could be complicated."

"Well, it is complicated for me." He thought of his sister, Aranea, and how easily she chose a side. She picked a faction without a second thought and yet here August was unable to make the same choice that she did. "I tend to stay away from politics. They're no fun and I like to keep my head."

Sanaa let out a small laugh. "That I understand. We never had to choose sides at the compound. We were all on the same side when I was younger."

"And what side was that?"

"We all hate Faeries and thought that they should have been erased from the land of Ettrea. But things are different now."

"And now?"

"Now there are factions in the compound. Some want to move on and some want to go back to the old ways."

"And what about you? What do you want to do?"

"I... I—... It's complicated."

August let out a chuckle at that and raise his eyebrows. "You see what I mean! It's hard to pick a side." Sanaa laughed and nodded her head.

She turned her eyes to him and August felt something warm rise up in his stomach. Her eyes were glittering in the moonlight and she was standing tall and strong on the branch.

Sanaa opened her mouth to say something, but a light flickered on in the temple. A flame flickered in the temple window. It flickered in the wind but then something odd happened, whoever was in the window covered the flame twice.

A rustling could be heard below them in the underbrush. August jumped up on his branch and watched as someone came from the underbrush below them. This person was covered in the same tattoos as the people that they had fought in the caves. They were small though and they moved quickly.

They reached the window in a matter of moments. August turned to Sanaa and their eyes connected. Sanaa nodded her head and made to move down her tree, but August raised a hand to stop her.

"Allow me," he said. August closed his eyes and fell into the shadow realm. Opening his eyes, he could only see the distinct shadows of everything around him. Everything was in shades of gray or black. August moved towards the house marking sure to steer clear of the shadows that the people at the window made. When he got close he began to make out what they were saying.

"—you can't rush this. I—"

"You promised that you would get us what we needed an—"

"And I said I would get it to you! The Hollow Ones aren't here yet—"

"You and the other witches go on and on about the Hollow Ones and we haven't seen them yet. Once they arrive we will get you what you need."

"And when exactly will that be?" His foot was tapping a quick rhythm on the ground and shifted his weight from one foot to the other. The flickering flame cast shadows all around them that flickered and shuddered. August was cautious coming towards those shadows. The harsh candlelight almost burned him with its brightness.

"When the Empress arrives we will have everything that we need. The Hollow Ones will be here and we will only need a moment alone with her before you can make your move."

The person standing outside the window nodded their head and moved away from the window then. August raced back to the darkness of the trees. He ran his way back up the trunk of the tree and materialized on the branch across from Sanaa.

He watched as the flame in the window disappear and Sanaa looked at him with wide eyes that flickered with excitement.

"What did you find out?" she asked without a beat of silence. It was hard to focus on her words. The shadows still called to him, wanting him to fall back into their dark and cool embrace. August ignored the mutterings of the shadows and focused his attentions on the moving flame as the witch and the candle moved from one window to another.

"August!" Sanaa tried again, this time with a little more volume. She looked back to the temple for the briefest moment and turned to look at him again. "What did you discover?"

"They are... planning something," August said. The call of the shadows were fading away. The shadows that clung to him were beginning to loosen and he could focus on the world of light that he was in. The world of light and shadow and people. "They are planning something for when the Empress arrives. They are looking for someone... They called them the Hollow Ones."

"Hollow Ones?" Sanaa asked. The words rang in his ears. The Hollow Ones. Who could the witch have meant when she said that they needed the Hollow Ones? What did that mean? He thought back to the brief snippets of the conversation that he heard but nothing made sense to him.

"At least now we know for sure that the temple of Roux is collaborating with the bandits. But why? What could the bandits have that the temple could want," Sanaa muttered under her breath.

"Do we still have to watch the temple for the rest of the night? I doubt that there will be any more meetings in the night," August drawled from his branch. Sanaa nodded her head and then jumped down from her tree. August jumped down also, landing on the ground without a sound.

"Come on, let's head back to the manse," Sanaa said and turned to go back to the path to the manse. August reached out and grabbed her hand.

"We don't have to go back to the manse," he said. Sanaa raised an eyebrow at him.

"Where else would we go if not back to the manse?" August let a smile take over his face and he tugged on her hand.

"Follow me."

August lead them down the path away from the temple but turned south instead of heading north to where the manse was. The farther south that they traveled the more lights they saw on in the windows. More and more faeries occupied the streets and until they were in the midst of a crowd of people.

Sanaa was pressed against his side to avoid the fast walking and talking people. Here they were stalls of people openly selling their wares and there were Husks in the windows calling out to the possible patrons in the crowd.

Sanaa pulled away from him then. "You brought me here to see whores and whoremongers?"

"I brought you here to relax," August said. He flashed a

grin at one of the whores in the window and watched as she flushed red under his attention. Sanaa was still stiff as a board at his side.

"I don't want to be here," Sanaa said, but her hand was still in his as he pulled her into one of the whore houses. He tugged on her hand, up the stairs, and into the house. Here people were laying on pillows and watching as a Husk woman danced on a stage.

August tugged Sanaa down onto one of the pillows and watched the Husk dance. He wrapped an arm around Sanaa's shoulders and pulled her in close to his side.

"You know, you dance better than that." Sanaa shoved him away and slapped his arm off her shoulder. August shrugged his shoulders and waved down the waitress to bring him a drink.

"We just came off a very important mission and you want to waste time with whores and drinks."

"I want to celebrate a victory!" August said as he claimed his drinks. The waitress was covered in nothing more than a thin gauzy material and August eyed the shape of her body through the thin cloth. "We just discovered that whatever hunch you had was right. Now we can sit back and celebrate."

"We cannot celebrate. There is work to do." August guzzled down the sweet wine that was in his cup and felt the familiar heat of alcohol settle in his stomach. He held out a glass to Sanaa and shook the cup lightly.

"Come on. Don't they ever tell you that it is bad to be so tense? You need to learn how to celebrate your wins! Is this against the rules that your commander gave you?" August took another gulp of the sweet faerie wine. It tasted like sweet things and flowers blooming on his tongue.

Sanaa looked down her nose at him and the way that he was sitting on the pillows. She loomed over him like a specter.

She was the only one standing as everyone else was sitting and laughing on the pillows.

Something passed over Sanaa's face at his words. Her face got a quiet look on it as though something in her had broken at his words. She nodded and then settled down next to August, grabbing the proffered cup of faerie wine. She took a sip of the strong wine and coughed. August let out a laugh and then clinked their glasses together.

# Chapter Twenty-Two

✿

The wine was sweet and blossomed on her tongue. The wine tasted of honey and sugary memories. The first sip that she took was a taste, the next a gulp. Sanaa drank down the wine with all the vigor of someone starving.

Why had no one told her that faerie wine tasted so good? Sanaa waved down a waitress for another drink. A warmth rose in her stomach and her head felt lighter despite the weight of her braids. She sighed and leaned back into the pillows, a smile rising on her face.

August let out a chuckle at the relaxed grin that rested on her face. "Enjoying the wine?" He asked.

"I feel good. Why does faerie wine taste so good?" Sanaa asked. Her thoughts felt fuzzy and she felt like her bones were melting in her body. Another glass appeared before her and Sanaa took the glass in one hand and rose from the pillows.

"No one knows why faerie wine tastes so sweet. Only the faeries do," August said with a hint of mystique in his voice. Sanaa laughed and drank down her glass again, enjoying the way that the smooth way that the alcohol ran down her throat.

The warm feeling in her stomach grew stronger and she let out another laugh as she watched the dancers on the stage.

"You know, you're right," Sanaa started. "I can dance better than that." She watched the way the woman ground and shimmied on the stage. It could barely be called dancing if it could be called that. Sanaa felt tears come to her eyes just watching her.

That was not dancing. That was barely dancing at all. And it was a disgrace to the word dancing for it to be even called that. Sanaa turned to August with her eyes determined.

"Dance with me," she said, placing her goblet down on the ground. August let out an incredulous laugh.

"What?" He asked.

"Dance with me," Sanaa demanded again. She reached out her hand and stared down his eyes. "Come on. Trust me."

August took a moment to look into her eyes and then looked at her hand again. Sanaa was shaking, brimming with energy. The warm feeling in her stomach had spread to her veins and made the woman giddy with energy. He nodded and Sanaa wanted to crow with happiness.

The sound almost escaped her mouth but she slapped a hand over her mouth and giggled loudly instead. August rose from the ground and Sanaa noticed that he was a lot taller than she was. Her head only came up to his chin and that was not even counting his horns.

The music ran through Sanaa. The beat of the drums thudding along with Sanaa's heart. It was an enchanting rhythm that she had to follow; she had to dance to. Sanaa let out a loud war cry. One that she had not given since she was fighting with her sisters.

She leaned in close, going on the tips of her toes to lean close to August's ear. "Follow along," she whispered.

She let out another war cry, bringing all the attention to them in the room. Sanaa began to sway her hips August followed her lead holding her close and following her lead.

Sanaa spun out of his hold, shimmying her hips and August followed after her just like she wanted him to. It was like they could read one another's mind, anticipating each move before the other did it. They danced with one another around the patrons and to the stage.

With a strong bump of her hip, Sanaa knocked the woman off the stage, and Sanaa and August danced against one another. Sanaa pulled at his clothing, bringing him down closer to her mouth. Sanaa pressed a searing kiss to his lips and Sanaa felt the heat explode within her.

The warmth pooled in her stomach traveled lower to her center and August ran his hands through her braids bringing her closer as their lips connected. Sanaa was the first to pull away and continued dancing again. Her movements were large and ungainly, nothing like the precise movements of the sword dance.

But this dance was much more fun so she kept dancing it. The drums beat on faster and faster, and Sanaa reached out into the crowd of people, pulling someone up on to the stage with her. She was dancing as though her life depended on it, changing from one partner to the other when she could.

Soon enough, everyone in the establishment was dancing, pulled into the chaos by Sanaa at one point or another. The drums beat wildly as Sanaa danced with a faerie who's green insect-like wings flutter out behind him as they danced around one another.

Sanaa could not keep her eyes away from his. They were the green of forest leaves in the shade and they seemed to glow in the low light of the room. Sanaa brought herself closer to the faerie and ground herself against him.

Her core rubbed against his leg and he wrapped her arms

around her. Their breaths intermingled with one another and Sanaa cried out as he inserted his leg between her own and pushed up against her core. Sanaa let out a breathy moan that rose from her core and pushed back against his leg, chasing the pleasure that he ignited in her.

The faerie man grabbed her face and brought her face close to his. Their breaths connecting and she brushed her lips against his asking for permission. He dove in, plundering her lips. She sighed into the kiss grabbed his face to bring him in closer and kiss him deeper.

Sanaa gasped as she was lifted into his arms and she ground her core into him. She wanted this man was the only thought. She wanted this man and she wanted him now. All thoughts about her mission and her family fled from her then.

The man slammed her against the wall and their kiss became harder. Tongues danced around one another twisting and tangling in a pleasurable haze that Sanaa did not want to rise from.

Sanaa thrusted her hips against him in a begging plea to bring her over the edge. The man walked out of the dancing mob and brought her someone darker and quieter, away from the drums and the heat of other people. Their kisses were frantic. Their lips smacked against one another, as the man tugged at the strings that held together her light armor.

The armor fell away and Sanaa reached backward trying to reach for the door knob. They fell through the door as Sanaa's hand found the knob. The man caught himself grabbing Sanaa by the waist to steady her.

Sanaa looked into his eyes and brought her shirt over her head in one fluid movement. The man replied by pulling his shirt off. They connected for another kiss but this one was a lot slower. The heat rose steadily from Sanaa's core.

The two of them fell back onto the bed. Sanaa shivering

as she reached up and cupped his neck in her hands, bringing him down to taste his lips again. His hand slid south, over her breast and into her breeches. Sanaa gasped at the first touch, his fingers cold against her heated core. Sanaa sighed though as his hands became warmer.

He set a punishing rhythm. His fingers plunged into her and Sanaa moaned loudly at the touch. His mouth was on her breast, rolling her nipple against his tongue. He paused his mouth in its ministrations and pulled at her nipple with his teeth. The pain of it went zinging down Sanaa's spine making her moan even louder.

Sanaa gasped as his finger plucked at her the bundle of nerves at the apex of her thighs and Sanaa was sent tumbling over the edge. She screamed out as she clenched around him. The pleasure washed over her form and all she could do was moan.

The man did not give her a moment to rest. He shucked off his pants. The considerable length of him throbbing and hard. Sanaa's mouth went dry as she stared at it. She wanted it inside of her. She wanted to put her mouth on it.

Sanaa never got the chance. As soon as the man's pants were off of him he was pulling Sanaa closer. His length bobbed as her brought her close and Sanaa thought of nothing else but getting him inside of her. The man held himself and guided himself inside of her. They both moaned once he was fully seated.

There was no time to adjust to his considerable length and girth. The moment he was done savoring the moment, he was plundering her. Sanaa gripped the sheets trying to hold on as the man drove into her. With every thrust Sanaa felt like she was forgetting parts of herself, slowly being consumed by the pleasure.

Thrust. She forgot her family. Thrust. She forgot her anger and hatred. Thrust. She forgot her own name.

Sanaa wrapped her legs around the back of this man, pulling him closer, allowing him to sink deeper inside of her. She lifted her hips and thrust them into the man's hips just as he was plunging into her, fucking him back.

"Harder," Sanaa begged. "Harder."

The man complied with her wishes and Sanaa could feel herself tipping over, so closed to finishing but not quite there at the edge yet. Sanaa moaned and thrust her hips harder against the man, chasing her pleasure. She needed something. She was there, but she couldn't quite finish.

The man reached down and tugged at that bundle of nerves at the apex of her sex and Sanaa was sent over the edge. She howled as she climaxed. That man's hips stuttering as he too finished inside of her, the warmth of their release mixing together.

Sanaa sighed, her eyes fluttering shut as her body relaxed. The man pulled out of her, leaving her feeling bereft and empty and settled on the bed beside her. Sanaa could not bring herself to open her eyes, as she was swept away by a wave of sleep.

Sanaa's eyes were crusted shut. It was with a snap that her eyes opened and she looked around the room. Her stomach rolled and churned, the sensation growing worse when she rose to sit up in the bed. Sanaa's head throbbed with every beat of her heart.

The ache in her body was unmistakable though and Sanaa pressed a hand against her aching back. She turned to look around the room and saw clothes strewn everywhere. She looked down, feeling a breeze pass through the room. Sanaa's eyes widened as she took in her nakedness and brought the sheets up to her chin.

She looked to the person beside her and saw a Fae man lying asleep beside her. Sanaa went over the memories from the night before. She was drinking with August and—

August. The very thought of his name made burning heat shoot through her. August was the one that brought her to this whore house and plied her with wine. Sanaa shot up, out of the bed, and began to gather her clothes. She zoomed around the room, careful not to alert the man sleeping on the bed of her movements. Sanaa shrugged on her clothing and tiptoed out the door.

A woman slept outside the door and Sanaa presumed that it was her room that she had slept in. Sanaa gathered her armor that was resting outside the door and launched herself out of the whore house.

The sun was bright when she entered the street. It was impressive with its power. Sanaa shaded her eyes as best as she could and began walking to the manse where she knew that Vorus and the others must be waiting for her.

Sanaa sped through the town. Did everyone know? Could they see the marks that the man left on her the night before? Fintan above why did this have to happen to her? She wanted nothing more than to sink into the floor.

The wine was stronger than she expected and it barely even tasted like alcohol. Sanaa could remember the fruity taste that slithered down her throat the night before. She only had three goblets and she was already conducting herself, unlike a Batsamasi.

And with a Fae man. The thought made her stomach drop. She slept with a Fae man. A Fae. It was one thing to sleep with someone but another thing entirely if it was a Fae. What would the others think? What would Mother—

Sanaa stopped that thought from blossoming in her mind. Why would Mother care? Who better to manipulate than those who have no choice but to love you? The words rang out in Sanaa's ears. Gods above she would never forget those words. The way that Mother made her feel when she said them.

Who cares if she slept with a Fae man? Greta said that times were different and that Sanaa needed to go out into the world and see that. Sanaa bit back the feeling of revulsion that rose in her. She should not feel ashamed. Her body had an urge and it was satisfied.

Sanaa laughed a little bit at the thought. Maybe when the Fae empress arrived she could find that man again. The thought sent shivers down her spine. She would stay away from the faerie wine though.

When she reached the manse, the house was in more disarray than when she had left the night previous. Maids and servants danced around the house. The maids were urgently scrubbing the floor like Roux was at the gates. Sanaa had to step over them to not interrupt their work.

Sanaa looked around the foyer. It was gleaming with how clean it was and not a single thing was out of place. What more did they have to clean? Taira came rushing down the stairs of the foyer looking put out.

"There you are!" she said as she reached Sanaa. Taira reached out and grabbed her arm and began to march her towards the stairs. Sanaa had to almost jog to keep with the brisk pace that Taira set.

"What is going on? Why does everyone look so... stressed?" Sanaa said with a twist of her lips.

"The Empress is here," Taira said without looking back. She kept marching forward. Sanaa stopped where she stood making Taira let go of her.

"The empress is here? But I thought that we had another day!"

"The empress is early. Though I suppose to her she is right on time," Taira snorted. "Now come on. You need to get dressed."

"What is wrong with my breeches?"

"There is nothing wrong with them, but they aren't fit to be seen in front of the empress. Now get dressed."

Taira shoved Sanaa into her room where a squad of maids were waiting for her. The maids grabbed her and ushered her into the restroom where a warm bath was waiting for her. Sanaa sunk into the bath and let the maids scrub at her tired skin.

"What is the empress like?" Sanaa asked one of the maids. They all paused for a moment in their movements before continuing.

"Crazy," one muttered under her breath. Other maids slapped at her hands and hushed her. The maid who spoke kept her mouth shut for the rest of the bath.

It had been a long time since she dreamed of meeting with the Faerie Empress. When she was young she dreamed that she would meet her in battle, blades drawn and ready. As she grew older she imagined burning the imperial city of the Fae to the ground the same way that they had burned down Mayara.

If only her younger self could see her now. She was being primped and primed to meet with the Empress and there was no burning city or blade to be seen.

One of the maids went to touch her hair but Sanaa stopped her. She grabbed one of her larger hair ties from the vanity and pulled her braids into a bun atop her head.

When she looked at herself in the mirror Sanaa barely recognized herself. The dress that they had put her in was of the softest lilac, the color of the sky when the night was just bleeding away. It flowed out behind her and shimmered slightly in the light. The sleeves were long bell sleeves stitched with cobalt blue embroidery.

Sanaa pressed a finger to the square neckline and looked at herself in the mirror. She looked soft and pliable. She looked like a flower. In the compound they never really wore dresses. They were hard to fight and maneuver in and when they wanted to look special they had their ceremonial garb.

But Mother had worn dresses a lot. No one questioned it. And when Sanaa stared at her face in the mirror she could see her mother in her eyes, the cat-like curve to her eyes and the bow like arch to her lips.

Sanaa sighed and gathered her thoughts again. She was going to meet the empress of the Fae. The thought sent tingles up her spine. Mother would have done anything to have a moment like this. Sanaa took a moment to breathe.

When she was ready, she opened her eyes and looked at herself in the mirror. With a sucked in a breath, Sanaa turned and walked out of the room, ready to face the empress for the first time.

# Chapter Twenty-Three

Taira's fingers could not stay still. They twitched and moved without her thinking. She clasped her hands together but that just descended into her wringing her hands together. Her hands passed over her fingers one after the other. Her foot tapped a staccato rhythm on the ground before she stopped it with a sharp look from Vorus.

The two of them were out on the lawn, the house sprawling out behind them, the brambles pulled aside so that they could see into the town. The dress that Taira wore was colored a deep mauve color and her hair was tied up in some intricate stylings that she heard was popular with the courtiers that surrounded the Empress.

Taira pulled at the curved neckline of the dress. It clung tight to her skin. Under the heavy sun, Taira felt like she was wearing pounds and pounds of clothing.

"Where are the others?" Vorus asked looking out into the town. The people were hanging wreaths of flowers in from their windows and the path from the gates to Vorus's manse was smothered with flowers. Taira tugged on the neckline of her dress again.

"They should be coming," Taira said with a look back to the manse. The windows shone in the light and the tree that the manse was carved into was blooming with small white flowers. Taira turned her eyes back to the horizon hoping to see the figure of the Empress make her way across.

There was still nothing there just the townspeople of Asren setting up for the arrival of the Empress. Taira's fisted her hands and put them behind her back, standing at attention. The fabric of her dress made it hard for her to spread her legs but she tried her best. Vorus looked back at her and grinned.

"It has been a long time since I have seen you in a dress," he said. Taira scratched at the material lining her neck. She sighed and tugged at it once again.

"I am more comfortable in armor," she said. Vorus let out a loud laugh at her words.

"Ah, but you wear a dress so well," Vorus said. His eyes scanned over her and Taira shifted in the dress. She could barely move her arms in such a thing. It would be difficult to fight in should something arise.

The belt around her waist felt more like a tightening noose. Taira tugged at it, but that only made the loop tighten around her and she stopped quickly.

"You look amazing," Vorus said. He walked over to her and brushed some hair behind her ear. Taira could feel the burgeonings of a blush starting from her neck. She slapped his hand away.

"I can't fight in this." Her eyes went back to the horizon. Where was the out-crier that made the announcement? It did not take that long to reach the town of Asren. But the Empress did have her whole retinue traveling with her. Maybe there was trouble on the road?

"Why would you need to fight?" Taira cut her eyes to him and then back to the horizon. The smile on Vorus's face slipped and morphed into a frown in a matter of moments. He gripped her arm and pulled her face close to his own.

"No," was the only word that he said. Taira shook her arm out of his grip and matched his frown with one of her own. "No, you will not."

"You cannot stop me," Taira said with a stiff chin.

"No, you will stop this nonsense. Taira, I thought that you had learned from the last time, the first time," Vorus said. Taira shook her head and looked out at the horizon. Where was she?

"You know what she did to me-"

"She did nothing to you! You're still alive! That's a lot more than I could say for—"

"Don't say her name!" Taira shouted at him. She finally turned her eyes towards him and took a good look at him. His hair was artfully tousled and his fingers were still in his hair, tugging at the roots.

He was looking at her with brown eyes that begged to be heeded, big eyes. Taira wished that her world could be as easy as Vorus's. Where things simply fell into place and he got to run a town without having to do the hard work.

Taira thought of the room and the door. She thought of the woman laying behind that door and for how long she had been there. Twelve be blessed, she would have been there for over ten years now. It was time for her to wake up. It was time for Taira to be able to open that door.

"I need to do this. I need to release her from that curse," Taira said turning her eyes back to the horizon. Vorus sighed and with another tug at his hair, dropped his hands.

"She is going to kill you, you know that. You're going to die because you can't just let this stupid vendetta of yours go." He didn't know how often Taira had felt like giving up. There were times when she thought that the curse would never be lifted and that she was fighting a losing battle. But Taira kept fighting, she had to.

"There is nothing worthwhile that she has not already taken from me," Taira said. Vorus sighed and shook his head. A wind brushed by rustling the leaves and Taira heard a commotion behind her.

"Ah, there they are!" Vorus called out. Taira turned her head and saw August and Sanaa making their way out of the manse. Sanaa's russet skin contrasted beautifully with the lilac color of the dress. And though the dress was out of season she still looked stunning in it.

August pulled at the eyepatch that they placed over his blind eye. His clothing was colorful just like Sanaa's with forest green breeches and coat. His hands were gloveless on account of the claws, but he looked handsome with his hair slicked back.

"Must I really wear this?" August said, pulling at the eyepatch over his left eye.

"Yes, you cannot show the Empress any imperfections. It would be unsightly," Vorus said. He offered an arm to Sanaa and she took it, her hand resting in the crook of Vorus's arm. August came up beside Taira.

"Look, I see something on the horizon!" August called. A thunderous sound of horses and shouts of elation could be heard. The Empress had finally arrived in Asren.

Petals danced in the wind as horses raced from the center of town down the street to the manse. The horses were followed by a carriage that was a brilliant white and gold color. Cheering could be heard as it passed by and Taira began to fiddle with her fingers again at the sight of it.

The Empress' emblem of a laurel on fire shone from the bright light of the sun. Taira put her hands behind her back and still fiddled with her fingers. The horses lead the carriage down the street and stopped in front of Vorus's manse and where they were waiting.

A man in a cobalt blue suit hopped down from one of the horses and made a brisk walk to the door of the carriage. He opened it and began to call out.

"Presenting King of the Spring Lands, First of His Name, King Gabriel Rhydderich!"

The man who stepped out was someone that Taira had never seen before despite her acquaintance with the Empress. He was tall with coiffed brown hair and emerald green eyes. He had a narrow face with a tapered jaw that Taira could see as he ground his teeth.

His clothing was fine as was to be expected. Embroidered vines rose to his pants and his jacket was a blushing pink that was cut to his figure. The crown on his head was dotted with emeralds and peridots and when he stepped out it was almost like he sucked the joy out of the atmosphere.

His eyes scanned over them all and the cold look in his eyes made something in Taira drop to her stomach. He sniffed at them and said nothing at all. Taira's hand held her wrist as King Gabriel took a long look around at the manse and the decorations.

"Presenting Tsar of the Dragons, fourth of her name, Reava!" The small man called out. From the carriage, he offered a hand. The hand that grasped it was covered in armor.

The woman that climbed out of the carriage was covered in the armor from her shoulders to her hands in armor. Spiked pauldrons were the first thing that Taira saw. They jutted out from her shoulders and the shine from them was so bright that Taira, Vorus, and the others had to avert their eyes for a moment.

When their eyes adjusted, Taira saw a small woman with brilliant red hair tied up into a top knot. Her eyes were a smoldering hue of blue. Her clothing was the standard clothing you would expect from a guard, a simple blue top and black breeches.

She hopped down from the carriage and looked around at all the flowers and the presentation. Her cheeks puffed out like she was holding in a laugh and she turned to look back inside of the carriage.

"They pulled out all of the stops for you," Reava said with a smirk on her lips. King Gabriel scoffed as he looked over them.

"Barely," he muttered under his breath.

The little man who was announcing readied himself again, straightening his stance and clearing his throat. Taira turned her eyes back to him and readied herself also.

"Now presenting, Empress of all the Seasoned Lands, the Light, and Dark Lands, first of her name, her Imperial Majesty, Empress Sorcha Fiore!"

The woman that stepped out was nothing less than stunning. Long curling locks of dark hair, eyes of melted amber, and a bow-shaped mouth that was curved up into a smile. Taira heard August suck in a breath at the sight of her.

Empress Sorcha wore a golden dress with a skirt that puffed out at the waist. The bodice of the dress was studded with various beads and stones that glittered in the noon light. The skirt looked like it was spun out of gold itself with the way that it shone in the light. Her wings fanned out behind her and they shimmered gold. Sorcha laughed.

"My, they really did try their hardest to welcome their Empress," she said in that way of hers. Taira grit her teeth when she heard her voice again. Sorcha talked as though everything was a game that she was playing. She never sounded like she took anything seriously.

Sorcha turned her head and looked over all the people gathered. Taira felt sweat drip down her spine. Did she look at Taira? Did she know what she was going to do—to ask? Taira shook her head of such thoughts. Sorcha was powerful but she couldn't read minds— that she knew of.

Taira waited with bated breath as Sorcha looked them over, never once diverting her eyes away from the empress. She looked them over slowly like she was measuring their worth in her mind and all with that maddening smile on her face. Taira could barely stand it.

She wished that she could lash out. That she could wipe the smile from Sorcha's face, but she kept her hands behind her back, standing at attention.

*"Murderer!"* A voice called out. Taira whipped her head around to look at the person that would be so bold, but everyone behind her was standing with their heads bowed, waiting for when they could be dismissed.

*"Murderer!"* The cry went up again. And Taira turned to look at Vorus and August but the two of them were looking at Sorcha. Was she the only one that could hear the voice?

Taira turned her eyes back to Sorcha who clasped her hands in front of her. Her amber eyes looked at the manse and she let out a small giggle that grated of Taira's ears.

"Thank you all for welcoming me to your town. I find it to be stunning. Everything is just so beautiful, I can hardly stand it," she said her smile blossoming into a large grin.

Sorcha turned to look at Gabriel and Reava who were standing only a little ways behind her. "Don't you just find everything beautiful?"

"I've never seen so many flowers," Reava said with a look around the area again. King Gabriel sniffed.

"The colors of these flowers are dull," was all he said. Sorcha clicked her tongue.

"Now, Gabriel you have to be a little more accommodating, not everything can be to your exacting standards," Sorcha chided. Vorus stepped forward then.

"Your Imperial Majesty, welcome to the town of Asren. I hope that your travels here were comfortable?" He started. The empress looked him over and offered her hand. Vorus bent at the waist to kiss it. Taira wanted to vomit.

"The travel here was like anything that you would expect: long and boring. I do hope that this little town will hold more entertainment than the others," Sorcha said.

"Of course, your majesty. You will have as much fun here as you do in the Imperial Court," Vorus said with a grin. Sorcha let out a little laugh.

"I certainly hope not. The Imperial Court can be dreadfully boring. I want to have Spring Court fun though I don't know how much fun could be had in the lands ruled by this dullard," Sorcha said with a tilt of her head.

A laurel of golden leaves circled her head and Taira could remember the way that the crown felt in her hands. Sorcha had not changed in the ten years that had passed by. She had not changed since she placed the curse.

Vorus stepped back away from the Empress and gestured towards the rest of them standing there.

"Allow me to introduce you. You remember Taira." Vorus brought that woman closer to her. Taira could hear voices clamoring in her head as Sorcha walked closer and closer to her.

*"Murderer!"* A voice cried.

*"Thief!"* Another voice cried out in her mind. Taira felt like she was being buffeted by a strong wind as the voices grew louder and louder, each voice fighting for dominance in her head and trying to get her to listen. Taira winced as they grew louder and louder in her mind.

"No," Sorcha said. "I can't say that I do remember her." She tossed Taira a knowing smile and Taira grit her teeth at it. The word struck something inside Taira.

Not a day went by that Taira did not ruminate on what

happened that night. She never stopped thinking about it and suffering from the consequences of that night. Taira felt as though she could spit fire at that moment.

The voices clamored louder and louder in her head. Each one vying for the chance to air their grievances. Taira gritted her teeth, her head pounding with every word that was uttered. She pasted a smile on her lips.

"Taira is the captain of the guard here in Asren," Vorus said, the smile wavered on his lips and he moved on to the next person.

"This is August, a contracted... helper," Vorus said with a grimace. Sorcha offered her hand and August kissed it.

"Can I say that you look very familiar," August said on a breath looking into her eyes. Her smile grew as she looked August over like he was a fine piece of meat.

"I get that often," Sorcha said. Vorus guided her to the next person.

"And this is Sanaa of the Batsamasi." At this Sorcha raised a brow.

"A Batsamasi? I thought your kind hated the Fae?" Sanaa looked down at her feet and then looked up again.

"Things have changed," was all that she said. Sorcha's smile returned to her face.

"Well I am glad that things have changed," Sorcha said. Sorcha turned to look at all the maids and servants who stood behind them ready to serve when she needed them. Taira balled her dress in her fists.

"Thank you everyone for giving me such a warm reception. I never would have thought that I could be treated so kindly by others," Sorcha began. "You run your town very well, don't you Vorus?"

She added the last bit with a cutting glance to Vorus. Taira, Sanaa, and August straightened where they stood. She knew. The empress knew about the problems that they were experiencing. Empress Sorcha's eyes were cool as she looked them over, the smile never once wavering on her lips.

Taira's hands tightened behind her back. They had not solved the problem in the caves. They were too busy running after the bandits when they should have been dealing with the siren. If Taira tightened her hands anymore she felt her hands were going to fall off.

Did she imagine that the Empress's eyes cut to her? Did she already know of their failure to keep the peace? No, there was no way that she could already know about it. Taira turned her eyes to the ground. Behind her back, she began to fiddle with her fingers.

"Yes, of course, Your Imperial Majesty," Vorus said with a downward tilt to his head. "I try my best to keep things in order."

The Empress nodded her head at that and Vorus made a gesture for two of the maids to make their way forward.

"Here, allow these maids to show you to your rooms. I hope that you find them to your liking." With a deep bow, the two maids made their way past Taira and towards the empress. Sorcha let out a low chuckle and turned to look at Reava and Gabriel.

"They really did try their best to impress me," was all that she said. With that King Gabriel, Tsar Reava, and Empress Sorcha made their ways inside the manse.

Taira let out a breath that she didn't know she was holding. August let out a gasp beside her when the Empress walked by. Taira turned her eyes towards him and saw a flush take over his tanned skin. Had the fool gone and fallen in love with the empress? Taira gave a sharp jab to his side.

"Don't even bother. The empress is the hardest person to get to in all the Faerie Courts," Taira said. August looked back to the carriage and then back to the manse where Sorcha had disappeared into.

"She looks so familiar," he said under his breath, but Taira still caught the words. She shrugged her shoulders and patted his back.

"There are plenty of whores that look just like her so you can slake your lust," she said. She turned and began the march back to her room.

Taira felt a wall building around her heart as the voices in her ears fought one another.

*"Killer!"*

*"Monster!"*

*"Trickster!"*

*"Whore!"*

The words blended together into one wordless howl of anguish and anger. They ached at the thought of Sorcha and they cried out to her wanting her to bring them justice. She sighed out through her teeth. What had that sphinx done to her in the temple of Arif? Was this the cost of power?

Questions burned in her thoughts, but she quieted her mind. Slamming the door to her room close, she rested against the hardwood. She would give their voices their vengeance and her own. It was only a matter of time.

# Chapter Twenty-Four

"They are looking for somebody called the Hollow One," August said from his perch on Vorus's bed. "They need to find the Hollow One for some reason, probably so that they can make their powers last in the light."

"Great," Vorus rolled his eyes, "Now we have another thing that we have to be guarding. And how exactly will be able to know who the Hollow One is?"

Sanaa shrugged her shoulders. "There is no way to know. I feel like this Hollow One business is something that we would need to look into."

Vorus rubbed his face and looked at all of them gathered around the room. "The empress cannot find out about this. She can never know that while she is staying here that we do not have everything under our control. That would cause madness and would make me lose my head."

Taira piped up from where she was sitting against the wall. "And what about the siren?"

"We need to deal with the siren and the bandits at the same time. There is no way to deal with one and not the other," August said with a shrug of his shoulders. Taira leaned back against the wall and looked put out.

Sanaa tugged at the collarbone of her dress. "Can we get out of these ridiculous things? I think we have already presented ourselves to the empress enough."

"Yes. You can change your clothes but discreetly deal with this. We cannot have the Empress finding out."

Sanaa nodded her head and made her way to leave the room. She walked out of the room and back to her room in a matter of moments. As she stripped, she thought about the empress.

She had met the faerie empress and felt nothing. She did not feel fear or anger as she expected but she felt nothing. This was not the faerie ruler that called for the deaths of her and her sisters. This was not the ruler that laughed as the city of Mayara was burning. She was just another faerie ruler, one that Sanaa had nothing to do with.

Sanaa knew for sure now that she was different. The world was different from the one that she had grown up in. The world had changed and evolved in the time that Sanaa spent stuck in stone.

The thought made something in her stomach curl up. The world had changed and yet Sanaa had not. Things were not the way that they should have been. Sanaa wanted to be angry, she wanted to be upset, she wanted to wish to fight the faerie empress, but she could not muster even the smallest part of herself to feel that anger.

It was anger that had driven her for so long. Anger at the Fae, anger at Greta, anger at her mother for what she had done to her and now? Now without that anger, Sanaa felt nothing; she just felt lost.

Who was she when she wasn't angry at someone? Who was she if there was not some righteous cause for her to throw her weight behind? Sanaa felt tears gather in her eyes, but she wiped them away. No, she couldn't be sad, not right now when there were things that had to be done.

Sanaa straightened her back and walked into the bathroom to undress. It a matter of moments, Sanaa was out of the tight dress and into a tunic and a pair of pants that she found to be much more comfortable.

She needed to find out more about this "Hollow One" that the temple of Roux was so set on finding. She needed to know more information. Sanaa remembered the library that was sitting in the house wholly unused and decided to make her way towards it.

Sanaa made her way to the other side of the house and walked into the dusty library. The same man from last time sat behind a desk looking deeply into a heavy tome. Sanaa cleared her throat.

"Oh," the man said, "I didn't notice you there."

"Sorry to disturb you," Sanaa said with a shake of her head.

"Oh no. I knew that you would be back. No one who makes their way here can stay away for long," the man said with a grin on his face.

"I need help with finding something out and I need your help with finding it in one of these books."

"I will help you any way that I can."

"I need something on monikers of the Twelve. I need to know the names that those that worship the Twelve would give to someone."

"Well, that would be difficult seeing as the Temples are very secretive with some of their practices."

"Yes, but you knew about the medallion that I had the last time that I was here. That must have come from one of the books here."

"Well," the man hummed. "I can think of one book."

"Can I have it?" Sanaa perked up at the thought. One

book was better than no book. They would be stuck otherwise if there was nothing that could be found in the library. The man rose from his seat and disappeared into the stacks of books.

Sanaa waited for a moment by the door before the man appeared back with books in his hands. The tower of books he held in his hand wobbled as he made his way to the desk. Sanaa raced over to his side and helped him bring the heap of books to his desk.

The books slammed against the desk with a loud smack that caused dust to rise in the air around them. Sanaa waved her hand and covered her nose, but the man seemed to think nothing of it and dived into the first book.

"This one here was written by someone who made it his mission to uncover the inner workings of the temples of the Twelve. Horus was his name. He entered each temple and wrote down everything that he learned. This book has been on my list to read for a while," the man said bringing up the first book in the stack.

Sanaa nodded and grabbed the book. "I think that this is all that I would need. Thank you."

The man sputtered and gestured back to the stack of books. "Oh, but there is more in here that could help you answer the question that you have."

Sanaa let a small smile grace her lips. "No. I think that this will be enough. Thank you..."

"Amos."

"Thank you Amos for helping me once again." With that Sanaa turned on her heel and exited the library. She looked through the book in her hands. The writing was a little faded and the paper was as delicate as an insect's wings, but it was readable.

Sanaa made her way to the gardens, flicking through the book to get to the section about the temple of Roux and their practices. When she found it towards the back of the books she began reading.

The book skimmed over how Horus got initiated into the cult and went into detail about one of the rituals that took place soon after the initiation.

"There are several people here who believe in the hollowness of the soul. They believe that we are all living vessels waiting for one of the Twelve to possess us to do their work. At night some of the initiated gather and howl into the night, hollowing themselves to be a fit vessel for one of the gods," a page read. Sanaa turned the page enraptured in the book.

The process of Hollowing was one that was simple, the book intimated. First one must empty themselves of all thoughts and desires. Then they must be "anointed with the power of the god." From there it was simply a matter of enacting the change that the god wanted to see in the world.

Sanaa sucked her teeth. So there was no Hollow One, but a process to make a Hollow One. So then why was the temple of Roux waiting for a specific Hollow One? What were they waiting for?

The questions bubbled up inside of her as she turned the page and began to read more. Sanaa's eyes ran over the page, taking in all the information that she could. The pages seemed to fly before her eyes as she read more and more until—

"Hello?"

Sanaa's head snapped up. She turned her eyes upward and saw Empress Sorcha standing with King Gabriel on her arm. The empress had a wide grin on her face while the king looked as though he was trying to swallow a lemon.

"Hello," Empress Sorcha said with a smile and a tilt to her head. Sanaa snapped the book close without a second thought.

"Hello, Your Imperial Majesty," Sanaa said rising to bow but the empress stopped her with a hand.

"No need to bow. That is too formal," Empress Sorcha said with a wave of her hand. "Come. Walk with me."

She offered Sanaa her other arm and Sanaa thought about it for a moment. The research in her hands was important. She should keep reading and find out what she can but then she thought of Vorus's words. The empress needed to be entertained and kept away from the problems that they currently faced.

Should she find about the Husk bandits and what they could do... Sanaa doubted that she could withstand the power of an angry empress all on her own. She reached out an arm and linked it with the empress.

Sorcha's smile grew bigger and she guided them through the gardens. She paused a couple of times to enjoy the flowers and comment on their fragrance. Sanaa's hand was a ball at her side, clenching the book in her hand that wasn't looped with the empress's. And her steps were stiff as she walked with the empress through the garden.

"You know I never thought that I would be in the same room as a Batsamasi one day." Empress Sorcha bent over to pull at some tulips that rose from the ground. Sanaa's eyes snapped to her lightning quick.

"Really?"

"Oh yes, I remember hearing about how they hated us. How you all claimed we burned down your city."

Thoughts of fire and smoke rose in Sanaa's mind but she squashed them down.

"Faeries did burn down our city. It was horrific."

"Gabriel, did you ever think that a Batsamasi would be in your court? Have you ever thought of something so wild?"

"Not even in my dreams," King Gabriel drolled from the other side of the empress. Sanaa nodded her head.

"I never thought that I would be here with the faerie empress under such... calm circumstances," Sanaa said with a tense smile. Empress Sorcha tossed her a brilliant smile over her shoulder.

"What were you reading?" she asked.

"What?" Sanaa said.

"What were you reading that had you so engrossed? I had to call out to you for you to even look away."

Both the empress and the king's eyes were on her and Sanaa felt the book weigh heavy in her hand. The words of Vorus ran through her head at that moment. Don't let them find out.

"It's a book about the practices of the Twelve," Sanaa said with a shrug of her shoulders. "Just some light reading."

"Thinking of becoming a witch," Empress Sorcha teased with a smirk on her face.

"I've considered it," Sanaa said with a tilt to her head. Devoting her life to Fintan is something that she had considered doing a long time ago. But Mother crushed that dream in a moment. She had wanted all her daughters with her, to enact her will.

Well, Mother was gone and now she could choose her destiny, her path in the world. Sanaa's thoughts broadened at the thought. She was free now. Free to make her own choices and mistakes and be who she always wanted to be. Mother was no longer there to stop her.

"Well, I have always thought that being a witch would be fun. I liked to pretend to be a witch when I was a girl. I think every girl has considered becoming a witch at some point," Empress Sorcha sighed. She turned her eyes toward King Gabriel. "And what about you? Ever consider becoming a warlock?"

"No," was King Gabriel's swift response. Sanaa thought

that he sounded curt and rude but Sorcha just laughed off the response turning to whisper to Sanaa.

"He's just put out because the marigolds here aren't the color that he wanted," Sorcha whispered.

If King Gabriel's face could sour more it did, "I told them that the colors I wanted this time are burnt sienna and maroon, but the ones here are yellow," Gabriel said with a flick of his head. He stared down at the flowers as if with his gaze alone he could wilt one of the marigolds. "These are golden yellow."

Empress Sorcha threw back her head in laughter. She laughed so easily. She had not a care in the world like she was not an empress but a girl. She gripped Sanaa's arm for support as the laughter wracked through her.

"I have never met a man who took the colors of his flowers so seriously. He is a dullard with everything else, but flowers..." Sorcha laughed. Sanaa felt a smile tick upon her lips as she watched the empress laugh. The laugh made her smile wider and made her shoulders relax. Sanaa let out a few chuckles at Gabriel's expense herself.

The king did not seem to mind, just rolling his eyes and looking with disdain at each flower that they passed. Sorcha straightened and gripped Sanaa's arm again, regaining her bearings.

Empress Sorcha smiled as she leaned to rest her head on Gabriel's shoulder. "You know I don't mean anything by it. You are just so serious Gabriel. Flynn would be aghast with how you run your kingdom."

"Well blessed be the Twelve that I run the Spring Court and not him," Gabriel said.

Sanaa let out a small smile, feeling the tension drip away from her now that the attention was not on her. This empress was girlish and fun. It appeared that all she wanted was to amuse and be amused. There was something young about her.

Empress Sorcha turned her eyes back to Sanaa. "Tell me how are you finding your stay in the Spring Court, Sanaa?" she asked as she gazed off into the sunset.

"I have found my stay here to be... enlightening," Sanaa said. She thought about everything that she had experienced so far. The Husks in the caves and the way that the Fae village was run. The world had changed a lot since the last time that she had walked the earth.

"Good. I do hope you have been enjoying yourself. Though I do wonder if everything has been peaceful." Sorcha's warm amber eyes grew slightly colder as she asked the question and Sanaa could feel her body tense up at the question.

She was asking if the problem in the caves had finally been dealt with. She wanted to know if Sanaa had done the job that she was hired to do. Sanaa felt the smile on her face wobble. She was never really trained on how to lie, to faint and misdirect she had experience in was one thing, but lying was Mother's domain.

"Everything has been at peace," Sanaa said with all the conviction she could muster. "The most work that I do is when I am training with August or by myself."

Sorcha looked her up and down with those lukewarm eyes of her before a smile broke out across her face. "Oh look, roses!"

With that the interrogation was over, Sanaa let herself be guided to the roses wishing that she was anywhere else than with the Empress.

# Chapter Twenty-Five

Taira stayed in her room for most of the day. From her perch on her bed, she watched as the sun sunk lower and lower in the sky. She knew that she was going to have to confront Sorcha soon and that she had to do it now.

But something stopped Taira. Her tongue felt heavy in her mouth when she went to say the words. All Taira could think about was the woman laying behind that door covered in dust and waiting for Taira to say the words and release her from the curse.

"No, I can't say that I do." The empress did not remember what she had done to Taira. She didn't remember that night when she took away the one thing that Taira treasured the most in this world.

*Challenge her,* the voice whispered in her ear.

*End her,* another voice insisted.

Things were different. Not only was she ready to face the empress, unlike the last time. This time she had her friends from the Void.

The voices that she was hearing were voices of Sorcha's

victims. Men and women who were angered at their deaths at the hands of the empress and wished for nothing more than revenge. Taira was going to give them their revenge and then she would be able to see her again.

A knock sounded behind the door. Taira could hear the whispering voices of two maids. She could hear the swishing of their skirts from behind the door.

"Taira," a voice piped up from behind the door, "Dinner will be served soon. Do you wish for us to bring your food to your room again?"

Taira rose from the bed and open the door, scaring the two women who stood behind it. The two short women, pixies no doubt, jumped back from the door. Taira straightened her clothes and looked at them both in the end.

"That will not be needed. I'm going to dinner," Taira said in a calm voice. The two maids nodded and then scurried away, disappearing down the hall.

Now that the words were said Taira had to keep them. Her knees felt weak when she thought of staring down the empress again. She did not want to look into those amber eyes and remember what happened that night. Taira wished with all her heart that she could simply kill the empress and be done with it. But she needed to look into those eyes again. She needed to see the empress one last time before she died.

Taira felt more comfortable in her breeches and tunic than she felt in her dress. Her sword was strapped to her side and ready at a moments' notice. She breathed in deeply from her nose. It would be now or never.

She marched down the hallway and to the dining room. The thick scent of seasoned meats and sweet fruits made Taira's stomach rumble. She had merely picked at the food that the maids had brought her earlier, too nervous to scarf anything down.

The dining room was polished to the point of gleaming.

The floor was white marble with grey veins running through it and chandeliers hung from the ceilings. Even the pillars of matching grey marble were shining in the candlelight. The table was stacked high with succulent meats and mouth-watering fruits.

Taira found her place, seated between Vorus and Sanaa, and sat down. The others trickled into the room one by one. August looked exhausted with his hair in disarray. Vorus saw that and began to push around August's hair so that it looked artfully tousled and not like he just woke from a nap.

Sanaa came in on the arm of the empress with King Gabriel lagging behind the two of them. Tsar Reava bringing in the rear.

The empress was chattering loudly, her arm wrapped around Sanaa's. "Oh, you would just love the Summer Court. The beaches there are amazing and everyone there is so much more relaxed. I think it has something to do with the heat."

Sanaa nodded along with her words but looked confused with the conversation. Taira gripped the armrests of her chair, her nails digging into the polished hardwood. Vorus sent her a testing glare and turned his eyes to Sorcha.

"Your Imperial Majesty, I hope that you found your rooms to your liking?" He asked.

"Oh, the rooms are just darling," Sorcha said with a flutter of her large golden wings. "Weren't they Reava?"

The dragon Tsar simply shrugged her shoulders, her eyes already on the food. Taira's hands were balled up into fists, gripping the wood so hard that she heard it groan under her hands.

Vorus sent her a withering glance that made Taira pull her hands from the armrests and placed them in her lap. She fiddled with her fingers as the empress sat down at the head of the table.

"The rooms are... adequate," King Gabriel chimed in with a sniff. "The colors go together nicely enough."

Vorus let out a soft laugh at his words, but Taira could see the way that he straightened his back and blood drew away from his face.

"I'm glad that you think so King Gabriel," Vorus laughed out. Taira rolled her eyes.

Why did they have to make nice with these people? The empress was a murderer and the king could do nothing as she murdered her way through the courts.

She looked around the room and saw that the maids were waiting for their chance to serve. Some of them looked on with bright eyes and a bounce in their step while others looked like death froze over. Taira felt closer to the latter of the two maids. Sorcha clapped her hands bringing the attention back to her once again.

"I just want to thank you Vorus for welcoming us into your quaint little town. It is so beautiful here and I wish to see more of it tomorrow," Sorcha said, raising her glass. "To Asren!"

The rest of the people at the table lifted her glass. Taira did so also with a shaking hand. "To Asren!" Taira mumbled out the words with the rest of them.

Taira took a deep drink of the wine that was in the cup. She finished the goblet in one gulp and then waved a maid to fill her glass with some more.

"I was thinking that it would be nice to have a tour of the town tomorrow," Sorcha said as a maid served her a helping of fruit. "I would love to see the town and maybe see the temples of the Twelve."

All their heads snapped up at the mention of the Twelve. The information about the temple of Roux first entered her mind. They needed to keep the empress far away from that temple in particular.

Sanaa looked at Vorus from across the table and sent him a panicked look. Vorus cleared his throat and then shook his head with a laugh.

"Then that can be arranged. Give me a day or so and I can have the tour arranged," Vorus said. The empress stuck out her bottom lip in a pout that she must have thought was cute but made her seem like a fish more than anything.

"A day or so? I think I want to go tomorrow. Is there any way that you can make it so that I can go tomorrow?" She asked with that pout still on her lips. Vorus cleared his throat from his seat. Taira knew that one should never say no to the empress, but Taira wanted to scream the words at her.

"Of course. I will arrange for you to go tomorrow with Sanaa and August." The two in question gave each other a questioning look from their chairs and then looked at Vorus. Taira frowned.

Why would he send two people who did not know the town as well as she did? Was this another attempt to keep Taira from challenging the empress? Well, it was not going to work.

Taira took another gulp of her wine and turned her eyes back to the empress. She let out a saccharine smile that she hoped hid her true intentions.

"Don't worry, Your Majesty," she almost spat out. "I can take you around the town. Sanaa and August will be there as your security detail so you can just focus on having a good time."

The empress laughed and clapped her hands. "Oh, this is going to be so much fun!"

"Yes," Taira agreed the smile still stuck on her face. The maid poured her another glass of wine and Taira chucked it back finishing the wine in one go.

The empress smiled as she fingered the food in front of

her, her eyes cooling from the warm amber to a cold golden fire. "You know something stuck with me today."

"What was it, Your Majesty?" Vorus asked.

"I asked Sanaa if the town was peaceful and she said it was. I assume that the problems that were preventing trade with the wolves has been dealt with?" The empress questioned.

"You would be right about that your Imperial Majesty. The wolves have been receiving shipment for weeks now, there is no delay. They receive what they ordered when they need it."

"That is good to hear. I was getting tired of getting letters from the wolf chieftains saying that they never received their orders. And accusations that we are reneging on our contract. It was getting to become very troublesome," Sorcha said with a flick of her hair.

"When was the last successful shipment?" King Gabriel said suddenly. Taira turned her head to him, her eyes wide. He was so quiet that he almost forgot that he was even in the room.

"The last successful shipment?" Vorus started, but then Reava giggled.

"It's a simple question. When was the last time that the wolves received their shipment?" She said with a mouthful of food.

"Oh. Well, it was not too long ago that they received the last shipment. Sanaa and August were there while they accompanied the shipment," Vorus said. Three pairs of eyes now narrowed in on August and Sanaa. Sanaa in particular seemed more uncomfortable with the attention.

Taira looked at Vorus and shot him a look, but the man's head was down looking at his food. August was the first to talk of the two.

"Yes, we were guarding the latest shipment. It was an easy

delivery and we killed the siren who was disrupting the trade," August said with every bit of confidence. Taira was a little surprised. He seemed calm and reassured about the victory that took place that night.

There was not even a hint of doubt in his voice and it never wavered. Taira raised a brow as the rest of the attention was turned to Sanaa. Sanaa was looking down at her hands. She was hunched overm looking at her food as if it was going to have the answers to their questions.

"Umm...What August said is true. We dealt with the siren and that was the end of it," she mumbled out.

"What?" The empress asked. She put a hand to her ear to leaned closer. "Sanaa I couldn't understand you?"

Sanaa seemed to sink lower into her seat, not taking the scrutiny that she was under well. Taira slammed her goblet on the table, bring all the attention that was on Sanaa to herself.

"You know, Your Majesty, something that you said stuck with me," Taira said. Sorcha tilted her head her eyes regaining that warm effect that made Taira's skin crawl. A slow smile slithered onto her face.

"Oh really? And what was it?" She asked.

"You said that you don't remember me. That was just—I cannot believe that you don't remember me," Taira started taking a whole mouthful of wine. Sorcha's smile faltered for a moment but it stayed on her lips. Taira frowned into her glass.

"I'm sorry, that seemed rude, but I meet so many people that I can barely remember them all," Sorcha said. "Reava had always been better at remembering people than I have been. Right?"

Reava nodded her head with a silly grin on her face. But Taira barely spared the dragon tsar a glance before her eyes were back on Sorcha.

"No, but it must be impossible to not remember me. I mean I was so close to killing you."

The sound of forks and spoons clinking against the bowls and plates stopped. Vorus turned his head to Taira with his eyes wide. August leaned back in his chair, arms behind his head, and Sanaa's eyes flickered between the empress and Taira.

"Yes, I remember it so clearly. I snuck into your palace— you have terrible security by the way—and I caught you sleeping. I was so close to killing you that I could almost taste your blood on my lips."

"I'm so sorry Your Majesty," Vorus started up. "I will have to reprimand her immediately and—"

The empress raised a lone hand, halting Vorus's words in his throat. Her warm amber eyes were not cool gold as she took in the Taira. She knew that in the empress's eyes she was not impressive. A spring fae with a lot of mouth is probably what she thought of Taira.

But Taira could remember that night with her and Cinder working their way through the castle and making their way to the empress' chambers. The empress was nothing more than a flower waiting to be plucked.

"If it wasn't for that guard coming into your room then you wouldn't be here. And I would be living in the lap of luxury," Taira said with another gulp of her wine.

The voices began to screech in the rears calling for death and murder. They wanted their vengeance right now. They wanted Sorcha dead and at her feet right now. Taira ignored the voices looking at Sorcha's face as the smile still stayed in place.

"I do remember you now," the empress said. "I remember how you and your little fried failed to kill me. And I cursed her since she was the one who came up with such a stupid plan. I remember you."

Reava smiled from where she was sitting, "But why bring this all up?"

Taira smiled and rose from her chair. The world spun for a moment but righted itself quickly. "Because I am calling for the right of brwydr."

The room sucked in a collective breath. The air in the room grew heavier at her words. Sorcha said nothing at the challenge she simply wiped her mouth with the cloth and placed it over her food.

"I accept," was all that she said. Another round of gasps went around the room. King Gabriel stood up.

"You must be joking," he said. "To accept the right of brwydr when you have no reason to do so—"

"Oh, be quiet Gabriel. This is going to be fun. Besides, this wouldn't be fun if there wasn't a little chaos," Reava said with a smile on her face. She was relaxed in her seat eating food and drinking wine like a challenge had not been issued at all.

"A daughter of Magni you are," Gabriel muttered, taking his seat once again.

Sorcha turned her eyes to Vorus again. "How quickly can you get the arena ready for the brwydr?"

Vorus sighed. "A week Your Majesty."

"Good." She rose from her chair and looked around the room. "In a week, we will have a brwydr between myself and... her. Tell everyone to be ready." She turned and walked out of the dining.

Taira could feel the wine still in her stomach but the worse of it was done. She was going to do battle with the empress, but this time she did not intend to lose. This time she had power on her side.

# Chapter Twenty-Six

✦✦✦

August was glad to be able to get out of the dining room. The air there was so heavy he could feel it weighing down on him. Leaving the dining room, August felt as though he was breathing fresh air for the first time.

From the corner of his eyes, he caught braids swaying and turned to charge after Sanaa.

"Sanaa! Wait!" He cried as he ran after her. Sanaa stopped where she was and then turned her head to wait for him to catch up to her. He was by her side in a matter of moments. He let a slow smile crawl up his face and slung an arm around her shoulders.

"Dance with me?" He asked Sanaa. She shrugged out of his hold, but she turned and smiled back at him.

"Fine." They walked together to the training pit. When they got there Sanaa wasted no time bringing the array of needles behind her. August stretched a little before he reached for the spear that was waiting for him at the rack.

They launched attacks against one another. One moment

August would be defending and the next moment he would be on the offense. Their bodies moved through the crisp night air together as they blocked and hit at one another.

"You know that night you kissed me," August said as he went in for an attack.

"What?" Sanaa asked as she went to block his blow. He fainted to the left and then struck out on the right, but Sana was ready for it, the needles gathering together in one spot to block the blow. Sanaa struck out again breaking the spear in half.

"Again?" August asked as all he was left with was the two parts of the broken spear. Sanaa sent him a cheeky grin and threw herself into another attack. "That night when you got drunk on faerie wine. You kissed me."

"I know," Sanaa said as she ducked under another attacked and slithered up in front of him. August locked his arms around her. Their faces were close together and August's eyes dropped to her lips. Sanaa struggled in his hold, but August simply tightened his arms around her.

"You kissed me. And I have to say you aren't a half-bad kisser," he said. He leaned closer his lips brushing against her own, but then she wiggled out of his hold and surprised him with an attack.

He rolled out of the way and his eyes went wide. He felt a laugh bubble up in his chest at the action. But Sanaa stood there with her array of needles behind her shining in the low light of the moon.

"What? You don't want to kiss me again?" he asked. He rose from the crouch that he had settled himself into and rose to his full height. "I thought I was a good kisser."

Sanaa rolled her eyes and her neck. She placed a hand on her hip. "I kissed you, so what? I'm not going to start falling all over you." August raised a brow at that.

"You know where I come from women would die to kiss me, to spend the night with me," he said with a tilt of his chin.

"Well good for them, but I need you to shut up and dance." Sanaa crouched low against the ground and shot back at him with another attack. They mired in the dance of fighting once more. Their attacks glanced off one another, sometimes just nicking one another.

He could see why she called this dancing. His feet had to be in an exact position or else she would catch him. His hand placement and the straightness of his back could mean that she was not supported with the next move that she was going to take.

Sanaa shot forward with all her strength and August caught her around the waist. They were both panting, Sanaa turned her face up to him and August looked down at her.

Her lips were right there, soft and plump. It was a siren song, trying to resist them and their bow shape. He let her go and she twirled back into position once again.

"Have you found anything about the Hollow One?" he asked as he jabbed out at Sanaa's side.

"I found out that the temple of Roux believes in the hollowness of the soul. It is a ritual that mainly anyone could do but I don't understand why they are waiting for a particular person," Sanaa said as she ducked under his spear.

"You know how witches are. They like to make everything a mystery. They love to speak in riddles and confuse anyone who happens to be listening," he said.

Sanaa slithered close again and August could feel the heat rising in him. He was burning with the need to get closer and closer still. He pushed her away and jabbed out a broken piece of wood from the split spear.

"I know that but I can't help but feel as though we don't

have the full picture like we are forgetting something," Sanaa said with a duck and roll. August struck out again his hand slamming against the wall next to Sanaa's head. The two were still panting. August looked down at Sanaa and took in her visage. From the way that her bosom heaved in her tunic to the way that her lips quivered.

"My that was a beautiful display."

August and Sanaa pulled away from each other to look at who was waiting in the archway. With her pauldrons gleaming in the low light of the room, Reava stepped inside the training pit. Her blue eyes smoldering as she took the two of them in.

"Oh," Sanaa dipped into a bow. "Your Majesty."

Reava waved a hand at the action. "No, no need to call me Your Majesty. My assistant is more ruler than I am. What do you call what you were doing right now?"

"I was simply practicing my sword dance with August," Sanaa said. August was wiping his face with a rag that he found strewn between the racks. He did not like the dragon that was among them now. And he found the empress to be suspicious with the way that she looked like Helia.

The empress looked far too much like Helia for it to just be a coincidence. There had to be a connection between the empress and Helia, but his mind could not fathom what it could be. As far as he knew the two of them had never met before and Helia hated the empress.

Reava nodded her head as she put her fingers to her chin. "Sword dance. We have a sword dance from where I come from." She paused for a moment. "It is a very old dragon tradition. Would you like to see it?"

"Of course, if you would be willing to show it to us," Sanaa said. August shrugged his shoulders when they turned their eyes to him. He did not care if he was shown the sword dance or not. He needed to know the connection between Sorcha and Helia.

Reava pulled two swords from her sides and readied herself. She turned to give Sanaa and August a wink. "Watch closely now."

This sword dance was not lingering in the way that Sanaa's was. It was more August's style with quick, powerful jabs and short swipes that were meant to lop someone's head off. But this dance was also unlike August's dance moves. It used her legs a lot more and the sword flashed over her head and her back several times.

The swords never stopped moving. One hand to the other, the swords changed hands and for a moment it looked like Reava was carrying more than the two swords that she had. August leaned back impressed with the way that the sword dance worked for the dragon tsar.

When the dance was over, all that was left was Reava panting where she was. She glowed in the moonlight, the light hitting off the metal pauldrons and the swords. She let out a laugh and put the swords back to her side. Sanaa clapped while August rose from his seat.

"That was impressive," he said.

"Why do I find that you are not someone who gives high praise," Reava said with a smirk on her face.

August raised his hand in defeat. "You got me."

Sanaa walked closer to Reava her hands shaking. "That was amazing Reava."

"Thank you," Reava said kicking the dirt. "It was nothing like your sword dance. It was so graceful."

"Thank you."

"You know I think that I can beat your sword dance Reava," August chimed in. Reava raised a brow but a smile grew on her lips.

"Really?"

"I don't think. I know," August challenged. Reava let out a short laugh.

"Fine then. Grab your weapon. Let's see who's fighting style is superior." She began to walk away to take her place in the pit.

"On one condition." Reava turned her head around to look at August. "You answer one of my questions if I win."

Reava shrugged her shoulders and got into position. Sanaa moved towards the edges of the pit so she wouldn't be in the way and August grabbed an unbroken spear from the rack of training weapons.

He settled into his position and waited. Reava did not move either, she stayed low crouched to the ground, and waited for August to make the first move. August's muscles began to twitch and burn from holding his position for so long, so he rose and charged at the dragon tsar.

Reava rolled out of the way and popping up on her feet and throwing out those quick jabs that he saw her do before on the sword dance. August remembered that the dance was mainly centered in the middle of the torso, very rarely straying from the center there.

August jumped away from her then and swiped low at her feet. The movement unmoored her and she was set adrift. He kept his attacks low to the ground aiming at her feet. Each attack made sure that she could not get ready for the next part of her sword dance.

"Hey, you're cheating," Reava said with a frown as she pushed away from August. A smile lit up her face as she pulled in her swords close to her chest. "I don't mind. That makes this more fun."

Two large-scaled wings unfurled from her back, the scales glimmered in the moonlight a blood-red color. She gave a heavy flap of her wings and she took off into the open air, going higher and higher into the night sky.

August unfurled his wings, flapping hard and rising from the ground. He needed to know why Sorcha and Helia shared a face. He needed to know so that he could sleep knowing that Helia was the person she claimed to be and not the monster that Nova painted her to be.

When he rose at the same level as Reava, she greeted him with a smirk. "Here we are equal. The only things that we can test are our skills. Do you truly believe that you can beat me?"

"I know I can," August said with an upturn to his lips. The two clashed together with the sound of steel hitting wood. The wood was holding well enough against Reava steel.

August launched into another flurry of attacks. Each hit landing squarely against Reava's precisely placed swords. She was never in a rush with her moves, it was like she knew where his hits were going to land before he even decided it.

He feinted left and then came to the right side with a heavy slam. The attack finally landed. Reava spun in the air for a moment, dropping a little bit but righting herself in a matter of moments.

"Good. Finally some blood," she said as she wiped at her lips. The blood smeared on her cheek but it seems like Reava thought nothing of it. Her blue eyes appear to glow as she looked back up to August.

She eyed him from her lower vantage point and shot up into the air. August barely had time to prepare himself for the onslaught. Each hit slammed into his body relentlessly. It was one after another after another.

Each hit jarred and sent his body spiraling down out of the air. But Reava would not give him a moment of rest. She kept on slamming her swords into his body as they traveled down.

August sucked in a deep breath as Reava reached back and slammed both of her swords into his stomach. The air was whipped out of him and his back slammed into the ground. He groaned and curled up into a ball.

Reava landed beside him and gave a short laugh at his pain. "What happened," she asked. "I thought you said you could beat my sword dance." She let out a loud laugh at that, but August just groaned from his point on the floor. Sanaa rushed over to his side and ran to see if he was okay.

"Oh, don't worry about him. I didn't kill him... Or at least I didn't try to," Reava said with a flick of her wrist. Sanaa got down at his side and brushed some of the hair away from his face.

August cracked an eye open and let a small smirk rise to his lips. "Can I kiss you?"

Sanaa who had been cradling his head, let it fall against the dense dirt of the ground. August let out another groan. August rose from the ground gripping his stomach as that was the area that Reava had focused on the most. He sighed and limped over to a pillar so he could lean against it.

"What was your question?" Reava asked as she sheathed her swords.

"What?"

"Your question? What were you going to ask me?" Reava repeated.

"I just wanted to know something. Sorcha... looks a lot like somebody that I know. I wanted to know if there was any connection between the two of them."

Reava snorted and then shook her red hair out. It was long and wavy making it seem like waves of fire were coming out of her head.

"Sorcha knows a lot of people. You are going to have to tell me who this person is."

"No, forget it. I lost." August said. There was no way that he could tell Reava, best friend of the Faerie Empress that he knew who Helia was, that he had seen Helia. She was a wanted criminal in all the Fae Courts and was considered the number one most wanted woman. He could not reveal that connection. What had he been thinking? That the dragon tsar would so easily wipe away any connection that he had with Helia. He bit his lip.

Reava shrugged her shoulder stretched her arms, and yawned. "Well, I'm turning in for the night. We get to tour Asren tomorrow. You should both go and get some sleep too." Reava turned out of the room and walked out of the archways and to her room.

August gripped the spear in his hands and threw it aside. Sanaa came up to him then looking at his stomach that he knew for sure was going to bruise over the next morning. Breathing was already becoming difficult as he stood there against the pillar.

"Why did you choose to fight her when you knew you couldn't beat her," Sanaa asked.

"I thought that I could beat her," August answered. "I was winning when we were on the ground. But the moment that we took to the skies I lost my advantage."

"Do you think you'll be fine?"

"I'll be okay."

"Okay." Sanaa turned and began to make her way to leave the room too, but she turned around to give him one last look. August could not name the emotion that was hiding in her brown eyes, but he knew it meant something. He felt as if his world shifted underneath his feet. Sanaa turned and left the training pit.

August slid down the training pit and rested his head against the pillar. His body ached with every breath that he took, but he felt alive, more so than he had felt in months and years. He had not even known that he was feeling so list-less and not... himself for so long.

But then his heart throbbed in his chest. The deal that he

had made with Helia was still intact. This was the closest that he was going to get to freedom for a long time. The thought made his heart stutter in his chest.

There was so much mystery about Helia about who she was and what she stood for. August hoped that the deal that he made would end soon. He did not know how much more of the fickle machinations of the faerie he could take.

# Chapter Twenty-Seven

Flowers decorated Sorcha's path. The people of Asren showered their Empress with the soft petals and Sorcha could only let out a laugh as the petals came down. They came down in all manner of colors from blushing pinks to deep maroons. Taira trudged in front of the empress guiding her from one place to the other.

Everywhere that the empress went she was showered with gifts, whether it be in the form of bread or the form of a bouquet. Gifts and flowers showered her every step.

The thought made something low and burning boil low in Taira's stomach. They did not know who their empress truly was. They did not know that their empress was more likely to curse them than to try and save them. The only thought that kept the anger at bay was the thought of the brwydr. She would get her pound of flesh and then some. Not just for her, but for the voices that murmured in her ear.

Patience. That was what she needed patience. Taira waved her hand in a vague direction in front of her.

"This is the shopping district for textiles. Where most of the seamstresses and their shops are," Taira drawled. The empress let out a large squeal, jumped, and clapped her hands.

"Oh, I'd been looking for a new fabric to make a dress. Come, Gabriel," the empress said looping her arm through the king's. She marched into one of the stores and Taira followed not a step behind them.

The empress was quick to go to one of the walls and examine the silk as the King took his time perusing around the shop. Taira stood a little ways away from Reava with her hands crossed over her chest.

"You know, you are a dreadful tour guide," Sorcha said without looking at Taira. She examined a bolt of cobalt blue silk. Taira frowned. She turned to look at the empress, but the empress's eyes never diverted from the silk. "Well, that is to be expected from a country girl."

Taira took a step closer to the empress, her eyes colder than ice. "Say whatever you want about me, but know this. When the brwydr arrives and our steel is drawn your head will roll. And it will have been a country girl that has ended you."

Taira pulled away then but the empress did not even seem taxed by her words. She simply looked at the bolt of silk and waved down the attendant.

"I would like this," she said with a flick of her hair over her shoulder. The attendant disappeared with the bolt of silk and Sorcha turned to face Taira yet again.

"Many people have thought that they could end me. I bet you and your little friends thought that you could end me to that night you snuck into my palace. But I am a child born under Sevan's stars and I will not be killed so easily. Dream all you want. But remember, I'm empress for a reason."

With that, the empress turned away from Taira and walked out of the store. Gabriel followed behind her and in a matter of moments, they had rejoined the retinue. The horses that they had brought with them were laden with the gifts and things that the people had given the empress.

Taira sighed and walked out into the crowd of people. The queen raised her hand.

"I would like to see the temples of the Twelve. I would like to pay my respects to each of the gods. I want to see Sevan." The empress said with a breathy effect to her voice. Taira winced at the sound of her voice and nodded her head.

She hopped onto one of the horses and pressed the side of her heels into the hide of the horse. The horse began to trot forward and Taira guided them to the temple of Sevan.

The temple of Sevan was different from the other temples in that it was a large smoldering metalworking guild. In every room, there was a burning oven made to melt metal and make weapons. The empress saw this and took in the smell of smoke and oil.

"I am never more at home than when I am in a temple of Sevan," she said without a backward glance. One of the shirtless metal workers took notice of them and pulled off his goggles to see them better.

The man was a warlock for Sevan. It was in the way that Sevan's squiggly symbol was branded on his shoulder.

"How can I help you today?" He asked as he came close to the group.

"I was born under Sevan's stars and I would like to pay my respects," Empress Sorcha said.

The man nodded his head and then escorted them past all the people smelting and banging at their weapons with tools, to the back of the temple. There it was just a pit with cascading benches.

"The rest of you could sit there while she pays her respects to Sevan," the warlock said with a nod of his head. The warlock took Sorcha's hand and led her down to the pit where she could pay her respects. In that puffy pink dress of hers, Sorcha looked almost ridiculous when compared to the hulking man that escorted her down.

Taira sat down between Sanaa and August and sighed when she sat down.

"You know I have been wondering this since last night but what is a brwydr?" August said with a tilt to his head. Sanaa nodded her head along and Taira let out another sigh.

"A brwydr is a battle right. It is one of the oldest traditions in the Fae Courts. It is made so those old families could settle disputes and now it extends to everybody," Taira said with a smirk on her lips. "And I intend to win this brwydr."

Sanaa nodded her head, understanding the concept but there was a frown on her face. "Are you sure you can win this? The empress is powerful and you fought her once before," she said.

Taira's thoughts were cast to that night when they had first confronted the empress. They had been sorely unprepared for the onslaught and the power that she wielded. She was someone who never second-guessed what she was doing. She was ready for everything.

"I have something that no one is expecting this time," Taira said with a smirk on her lips.

Taira turned her eyes back to the stage where they had handed Sorcha a sword. Drums started to play in a hard rhythm and men with swords came out and surrounded her. They stared each other down for a moment and then Sorcha pounced

It was nothing but a one-sided slaughter on Sorcha's part. Every move was calculated and well placed. She moved between the men as quick as a shadow and the men could not get even a hit on her body. The cuts that she landed were shallow, nothing more than flesh wounds, but she landed them with precision and brutality.

Every hit that she landed was a slam against the men's

waiting bodies. In a matter of moments, she was done with them. The men were strewn around her like broken toys.

For a brief moment, Taira felt her heart stutter in her chest. This was the empress that she remembered. The easy way that she fought and how she toyed with Taira and Cinder that night. The only reason that they lasted so long was that she enjoyed the game.

Taira steeled her spine. There would not be a repeat of what happened that night. This time she would get revenge for what happened to Cinder. She settled into her seat as the empress came to where they were all seated.

"Sometimes I wish that I was a daughter of Sevan, but it is too structured," Reava said when her friend was in range to her.

"Don't worry Reava. You honor Sevan every time that you go into battle and every breath you take when you fight. He isn't picky as to who worships him," Sorcha said as she neared the group. "Where are the other temples? I would like to pay my respects." This was directed at Taira.

"Your Imperial Majesty I think that we should only make one more stop. The sun is starting to get low in the sky and there is no way that you can visit the rest of the Twelve before nightfall," King Gabriel said. It was with a quick look at the sky that Taira confirmed that he was right.

The sun was beginning to hang low in the sky and get that brunt orange color to it. The sky was a pastel of pinks and yellow hues that marked the beginning of sunset. Taira nodded her head in agreement.

"One more temple," Taira agreed. Sorcha stick out her lower lip and crossed her arms. She looked put out by the knowledge that they were not going to be able to visit all the temples that she wanted. But she quickly uncrossed her arms and turned her frown into a wide grin.

"I would like to visit the temple of Roux," Sorcha said. It

took everything in Taira not to let her face drop. Why out of all the temples that she could want to go and see it had to be that one? The thought of going to that time that was colluding with the bandits was something that she knew Vorus was going to be against.

But how do you say no to an empress? How to deny access to the most suspicious place without rising suspicion yourself? Taira's eyes darted to Sanaa and August, and the two of them were mostly holding it together. Sanaa's smile looked a little strained but they had it together for the most part.

Taira let a smile spread across her face, "Of course, Your Majesty. Right, this way."

They made their way back through the forges and to their waiting horses that were grazing in the grass. Taira hopped on to her horse and held the reins in her hands. She soothed herself with the thought that this would end soon and then sent the horse into a light trot.

The horse followed along the path and Taira thought of ways that she could hide how suspicious the temple of Roux was for them. The temple had been silent for a long time. They ceased strolling through the town at their designated hours and had stopped calling for worshippers.

The temple had completely isolated itself from the rest of the world and no one knew why. But now Taira knew that it was because they were helping the bandits for some reason. They were assisting Husks in escaping from their betters and stalling the movement of the town.

Taira shook her head. She could never understand why the temple would take the side of Husks, mortals, over people who wielded the same power that they did. It did not make sense. There was something that they were missing.

Sanaa pulled up beside her and ducked her head as she said, "Do you think that taking her to the temple of Roux will be a good idea? I mean they're—"

"I know what you mean. And we cannot say no to the empress when they aren't supposed to know anything about this. We just have to keep a low profile. Maybe we can even investigate the inside of the temple," Taira whispered back. Sanaa nodded her head, but still looked sick at the thought of going to the temple of Roux.

"You're nervous," Taira said as she led her horse down the path.

"No, I'm not," Sanaa insisted.

"That why are you holding on to your reins so tight?" Sanaa's were two balls in front of her. She was gripping the reins so tight that her knuckles lightened from the golden-rust color to almost a pale tan color. Sanaa let go of the reins and flexed her hands, looking at them.

"In the compound, we were not trained to lie."

"What if you got captured by the enemy?"

"Death would be the only way that we could leave such a situation. Mother made sure that we knew that." Her hands were fists on the reins again and Taira tried another route.

"Tell me about your magic. It is very different from my own," Taira tried again. Sanaa's head shot up and she gave her a queer look, but Taira nodded her head, encouraging her to continue the conversation.

"My magic deals with potential, we call it monyelta. I can manipulate that potential and make it do things that I want to do. Though the more complex the object the harder it is for me to manipulate," Sanaa began.

Taira noticed that her grip was lessening on the reins and her eyes flickered back to the empress, the tsar, and the king. The three were talking amongst themselves and not a care in the world. Sanaa grew less and less tense the more that she uttered about her magic and how it worked. Taira let out a sigh of relief.

With Sanaa talking about her magic, it looked less like

they were having an important conversation and more like a conversation between friends. Sanaa went on about her magic and Taira tuned back into the conversation.

"—Mother was the best at working with monyelta—"

"And we're here!" Taira said. She hopped off her horse and gestured to the hulking metal sphere that was the temple of Roux. The temple was a fixture in the ground with crisscrossing semi-circles that told of the positions of the stars.

Taira tied her horse to a tree and walked closer to the entrance. She slammed her fist against the warm metal and waited. The semi-circle twitched and then jumped into action. Each semi-circle swirled around the golden circle before each lined up perfectly revealing an opening. A white-robed witch stepped out of the opening and smiled as she looked at all the people gathered in front of her.

"Hello, Your Imperial Majesty we have been waiting for you to grace our doorstep," the witch said her voice low and lilting. She stepped and aside and gestured for them to enter the temple.

Taira stepped in first and let out a gasp at what she saw. The inside was not gold like she thought but an opaque golden glass that was transparent on the inside. The world that was reflected through the glass was large but bursting in a kaleidoscope of color. The sky looked so close that Taira was sure that she could touch it if she reached out.

The others came in with equal exclamations of awe. Taira spun around the room looking at the setting sun and the pastel colors of the sky. The witch that had let them in hid a laugh behind her robe.

The witch swept into the front of the room and clapped her hands. She caught the attention of them and smiled a smile that spoke of nothing and everything all at once.

"I am glad to see you here Your Majesty," the witch said.

"We have been expecting you today. Come we already have a room prepared for you."

The witch led them deeper into the temple, they escaped the colorful room and went down a dark pathway that was dotted with candles that imitated starlight. Taira looked from side to side, her eyes darting to each side of the long hallway.

The witch opened the door and lead them into a room that was dark just like the hallway. There was a lone light from the window and there was a pillow against the ground and two metal rods that poked out of the ground. The witch ushered the rest of them into the room.

Taira looked around the room but the room was swatched in darkness. The darkness was impenetrable. There were no candles and all the light came from the lone window in the room and it spotlighted the pillow and the two metal rods in the center of the room.

"Your Imperial Majesty if you'd kneel on the pillow please," the maid gestured to the pillow. Sorcha did just that and the witch smiled. "Hold on to the metal rods in front of you."

"So how will I be showing my devotion to Roux today?" The empress asked with a grin.

"This process is called Hollowing. We witches here in Asren believe that the Twelve could work through us, we just need to get rid of some of the clutter in our bodies. This process is easy and simple. Just scream," the witch instructed.

Sorcha turned back to look at the witch. "Just scream?"

"Yes, and that will be all."

Sanaa stepped closer to Taira and whispered in her ear, "I don't think this was a good idea." Taira hushed her and sent a tense smile to King Gabriel who sent her a questioning look. Taira turned to see Sanaa behind her looking at where the empress was with trepidation.

"Everything will be fine. If she dies then that will be a

blessing sent down from Kai himself. And that means that I will not have to face her in the brwydr," Taira hissed between her teeth. Sanaa looked shocked that she could even wish such a thing on her empress, but the words were out of her mouth before she could even think about it.

She noticed then that her hand was gripping Sanaa's arm tight and she pulled away from the woman, straightening up her back and turning around to face the empress once again. She had lost control of her anger. She could not afford to lose her calm so easily when the empress was around.

She looked around and it seemed like no one noticed the fact that she pulled Sanaa aside to hiss at her. Sorcha held the two rods in her hands and then turned to look at the witch again.

"Okay I think I'm ready to start," Sorcha said. The witch clapped her hands and the rest of them fell into silence. Sorcha turned her eyes straight forward and then she began to scream.

The first one was one long howl. It was long and drawn out and sounded like that of a wounded animal. She let loose a few more screamed like that, but then the witch got close to her.

"Is that what you call screaming? You need to lose yourself in the howl. You need to scream like your dying," the witch berated her.

Sorcha let out another round of howls this one worse than the ones before. Her voice cracked and broke in some places and she barely took a moment to take in a breath before she let out the next scream.

"Scream like you have lost your son as if the world that you know has been torn asunder!" The witch shouted over her screams.

Sorcha let loose scream after scream, each one overpowering the one that came before it. The witch shook her head at the screams that Sorcha was letting out and then tapped her lightly on the head.

The screams morphed after that tap. These were truly agonized screams. They spoke of pain and trouble and darkness. These screams were drenched in sorrow and sadness. Sorcha's wings unfurled behind her back, large and golden and glowing, sending her light around the room.

Power swelled in Sorcha's throat and it blasted everyone onto their backs. The witch was the first to rise from the ground and clapped happily.

"Yes! This is true hollowing!" The witch shouted from the edge of the room.

Taira rose from the ground and noticed a golden aura surrounding the empress. It shimmered and shone and her hair whipped in the wind that her power was creating. Then one side of the aura turned pitch black. The black infected the golden aura consuming it and taking it over until half of Sorcha's aura was black and gold. One of her wings became black and mottled, the black aura dripping like ooze from the wing.

The hair on one side of her head unraveled from the loose curls that she sported and became jagged and straight. Sorcha let out a loud howl as she gripped the two rods in her hands.

"Sorcha!" Reava shouted from her post. She rose from the ground and with a strength that Taira would not dare muster began to fight against the wind to get closer to her friend.

King Gabriel lay close to the ground and Taira rose to help him up. "We need to get out of here!" Taira said without a backward glance to the empress.

"No, we need to get Empress Sorcha," Gabriel said.

"She'll tire herself out. We aren't safe here," Taira said over the whipping winds.

"Helia?" Taira turned and saw August rising from the

ground. She grabbed his hand and put it on Gabriel's shoulder.

"Get everyone out of here! I'll stop the empress." Empress Sorcha was still howling into the wind, her hands wrapped tight around the metal rods in front of her. Taira cast a glance at Reava who had her claws out, a hand digging into the ground to keep her where she was.

A part of Taira wanted the empress to tire herself out. That way it would be easier to fight when it came to the brwydr. But she knew that if she did nothing with Reava here to watch the dragon tsar could testify that she did nothing in the empress's time of need.

So she dug a boot into the ground and pushed herself against the wind. She made it a couple of feet, but the closer that she got to the empress the stronger that the winds grew. Taira was flung back and her body slammed into the wall of the room.

She bit her lip. She needed to get close to the empress but the wind was tough to get past. If only she had more power. She tried to call on the voices of those that hated Sorcha, the ghosts that wanted nothing more than her downfall, but they were silent. Not a whisper was uttered. There would be no help from them.

Reava dug her claws into the ground and used them to moor herself as she crawled towards her friend. She dug her claw into the ground, but it was loose and the tsar was sent hurling back into the wall.

Maybe...

"We have to work together!" Taira shouted over the howling winds and the screaming. The tsar looked at her for a moment and then looked at her friend who was howling like she was in pain. Reava turned back to Taira and nodded her head. "Good. I need you to toss me with all your strength. I think you're strong enough to get me through to her."

When those words were out of her mouth. Reava did not waste a moment. She grabbed Taira's forearms and spun around, picking up momentum. Taira let out a small scream when the tsar gripped her arms and started swinging. But then she focused. She needed to get as close to the empress as possible.

"I'm going to let you go now," Reava shouted with a huff of breath. Taira nodded her head. She was flying through the air, the wind whipped her hair from her face, but she was making her way through the winds. The wind that Sorcha whipped up was weaker than the force that Reava had tossed her with.

Taira stretched out her arms and crashed into Sorcha. The two of them went flying past the metal rods and slammed harshly into the ground. Sorcha grunted and writhed underneath her body and Taira pulled her up, flipping her over so that she was laying on her back. Taira wiped some black looking chalk off her forehead and the screaming settled into silence.

The chalk evaporated from her hand, spreading into the wind. The wind settled down and all was silence in the temple.

A group of witches in white robes burst into the room. Their eyes darting around the room. They landed on the empress and Taira and rushed towards them both.

"I am so sorry," one of the witches muttered. "I am so sorry that this happened—"

"She's a new novitiate and—"

"That's no excuse she shouldn't have done that!"

One of the witches hung back from the rest. They simply went to the girl who was running the devotional and gave her a hard slap that rang out around the room. The slap silenced the rest of the witches.

"You will be dealt with," was all the head witch said. She

turned to Taira who was cradling the passed-out empress in her arms. Her hair was back to the way that Taira remembered it, in soft curls. But Taira remembered that night that she and Cinder fought the empress.

She had not always been that golden woman that everyone saw. She had a dark side. A side that very few people got to see. It was this side that had cursed Cinder. That darkness of her wings and the jagged straight cut of her hair. Whatever that shadow, that black aura was, that was what Taira remembered.

"I think it'd be best if we go." Taira gathered the empress in her arms and without a look back made her way to the door.

That black aura was the closest that Taira had seen Sorcha been to being herself than in her whole time in Asren.

# Chapter Twenty-Eight

T he air was whistling and there was a slight chill in the air. Sanaa wrapped a shawl around her shoulders and closed the window to her room. She closed her eyes.

After what happened in the temple of Roux the empress was ushered into the manse with no small sense of urgency. The empress came to the manse in Taira's arms and she was quick to shout out demands that they ready the empress's bed for her and to call a medic. With a quick assessment, the healer was able to tell them that the empress was merely exhausted and that she was to simply rest and that would recover her.

Sanaa sighed as she thought back to what happened in the temple. The fact that her aura split in two the black offset by the gold. Sanaa thought she would never get the image out of her mind. She sighed and slumped down against the wall. On her way down she sent a book tumbling down in front of her.

She lifted the book to her eyes and saw that it was the hefty tome that Amos had given to her. The book was littered with stray pages and notes that she had written on scraps of paper that jutted out like angry people. She lifted the book and turned the page to the one about hollowing.

Did the whole temple believe in hollowing? And why had Sorcha been so affected by the process? A knock sounded at her door and Sanaa rose from the ground. She just hummed and the door opened.

"Brief meeting in Vorus's room," August poked his head into the room. Sanaa sighed and drew the shawl tighter around her shoulders. August took this moment to enter the room.

"What's wrong?" He asked as he neared her. From her point on the ground, Sanaa had to look up to see into August's eyes. The left eye was a milky white color that signaled his blindness, but Sanaa found that she liked staring into it now. That it was easier to stare into someone's face when they weren't staring back at her.

Sanaa sighed, "I feel like I am missing something. Why would the temple work together with Husks of all people? Who are these hollow ones that they seem so sure that they have? I just wish that I knew more. And now this nonsense with the empress." Sanaa brought the shawl over her head and gathered herself as much as she could.

She heard things shuffled around her and then felt heat close to her side. She turned towards the heat and let the shawl go. It lifted and she saw August's long legs next to her. He sat back with his arms behind his head and his legs crossed over one another.

"The way that I can see it you can worry endlessly about what you don't know. Or you can deal with the problems in front of you. Don't you want to go home to your nieces?"

"Of course I do more than anything." The thought of Greta and the rest of her nieces flew through her mind. It had been so long since she had thought about them. Her stomach ached at that realization and she drew herself closer into the shawl.

"Then you need to focus on what we do know. The only way that you and I get to go home to the people waiting for us is if we keep going forward. We cannot be distracted by what we do not know. There can be no looking back," August said with a clenching of his fist. Forwards there was no turning back if they wanted to go home. Sanaa nodded her head and rose from the ground, the shawl falling away from her shoulders.

She shook out her braids and made her way towards the door. "Are you coming? You said that there was a meeting in Vorus's room." August rose from the ground with a grin and the two of them made their way outside of the room. They walked down the long hallways and they made it to the ornate door that was Vorus's room.

Sanaa knocked once and the door opened immediately with Taira pulling them inside of the room. She looked frazzled with her hair coming out of its top knot. Her clothes were wrinkled and she ran her fingers through her hair as she paced from one side of the room to the other. Vorus sat on his bed.

The room was in a state of disarray. The dresser was toppled over and the mirror was cracked. The ground had several scratches. The bed was split down the middle. It appeared as though a tornado had gone through the room.

Sanaa looked around the messy room with wide eyes while August let out a low whistle as he took in all the carnage. Vorus sat on the bed overlooking it all with a droll look on his face as though the messy room barely bothered him.

"What happened in here?" Sanaa dared to ask, but Vorus waved off her question.

"What happened in the temple of Roux?" Vorus asked. He looked around the room like he was now realizing the mess that his room was. Sanaa squared her shoulders and took a step forward.

"They wanted Sorcha to partake in a process called Hollowing. And then witch was berating her saying that her screaming wasn't enough-"

"What is hollowing?" Vorus asked from his position by the door.

"Hollowing is the belief that we can all be vessels for the Twelve to work through us. But before they can do that we have to hollow ourselves out and they do that by screaming."

Vorus waved his hand again, "So they wanted her to take part in this process of hollowing."

"Yes they wanted her to take part and things were normal for a while. But then I have no clue what happened the witch touched her and she went wild."

"The witch smeared something, like this black chalk on her head. It disappeared the moment that I touched it," Taira added.

"This isn't good. The empress injured while in my town, my city. This is not good."

"Who cares? She is still alive and she is going to be fine with some rest," Taira said in a brusque tone. Vorus turned his eyes to her and all Sanaa could see in those eyes was pure fire. They held the very depths of hell itself. Vorus stalked towards Taira and loomed over her. His shadow over her seemed to consume her own. Sanaa looked on with bated breath.

"You and your little vendetta against the empress. If you weren't bound to me I would cast you out in a moment. A brwydr and now this. You have no consideration for the people that help you," Vorus breathed so low that Sanaa had to strain to hear what he was saying.

Sanaa straightened her back when Vorus cast his eyes on

her and August. "And what were the both of you doing when all this was going on?"

"We were getting everyone else out of there. We had no way to tell if she would hurt anyone else," August said.

"Good at least some of you have some sense," Vorus spat out. He walked over to a lounge chair that was split in two and laid down in it. "That will be all for this meeting. I just needed to know what happened. You can all leave. Except for you Taira, you stay."

Sanaa turned to exit the room, but while she did she gave one last glance to Taira who seemed frozen where she stood. The door closed on her and then Sanaa and August were outside of the room.

Sanaa wanted to stay by the door and hear whatever conversation was going to go one between the two of them but August grabbed her hand.

"Dance with me?" He asked with a half baked smile on his face. Sanaa shook her head and pulled back her hand.

"No. Not tonight. I'm too tired to dance tonight," she forced the words out of herself. Her muscles ached with the urge but her heart was not with them. Instead, it wanted to be alone. Somewhere quiet where she could sit and think for a while. August nodded his head in understanding and Sanaa let her feet whisk her away.

She had no destination in mind. She simply wanted to be alone. Her feet brought her to the large ornate doors of the library. They shuddered when she opened them. The candles in the library were already lit, brightening the gloomy-looking room.

"Ah. I expected you." She turned with a gasp but was met with the simple smile of Amos. She rested a hand over her fluttering heart. "No one who makes their way here ever truly abandons it. They are simply gone for a few moments."

A smile curved up Sanaa's lips, "Oh really are you saying that this library is cursed?"

"Not cursed. Simply that those who love books will always find their way back here."

Sanaa walked over and settled herself into a seat. The table was stacked high with books and dust. There was such a thick layer of dust that when Sanaa wiped her finger against the table it came away dirty with residue.

"I was never really one for books. I grew up in a more... active way."

"Oh really? Do tell. I have always been fascinated by the Batsamasi and their abilities. Tell me what was it like to grow up as one of them." Amos was busy shelving books and checking them off some list that he had in his hands. Sanaa leaned back in the chair and thought back to her girlhood when she was young.

"Our Mother served as commander. Everything that she said was the law. Slaves, warriors, she was the most powerful of them all. We all loved and feared her. She was everything that we wanted to be when we were older. Powerful and strong. No one could touch our commander."

"I have a feeling that there is a but there."

"Our commander is not who we thought she would be. She was a liar and we found out all her secrets and her lies. And then she died."

"And what about the title of commander who did that go to?"

"The title of commander went to my sister Kala who served as commander for two centuries before she passed and the title went to her daughter and so one and so forth until it has reached Greta, my niece. She serves as commander now."

"Why don't you serve as commander?"

Sanaa paused. There was a moment where she thought about overthrowing Greta, taking it all for herself and guiding the others as she saw fit. But then she would have been like Mother, doing what she wanted for her selfish desires. Sanaa wanted to be Sanaa. She wanted nothing to do with her mother.

"I am not suited to lead others," was all Sanaa said.

Amos came out from behind a stack of books, his eyes roving over the list and checking everything that he had just done.

"What are you doing?" Sanaa asked with a quirk to her eyebrow. Amos looked over his list once, twice, before rolling it up.

"I'm organizing the books. Or at least trying to," Amos said with a quick look to the shelves. "Some of these books are so old I don't think that they have them in libraries anywhere outside of this one."

"Let me help." Sanaa rose from her chair and stretched. "I need the exercise. Especially since I haven't danced today."

"Oh well. I have the selves all labeled. Just place the books on the proper shelf." Sanaa walked over to the desk and grabbed a roll of paper off his desk. She unrolled it to find a list of books that needed to be shelved. She found the pile and went into the stacks.

The shelves were empty, though where Amos put most of the books she could not fathom. She went to the shelf where the books were marked to be and began to shelve the books. She repeated the process as many times as the piles allowed her. Soon there was only one pile left. Amos lifted it and Sanaa held the roll of paper in her hands.

"It says that this one had to go in the mythologies and legends shelf while the last two of the pile go into informational," Sanaa read out as she looked over the paper. His handwriting was short and spiky but easy to read. She looked over at the other shelves and though some of them only had one or two shelves full they were looking better than the original mess they were before.

They made it to the library that had the sign mythologies and legends on it and put the books away. The last two were farther in the back so Sanaa walked with Amos to the back of the library.

"Where did you store the rest of the books?" Sanaa asked.

"There is a large storage closet not too far from here. It was only a matter of a little magic to make sure that all the books—"

A loud howling rang out in the night. The sound was so loud that Sanaa had to cover her ears. When the howling ended Sanaa rose from the ground with a look of astonishment on her face.

There could only be one person who screamed like that. Without a second thought, Sanaa bolted out of the door and into the hallway. Another scream went up and Sanaa covered her ears but kept moving.

The closer that Sanaa got the more shattered windows she was seeing. Glass covered the ground in multicolored shards but Sanaa kept pushing forward. Another scream rang out into the night and Sanaa was in front of the empress's door with two guards slumped over on either side. Sanaa flung it open and saw Sorcha.

Sorcha's feet could not find purchase on the rug so her legs flailed. And she shifted her weight recklessly from one side to the other in a bid to get the arms off of her.

Without a second thought, Sanaa made the needles rise from the sheaths on her legs and jumped into the fray.

# Chapter Twenty-Nine

The scream was unmistakable. He had just spent a whole hour listening to her screams. August vaulted up the stairs and into the most decorated hallway where the empress was sleeping. It had to be her.

The door was already agape when he got there and when he looked inside Sanaa was fighting with two of the kidnappers. They danced around one another, but Sanaa was limited by the space in the room so her movements were short and jerky.

The kidnappers had the same tattoos rolling on their skin as the bandits did. August went back into the hallway and returned with one of the candles and jumped into the fray. He pulled a broken shaft from the bed and used it as a spear.

His first jabs were to the head, but the kidnappers kept ducking away. He changed up his style adding leg sweeps and jabs towards his torso. This caused the man to move backward. When the man tried to use his shadow August was quick to shove the candle close to his skin, intent on seeing the shadows squirm away from the light, but they didn't.

August looked up and he could see the smile in the kidnapper's eyes. "That won't work this time," is all the kidnapper said before the shadows slithered off his skin and rose like the head of two black snakes.

August cursed and dropped the candle. The snakes shot out at him, and August used his shaft of wood to hold them off. The two snakes bit down on the wood almost splintering it in their grasp.

August danced around the room, trying his best to block the attacks and make sure they did not splinter his only weapon.

Why was the light not working now? Had they found a way to make their powers last in the daylight? But how? The questions rolled around in August's head. Their powers depended on the darkness, it thrived in the darkness. There was no way that they could solve that issue so quickly and without anyone even knowing. Where had they gained the knowledge?

August jumped in front of Sorcha, blocking a blow that was heading straight towards the woman. "We could use your help here!" August shouted and he pushed back against the tattoo snakes.

Sorcha looked at him through tousled curls. "I would, but my powers are still exhausted. If I could I would have done more than scream."

He pushed the snakes off and turned his eyes back to the kidnapper. He was dressed head to toe in black, with armor that fitted him somehow despite the mismatch. The man called the snakes back to his skin and whipped his arms around. The darkness whipped out of his skin like a whip, cutting into the ground and gorging it.

August readied himself, calling upon the hellfire that burned bright in his stomach. His nails lengthened into claws and his breath was more smoke than anything else. The two ran at each other. August had more raw strength behind him so he pushed the man out of the window and unfurled his wings.

The man let out a shout of surprise, but August held on. He flapped his wings once, twice, and then slammed the kidnapper's body into the trunk of the tree that made Vorus's manse. The man let out a small grunt of pain but still rose. August stayed in the air circling over where he was settled.

His tattoos writhed on his skin for a moment before they reached up and caught on one of the branches of the tree. August cursed as the man was pulled up into the branches. August went headfirst into the branches looking for where the man had disappeared to.

A branch shook and August blasted it with the heat of hell. August scanned the area looking for the man, waiting for him to come out of hiding. The man shot out from the trees his hands whipping and August knew what would follow.

The shadows slammed into August with all the strength of a horse's kick. It flung him backward out of the branches, but August righted himself and headed back into the branches. He knew what to do.

With no thought, August sunk into the shadow world. The shadow world was a mixture of black and grays and the stark white of light. August slithered along, waiting to see the shadows move and dance. To his right, something caught his eye. The shadows did not sway in the right direction there, they were being manipulated.

August followed the man as he swung through the tree-tops using the branches as bars so that he could swing from place to place. When the man had made his rounds and thought that August had been dealt with that was when he struck.

He pushed himself out of the shadow world and into the world of light and living once again. It was with a huff of breath, August burst forth, his breath burning hot and flames coming out of his mouth.

The man barely had a moment to scream before the flames of hell overtook him. With that, it was done. His body crumbled to ashes and August leaned back with a grin on his face.

It had been so long since he had eaten a fresh soul. Let alone eaten one of a Husk. His body felt heavy, warmth spreading through his veins. It felt so good to have consumed a soul again.

He thought back to the other person that was in the empress's room and rose from the branch that he was laying on. He needed to help Sanaa. He needed to deal with the disgusting Husks that thought that they could stand up to a demon and a Batsamasi. The thought made him laugh. He unfurled his wings and with a flap made his way back to the rooms where Sanaa and Sorcha were waiting for him.

◌⚬◌

The needles that she used for battle were perfect for this setting but the sword dance was not. Her body kept hitting against dressers and vanities and beds, that Sanaa knew that she would be sporting bruises for days to come.

The array of needles danced around the kidnapper, cutting into their legs and their arms, but they were merely flesh wounds nothing deep enough to truly hurt. Sanaa grunted as another hit landed on her. This man was merely toying with her, testing her limits to see how far she could go, how much she could take. His hits were weaker than what she was expecting more like hard taps than real hits.

Sanaa changed her style, making her movements shorter

and quicker, the needles flew through the air and landed harshly in the man's side. He let out a howl of pain at the needles embedded in his skin. Sanaa shot forward, landing hits to his stomach and jumping up to kick at his head.

The man was sent spiraling into the wall and Sanaa pulled out her needles with a quick jerk of her fingers. The man let out a howl of pain as blood gushed from his shoulder.

Sanaa was quick to run on with her advantage. She pulled on the red string of monyelta and the needles began to glow. She sent them after the man, landing hit after him, the wounds being burned as they were being struck. The man let out a howl of pain and the darkness hoped off his skin to coalesce around him creating a dark bubble around him.

Sanaa tried to land hits on the bubble but her needles bounced off. She back away from the bubble and looked at it closely. It was a heavy black color that Sanaa could not see through. Sanaa walked the perimeter of it and returned to where she was standing before.

"Well don't just stand there! Do something!" Sorcha shouted out from her perch across the room. Sanaa turned to her to give her a droll look before she turned her eyes back to the ball. Sanaa tapped it with one of her hands but nothing happened.

Then with the sound of something cracking the bubble expanded. It was consuming everything in front of it. Sanaa back away a couple of steps but soon she was in the grasp of the power. It was darkness. Pure darkness.

"Sorcha?" Sanaa tried calling out. Her voice did not even echo, it was swallowed by the darkness.

"What you did might have worked out there, but in here I'm the master," a voice trickled down to her ears. Sanaa turned around looking for the voice but was only meet with more darkness. Her eyes scanned everywhere but there was no horizon, no point where some of the light came in. It was darkness and darkness alone.

Sanaa did not move from her spot. All her training telling her that to move first would be to concede defeat, but where would she go if there was nowhere that she could see?

It was in the darkness that she heard the rushing of the wind and then the first hit landed on her. It was a biting slash to her leg that sent Sanaa down on one knee. She gasped out at the pain of it and rose again.

The wind rushed again and another hit appeared on her side. Sanaa's eyes widened as the pain burst within her.

Where had they learned to fight like this? Who was training them? The thought rang out of Sanaa's head as she became littered with wounds. How had they gained the training and these abilities? Husks were the lowest of the low, mortals whose time in the world was brief.

Sanaa cried out as another hit landed on her. She fell to the ground clutching at her side. The wind rushed again and Sanaa knew what she needed to do this time.

Sanaa flipped onto her stomach and she gripped the ground beneath her. The floor was heavy and matted with her blood and she knew she was on the rug in the room. Sanaa crawled backward and the hit barely missed her, scraping her stomach as she pulled herself forwards.

"This is going to be the last one. I'm done playing with you," the voice said. The air rushed again and Sanaa pulled at the red string of monyelta that shone before her like the sun.

Flames rose all around her as the carpet was set aflame. The man reeled back and covered his eyes as the light shocked him, but it was all the opening that Sanaa needed. She rose and called the few needles that she had to her. They zinged through the air and embedded themselves in the man's throat. He gagged as blood filled his mouth.

The darkness began to peel away and the room came to

light. Layer by layer Sanaa could see more and more of the room and she sighed when she saw Sorcha's face again sitting in the corner.

Sanaa touched her body, she was bleeding and littered with wounds, the clothes that she was wearing in tatters and what remained was covered in oozing blood. Sanaa dropped down to the ground and let out a laugh.

August came in through the window, the breeze that he brought with him felt like a cooling balm on her mutilated skin. Sanaa looked herself over again. The cuts were luckily shallow and no new scars would make their way on Sanaa's litany of marks.

August closed his wings and Sanaa reached out a hand. He grabbed her hand and helped her up from the ground. Sorcha, with her tousled hair and golden eyes, looked displeased with the state of her room.

"Who were those people?" Sorcha asked in the most dignified way possible. She held her sheets to her chest and raised her chin at the both of them. Thudding could be heard as Taira, Reava, and Gabriel made their way to the door. They took in the state of the room; the smoking remains of the rug and the broken window.

"What happened here?" Reava asked with a low whistle. Sorcha raised a hand.

"Who were those people? And don't even bother lying to me," Sorcha said again with a stiff lip. Sanaa and August looked at one another and then looked to Taira. She sighed and slapped her hands against her legs.

"This is something that you are going to have to sit down and listen to. I need to go get Vorus," Taira said. The woman looked like she aged considerably when she said those words. She turned and left the doorway, leaving Sanaa and August with the Sorcha.

Sorcha walked over to her bed and sat down with

elegance. She tossed her hair over her shoulder and stared down at both Sanaa and August with a smile that seemed more like a baring of teeth. Sanaa felt her body tense at the action.

"Please," she drawled, "tell me everything."

# PART THREE
# CATACLYSM

# Chapter Thirty

❦

"So you mean to tell me that we are possibly dealing with a Husk rebellion on our hands?" Sorcha leaned back. They were still in the remnants of Sorcha's destroyed room. Taira was closer to the door, but it was being barricaded with Reava and Gabriel's bodies.

Any chance that she got her eyes darted to the door and her hands twitched. The empress's stare was heavy. Every look that she delivered in their direction compounded on one another, each look growing more and more weighty until Taira could feel her knees tremble underneath the pressure. Sanaa and August looked as though they were faring better than her.

They each looked like they could not feel the weight of the empress's stare and Taira wished that she could be like them and feel nothing. The two of them looked at the empress and stood at attention with their hands behind their back and their feet spread apart. Taira wondered at how Sanaa was doing it littered with wounds that she was.

"No, not exactly, I placed an edict—" Vorus started, but the empress was quick to cut him off.

"Your edict did nothing but stem the flow of Husks to the group. It did nothing to solve the problem," Sorcha said. The empress was lounging on her bed now, she did not seem to mind the stiff breeze that was coming in from the window, though Taira shivered with every buffet.

"Well, we found that the temple of Roux was working with them—"

"You found this. You found that. All I hear is a lot of discovery and not enough action," Sorcha said with a hard look at Vorus. "Get to the part of the story when you do something about all this."

Vorus and the rest of them all fell silent at that. Taira shifted her weight from one foot to the other. Sorcha raised her eyebrows and looked from one side to the other.

"Oh wait. Do you mean to tell me that you have done nothing in the time since you discovered a rouge group of Husks were squatting in the caves? You haven't done a single thing to stop them?" Sorcha rolled her eyes and shared a look with Reava. "Men."

"Only good for one thing, I say," Reava replied. Taira placed her hands behind her back and began to play with her fingers. What had they done to deal with the husks in the caves? Nothing. They had not done a thing let alone deal with the siren that they had to kill.

"Where are the people who had been affected by the siren?" Sorcha asked, rising from the bed.

"They are in the basement dungeon," Vorus replied.

"Show them to me," Sorcha said, shrugging on a robe. Reava and Gabriel moved aside from the door and Vorus led them throughout the house. It was a long walk from the empress's room to the dungeon and the whole time Taira could not help but play with her fingers and hope that the empress did not level her gaze at her.

The voices in her head were quiet now, silent in their

mutterings and murmurings and Taira wished that they would speak up so that her thoughts were not the only thing that she had to listen to.

They descended the steps to the dungeon and Taira went for the wall, digging her hands into the dirt of the wall and allowed her powers to surge into the tree. There was a loud groan as the roots lifted to let some of the moonlight in and Taira let out a gasp when she looked out to the cages.

All the cages were hanging ajar. Their thorny doors hanging open with none of the Fae inside. Taira willed the tree to listen to her and bring back even the oldest of the prisoners, but they were all gone.

"What happened to them all?" Sanaa said. She walked a little farther in, her eyes wide like what she was seeing was a mirage. Taira dislodged her hands from the dirt wall and looked around. All the cages where they kept those affected by the siren were empty.

Taira turned to Vorus and she could see the temper smoldering in his eyes, but then like a magnet her eyes were brought to the empress. Her face was cool and Taira could glean nothing from her expression. The empress simply nodded her head and turned to Vorus who was standing by her side.

*THWACK!*

Sorcha landed a fierce slap on his face that set his head-turning. Taira felt a gasp get stuck in her throat. In all her years working with and for Vorus she had never seen him get physically reprimanded before. He was also so crafty and sly that he always avoided punishment.

Time seemed to freeze at that moment and Taira brought her hands out in front of her, her fingers laced together.

"You are a fool," Sorcha hissed through her teeth. "An absolute fool! You couldn't deal with one simple threat and now look what it has spiraled into. You had one task. One job that you needed to achieve and you couldn't even do that much!"

A gasp went up and everyone turned their eyes to Sanaa. Her face was bright and open, something was dawning upon her.

"The prisoners. They were the Hollow Ones that the temple of Roux was waiting on. They were already in a constant state of hollowing themselves with their constant screaming and now they have them," Sanaa said, putting the pieces together.

Sorcha clapped her hands. "Thank the gods above that you finally figured that much out. Where would we be without you?"

Taira turned her eyes to Sorcha and noticed that the empress looked duller than usual. Her ringlets weren't perfectly coiffed making her hair loose and wavy and her glowing amber eyes were a muddy orange color. Sorcha turned her gaze to Taira.

"What about you? Do you have any idea about these shadow bandits?" Taira sent her gaze back down to her fingers and shook her head. Sorcha nodded and turned her gaze to Sanaa again. "Any other enlightening epiphanies?"

"No," Sanaa replied.

"Good. I came here to make sure that trade was running smoothly between us and the lycans on the other side of the mountain. Now I have to deal with a possible uprising from Husks. Husks of all things," Sorcha muttered to herself. She turned and pulled her robe tighter around her frame.

"Come. Now I'll make sure that these Husks are dealt with," Sorcha said. She turned and marched up the steps out of the dungeon. Reava and Gabriel followed after her.

Taira walked over to Vorus. She reached out a hand but Vorus slapped it away, his hand pressed against his cheek.

Taira looked up at the shadow that the empress cast and then she could hear the voices muttering in her ears.

"*Get her! While she is still weak!*" The voices muttered in her ear. She was tempted to listen to them. She wanted to lash out with all her power to the empress and put an end to her reign right then and there, but she was right. They had done nothing to deal with the rise of the Husks in the caves or deal with the siren.

Taira followed the empress up the steps and out of the dungeon. Sorcha walked into the dining room and cleared the table. She snapped her fingers and a maid was by her side.

"Bring me a map of the caverns below the mountains," Sorcha said without even looking at the maid. The maid scurried off the find the map, and Taira marveled at the way that the empress held herself. Though she was shorter than Taira, the empress seemed to be the tallest person in the room.

The maid returned with the map in a matter of moments. And Sorcha rolled out the map, placing candelabras to hold down the corners. Sanaa and August came up on the other side of the table to look at the map and Taira dared to come closer. Vorus stood listlessly by the door.

"August, you said that you possessed one of the people that worked for this Nova person right?" Reava asked as she looked down at the map. August nodded his head. "Can you tell us where they were hiding?"

"No, my soul was cast out. Violently at that, I barely made it back to my body as it is," August said.

"And what about when they carried you to their hideout?" Gabriel asked.

"I had to pretend to be asleep as to not alert them to the possession," August added. Gabriel shook his head and looked down at the map again.

"So we know nothing about where this enemy is located," Reava sighed out. Sorcha held up a hand and pointed.

"We do know that they have to be close to the path that the shipment travels on. How else would they use the materials from their raids? They have to be living in one of the caves closest to the route," Sorcha said.

"You're right. They would have to be close by to keep watch over the route and then alert the others when they see a shipment coming through. Now it is just a matter of finding a cavern big enough to house them all," Reava muttered.

Taira looked down at the map, her eyes scanning over the caverns on the map. She pointed out to one.

"This one may be big enough to hold them all," Taira said. Her eyes flickered up to Sorcha and Reava before returning to the paper. "This one is big enough to hold all of them and it isn't too far away from the route used to trade with the lycans."

Sorcha looked over the place that Taira was pointing to on the map and nodded her head. "Fine, the three of you will head there tonight with the Imperial Guard there to make sure that everything goes the way that it should."

Taira's eyes widened, "Tonight?"

"Yes, tonight. What better time to strike then when they are least expecting us to attack them back?" Sorcha said with a toss of her hair. "They probably think that we are still reeling from my attempted kidnapping and the loss of all the people in the dungeon. They would never see us coming."

"But walking through the town at night with the Imperial Guard will cause some concern. One of the things that we have done is keep the citizen concern low and—"

"The citizens should be afraid," Reava said with a slap against the table. "The citizens should be shaking with fear. Do you know what will happen should we fail here tonight. Thousands of Husks will flee to this Nova person in droves and use her abilities to gain some power. The Husks out match us five to one. Do you think that this is a war that we can win? That anyone in Ettrea can win?"

Taira fell silent. She knew that what they were going up against was something important. She knew that the Husks were outmatching them but she had never thought of this issue as something that was uniquely Fae in nature. She had never thought of it as something that could spread outside the borders of the Spring Court.

"You have done a commendable job in keeping the peace of Asren together. But this is something that needs action and immediately," Sorcha said, her eyes scanning over them. "But what we need now is action and not keeping the peace." With a spin of her heel, Sorcha began to saunter out of the room, her commands delivered. Reava and Gabriel trailed out behind her. "You leave within the hour," were her parting words.

Vorus still stood by the door, holding his cheek. Taira turned to him and looked at him with wide eyes. She gestured to the table.

"You're okay with this?" Taira asked. Vorus stood by the door without so much as a word to say. Taira stalked over to Vorus. "The peace of Asren that you tried so hard to preserve is now being defiled. We are being sent out within the hour to take out the bandits and the Imperial Guard will be marching through your town tonight. Don't you have anything to say about this?"

Vorus still kept quiet. His eyes not wavering from their place on the floor. Taira shook her head and stormed out of the dining room. Vorus had nothing to say and could do nothing, so what was she expecting from him. The empress had already made her decision and it was going to be carried out whether she liked it or not.

# Chapter Thirty-One

❧❀❧

The Imperial Guard was roused easily enough. They stood at attention in the foyer of the house. Their boots mucking up the polished marble of the floor. August looked down at them from his vantage point on the stairs. He was already dressed for battle, his clothing changed out for the worn leather armor that he wore. Sanaa came up beside him, her eyes roving over the Imperial guards and their white and gold armor.

"This is going to cause some problems for the people of Asren. They're going to wonder why the Imperial guard is marching through their town at night," Sanaa said as she looked down at the guards. August shrugged his shoulders.

"Reava and Sorcha are right. We have to do more than try to discover everything that our enemy is doing. We need action," August said.

"It is foolish to head into battle without knowing what your enemy can do."

"It is even more foolish to allow your enemy to recruit more and more people to their side. What Sorcha and Reava are doing is making sure that there is action. We need decisive action. And they are providing that."

Sanaa raised an eyebrow at his words, but August kept his eyes on the Imperial guard. "Since when have you been someone who followed the rules of others?"

"I'm not. I want this to be done as soon as possible. Don't you?"

Sanaa got that look on her face then, the one that let August know that she was thinking of her family. She sighed and shook her head. August turned his eyes away from her and back towards the Imperial Guard.

Sorcha came out of one of the rooms with Reava and walked down the center of the stairs. She looked out around the Imperial Guards and clapped her hands. The sound made everyone fall silent and August even held in his breath. Sorcha's back was straight and her hair was perfectly coiled once again and she was in a simple black dress.

August looked her over again, examining her features, and could find nothing of the hints of Helia that he saw in her face. Her eyes were a burnt amber color and she took her time to look over each guard that was in her presence.

"I know you are all wondering why you have been called here. In the middle of the night when you should be warm in your beds, awaiting the next day to begin," Sorcha started. "Well, I am here to tell you that you have been brought here tonight to deal with a threat not just to the Spring Court but to all Ettrea. You have been called to destroy a rebellion that threatens all of us. A Husk rebellion."

The crowd of guards descended into a flurry of shouts of disgust and general malcontent. August felt his hands tighten around the banister that he was leaning forward on. Some of the guards even dared to laugh, the thought of Husk rising up against them was so ludicrous to them that they could not fathom it.

Sorcha quieted them all with a wave of her hands. "I know that the thought sounds ludicrous. The very thought of Husks, of mortals rising up against us, is something that you all may have never even dreamed of happening. But I am here to tell you that this is the reality that we face. That Husks are rising against us and they have power behind them."

Another round of gasps and general astonishment went up. August turned to look at Sanaa who was stone-faced. "Wait until they hear about the shadow magic that they use," August whispered to Sanaa. She cracked a smile.

"Yes, they have somehow gained power and plan to use that to erase the rest of us from the map. They plan to go into every home here in Asren and slaughter us. They tried to kidnap me, your empress."

The crowd reeled back at the admission and Sorcha nodded her head as they descended into angry mutterings and murmurings.

"Luckily I was able to get away with the help of others. But they have plans to murder every person here in the town of Asren. And do you think they are going to stop there? No! They have plans to convert more Husks to their side and kill all of the Spring Court and then the Light Court and then the Imperial Court and all of Ettrea. If we do not stop this terror they will extinguish our light from the map. Do you want that?"

A resounding no was heard in the foyer and each guard stood at attention, their hands grasping their swords and spears.

"Then do this for your empress! Kill them before they kill us. Free us from this scourge and return heroes!"

The guards unsheathed their swords and a cheer rang out in the room. Sorcha smiled and she looked like she was basking in their cheers and praise. August clapped his hands and Sanaa sent him a questioning look.

"What? It was a very convincing speech," was all that he said. Sanaa shifted from one foot to the other.

"How are your wounds?" August thought to ask. Sanaa shrugged her shoulders.

"As good as they can be. I'm wrapped tightly under these leathers," Sanaa said.

Taira walked up to them, with her hands fists at her side. August greeted her with a wide smile.

"You missed a riveting speech," August said. But Taira did not stop to converse with them. She marched down the stairs and went straight to Sorcha. August and Sanaa followed after her. They were more cautious in approaching the empress than Taira was.

"I want to be in charge of this expedition," Taira said with her chest out. Taira stood to her full height and loomed over the empress, but Sorcha looked at her with still water eyes.

"No, you've had your chance to deal with this. My guards will be in charge of this one," Sorcha said with a toss of her hair. Taira's face grew red, but she did not relent.

"Unless your guards know all the hiding places and where that cavern is exactly then they shouldn't be the one leading this expedition," Taira said with a smirk on her face.

Sorcha rolled her eyes and sighed, her shoulders sagging with the action and making her look very un-empress-like. She snapped her fingers and one of the guards was by her side. His white and gold armor was polished and shone in the candlelight.

"Yes, Your Imperial Majesty?" He asked on a bent knee. Sorcha did not even bother to look at him, her eyes trained and narrowed in on Taira who stared back defiantly. Taira looked down at Sorcha and green eyes trained on the burnt orange eyes and they stared one another down. Sorcha sniffed and turned her head to look at the guard who was still bent over before her.

"You are in charge of the assault but the reconnaissance will be under Taira's jurisdiction. Is that understood Captain?" Sorcha wrapped her shawl tighter around her shoulders.

"Of course, Your Imperial Majesty." He nodded. Sanaa and August shared a look and Taira straightened up her back and turned to look at the both of them.

"Well come on, we don't have all night," Taira said. Taira headed for the door and August and Sanaa had to run to catch up with her. Sanaa shook her head.

"You were foolish to approach the empress like that. What would you have done if she decided not to give you the charge that you wanted?"

"Oh she was going to give it to me," Taira said with every bit of confidence. August raised a brow at that. Though he was not a Fae he still feared the small empress. She was powerful. All the more reason to stay out of her way.

"And how do you know this?"

"Because she had an image to uphold," was all that Taira said. Sanaa sent August a look, begging to understand what was going through Taira's head, but he was as much for a loss as she was.

They stood outside as the guard began to trickle out of Vorus's home. Their shining armor made them beacons in the night and it was with a loud shout that they were sent marching down through the center of Asren.

The guards marched perfectly in time together, they trampled every flower and knocked overhanging fruits with ease. August, Taira, and Sanaa led the charge as they marched to the caves.

As they marched, August caught people looking out the window and hiding behind the shutters to stare out at them. The people of Asren were scared that the Imperial Guard had been set loose on the town. And they should be scared.

When they made it to the mouth of the caves, Taira stopped in front of them making the Imperial guard stop behind her.

"Let's go inside," one of the Captains said gesturing to the mouth of the cave.

"No," Taira said with a shake of her head. "They would hear all of us coming if we all went inside. Let me, Sanaa, and August go into the caves first and tell you how many to expect, and then you can go in after us."

August found himself blustering at her words. "Who cares if they hear us coming? We have the Imperial Guard behind us. Let's slaughter them all!"

"No, if we are going to do this, we are doing this my way." August stared and could feel the weight of her stare. He stared back defiantly. Before the tension could rise, Sanaa inserted herself between them.

"Let's bring a small group of guards with us. The rest of the guard can wait in the cave on the route so that when they hear the sound of fighting they know to come to us," Sanaa said in a cool tone. August took his eyes off Taira but nodded his head.

"Fine," Taira said. Sanaa nodded her head and they entered the caves. They guided the guards through the route that was usually taken when trade commenced. August knew they stopped in the exact place where they had been ambushed before because the carts were still there, though now they were empty.

"You can wait here. We shouldn't be too far. If you hear any fighting, then come in after us," Taira said with a nod of her head. She chose five guards who shed their heavy clanking armor. They climbed the slope to get into the tunnel that would lead them to Nova and her shadow bandits.

They crept along, stopping when they thought they heard something. They continued to creep through the caves until they heard the rhythmic beats of drums. August was the first to hear it. With a shushing noise, he quieted the others around him and they listened.

Each beat of the drum was like a heartbeat that they could follow. They followed the tunnel that widened up into a cavern. The cavern was decorated with fire and flames. A big bonfire burned on a makeshift stage and people danced and laughed as they celebrated.

"Over here!" Sanaa gestured to them from behind a gathering of rocks. They rushed to her side and watched as the bonfire and the drumming grew faster and the people dancing around the fire danced quicker, their movements almost becoming a blur. Like last time, every one of them was decorated in the slithering tattoos from before. Though this time there were people in the crowd that were wearing heavy cloaks over their bodies as they mingled with the other guests.

The drumbeat stopped and Nova stepped forward. She was covered from head to toe in the tattoos that she bestowed on the Husks. They slithered and snaked around her body like an odd embrace. Her eyes were still pitch black and they shone in the fire light. She lifted her arms.

"Welcome! Brothers and sisters to the night of our anointing!" Nova shouted.

A cheer went up all around.

"Tonight, we stop dwelling in the darkness and ascend into the light. Tonight we take the first step on our mission to go home!" Nova basked in the cheers for a moment before she spoke again.

"I know that the journey here has been long and hard. And that we have all lost many things, many people, on this journey. But tonight that all changes. Because tonight we will be the ones with power. We will be the ones on top!"

"But for us to do that, we need one more thing. One more person I should say. Bring her out!"

The crowd roared as they rolled out Nox in one of the cages. Her ears were still bloodied and she moaned pathetically at every jostle of the cage. The cage rolled to a stop in front of Nova. The crowd's cheers rivaled that of the drums but Nova silenced them with a wave of her hands.

"Tonight we use what they love against them! We kill them using their gods!" Nox was dragged out of the cage and placed on her knees in front of Nova. Nova placed her hands on Nox's head and closed her eyes.

Nova started to chant. The words were in a language, unlike anything that August had ever heard before. The chant was rhythmic in its song, heavy on grunts and brutal sounds. The necklace that hung around Nova's next began to glow washing the area in a brilliant pink light. The light focused then taking the visage of a woman. It slithered around Nox and Nova's chanting became faster as she held on to Nox's trembling body.

Nox let out one last final scream and the light entered her. Nox sagged forward, her head bent and her body twitching. Nova still chanted over her, gripping the necklace that she had in her hands and that same pink light began to glow in Nox's tired eyes.

Nova finished her chant with a flourish of her arms and turned back to the crowd. "Now, I present to you, Roux! Goddess of Death and the Forgotten."

Nox rose but it was not the trembling form that it was before. It was the rise of a woman assured of her place in the world. Her eyes glowed pink and power sparked at her fingertips. Nox turned her head to Nova and spoke in a voice that was unlike Nox's.

"Who has to awaken me from my resting place in the stars?" Roux asked. Everyone fell to one knee, their heads bent, all except for Nova who stood before her with her head held high.

"I did." Nova held the necklace in her hands showing her the still glowing pendant in her hands. Roux looked down at it and twisted her lips.

"So you have called me. What do you wish for me to do?"

"Roux we are your forgotten people. We have been forgotten, tossed aside, and overlooked our whole lives. We only ask that you help us gain the recognition that we deserve."

August leaned closer then, waiting to hear how Roux would respond but the woman rolled her shoulders.

"You hold my talisman. I am bound to do as you please." Roux tossed her hair over her shoulder. "Rise all of you."

The crowd rose at her words and some in the crowd murmured amongst themselves at her words. Talisman? Bound? August felt his heartbeat like rapid-fire in his chest. Nova was able to summon a god and bound her to her will. How had she found that talisman? Where did it come from?

Taira began to rise from her position, but August snatched her hand and pulled her back down to the rest of them.

"Are you crazy?" He whispered to her. "We are outnumbered and outclassed. You just saw, they were able to conscript a god to their cause. We need to go back and get reinforcements!"

"I will not stand here and allow them to defile everything that we hold dear. Roux is scared and for them to conjure up this mockery... it goes against everything I stand for. I will end this here and now." Taira shrugged off August's hold and marched out into the crowd. August cursed under his breath. He tensed his muscles and prepared to go in after her.

# Chapter Thirty-Two

✿❀✿

"How dare you defile Roux! Have you no shame Nova!" Taira pointed her sword at the woman standing next to the bonfire.

"Oh look if it isn't the town protector," Nova said with a grin. The crowd readied their powers, their hands ready to let the shadows leap from their skin, but Nova stopped them.

"You have no shame! Calling this person Roux. It is a disgrace." Taira spat. Nova's grin grew bigger and bigger with every word. Taira neared closer and closer to Nova. Taira never once let her sword drop. When she was face to face with Nova her sword grazed the woman's neck but the smile never wavered from her lips.

"You don't believe that this is Roux?" Nova said with a smile that would not stop growing. Taira shook her head.

"I believe this as much as I believe that you can take the town of Asren," Taira said with a stiff lip. Nova laughed at her words and the crowd laughed along with her.

They thought that this was funny? They thought that defiling one of the Twelve was something to be amused about. Nova played with her pendant and Taira saw the talisman for the first time.

It was a small bauble, a craved glass figurine that looked like a woman pouring water into a river. It could have been no bigger than the palm of Taira's hand. She looked into the eyes of Nox, the blood still drying on her ears.

"Nox, stop this nonsense."

"I think you need to give her a demonstration of your power Roux," Nova said with a silly grin on her face.

"If that is what you wish," Nox said in that voice that was not her own. It was the light. After that light entered her she had changed. She was no longer that small woman who shivered in the back of her cage, but something more confident and self-assured. It was almost startling how quickly she had changed.

Nox raised a hand to Taira's weapon and flicked her finger against the blade. It gave a small ringing sound and Nox matched the tone with a hum. Then she screamed.

The scream was loud enough to knock Taira back, the air swelling with noise. The sword in her hands shattered into shards of sharp steel. Taira fell back to the ground and covered her ears as the voice rang out the air vibrating with her voice.

Taira looked at her sword after she had finished her scream. Barely the hilt was left, the blade had shattered. She looked to the woman that was standing next to Nova and examined her. She had Nox's matted black hair and her clothing, but that was certainly not Nox. The only person who had the power to shatter swords with their voice was—

"Roux," Taira breathed. Nova laughed and nodded her head.

"Don't you see? You and your little town are doomed. We have the advantage."

Taira felt a stone drop in her stomach. How could they

stand against this assault? Would the reinforcements from the Imperial guard truly be enough?

"Hey, Nova! Watch this!" called a voice.

Taira turned around and watched as August took to the sky his huge wings flapping. He opened his mouth and a stream of hellfire came out. People screamed and tried to dodge the fire that was falling from above. The flames caught on the clothing of one person and they tumbled to the ground, patting away at the flames.

Taira got up from the ground and began to run back to the outcropping of rocks where they were hiding before. Sanaa and the others had already jumped out, their weapons at the ready and killing those who stood in their way. One of the guards tossed Taira another sword and she grabbed it out of the air.

"We need to get back to the reinforcements," Sanaa said when she reached her side. Taira sent a hacking slash to one of the followers of Roux who were in attendance and spun around to slash at another person who was trying to escape.

"No! First we need to get that talisman away from Nova then we can get to the reinforcements," Taira said.

"Get him down from there!" Nova howled, pointing a finger at August.

August weaved through the air, spitting balls of green hellfire wherever he could. The fire spread fast, but people were beginning to gain their bearings. Shadows rose from the plumes of smoke in the air and snapped at August but he maneuvered out the way.

Taira wanted to keep her eyes on August, but a man charged at her with a sword. Their swords beat down against one another with the man pushing Taira back with his impressive strength. The tattoos slithered off his skin and snapped at her like vipers.

Taira backed away but when her back touched the rocks

she knew that she was pinned. The shadows rose trying to snap at her but Taira pushed against the man's monstrous strength.

The tattoos were still snapping at her, but the man was slowly being pushed back. Taira braced her hand against the blade of her sword and with a shout, she dislodged the sword up into the air and out of the man's hands. For a moment she looked confused, surprised with the sudden burst of strength that she had, but Taira wasted no time. She felt the resistance of the sword for a moment and then the sword gave way as it entered the man's stomach.

Blood splattered out of the man's mouth and some fell on Taira's face but she kept pushing. The tattoos seemed to whimper in his hands and then evaporated from his skin. Taira grabbed the sword that the man had dropped and headed back into the fray.

"Stop him! Get him down from there!" Taira turned and saw a line of archers taking their place in one of the few places that August's hellfire had not reached yet.

"No!" Taira shouted. She ran hard, her feet slapping the ground and her swords never stopped moving. She slashed and hacked away at those that tried to get in her way. When she reached the archers they had already nocked their arrows, following August as he zigged and zagged through the air. Taira was on them in a matter of moments.

The air sang as her steel cut through it. She cut down the first archer with ease and then the next. The archers turned their attention to her then, nocking their arrows at her.

The first shot was the easiest one to block. The next that came after was a little harder. Her muscles were screaming at her when she dodged the third. It was the fourth one that got her. The fourth one landed squarely in her thigh and Taira gave a loud howl of pain at the burning that she felt when it entered her skin.

She did not fall to one knee though, she kept her head held high and charged the archer who made the lucky shot. The girl loosed more and more arrows but Taira swiped them out of the air with the strength that her aching muscles could muster. It was with a snap of her fingers, vines sprouted out from the ground, their thorns red like blood. They wrapped around the girl and she dropped her weapon.

Taira wanted to laugh then. They wanted to take over Asren, but they could not even learn the basics of combat. Never drop your weapon, no matter what. Taira gripped the two swords in her hands and plunged them into the girl's chest. She gave a pathetic moan of pain and then her life was extinguished.

She turned to where Nova was standing with her hands wrapped around the babble around her neck. Taira needed to get that talisman away from her. If Nova had it, there was no telling what she could do to the rest of the town.

With August still belching fire above her, she turned her eyes to Nova and what was held in her hands. She limped over as fast as she could. Pain zinged up her spine and her leg ached every time that her foot hit the ground, but she did not stop moving. They needed to win this. This was more important than the paltry pain that she was feeling now.

"The people of Asren should be afraid." The words of Reava rang out in her head. The people of Asren should be afraid. These Husks had powers and could conjure gods. Taira held her swords tighter in her hands until her knuckles turned white.

She charged at Nova with a shout. Roux slid into view and it was with a hum from her throat that her weapons were stopped. The air vibrated but no matter how hard Taira tried she could not move her weapons forward to cleave Nova in two.

Roux hummed another note and her weapons were released from the air after Nova had moved back a few steps.

"Do you think that killing her would be that easy?" Roux asked with a quirked eyebrow.

"I was hoping," was all Taira said. Taira and Roux circled one another. Taira twirled her swords around, loosening her wrists for when she attacked.

The two charged at one another. Every move that Taira made was blocked by a wall of shimmering air, her swords repelled by the sounds that Roux was making deep in her throat.

But Roux was on the defense and Taira could take advantage of that. Taira shouted with every harsh clash of her weapons against the air. She pulled away and charged at her, lunging forward with the point of one sword. As expected Roux hummed low in her throat and then the weapon was blocked by the sound in the air. Taira adjusted her stance with the other sword and sent in whizzing past Roux's ear.

Roux was not expecting that and barely had a moment to move her head. The sword still grazed her cheek and blood slid down her cheek. Roux's eyes grew wide. She brushed her hand against her cheek and when it came away with blood she looked at Taira as if she had done something amazing.

"You hurt me," Roux said. Taira settled into her fighting stance.

"That was the plan," she said, blowing some blonde hair out of her face. Roux began to laugh. She brushed a hand against her cheek again and when it came away with blood yet again, she let out a laugh.

"This is amazing. I haven't felt pain in so long I almost forgot how it could feel," Roux laughed. She turned to Taira smiling bright, backlit by the murder and chaos behind her. "You are going to be so much fun."

The woman launched herself at Taira with a manic grin on

her face that stretched from ear to ear. Taira readied herself to block each blow. Roux shot out her hand and it was like being bombarded with a cacophony of sound and wind. Taira braced herself against the sound, but she could feel herself sliding back inch by inch on the ground.

Taira could barely see a thing in front of her, but when the sound and the wind stopped, Roux was right in front of her. With a smack, Taira was battered with sounds and wind again that knocked her off her feet. Taira was sent spiraling to the ground.

She skidded, her body tumbling against the rocky ground of the cave. Taira groaned as she rose again, her muscles begging her to stay down, but still, she rose.

"Don't you get it? I am a goddess. There is no way that you can defeat me," Roux widened her arms. Taira took in all the madness that was happening around her, from the flames to the battle. They were outnumbered and their opponents even had a goddess on their side.

Taira bit her lip and braced her sword. "Your body is mortal. And that is all I need to know."

Roux let out another laugh and Taira braced for another hit.

# Chapter Thirty-Three

August weaved between plumes of smoke and the snapping shadows that rose from their skin. He felt his stomach burn with heat and tossed out a smattering of flame. It hit a group of people who were charging towards Sanaa and the men that were with her.

Sanaa was holding her own against the followers of Roux and Nova's powered Husks. And Taira... his eyes darted to her form. She was battling against Roux with all the strength that she had, but the goddess was batting her between waves of sound.

August tilted his wings and made his way over to where Taira was. The two were doing battle before the large bonfire that Nova had stood in front of. The cave was a mess of shadows and smoke. August closed his wings and dived head-first into the shadow world.

The shadows were cooler than the world of light. August swam through the shadows and slithered to where Taira was fighting with Roux. She was battered and rising from being thrown into the side of the cave. Nova stood at the side, cheering and laughing away like everything was still amusing to her.

"Finish her Roux!" Nova cheered from a little ways away. August slithered closer to Nova his hand leaving the shadow world to grip Nova's hair. His fingers elongated into claws and he gripped Nova's throat in his hands.

Nova gasped at the touch and August placed his other hand on her shoulder. "Stop. Do not harm her any further or else, Nova's life ends today!" Through the smoke, August saw Roux's head raise and turn in his direction. Her eyes were wide and she took a step in her direction before stopping. August drew a thin line of blood around her throat. When he looked down at Nova she was still smiling, her hands clasped around the talisman that sat squarely on her chest.

"Don't worry about me. Do what you intend to do," Nova said. August pulled back to look at Nova. Could this woman be serious? She was so unconcerned with her life that she would rather Roux keep fighting than save her?

The ground rumbled underneath their feet and August could hear the roar of people over the din of burning. The reinforcements had finally arrived. He gripped his hand around Nova's throat tighter, turning her to look into her eyes.

"The Imperial Guard is here. You have lost," he said to Nova. Nova's smile just grew wider.

"Not yet."

August turned his eyes to Roux and saw that she was stalking towards Taira. She lay on the ground struggling to bring herself to her knees. Roux kicked her hands out from under her and Taira was sent tumbling to the ground.

Roux began to sing then. Her voice was husky and low. It was a bittersweet song of things promised yet never realized. Taira looked on and said nothing.

August touched one of his ears and it came away with

blood. He pulled away from Nova as the song continued. All he could hear was the notes that she sang and he could almost feel the yearning in his heart for the things that he lost.

Something in him was howling, telling him to think of anything else, to stop listening to the song. But as her voice got lower and lower, August found himself straining his ears to catch even a hint of her voice.

It was then that August remembered the words of Vorus. The siren had no song, but a select few could hear her singing. This is what he had meant when he said it. Before while trapped in that talisman Nova had only had access to a small bit go Roux's power. And now all that power was unleashed.

That was the last coherent thought that he had before he was consumed by the song. It washed away everything that he was, all his thoughts and desires, his hopes and fears. All were consumed by the song.

When the song ended, August's hands were flat against his sides. The song was the only thing that he could hear.

Taira stared up at Roux unaffected by her song. Roux frowned and turned away from her.

"Stupid vessels," Roux muttered under her breath. It was with a wave of her hand that a sharp ringing sound rang out and slammed Taira against the opposing wall of the cave.

The song echoed in his mind. His body ached with the desire to hear Roux's voice again. He wanted to hear the low tones of her voice and the ache that the song brought on in him. His muscles tensed when Roux stalked towards him.

Was she going to grace him with a song? Roux stalked closer and took a close look at August. She pressed a hand to his ear and August sagged into the touch. Her hands were so cool against his burning skin. It felt heavenly. She smiled when she pulled her hand away and it came away with blood.

"Well at least I have a new thrall," she said. Nova giggled beside him.

When was she going to sing? Will he finally be able to hear her voice again?

"You have more than one thrall," Nova said. She went somewhere behind the bonfire and August saw cage after cage of people.

A faint shivering part of him knew that he should be concerned, but hearing the song overtook his mind. He needed to hear Roux's song again. He needed to hear her voice in him again.

Nova unlocked the cages and swarms of people were in front of Roux, each clamoring to hear a song from her. Roux gave a laugh that sounded like the notes of a song. It soothed the ache in his chest a small amount but August needed a song, not the opening hints of it.

"Come now my thralls. Destroy my enemies and I will sing for you once again." Without a thought, August unfurled his wings and took to the ceiling. He knew that the ones in the shining armor were not on the side of Roux.

His stomach burned and he reigned down hellfire on them. Some of the Fae reached deep into the Earth bringing forth huge thorns that cut and tangled in the men where they stood.

Roux's enemies were his enemies. He would kill them all for a song.

# Chapter Thirty-Four

W hen the fire hit the reinforcements Sanaa at first thought that it was a mistake. With everything going on and all the smoke and ash that was in the air, she wanted to forgive August for the mistake of attacking their allies. It was when the fire hit them for a second time, that was when Sanaa knew that something was wrong.

The captain shouted for his soldiers to raise their shields when August had another pass over them. Sanaa rushed over to the captain who was huddled under a shield being battered by hellfire.

"What is going on? Why is one of our own attacking us?" The captain asked. Another bout of flame battered against the shields above them and Sanaa took a peek out from under the shield. She could see August's form gliding through the air through the plumes of smoke and ash.

"I don't know why he is attacking us," Sanaa shouted over the din of battle.

"Captain!" A man shouted. "More hostiles incoming."

The ground shook under their feet and vines sprouted

from the ground where they were standing. Sanaa hopped away, but the captain was caught in the vines and the thorns that stuck out of it like serrated blades. Sanaa turned her head and from the smoke, she saw the other prisoners that had disappeared from their cages.

Sanaa looked around and the air shimmered before her. She could see the strings of monyelta before her. She reached out a hand and tugged on the red string. A line of flame shot up between the prisoners and the Imperial guards. Sanaa smiled and looked to the sky again.

August gave another pass and belched out another plume of hellfire. There was no way that the Imperial Guard could fight off the prisoners while taking the onslaught of hellfire that August was raining down on them.

Sanaa braced herself and pulled on the strings she saw before her eyes. The ground trembled and Sanaa jumped as a column of earth rocketed into the sky. She jumped again and another column of earth sprung to catch her feet. Each jump took her higher and higher than the one before and soon Sanaa was in the world of smoke and heat that August was occupying.

Sanaa turned on her column of earth looking for August amidst the smoke. She saw the tip of his wing dip behind a cloud of smoke and she grabbed the silver string of monyelta and pulled with all her might. A great gust of wind spread the smoke and cleared the path for Sanaa to see. But the air was clear.

She turned her head this way and that in hopes of catching sight of him again when hands locked around her waist and she was hoisted higher into the air. Sanaa let out a small scream of surprise, but when she turned her head to see who it was, she saw the mop of black hair that was August.

"Let me go!" She struggled in his hold. She looked up again and noticed the blood against his cheeks. She reached up and wiped some of his hair away from his ear and saw that it was bleeding. Shit.

August smiled down at her with eyes that were blown wide. He tossed her and she slammed against the wall with a grunt. She tumbled to the ground, seeming to hit every rock on the way down. She landed flat on her face, but she was up in a matter of moments.

"August stop! This isn't you! This is all Roux's doing!" Sanaa said. She wanted to be cautious with him, but his hands were already grabbing at a fallen soldier's spear.

"She said that if I kill you, she will sing for me," was all he said before he charged. Dancing with August like this was completely different from the way that they had danced previously. Before the moves were fluid, flowing into one another with ease. Now it was going to a more staccato beat with harsh jabs and quick dodges.

Sanaa wrapped her fingers around the strings of monyelta that tied her to her needles and thrust them forwards. They sang through the air and embedded themselves in August's shoulder. He grunted at the pain and pulled them out. Sanaa pulled at the strings again and the needles glowed red with heat. She tried to attack him again but August blocked each attempted hit.

"I need to hear the song. I need to hear her sing again. And you're in the way!" August charged at her, his spear pointed at Sanaa's stomach. Sanaa danced backward from the hits and the jabs and pulled on another string. The ground rose between them blocking a blow that would have pierced through Sanaa's stomach.

Sanaa pulled on the brown string again and the wall of earth moved forcing August back as it made its advance. Sanaa could breathe if only for a moment. August was enchanted by Roux and there was no way to break it. The banshee was known to create thralls to do her bidding. Sanaa's eyes flickered over to the Imperial Guards.

They were holding their own against the other thralls of Roux, but it seemed that they were not prepared for how little pain they felt. No matter how much they tried to harm them but just kept getting up and kept on charging. They were slowly but surely being pushed back.

How could they win this? It seemed like everything was against them. Fuck, even the gods were against them. Sanaa felt consumed by the battle and the rage, she did not want to be here. She wanted to be with her family again. She would even take being with Mother again over this.

August broke down the wall of earth that had been pushing him back and charged at Sanaa again. She rose from the ground and readied herself for the second onslaught.

August came at her with everything that he had. His movements were fast but reckless. It seemed that August was not thinking out his moves and more desperate to end the battle as fast as possible. Sanaa kept calm and let all her training guide her.

Dodge. Parry. Lunge. It was all coming together. This was a new dance that she was learning, a new rhythm that she was learning the steps to. She spun around August and embedded some of the needles in his thigh. He let out a howl of pain but Sanaa was faster, with a strong push she was able to grab him around the neck and held him close.

"You have to fight this August. You cannot let her control you," Sanaa said. She cried out when August bit at her arm and she released her hold on him. A cry went up and Sanaa spared a glance beside her to see what the cheer was for.

They had broken the ranks of the guards, they were leaving the cave. Sanaa cursed under her breath before August was on her. Pinning her down by her shoulders, August grabbed a rock and slammed it down on her face.

She felt her nose cave inwards at the hit, and her brain was rattled by the action. Her face ached. The first hit though was the only one that was able to land, as August reared back for another hit Sanaa pulled on the sandy-colored string that connected to the rock. The rock turned to sand in August's hand before he could slam it down on her face again.

Sanaa reared up and pushed August down on the ground. With a snap of her fingers on the string of monyelta, the ground rose around August wrapping around him until he was cocooned in a wall of earth. He struggled in vain to get out, but Sanaa's eyes were on Nova and Roux besides her.

The two of them were walking through the broken line. Roux giving quick shouts to clear them a path. Sanaa rose from the ground and grit her jaw.

If she could just get that talisman away from Nova then this would all end and August would be freed from being Roux's thrall.

Sanaa kicked up dirt as she ran with all her strength to catch up with Nova and Roux. Her arms pumping by her side she was so close to reaching Nova. Sanaa's hand grazed her clothing but something slammed into her body.

A man with a crazed smile was atop her. His fists reigned down on Sanaa's chest and she struggled to breathe. Every time her chest wanted to rise to suck in air, the man's fist came down with a hard slam. Sanaa tossed him off of her, panting harshly. The man made to grab her by the ankle but Sanaa pulled on a string of monyelta and a streak of flame rose between them.

Sanaa turned her eyes to the path that Nova and Roux had taken, but the moment was gone. Nova and Roux were gone from where they had been standing. Sanaa sucked in a breath and screamed. She pounded her fist on the ground and let the scream drain out of her.

Of all the times that her luck had to be in Arif's hands!

Sanaa rose from the ground her hand fisted at her sides. The needles flew to her, the strings of monyelta tied tight around her hands they almost burned her. With a wave of her hand, Sanaa lopped off the head of a man that was charging towards her.

In another swift movement, she lopped off another head. Sanaa committed herself to the fight, to this dance. She was untouchable in this moment. She moved through the crowd of thralls and followers. She cut off heads and limbs, her hands never stopped moving, manipulating the needles with brutal waves and slashes.

Several of the thralls and followers had escaped with Roux and Nova. But there were a few left in the cave with them fighting the Imperial Guard. Sanaa finished the last of the thralls and she stood there panting with her hands two tight fists at her side.

She turned back to look at the soldiers. They leaned on one another. Another soldier had his hands on his knees, he was hunched over gasping for breath. They were tired and Sanaa looked down at the body of the captain. He had long since passed on to the Void.

Sanaa climbed onto a rock. "You are all tired. I know you are all tired because I am tired too. We fought valiantly but the work is not done! Nova and Roux have escaped into Asren and plan to harm anyone that they can get their hands on. We have to stop them."

One of the soldiers looked up at her and squinted his eyes. "And who are you? Why should we listen to you?"

The rest of the Imperial Guard agreed with him. They all nodded their heads, their heads drooping down into their chests with the actions.

"I'm no one. You have no reason to listen to me. I am not one to you. But those people in Asren have to mean something to you. They are mothers, fathers, workers, guards, children who hope one day to be part of the Imperial Guard just like you. They have to mean something to you. If that doesn't move you then think about the chaos that they can create when they reach the courts that you all hail from."

"But they have a goddess on their side. How are we supposed to fight against a goddess?" Someone piped up from in the crowd. Sanaa shook her head.

"The gods may be against us this time, but I will take care of that. I have a plan to deal with Roux." A smirk crawled upon her features, but her face ached with pain at her broken nose. "But we must get out of these caves and fight against Nova and her plans. Are you with me?"

The guards raised their swords and cheered. Sanaa let her smirk stretch into a smile. Now she needed to come up with a plan to defeat Roux.

# Chapter Thirty-Five

H er whole body was a pulsating point of pain. Everything hurt her, from breathing to even fluttering her eyes. But Taira grit her teeth and rose from the ground. Her hand slapped against the earth and she rose from the ground with a grunt of effort.

Taira looked up and saw her sword a little ways away from where she was laying and struggled towards it. The cave was practically empty. The only other person that was inside was August who was muttering to himself, held in an earth cocoon.

But where was everyone? The last thing that she remembered was being slammed against the wall and then... nothing everything went black.

Taira's eyes went wide. The only reason that they would abandon the cave was if... Taira ran out the exit of the cave, sword in hand. She charged out of the cave and as she neared the exit of the cave she could hear the din of battle.

When Taira exited the caves all she could see was the fires. Fires consumed the tree houses and the earth was torched. Taira's heart broke as she watched a treehouse crumble in itself.

Taira had done everything she could to keep the people of Asren out of this mess and away from the madness. And in one night all of it was ruined. Taira frowned as she thought of it. The empress, this was all her fault.

"*She did this. You did everything that you could and she ruined it*," a voice muttered in her ear. The voice was right. She and Vorus had done all that they could to keep the peace in Asren and look at it, the city was burning all because the empress thought that she was so smart.

She flapped her wings. She needed to find the empress. She flew through the smoke and the char, her wings never once faltering. She made her way to Vorus's manse. The manse was still standing but the windows were broken. Taira landed in front of the manse and saw one of the maids laying against the stairs of the manse. Taira neared her, but her body had the waxy pallor of death and Taira moved on.

She tiptoed into the manse. It was silent in the house. So quiet that Taira barely dared to breathe in the silence. Taira walked passed the dining room and found no one there, she moved from one wing of the house to the other and found no one there. Where had everyone gone?

A shock rocked the house, shaking everything and knocking Taira to the ground. She soon shot up from the ground and ran to the one place that she had not checked; the gardens.

The gardens were on fire. The rose bushes burned and the tulips were already scorched. Above it, all flew Sorcha. But this Sorcha was not the one that she had left behind earlier that night.

This Sorcha had long jagged black hair instead of perfectly coiled ringlets. Her wings were no longer the shimmering gold instead they were a dark black that looked almost purple in the firelight. Her wings appeared to be covered in a dark sludge that looked like oil but she was flying just fine.

And her eyes, Taira knew that those eyes were going to be a brilliant carmine red instead of the warm amber color that they were before. That was the empress that cursed Cinder. This was the empress that ruined her life.

"*Kill her! Take our power and kill her!*" The voices seemed to coalesce into one voice. Her aches and pains began to ebb away and strength filled her veins. She no longer felt like one pulsating point of pain and anguish. Instead, she was strong, she could feel the muscles bunch together under her skin.

"*Kill her. Get us our revenge!*" The voices said together in her ear. She heeded the words of the voices. Her wings fluttered on her back and Taira shot herself into the sky.

Her wings beat a furious rhythm on her back and though usually going this fast would pain her. But she could feel nothing. Ghost white power glowed at her fingers and Taira shot them out to Sorcha.

The empress was fast though and dodged the hit before it could land on her. She turned her head and her eyes went wide when she took in Taira's form.

"Taira!" Sorcha gasped. "Thank the Twelve that you are here. This imposter claims to be Roux and she has been assaulting me since she came out of the caves. As your empress, I request your help." Sorcha flew a little closer to Taira, her eyes that carmine red color that she knew so well.

Taira could feel her stomach roll at every word that she delivered. How could the empress just sit there and demand that she fight for her? Had she no thought of her citizen's safety? The town was burning around her and all she could think of was herself.

"Brwydr," Taira muttered under her breath. Sorcha looked up at her.

"What?"

"You know we never did have the chance to have our brwydr. Don't you think that it is time that we settled the score?" Taira said, the white power of ghosts lighting up her hands. Sorcha looked at her with a curled lip.

The voices were clamoring in her head. Each one was airing out a grievance, a reason that they hated Sorcha and everything that she stood for. Taira pulled away from the empress, her hands growing cold with the power that the ghosts were pouring into her.

"You cannot think to have the brwydr now. The city is burning! There are Husks assaulting everything that you have worked so hard to protect. You cannot be serious," Sorcha said with a gasp.

To the right of the empress, Taira could make out the form of Roux floating in the air, her arms at the ready to attack. Taira said nothing but simply nodded her head in Roux's direction.

"I intend to have my brwydr. Right now," Taira said. Sorcha opened her mouth to say something else, but Taira did not give her the time to speak.

With a great push, Taira pushed the power out of her hands and two blasts of glowing white power made their way towards Sorcha. Sorcha's eyes widened and she dodged to the side, her large wings beating furiously. Taira and Roux both gave chase after her.

"It appears that we are both working together," Roux said with a flick of her hair over her shoulder.

"Only on this," was all that Taira could answer.

They zoomed through the treetops and the burning branches of trees, Taira never let up her assault sending blast after blast of power out in her direction. Her power bit through everything, leaving a frozen mess where it landed. Sorcha's wings beat fast as she tried to dodge and evade all of their hits.

Roux never once let up with her sounds. With the smallest hum, she capsized a sturdy looking branch and caused it to go tumbling into Sorcha's path. The empress cut through it with a blade of shadow.

Taira narrowed her eyes and beat her wings harder, pulling in front of Roux. She aimed at one of the wings and sent the smallest shot that she could muster to that wing. The hit landed and Sorcha let out a painful screech of pain. She was sent tumbling to the ground. Taira and Roux went diving after her.

Sorcha landed on the ground, feet first, settling into a crouch. Taira settled into the ground next to her with her hands open to send another shot to Sorcha. Sorcha reached back to touch where she was hit and pulled away with her fingers tinged with a black ooze like substance.

Sorcha grit her teeth and stood at the ready. "So you both want me dead? Fine. Let's see who dies first."

Taira settled herself into a crouch, hands splayed at her side, ready for whatever Sorcha could throw at her.

# Chapter Thirty-Six

S anaa could feel her muscles screaming at her. They needed a break; they needed rest. But Sanaa could not help but to keep her body moving. She was escorting people to a safer location and bringing herself to fight against the thralls and followers. Her body needed a break, even she was not made to dance this long. Sanaa found some comfort in the thought that August was being contained in the caves. The likelihood of him getting out and contributing to this havoc was minimal.

Sanaa ran forward grabbing a baby out of the hands of a follower of Roux and slammed her hand into his stomach. It was with a quick twist of her body that she kicked him in the head and sent him sprawling on the ground. She returned the baby to its mother and told the woman to hunker down in the nearest building that wasn't on fire.

With that Sanaa was sent running again, looking for the next person that she could help. Her hands were burned from pulling on the strings of monyelta and her hands ached fiercely with the pounding of her heart. A man cried out as he was brought down by two of the thralls.

Sanaa summoned what little power she still felt within her and pulled on the strings of monyelta. The strings burned through the scabs that had grown around her knuckles. The needles that she favored wobbled in the air as they shot out towards the two thralls that were attacking the man. They zipped around and embedded themselves in their necks, drawing their attention away from the man to the pain.

They screamed and cried out and Sanaa was quick to jump in front of the man. She turned and looked at him. "Run," was all she said as she helped him up and pushed him off.

The thralls ripped the needles out from their necks and turned their eyes to Sanaa. She quickly turned and ran away from the thralls. They gave chase after her. Her feet pounded against the ground. Her feet leading her in the opposite direction that she had seen the man run in.

The blisters that covered her finger popped and burned as she fisted her hands and kept on running. She could hear the thralls chasing after her. Sanaa turned a corner to escape from them but the turn that she took only led her into a smattering of homes with no road leading out.

Sanaa turned around and saw the thralls rushing towards her. She readied herself, the strings of monyelta ready to pull at the needles that she always kept with her. But when she looked down at the boxes where she kept the needles she saw that it was empty. Sanaa looked and saw the thralls nearing her and she sighed.

She never thought that she would die defending a home of the Fae. But she had always known that she would go out in battle. It was fitting for a Batsamasi, it was what she wanted the most. She settled into a fighting stance. If she was to die here, then she would not go without a fight.

The thralls neared and Sanaa readied herself. But before she could, a gust of wind knocked back Sanaa and the thralls. Sanaa turned her eyes upward and saw the large form of a dragon descend from the sky. With a roar, the dragon landed on the ground and breathed fire on the thralls. The thralls did not even have a moment to scream before they were burnt to ash.

The large maroon red dragon turned around to look at Sanaa. Sanaa braced herself for the flame but the dragon only stared at her. Steam began to expel from the dragon's mouth and it grew smaller and smaller. Soon enough what took place of the dragon was the small form of Reava, her red hair shining brilliantly despite all the smoke and ash.

"Reava," Sanaa breathed. She walked over to the woman and the two of them clasped hands. "Where is King Gabriel and Empress Sorcha?"

"Lost them in all the fighting. I'm going to look for Sorcha now but then I saw you and decided to drop in and help," Reava said. Sanaa nodded her head and looked around at the chaos that was reigning in the town of Asren. It had been so peaceful at the start of the night.

"Maybe I could help you find the empress," Sanaa suggested. Reava only nodded her head.

"Please. I can barely see anything with all the smoke and these burning trees," Reava said. A large sound rocked the earth and Sanaa had to grip Reava's shoulder pauldron to make sure that she did not fall. Sanaa and Reava shared a look.

"That has to be her," Reava said with a nod to her head. Sanaa nodded her head in agreement. Reava sighed and tensed her muscles, it was like watching someone grow too big for their skin. The tusks were first with them jutting out of her mouth. The wings were next with them protruding out of her back and curving out around her body. In a matter of moments, Reava was the large red dragon that she was before.

Reava leaned down, allowing Sanaa to clamber up on to

her back. With that, the two of them were off. Sanaa scanned the skyline looking for something that she could say was Sorcha.

A spear of darkness flared up shaking the earth. Sanaa pointed in the direction of the power. "I see something over there!"

With a tip of her wings, they were flying in the direction of the shaking. Spears of pure darkness flared from the ground, each one a harmful spike that Reava had to dodge. Sanaa scanned the ground looking for the source of the power.

"There!" Sanaa pointed to a clearing where she could see people standing. Sounds of battle could be heard from the clearing. Reava hovered over the space and the place where Sanaa had directed them and landed on the ground with a heavy bang.

Sanaa slid off the side of Reava's neck and made her way over to the woman that looked most like Empress Sorcha. "Empress Sorcha?" Sanaa ventured to ask.

When the woman turned, it was Empress Sorcha's face but the coloring was all wrong. Sorcha's hair was not pitch black, but a deep brown color. And her eyes were amber, not this bright vermillion color that Sanaa was seeing.

The empress grabbed her hand and pulled her close. "I don't know how much longer I can hold them off," Sorcha said with a heavy sigh. Sanaa turned to look across the field and saw Taira and Roux standing ready to one another, ready for anything that was coming their way.

Roux she could understand, but why was Taira siding with the enemy? Why was she attacking the queen? Nova stood a little ways behind them both, her face lit up. Sanaa looked at Sorcha and nodded her head. "Don't worry, I'm here to help," Sanaa said.

"Thank the Twelve that you're here," Empress Sorcha

said. With a flick of her wrist, she sent a wave of darkness careening towards her two assailants. They both moved out of the way. Sanaa could see Taira, her eyes were glowing white with power. Sanaa scrambled to return back to Reava. She climbed the scales on the dragon's back and they returned to the skies.

"You know you can't win this right?" Roux floated before the dragon. Her eyes level with Sanaa's own. "We have the advantage and they have a goddess on their side. Do you intend to fight me? Fight the gods?"

"I'm willing to fight whoever I need to to get what I want," Sanaa said.

"And what is it that you want?"

Sanaa thought back to all the things that she had wanted. She wanted to be the daughter that her mother loved. She wanted to be a good example for her nieces. She wanted to be able to grow old with those that she loved by her side as her sisters had done so long ago.

"I want to go home." With that Reava opened her maw and let loose a stream of fire so hot that Sanaa felt the heat from where she sat. It was with a howl of her voice that Roux split the fire in two and forced it to go around her.

Sanaa grabbed at the strings of monyelta in front of her and gathered some of the fire above her head. The strings of monyelta rubbed harsh against her hands and opened blisters on her fingers. Reava snaked around Roux. From the flame above her head, Sanaa sent blast after blast of pure fire to Roux. Roux seemed unaffected by the flame merely tossing them aside when they got close to her.

"We need to get the talisman from Nova," Sanaa shouted over the wind that whistled by. "That is how she is controlling Roux. I need to get it."

Reava only nodded her large hair and continued to fly through the sky. With another roar, Reava reared back and sent a mouthful of flames towards Roux. The woman was unaffected by the attacks and Sanaa sent a ball of fire flying in her direction.

Sanaa turned her eyes downwards looking for Nova amidst the trees and the foliage. Her eyes caught on the glowing form of the talisman that was around Nova's neck. Sanaa narrowed her eyes and readied herself.

"Cover me," Sanaa shouted. Reava shot another mouthful of flame towards Roux, but it blocked as easily as the rest. Sanaa let her body slide off of Reava's massive back.

Sanaa fell through the air as Reava did battle with Roux in the air. Sanaa used the strings of monyelta to anchor herself to the trees. They slowed her descent and when she landed she landed right on top of Nova. Their bodies crashed into one another and Sanaa went for the talisman that glowed at her throat.

She was able to rip the talisman from around her neck. The talisman slid off the leather strap and was sent careening towards the ground away from them.

Sanaa and Nova connected eyes and then they both looked at the talisman. Sanaa pushed down Nova's face and began to rise from the ground. Nova's leg shot out, catching her ankle and sending Sanaa tumbling to the forest floor again. Nova struggled underneath her, her arms reaching out and dragging herself from under Sanaa and towards the talisman. Sanaa reached out and slammed Nova's face into the dirt.

The two of them struggled towards the talisman. Just when one thought that she overcame the other, their advantage would be thwarted. The two inched closer and closer to the talisman. But when Nova sought to claim it, Sanaa reached out, pulling on a string of monyelta. The talisman twitched and jumped from the ground and into Sanaa's waiting hands.

Sanaa pushed off the ground and rose, her hand rising with the talisman. She knew the first thing that she was going to do.

"Stop!" Sanaa's voice rang out. The talisman glowed in her hands, the light growing brighter and brighter as she held it. Roux stopped where she was and held still in the air as Reava's fire brushed past her.

Roux turned her eyes towards Sanaa and descended from the air to where Sanaa was. She looked at Sanaa with a smirk on her face and her arms crossed in front of her.

"And what will you command me to do?" Roux asked as she looked at the talisman. Sanaa panted where she stood. What should she ask for first? She thought of August who was still in the caves and knew what her first request would be.

"Release all these people from your thrall," Sanaa commanded. Roux rolled her eyes and then snapped her fingers. She looked at Sanaa and with a plain look on her face.

"There. It is done," Roux said. "Your next request?"

Sanaa turned her eyes to Sorcha and Taira who were still doing battle in the air. Sorcha blocked a blow from Taira's fists and landed on the ground. Taira landed on the ground after her. Sorcha moved with her hands and a dark lattice formed on either side of Taira, pushing in closer and closer to Taira. "Stop them."

Roux's smirk grew into a smile. She appeared behind Taira and with a quick hit, smacked her into the ground and out of the way of the dark lattice. Taira was sent crashing into the tree line, to where she downed trees and brush alike. Sanaa gasped as she saw the ghost-white glow leave Taira's body and she stayed down.

Roux floated to Sanaa. "I have always hated vessels. They always cause problems," she flicked a piece of hair over her shoulder. "Any more commands?"

Sanaa turned around and looked at Nova who cowered under her gaze. Tears gathered in Nova's eyes as she looked at Sanaa.

"Please. Please don't hurt me." Nova pleaded. "I just want to go home."

Home. Sanaa had been fighting for so long she had almost forgotten why she was doing this. She wanted to be home with her family. She wanted to be with people who loved and cherished her. She wanted the same thing that Nova wanted; she wanted to go home.

"Home," she muttered the word under her breath. Nova nodded her head.

"Please. I just want to go home," Nova said through tears. The whites of Nova's eyes lightened from the pitch black to the white color they should be. Sanaa nodded her hand and her hold slackened on the talisman. Nova struck then.

Her foot raised and knocked the talisman from Sanaa's hands. The talisman went flying through the air and Nova jumped up and caught it in her hands. She sighed when it was back in her hands and Sanaa stared at her hands where the talisman just was.

"I know when to retreat." Nova brought the pink talisman close to her face. "Roux, we're leaving." The whites of Nova's eyes darkened back to the pitch-black color.

"Of course," Roux said walked past Sanaa to hold on to Nova's shoulders. She grabbed the girl and held her tight in her arms.

"Goodbye for now Sanaa," Nova said. The two of them fell backward and a void opened up behind them. It was pure black and nothing could be seen but darkness. The two of them fell in and as quick as the void opened up it was gone.

Sanaa slammed her hand against the tree and let out a small scream of frustration. She had the talisman in her hand and she allowed herself to be distracted by Nova and her pleas for home. Sanaa shouted out as Reava and Sorcha landed next to her.

"Where are Nova and Roux?" Reava asked as soon as she was in her humanoid form. Sanaa shook their head.

"Gone," was all that Sanaa said.

"Well, we have to chase after them!" Reava shouted. But Sorcha held up a hand.

"I need to look after my people. The people of Asren must be scared and tired after tonight. We need to regroup."

Sanaa sighed and turned her eyes to the sky. The blue-black of the night was ebbing away to make way for the pink dawn. It was the start of a new day in Asren.

# Chapter Thirty-Seven

ugust came to in a bedroll. He opened his eyes and found himself in the bed of the infirmary in Asren. He rose from the bed with his back and head aching something fierce. He turned his eyes to the light but even that was too much for him. He raised a hand to block the light.

August closed his eyes and took a moment to breathe. In, out, in, out. He could feel the air whistling through his chest and it was the steady beats of his heart that brought him back to himself. He could scarcely remember what happened before he woke up in the infirmary. He breathed out through his mouth and tried to pull his thoughts together.

He was in the infirmary that much he knew as he saw the sigil of Asren stamped everywhere. But what happened before that? The night before he was fighting with Roux and Nova. He was fighting them because they were making designs to attack the town of Asren. And then... From there, his memories became a blank void. He could remember no more.

August opened his eyes and tried to rise from the bed. He

needed to find the others. He needed to know what happened. Sanaa and Taira would know what happened in the caves. He tried to rise from the bed, but his legs shook and he fell forward on a vacant bed. He gripped the sheets and used the bed to gather his strength and try again.

This time with the support of the bed, August was able to put one foot in front of the other. His steps were shaky, but he was moving. Someone opened the door and the healer looked alarmed to see him up. The healer rushed to his side, helping to support August's weight.

"You shouldn't be up. You need more rest," the healer said with a gasp of surprise. He tried to turn August around, but August refused to be moved. He planted his feet into the ground and gripped the bed with all his might, paltry that it was. The healer was able to turn him slightly but he was unmoved.

"I need to speak with Empress Sorcha and the town guardian, Taira. I have business with them." August said. He took another step forward and the healer let go of his clothing.

"Fine. I can see that you are set on this. Let me get you a cane." The healer turned and grabbed something from under one of the beds and pulled out a gnarled piece of wood. He handed August the cane and August tried it out with a step or two. The cane was something that he did not want to be seen with, but there was no way that he was going to be able to walk on his own.

He set off, walking out of the infirmary and into the hallway of Vorus's manse. The manse was in a state of total disarray. Maids and servants flew from one side to the other, everyone trying to tidy the manse into its previous grandeur. The windows were fixed and a servant was sweeping up the dust and debris on the floor. Though August had been asleep for some time, he could only imagine the havoc that Nova and her followers were able to enact.

Hobbling as fast as he could, August took in the manse that was being reconstructed in front of his very eyes. He looked out one of the windows and saw that gardeners were hard at work pulling out the old weeds and planting new saplings. August moved on. The foyer was already clean and restored to its former glory. It seemed that the outlying wings of the manse were the ones that needed restoring. August crept down the stairs and could hear voices coming from the dining room. He crept closer and could hear the voice of Sorcha pouring through.

"-armies. I need to rally the council and make sure that our defenses are fortified."

"I should alert all the other dragons." August heard Reava's voice say. "We should all be at the ready for when she decides to strike again."

"August?" A hand touched his shoulder and August jumped at the touch. He whirled around and saw that Sanaa was behind him. Her hands were wrapped in gauze and her braids were pulled back into a top knot on her head. Her eyes were soft as she looked at him. "You're awake."

"Yeah, and I can barely remember a thing that happened," August said with a cut of his eyes to the door. Sanaa looked at the door.

"Maybe we should go inside," Sanaa nodded her head to the door. August pulled the door open and gasped at what he saw. Sorcha had long straight black hair, and with her were those eyes, the same vivid red color that he stared into adoringly when they were in bed together.

"Helia," he breathed. Sorcha looked up at him and a smile made its way onto her features.

"You know I always wanted to tell you, but this. Well, I could not have imagined a better way to tell you."

"Then the Brownie brothers, the rebellion in the Summer Court—"

"All failed because of me. Because they were threats to my rule." Sorcha said. "Besides who better than to unite against than some faceless vigilante."

August felt like the floor had fallen out from under him. The whole time, Helia had been the Empress or the Empress had been moonlighting as Helia. August felt his stomach drop. They were never going to face the empress, everything that she had ever done. It was all a ploy. They were pieces for her to use and dispose of.

"Now, if you are ready to speak about more important matters then sit," Sorcha said. August's mind was whirring but he took a seat next to Sanaa.

"Nova got away and she has Roux's talisman with her," Sorcha said with a look like storm clouds. Sanaa bowed her head and August's mouth dropped open.

"How did she get away?" He asked.

"That is not important. The fact is that she got away and she got away with Roux still under her control."

"If there is one talisman that can control a goddess we must assume that there is more," Gabriel piped up from his seat. August flicked his head to the side and saw the King of the Spring Fae sitting there looking unruffled. His clothing was impeccable while everyone looked distraught with their clothing in various forms of disarray.

"Do you think that she must be going after the rest of them?" Reava arched a brow.

"Without a doubt. What better way to bring us all down than with the Twelve Gods of Ettrea. It only makes sense," Gabriel nodded his head. Sorcha let out a string of curses and slammed her hands on the table.

"The last thing that we need is the Twelve aiding Nova in her plans to harm the rest of us," Sorcha slapped her hands down to the maps on the table before her. "I think we are going to have to enlist soldiers to search for the talismans."

"Search for the talisman and be on the lookout for Nova? That is a lot of work you are going to put on the Imperial Army," Reava said with a look at her map.

"They can handle it."

Sanaa cleared her throat and Sorcha and Reava's eyes snapped away from the maps and letters on the table to land on her. She shifted in her seat a little bit, but then straightened her back.

"May I ask what is going to happen to Taira?" She said with confidence. What happened to Taira? August felt his mind whirring as he thought up what could be wrong with Taira, but his mind was drawing a blank. He tightened his hands into fists.

Sorcha let an oily smile slip onto her lips. At that moment she looked more like Helia than he even remembered and his heart stuttered in his chest. Sorcha crossed her arms over her chest.

"Why don't we go see her?" Sorcha said in a low tone. Sanaa rose from the chair and August grabbed his cane and rose too. The three of them left the dining room at a leisurely pace. Sorcha opened the door to the dungeon below and August felt his eyebrows raise. Why was Taira being kept in the dungeons?

They walked down the stairs and into the dungeon. There were no other people other than one trapped in the cage above. Sorcha dug in hands into the dirt wall beside her and the tree moaned as the roots shifted. The lone cage lowered down to the ground and a head of blonde hair shifted and Taira looked up.

"What is this?" August asked as he watched Taira rise from her corner of the cage. Sorcha came close to the cage and knocked her hand against it.

"This is what happens when you try and kill your empress," Sorcha said with a grin on her face.

"I can still kill you if that is what you want," Taira muttered from inside the cage. Sanaa nodded her head.

"What do you intend to do to her?" Sanaa asked.

"Well, she tried to kill me because I cursed her lover a long time ago. So I've decided I'm going to lift the curse." Sorcha examined the edges of her hair.

"That is very giving of you," Sanaa said with a twist of her lips. Taira looked on with her mouth dropped open in surprise. August felt something akin to pity rise within him. He understood Sorcha and her fickle moods. This was a blessing as much as it was a curse. Sorcha opened the cage and allowed Taira to walk out.

"And you," Sorcha turned her eyes towards Sanaa. "You hesitated."

"Me?" Sanaa asked with a tilt to her head.

"Yes. You had your chance. You could have killed Nova the moment that she was cowering on the ground there, but you hesitated." Darkness coalesced in Sorcha's hands and August took a step back, knowing that Sorcha was about to do.

"That is preposterous," Sanaa said with a shake of her head. But Sorcha was quick. With a clenched fist she launched forward and landed a strong strike to Sanaa's midsection. Sanaa doubled over in pain and August could see the darkness slipping inside of her.

Sanaa coughed and Sorcha retracted her hand, shaking it out. "There. That will make sure that you don't hesitate at all next time."

Sanaa coughed, "What have you done to me?"

"I left a little bit of my power in you. Make sure that next time you have the chance to end somebody you take it."

August leaned over and patted her back. When he made

the deal with Helia the same thing happened to him. He knew what she must be feeling right now. Like ice was sinking into her body.

Sorcha let out a laugh and clapped her hands. "You all will be coming back with me to the Imperial Court. I need to plan and you will need to be a part of that."

Sanaa reared back and shook her head. "No. I need to go home. I was hired to deal with the siren and the siren has been dealt with and—" Sanaa let out a horrifying scream. It ripped straight out of her vocal cords and August reared back when he heard the sound. Sanaa collapsed onto her hands and knees panting to gather her breath.

"You see as an empress, no one has ever told me no before. And today will not be that day. You are coming with me to the Imperial Court. We need to fight off this Husk threat and we are doing it together," Sorcha said. She patted Sanaa's head and made her way to the stairs. "We leave tomorrow." And with that, she was gone, headed up the stairs and away from them all.

The three of them stood in the remnants of Sorcha's action each one of them not knowing what to do next. But August was not going to let it end there. With a great mustering of all his strength, August hobbled after the Empress, his brow furrowed.

He chased after her, with all the determination of a man on a mission. He caught Helia or should he say Sorcha, a little way away from the entrance of the dungeon. He grabbed her arm and whirled her around. With one hand gripping his cane and the other gripping the forearm of the empress, he knew the striking position that he had put himself in.

He didn't care.

He pulled the empress close to his face so that the two of them were nose to nose and he hissed, "You lied to me."

Sorcha pulled herself out of his arms, slapping away the

hand that had dared to reach out for her. "And what, pray tell, did I lie to you about? I lie about many things."

"I swore oath to Helia and Helia alone. Our deal is off!" August growled. Everything felt like it had been unmoored. The world that he knew was tilted and sliding and August could fine no purchase to hold himself. Sorcha cut those muddied eyes to him. They were no longer the brilliant carmine red or the soft amber, they were a muddy orange color. And in-between state just like she was now.

"You swore an oath to Helia and any face that she may wear. You swore an oath to me," Sorcha said while looking at her nails. "You can still feel it can't you. My power resting inside of you," she walked closer, "You will always be under my thrall."

August pulled away from her with a sneer. His stomach was rolling, he felt the heat of hellfire in his veins at the very thought of Sorcha burned him.

"You lied to all of us. Not just to me, but to Luz, and the people who follow you. You are lying to all of us! Have you no shame! We all believed in you. We all trusted you. And you would march us to our graves for what."

"All in the name of the Empire of the Fae," Sorcha said, not even bothering to look up from examining her nails. "If I have to create some fake threat in order to keep them on their toes and make sure that everything runs smoothly in the Empire then so be it." Sorcha looked up from her nails and leveled August with a stare that he had only ever seen on Helia's face. Sorcha with her one black wing and one gold wing, looked nothing like the woman who he had spent many nights with.

Sorcha's lips ticked up in a smirk. "Were you worried? Is that what this is? Were you worried that I would have left you to be captured by some wandering guard." She stepped closer to August again. She was so close that August could smell the perfume that she wore, something sweet and cloying. The scent was stuck on his tongue.

"I would have never left some who fucks as good as you do to hang. No need to worry," Sorcha said in that husky tone. If she was Helia that tone would have been one that sent shivers down his spine and would have him dragging her to their bed. Now it made his stomach turn.

"Our deal is off," August bit out.

Sorcha's face turned sour and she pulled away from him then. Her lips turned down in a frown. "You want to go back to the way you were before. Cursed by your own family and half dead. You want to go back to that? I've given you a place to rest and a sense of purpose. You should be grateful to me. The deal stays."

With that Sorcha turned on her heel and walked away leaving August with only the disgust and shame that came with broken promises.

# Chapter Thirty-Eight

She could scarcely breathe as she stood in front of the door. She never dreamed that there would be a moment where she could stand in front of the door to open it, but here she was. Taira's hands were fidgeting at her sides as she stared at the door.

The door seemed to loom in front of her, growing larger and larger with every breath that she took. Sorcha said that she would remove the curse, that Cinder would be okay. That she would be able to see and speak once again. Taira placed her hand on the doorknob.

What would she say? The thought rose inside of her unbidden. It had been so long since she had heard Cinder's voice and it had been so long since the two of them have spoken. What would she say to her after everything that she had been through because of the curse? Would Cinder be able to talk considering everything that she had been through? Taira shook her head.

She needed to enter and see Cinder. She needed to feel the woman in her arms again and be with her. Being with

Cinder again would bring all the clarity that she needed. She gripped the doorknob and twisted it.

Taira pushed the door open. The room was modest though dirty. Everything was covered with a layer of dust. Taira's wings fluttered behind her as she took it all in. On the bed sitting up was Cinder. Her hair was long and dark like night, her eyes were a beautiful blue that made her heart stutter in her chest.

Cinder's soft features made Taira's heart melt in her chest and Taira could not hold back the tears. She ran into the room and brought Cinder into her arms. The tears were running down her face and she laughed as she felt Cinder, solid, and there in her arms.

Taira laughed and pulled away to cup Cinder's face in her hands. "Look at you. Look at you."

She pressed a kiss to her lips and pulled away to rest their foreheads together. This is what she had been fighting for. For so long she had fought and strived for this moment and now it was finally here. Taira opened her eyes to see Cinder still had her eyes open.

Cinder's eyes were wide and she was shivering in her spot. Cinder was gripping the bed sheets tight in her hands that her knuckles were going white. She looked at Taira with eyes that showed nothing but abject horror.

"Please... please don't hurt me," Cinder whispered under her breath. Taira felt her stomach drop. "P-please don't hurt me."

Taira fisted her hands in the bedsheets. She shrunk back from Cinder laughing lightly at the words.

"I would never hurt you," Taira tried, but when she made to touch her again Cinder shrunk back from her hand. Taira let out a laugh.

She knew that this was too good to be true. Sorcha always had to give you something that you wanted and take away something that you didn't know you valued. Taira rose from the bed with her hands fisted tight at her side. Cinder shrugged away from the action, but Taira paid her no mind. She stalked out of the room and into the hallway.

Sorcha always found a way to twist the knife.

The air was stirred by a light breeze that ruffled the air. Sanaa welcomed the breeze as she sat down on the lawn in front of the manse. Vorus was off looking for new pieces to decorate his home and Taira was off doing something to a similar degree, she assumed.

Sanaa looked down at her bandaged hands and sighed. She had fought so hard that night. The power had burned her hands and caused blisters to pop up. Her hands still ached despite her doing nothing. It would be a while until she would be able to dance again.

"You won't be practicing your sword dance for a while," a voice piped up from behind her. Sanaa turned around and spotted August as he neared her. He sat down beside her and gave a pointed look to her hands. "Do they hurt?"

"They ache. Even when I'm not doing something my hands ache a lot. But they will heal and I'll dance again," Sanaa said turning her eyes to the rebuilding town.

Asren had been dealt a heavy blow by the battle that night. So many trees had been burned down and many had been lost in all the fighting. Sanaa watched as new trees were erected with a snap of their hands. The new trees were not as wide or as tall as the old ones, but surely they would grow with time.

"I'm upset that I missed all the fighting," August said as he looked over the town with her. "I could have helped stop this, but instead I was trapped in the cave under Roux's thrall."

"You couldn't have helped it. Roux is a goddess and I imagine that her power is something that we cannot imagine. You are not at fault here," Sanaa said. She turned her eyes to him and made a point to look into his eyes. "Roux is a goddess and now she walks amongst men. Mother Darkness above that doesn't get easier to say."

"Taira was there too and she didn't fall under her thrall," August said with a pout on his lips.

Sanaa shrugged her shoulders and turned back to the town reforming itself. "From my understanding, Roux said that Taira is something called a vessel. I have no clue what that means, but it made her unable to be controlled."

August nodded his head and the two stayed silent for a few moments. The gods were real, was all that Sanaa could think about. They were real and tangible things that they could interact with and fight. There had always been some small part of her that had distrusted the twelve gods that everyone was so keen on worshipping. She questioned if they were even real or some fiction that they were all following.

But Roux was there in front of her. How was she supposed to deny the existence of the gods now? Sanaa let out a sigh from her nose. The gods were real and they were people that they could fight. The tales were true.

Sanaa flexed her hands and winced at the pain that went zinging up her spine. She knew that the pain would go away but she wished that she could heal faster.

"So we are going to the Imperial Court. Home to the Empress herself," August said as he looked down at his hands.

Sanaa shrugged her shoulders and touched her stomach where she could still feel the remnants of Sorcha's power lingering. It felt like a cold stone was in her stomach.

"Don't worry. You'll get used to it," August said when he saw where her hands were.

"I just want to go home," Sanaa said falling back into the grass. August fell back with her and they stared at the clouds that drifted by. "I did all this just so that I could go home."

"Well think of this as a short vacation from your commander and following orders."

"We'll be following Empress Sorcha's orders."

"Don't think too hard about it."

Sanaa let out a small laugh at that. She did not know what new adventures the world was going to bring her way but nothing was going to stop her from going home and being with her nieces. She was going to leave this thing alive, Sanaa determined. She was going to go home no matter what.

# Acknowledgments

In the nine years that it has taken me to write this book there has come and gone a plethora of people that have helped me to write this book. The first person I would like to thank for helping me write this book is my brother.

Jovi you have been the best sounding board and my biggest supporter. You've helped me through some of the toughest plotholes and you have been there for every iteration of this book. You have been patient and kind and a credit to your faith. Thank you for trusting me with your character and you know that when he finally arrives in the story you will be the first to know.

Next, I have to thank my parents. I told you I could finish a book! But honestly thank you for your support and your investment in me. Thank you for believing that I could become anything I wanted in the world and supporting my vision even when you didn't really understand it yourselves. I know that you are excited to see what I wrote and I hope that what I wrote doesn't disappoint.

To my best friend Leslie, thank you for always laughing with me and listening to me even when you had no interest in what I was saying. And in the time it took for us to become best friends I wrote a book. Ha!

Thank you Arleene and Annette. Who would have thought that two characters that you pitched to me so long ago would end up being the my most favorite characters ever in this story. I love Reava and Sorcha more than I love the whole world of Ettrea and I am so glad that you have entrusted me with these two characters. I hope I do them justice.

I need to thank Ameena, Lindsey, and Jessica. Without your helpful contributions in editing and getting my story together. None of this would be possible. I loved reading your stories and I hope you at least enjoyed reading mine while you edited it.

Last but not least, I would like to thank everyone who followed me and encouraged me when I was writing fan fiction. To every user who left behind a comment and encouraged me and pushed me on this writing journey. I could not have made it to this point without you. Thank you.

# About the Author

Tiffany A. Joissin is an emerging author of fantasy novels. When she isn't diving deep into the world of dragons and magic she finds herself enjoying anime and other books. She is currently diving deep into her TBR list in an attempt to cull the amount of books she has to read.

And when anime and reading get a little too much for her she likes to relax at home with her cat Cupcake and her dog Snow listening to music and watching the world pass by. This is her first novel.

*For more information about Tiffany A. Joissin, future books, or you want to interact with other fans visit: www.tiffanyjoissin.com*

facebook.com/1000067123433002

twitter.com/iris_eyez

instagram.com/iris.eyez

goodreads.com/iriseyez

CPSIA information can be obtained
at www.ICGtesting.com
Printed in the USA
BVHW050728210721
612416BV00013B/1301/J